RULES
OF THE
STREAM

By
Sandi Soendker
And
Nicci DeMint

Llumina Press

Copyright 2003 Sandi Soendker and Nicci DeMint.

All rights reserved. No part of this publication may be reproduced or transmitted in any form or by any means electronic or mechanical, including photocopy, recording, or any information storage and retrieval system, without permission in writing from both the copyright owner and the publisher.

Cover design by Debbie Johnson.

Requests for permission to make copies of any part of this work should be mailed to Permissions Department, Llumina Press, P.O. Box 772246, Coral Springs, Florida 33077-2246

ISBN: HC 1-932303-01-4
PB 1-932303-00-6

Printed in the United States of America.

Library of Congress Cataloging-in-Publication Data

Soendker, Sandi.
   Rules of the Stream / by Sandi Soendker and Nicci DeMint.
      p. cm.
   ISBN 1-932303-01-4 (alk. paper) -- ISBN 1-932303-00-6 (pbk. : alk. paper)
   1. Horses--Fiction. 2. Horse breeders--Fiction. 3. Horse breeding--Fiction. I. DeMint, Nicci. II. Title.
   PS3619.O378R85 2003
   813'.6--dc21
                                          2003005109

ACKNOWLEDGMENTS

Honest horse stories are hard to find and mostly neglected by writers of fiction. The reason? Perhaps it's because the link that must be established when "partnering up" with a horse is an astounding culmination of trust, respect and control. Without actually experiencing it, it's a spiritual bond nearly impossible to capture.

We are two friends who share lives full of horse stories, newborn foals, painful losses of beloved horses, good rides and bad rides. For the opportunity to become part of the world of horses and to experience that spiritual bond, we owe our parents. Also, a special acknowledgment to our husbands, Jim Soendker and Greg DeMint, who share our passion for quarter horses and our commitment to this lifestyle.

We also wish to thank all of the friends, trainers and competitors who shared details and personal experiences. A special thanks to Gary Griffith, Executive Director of Registration of the American Quarter Horse Association for reviewing certain suppositions in the book and others within the AQHA structure who offered encouragement and advice.

A very special thanks to the roster of vets who supplied valuable expertise, and the dedicated staff at the University of Missouri veterinary hospital.

Dorothy Heckmann Shrader, author of "Steamship Treasures" and other award-winning books about the Missouri River, provided encouragement and a factual source for Missouri River tales and we are indebted to her.

The raising of an orphan colt is not an experience one can adequately fathom without real life knowledge. For that, we must acknowledge our longtime friend Carolyn Cooper Wright and her tribulations with her orphan.

We can't recognize those who inspired this book without acknowledging the horses. The equine characters in "Rules of the Stream," while purely fictional, were mostly inspired by horses we have owned or known.

--Sandi Soendker & Nicci DeMint

AUTHOR'S NOTE

All human characters depicted in "Rules of the Stream" are fictitious, as are the horses. While they may have been inspired by horses we know or have known, our equine characters do not exist. The names of the horses may implicate actual popular bloodlines, but the horses should be perceived entirely as fictitious characters. Any name that duplicates or is similar to an actual registered American quarter horse is purely unintentional.

While parts of the novel contain fictional suppositions regarding specific action of the American Quarter Horse Association, we have meticulously endeavored to stay true to the safeguards and high standards of integrity established by AQHA.

Historical references and bits of Missouri River lore are primarily factual, but names of places and described events are a mix of fact and fiction.

--Sandi Soendker & Nicci DeMint

CHAPTER ONE

The occasional nickering and the clatter of ironclad feet on concrete mingle subtly with the pungent smell of cured hay and saddle leather. Uniquely identifiable by a collage of sound and smell, a horse barn is a remarkable place where dreams flourish or fail and where sometimes, extraordinary partnerships are born.

The new barn was long and low-raftered, bright with natural light streaming through skylight panels in the roof. Against a spacious stall housing her favorite mare, Jeff Day's daughter slouched on two stacked bales of bright straw. She soaked up the tranquility of the place.

The bottom half of the stall was walled in solid oak planks. The upper part of the front was open, with vertical iron bars set in the oak frame. Inside, a bay mare named Stella Dora pressed her nostrils against the bars and looked down at the young woman. Christine, feeling the hot breath and sensing companionship, spoke to her.

"Long day, eh, sis?" she murmured, reaching through the bars and touching Stella. The mare's neck was a little damp and the hair on her shoulder and sides was dark and moist to the touch. Perhaps this was some kind of sign of beginning labor, mused the watchful girl. Stella simply stood and gazed back with patient eyes, the dark round orbs guarding her secret.

Chris leaned against the foaling stall and looked out of the massive barn door. Freeze frame. The scene appeared to be a snapshot of her home. The Missouri farm had been the pride of the Day family for three generations. Large old trees lined the gravel circle drive and the buttery rays of the evening sun softened the starkly painted white fence and dulled the green clipped lawn like a fading photograph.

It was a place that was easy to call home. The farmhouse was more than a century old and well cared for by the Day family. The two-story structure faced west and was surrounded by large budding oaks and clusters of early blooming shrubs. The front of the house was crowned by one large, deep gable, flanked by symmetrical, multi-paned dormer windows. Horizontal clapboard siding, white, with dark green shutters, was simple dressing for the varying roof planes. Wrapping around the face of the house, the abundant porch was warmed by scattered tables, wicker chairs and porch swing. It was unmistakably the family hub and never failed to provide a "sit-down-a-spell" for visitors.

A shaft of light filtered through double screened doors and the girl's eyes followed the incandescent stream inside, where she could see her mother, Joanna, moving about. Supper must be over. Soon Jeff would walk down and ask her if she wanted to be relieved of her long watch, but Chris didn't really want to go to the house. She knew Stella's time was close. She stretched her long legs and tapped the toes of her old boots together, then scooped up handfuls of long blonde hair and clipped it on top of her head. Half of it fell down again, but she let it go. She shifted her position quietly and stuffed her hands into the pockets of her worn canvas barn coat.

Discarded beside her on the floor lay the quarter horse *Journal*. She had read it cover to cover, scanning with new interest the names of the horses in the magazine. She had been watching Stella since early morning and had passed the time by building a list of imaginary names. Horse colt names … filly names. So far, none were just right.

"I guess you're not gonna do this while I'm on watch, are you?" She whispered in a silky, girlish voice. "You think you're gonna wait for Dad, aren't you?"

She had witnessed the birth of several foals, and had been allowed to assist with a few. But the stately Stella was special compared to the other brood mares and Chris was determined to share the impending miracle that would certainly bring forth a remarkable arrival.

"I'm not leaving here until you do it," she warned.

The other horses in neighboring stalls looked up and pricked their ears, always interested in a private conversation. Inside the roomy stall, the big bay mare swayed with the ponderous weight she carried. She moved around in the straw and Chris knew she would be nestled down in it again soon.

Eighteen-year-old Christine Day was a good hand and schooled in normal foaling procedures. Beside her was the medicine box. Every horse family had one. Inside was a bottle of alcohol, an assortment of topical medications, syringes, cotton, some clean leg wraps. In a separate bag was a horseman's basic equipment for foaling. Clean towels, iodine, two infant enema packs and a sterilized shoestring in a sandwich bag. The shoestring was old-fashioned, but a tradition at the Day farm.

She sat back, immersed in the serenity surrounding her. In nearby stalls, the other horses stood quietly, listening intently to the sound of the constant shuffling emanating from the foaling stall. Two cats observed from their perch on a feed barrel and a blue merle Australian shepherd named Josephine stretched out on the floor, her head between her front paws. Although she appeared to be in a sleeping position, her eyes were open wide and Chris knew she was fully alert. Josephine belonged to Chris' older brother Wes, who was away at college.

Stella was by far the finest quarter horse mare in the Days' string of handpicked brood mares. In the show ring, she had proven herself and her gentle personality made her a favorite to handle. Stella, whose exceptional bloodlines imparted respectability and whose comeliness was admired by all, was a joy to own.

Another long groan made Chris stand up and peer at the mare. Stella was now down and lying on her side with legs straight out. She threw her head up and gave a startling grunt, causing Chris' attention level to jump from "just checking" to "does this mean something?" But then, the mare rested her head in the straw and heaved a miserable sigh of acceptance.

When Chris had checked Stella after breakfast, the wax on her udders was glistening in huge drops. The substance was now milky and had begun to drip, announcing that the coming of the foal was close. How many hours until the birth was anybody's guess.

Motherhood was not new to the mare. She had already produced a number of foals for her previous owners and two of her sons were particularly accomplished, setting show records of their own. Chris smiled, recalling how excited she was when her parents acquired the mare. Needing a top-producing mare to mate with their young sire, Jeff and Joanna Day studied bloodlines, shopped prudently, and then made the leap of faith. They borrowed the money and bought Stella.

She was the Days' first World Champion producer and Jeff exulted in the acquisition. While he thought of her in terms of dollars and cents, the rest of the family considered her a celebrity. The mare's name was well known to quarter horse exhibitors nationwide and Chris regarded her with awe. For the girl, it was an honor to know the great Stella Dora.

Chris picked up the *Journal* again and flipped to a page featuring a large photo of a handsome gelding surrounded by proud owners. Red, white and blue roses encircled his fine neck.

"Look, Stella, here is one of your sons."

She held the open magazine up to the stall door, carrying on the one-sided dialogue as if the mare would be interested. It was childish, she knew. But she had always connected to horses that way. She knew they weren't pets. But Chris had been raised with horses and to her, they were companions. They were individuals.

She was certain none of Stella's babies could ever be as special as the one the mare had carried for nearly a year now. The foal would be among the first by the Days' young stallion. The family's expectations for the stud and their respect for Stella made for a sweet promise.

Chris rose from her position in front of Stella's stall, stretched and sauntered down the alleyway. She paused and stood before a large stall and fingered the brass nameplate that read "JJ Invincible."

She leaned up against his stall and whispered, "You're gonna be a dad, big guy, probably tonight."

She remembered the first day she saw the stud four years ago. It was at the World Championship Show sale in Oklahoma City and he was a nine-month old unnamed weanling, black with a big white crescent on his forehead. The sale, always held in November, attracted consignments of the breed's finest bloodlines. The colt was the best of the topnotch weanlings and Jeff Day knew the price tag would make his wife cringe. But Jeff had waited for a stallion prospect like this for a long time and the determination on his face told the family they were not going home without him. Chris promptly nicknamed him "Vince" and the black stud's reign over Day Quarter Horses began.

CHAPTER TWO

Chris wandered impatiently down the concrete alleyway past Stella's stall and to the open barn door. The moody sky looked like a bulging canopy of dark clouds, ready to rip open at any moment and release more rain. As a few large raindrops signaled the impending downpour, instantly her mind flashed back to the events of the previous year.

Jeff bred Stella and three other Day mares to Vince. Ten outside mares were accepted. Nine went home in foal. While the breeding season was successful, the following months brought a calamity Chris would never forget. The Missouri River and its tributaries raged from their banks, inflicting disaster throughout ten states. It seemed like the entire Midwest was under water. People called it the Great Flood. Chris watched in horror as the heartland where she grew up filled with filthy brown, ruinous water.

New Winston was a small town perched on the south banks of the Mighty Mo. It flooded in July. While the Day farm, sitting high on a bluff above the town, did not fall prey to the river, all roads leading to it were flooded. As the water rose, the bluff became an island. To leave the farm, the family drove to a point where the road was underwater and took a rowboat to higher ground where Jeff's truck was parked. While floodwaters claimed the access roads for only three weeks, it was fall before all vestiges of the flood had receded. The girl shivered as she remembered the wasted crops and dead livestock, endless sandbagging and the awful cleanup.

Wes, just finishing his freshman year at college, returned home to New Winston that summer to a full-time job at the farm. Chris had no interest in college. She often begged Jeff to let her stay home after high school and work for Day Quarter Horses.

"When we have a couple of Invincible two-year-olds, we'll get them broke to ride and go on the road, show some futurities! Let people see our stud's babies. Just you and me," she appealed to her father.

"We'll see. You have to make it through high school first," he teased her. While he acted like it was a farfetched idea, he smiled every time she spoke of it and in his heart, he would have liked nothing better. He was proud of his tall, athletic daughter. It was the ultimate compliment to hear his friends remark how well she could show a pleasure horse. In his eyes, her gift was an extension of his own talent and her accomplishments a direct tribute.

Of all the quarter horse events, Chris favored western pleasure and was completely absorbed by the level of finesse she found there. Walk, jog, and lope on the rail. Perfectly executed, no mistakes allowed. Line up, back your horse, be judged. Western saddle, chaps, long-sleeved shirt, hat shaped just right ... maybe a fitted vest and matching scarf or pin.

She chuckled to herself as she recalled her first years in youth competition. Until she was fourteen, she was mounted on an exceptional old gelding named Leroy. He was a birthday gift from Joanna's Uncle Frank and Aunt Lil, who lived on a small farm adjoining the Day place.

Frank, in his early sixties, was an affable man with thinning blond-gray hair and boyish face. He talked like an easygoing cowhand, but beneath the ball cap he preferred to wear daily was a brain that could have functioned well on Wall Street. His wife was a robust woman, a bit younger, with smartly coifed brown hair sprayed so intensely it never moved, no matter how strong the wind. Both were an integral part of Day Quarter Horses.

Uncle Frank had owned Leroy for years and bragged that "he never took a bad step." Despite the gelding's plain head and too-short neck, Frank guaranteed he was solid as a rock in the show pen. Chris rode him in beginner classes and when she was ready to move on, Leroy proved he could do that, too. He was a youth exhibitor's dream. Chris had howled when Frank called him an "old babysitter." Leroy was retired for the second time when Chris was fourteen. Only now, in hindsight, did she truly appreciate his faithfulness all those years.

Soon, she would leave the world of youth competition and go on to another level. For the past several years, she had ridden several of her parents' pleasure horses, but she never really clicked with any of them. She knew one day she would have a truly great horse, but the partnership required for greatness was elusive.

Maybe the foal Stella was soon to present to the world would be the one. *Colt or filly? What color?* Chris reclaimed her post outside the mare's stall and leaned back against the oak planks, giving full rein to her imagination.

***

A rustling breeze swept through the barn's long alleyway and Chris' drifting mind snapped back to reality. It was nearly dark. Stella was standing again and had begun to sweat profusely. Her breathing was labored and her body began to weave. Suddenly, her water broke, gushing, soaking her long black tail. The sound of it splattering the straw bedding brought Chris to her feet.

Abruptly, Stella dropped to the floor and rolled. Then, she lunged to her feet and threw her huge hip toward the wall, backing into it violently and thrashing back and forth. In instant panic, Chris slid the stall door open and stepped inside, only to be knocked backwards by the force of the mare's heaving body. The mare hit the wall again, this time with such force it knocked clumps of dirt and dust from the rafters.

The shocked girl scrambled to her feet and dragged the stall door closed. She rushed to the open barn door as Jeff stepped out on the porch. She motioned frantically and he was at a dead run in seconds. He stopped as he entered the barn and walked quietly to the stall. Should the mare be down, he wouldn't want to disturb her and cause her to jump to her feet. But Stella was up and pacing the stall nervously, pausing only to stomp her hind feet hard and shake her head from side to side. Jeff slipped inside and cautiously approached her.

Stella backed her ears in painful defiance and snapped at him. He grabbed a halter, slid it over her head, buckled it and stepped back.

"Get back, honey," he spoke sharply to his daughter, "go call Doc and fetch your mom."

As the girl sped to the barn phone, she heard the mare let out a long groan, culminating in a grunt as her heavy body dropped to the bedded floor. After phoning the vet, Chris raced toward the house. She could hear Stella, back on her feet, crashing into the wall again and again.

Jeff was trying to hold the mare's head and keep her from injuring herself, but her weight and strength made her unmanageable. She began to circle around the center of the stall, pulling away from him. Despite his presence in her foaling place, the mare buckled and went halfway to the floor. In minutes, Chris was back by his side. Her pounding heart exploded as she saw the bubble of the amniotic sac, pale and bloodless, protruding from under the mare's tail.

"Dad! The baby's coming. I can see something!"

Fifteen minutes later, push as she might, Stella's foal remained unborn.

Jeff wiped his face and muttered. "I can't wait for Doc. Hold her head and don't let her knock you down!" He lifted the mare's tail and slid his hand partially inside her.

"I'm gonna have to help her," he said, trying to be calm. "The foal is in a piss poor position."

The contraction passed and the mare clambered to her feet. Jeff used this opportunity to move closer.

"There," he muttered, "I can feel its head. I need to get it between the two front legs. Damn! Hold her, Chris. I think I've got it!"

He removed his hand and a tiny pale hoof was suddenly visible. Then, the other. In seconds the nose came, between the legs as it should be. Stella gave a mighty heave and half the baby was out. Joanna, whose presence had gone unnoticed, joined her husband and daughter inside the stall and with towels, grasped the emerging foal. The membrane over his face had torn and Chris could see a small wet head, eyes closed and ears folded. A bluish tongue protruded from his mouth. The straining mare was still on her feet and half his body and hind legs remained inside her.

"Don't let her fall on you," Joanna warned her daughter, as Stella staggered, front legs buckling. In Jo's arms, the foal twitched its head slightly.

"Thank God, it's still alive. Jeff, help me!" she cried as the mare gave another push and expelled the foal, which now began to slip from her arms, "I can't hold it up, and the cord's gonna break!"

The slippery baby dropped to the bedded floor. A blood-engorged mess hung heavily from under the drenched tail of the torn mare. The cord, still attached to the placenta with precious blood for the foal, was now broken off near the navel. Jeff winced.

"Get the foal out of the way," he ordered, "She's going down."

As Joanna dragged the fragile foal toward the outer edge of the stall, the exhausted mare staggered and dropped. Jeff picked up the baby and placed it near her head. She nickered weakly and the newborn wiggled.

"It's a stud colt," observed Joanna.

"Look at the size of him!" Jeff knelt and ran his hands over the wet foal. "Get the iodine, Christine."

Thirty minutes later, Dr. Mike McGraw's pickup screeched to a stop outside the barn door. Inside her stall, the mare struggled and stood up. Minutes later, McGraw was beside her with the stethoscope, listening first to the mare's flank area, then at the girth area.

"Whoa, sis," he mumbled gently to the sweat-drenched mare.

"I need to get some painkiller in her to try to get her heart rate down." The vet's voice was calm but he was unable to disguise the concern on his face. He muttered to Jeff. "Bad news. I'm afraid she's colicking. There are no gut sounds."

At the mention of the word "colic," Chris saw panic spread across Joanna's face. Although colic in humans was painful, it was not life threatening. In horses, however, colic was normally due to impaction or a twisted intestine and usually meant real trouble. Rupture from this condition Chris knew to be a leading cause of death in horses.

After examining the mare, Doc sat down on the floor and shoved hands through his hair.

"Damn the luck," he muttered.

Chris knelt in the soaked straw beside Jo and stroked the wet foal. The colt was feeble from the rough birth but tried to suck on Joanna's fingers. He still had not tried to stand.

"We need to get him up on his legs and hope she'll let him nurse. He needs that first milk for the antibodies." Mike injected the mare in an attempt to ease her pain.

Twenty long, tortuous minutes passed, but eventually the painkiller began to ease Stella's suffering and she stood and nickered for her baby. He reacted weakly and floundered, spindly legs trying to respond. Joanna moved in to help. Finally, he stood and began to nose around between Stella's front legs. She sighed.

"The mare seems better, but I don't know," the vet said after he studied the pair for a while.

Mike McGraw played a dual role as trusted vet and close family friend. He placed a reassuring arm around Chris. "It's a good thing you were watching her so close, Chrissy."

He gathered up his equipment to go, leaving Jeff with somber advice. "The painkiller can sometimes mask what's really going on. Keep an eye on her and call me in the morning."

The gawky colt stood swaying beside his dam. Stella nudged him gently. Relief spread over Jeff's face as he watched the colt instinctively find his way to a dripping udder. After some practice, the foal was swallowing the warm milk.

"We've done all we can," said Jeff as he rolled his sleeves down and beckoned to his wife and daughter. "Let's go wash up."

"Not yet," Chris mumbled. She was still mesmerized by Stella, standing quietly in one corner, eyes closed. Her head drooped protectively over the foal now stretched out in the straw. Hours later, the girl switched off the light and left the barn.

Before dawn, she pulled on her clothes and hurried back. She stood quietly outside the stall and peered in. Stella stood patiently, shifting her weight occasionally, as the colt nursed. Chris spoke to her, but the mare didn't respond. The girl noticed Stella's bucket of water was untouched.

"Feeding time!" Jeff's voice called from the barn door, startling her. He stepped inside.

"How's the foal? I checked on them about three hours ago and he seemed fine. How's Stella?"

"Well, I'm not sure," Chris replied, walking down to help him get the feed ready. "The little guy looks okay, but Stella seems funny. I still don't think she feels too good. She didn't drink any water."

"Let's see if a little feed doesn't make her perk up." As Jeff dumped the oats to each horse, Chris followed with flakes of hay. After the chores were done, they stood outside Stella's stall. Jeff's eyebrows pulled together and his mouth was twisted in a troubled expression.

"She doesn't seem interested in the oats. And she needs to be drinking plenty of water right now." He paused and scratched the back of his neck.

"How goes it?" Joanna called out brightly as she joined them, the dog padding faithfully at her side.

"I'm not sure," Jeff called to her in a low, flat voice. "What do you think of this?"

Joanna watched for a minute and eased inside the stall. Stella didn't move. The colt skittered clumsily around the mare's rear end. Stella still didn't move, dull eyes fixed on the floor.

"Something's definitely wrong." Jo and Jeff exchanged a singular expression of silent alarm. "I'll go call Mike."

Within the hour, the vet was back. Stella was now beginning to sweat and her breathing had quickened.

"Her heart rate is way too high. She's either in tremendous pain or she's losing blood," he said despondently. "She's not bleeding externally, so it could be internal. If that's the case, the blood is pooling inside her." He reached for a large syringe and with the needle, tapped the mare's distended belly. The syringe immediately filled up with blood.

"You're in big trouble, lady," he mumbled to Stella. Pushing his glasses back on his nose with his thumb, he turned to Jeff. "The university might be able to save her." His voice was calm, but urgent. He could do no more. "But you need to get her in the trailer and get her down there now."

"I've got a lot invested in this mare, Mike. I hope to God she doesn't go down on the way." Jeff swiped beads of sweat from his forehead. "Joanna, can you and Christine hook up the trailer? Doc and I'll try to load Stella."

The trailer was hooked up in minutes and Chris and her mother lifted the foal in, followed by the two men leading the faltering mare.

"I'm gonna leave her untied. You ride in the back and keep the colt out of her way," Jeff instructed his wife as the vet looked up, surprised.

"That could be pretty dangerous, don't you think, Jeff?" he ventured. "I mean, if the old gal goes down. If I were you, I'd just … "

Jeff cut him off. "Joanna will be fine." He closed the door.

Inside the trailer, Joanna braced herself against the padded sidewall. She would ride this way all the way to Columbia, where equine specialists at the university vet school could provide the latest technology to try to save the mare. Joanna's job was to keep the squirming foal safe from possible injury under the hooves of his staggering dam.

"Good luck," McGraw called loudly as they pulled out, "I'll call M.U. on my cell phone and let them know you're on the way. And I'll stop by Frank's and tell him what's going on. Joanna, be careful back there!"

In the front seat of the pickup truck, Chris was silent as they rolled down the highway toward Columbia. Jeff drove the truck like he was in another world. Concerns for his investment and visions of an astronomical vet bill preoccupied his mind. On the other side of the pickup, his daughter slumped in the seat, aching for the ailing mare and her mousy gray colt with the white half moon on his forehead.

In the back of the trailer, Joanna stroked the colt and crooned to Stella.

"Whoa now, sister. Easy, big mom," she murmured to the sweating mare. The colt sucked on her hands, fingers and sleeves. Stella was in too much pain to allow him to nurse.

Chris stared out the window of the truck, numbly observing the farms and billboards flashing by, trying not to look at the speedometer. Raindrops peppered the windshield and the road began to look shiny. Suddenly, from the back of the trailer, a resounding crash rocked the truck, followed by a prophetic silence. At first, Chris thought lightning had hit the trailer, but Jeff, knowing exactly what it was, eased to a stop and leapt from the truck. He growled an order for Chris to stay in the front seat, but he couldn't stop his daughter as she jumped to the pavement.

Inside the trailer, Joanna clutched a struggling, frantic colt. Stella was still, her massive body in a lifeless heap. Her deep soft eyes were now fixed and bore no resemblance to the regal expression Chris had come to know. As she stared at the huge corpse, the frightened foal exploded from Joanna's arms and crashed onto Stella's body, pushing desperately under her belly in an instinctive search. He was whinnying now, high and shrill.

"We're going on to the university! Get back in the truck. You, too, Joanna. Leave the colt alone," Jeff commanded, pulling his wife from the trailer. "They can do the autopsy and give us paperwork for the insurance company."

He looked at the wet asphalt. "And we'll just donate the colt to the vet school. At least we can get a good write-off out of this whole mess."

This prompted an anguished scream from Chris, who refused to move. Gripping the trailer door, she pleaded for a reprieve for the colt. Jeff sharply cut her off.

"We're a working family. No way we can bottle-feed him 'round the clock!"

"Orphan colts are usually problems, anyway. They don't behave like normal horses," Joanna spoke in a defeated voice as she attempted to shut the trailer door. Chris stopped her with a loud cry. She shoved past Joanna and scrambled inside the trailer, climbed over Stella and put her arms around the floundering baby.

"Come out of there, Christine," ordered Jeff loudly over the now full-fledged cloudburst. "Try to get hold of yourself! The last thing I need is more vet bills trying to keep this little bastard alive. And if he does make it, he'll be spoiled rotten!"

"Dad, please! No!" Defiant words were wrenched from Chris' throat. "He's one of Vince's first and Stella's last! We gotta take this chance! I'll raise him. I'll teach him. I won't spoil him. Please!"

"Honey, stop," said Joanna, "Listen to your Dad. He's right, most orphan colts are lunatics! And this little guy might not even make it. He hasn't had much milk."

"I'll be graduating soon. You asked me what I wanted to do," she pleaded, "I want to raise this colt. Let me try. Please! I'm not a child anymore and I can do this. Dad! Stella died giving birth to him. She didn't ask to be bred. You made that decision for her!"

Jeff was totally exasperated with her now. And he was soaked. He curled his lip and shook his head.

"*I said no!* You are gonna get yourself in over your head and then I'll be stuck with the little bastard. And nobody's gonna bail you out!"

On the face of the young woman glaring at him in the dim light of the trailer, there was no trace of capitulation. Instead, there was an unreasonable fury in her eyes that made him look away. He was numbed by a fleeting moment of indecision and she grabbed at the opportunity.

"I'll be out of school next month! Uncle Frank will help me until then." She wiped away hot tears and seeing the hesitation on Jeff's face, knew he would cave. She was all business now.

"He's gonna make it. And he won't be like other orphans. You'll see."

She knelt and laid a hand on the clammy hip of the dead mare and whispered a last message, choking with finality and emotion.

"I'm going to take care of him for you, Stella. I promise."

CHAPTER THREE

Weston Day tried to open his eyes, but each eyelid weighed ten pounds. He tried again and the left one reluctantly obliged. Head throbbing, body chilling, he realized he was lying in a back seat full of beer cans. He didn't recognize the car.

He pulled himself up on one elbow and felt a little sick. It was daylight and it appeared the car, a much-abused old Corvair, was parked at the back of a lot somewhere. He scanned the huge empty expanse of asphalt. As the cobwebs cleared and he recalled last night's blues concert, he wondered what had happened to his date, Susan. *What the hell was her last name?* A groan from the front seat served as a crude introduction for a young man with bright red hair. He was trying to sit up. Wes observed the earring in Red's pierced eyebrow and marveled at his haircut. It was a haircut that would turn heads even in the most unusual crowds.

"Hey, man. What a night!" Red said, grinning. "Those dudes musta played for hours. Jees-us. I feel like dog shit. I shouldn't have switched from beer to whiskey after the concert."

Wes was upright now and his senses began a slow revival. He smelled like somebody had puked all over him.

"Man! Do I know you?"

"You didn't before last night. Me, some friends, you and your girlfriend, we were on the fourth row. Remember? I got a little screwed up and we, uh, got into this major altercation with some assholes who said all of us were in their seats. Then, the shit was on and I guess somebody got the best of me. You helped me outta there and to my car!" Red pursed his lips like a duck's bill. "Your girlfriend was here for a while, I think, but I don't know what happened to her. Didja check under the car?"

Wes chuckled at the idea of Susan being passed out under the car, feet sticking out. But he could see it was a serious inquiry from Red.

"Nah, she probably got pissed and split," he replied. Simultaneously the weightlessness of his right front pocket notified him of another predicament. "Looks like she took my truck … Sonofabitch! My truck! And now I'm stuck here in *goddamned* St. Louis!"

"Come on, let's try to get our shit together. We need to get outta here," the redhead said. "Man, you got a hair trigger when it comes to a fistfight. I thought we were in the wild, wild, West."

Wes ran his fingers over a scraped cheekbone.

"My place is pretty close to here," Red offered. "We can go over there. Then we can try to get your truck back. I take it you don't live here."

"Naw. Actually, I'm supposed to be at school in Kirksville."

"Oh, yeah? You a college boy?"

"I guess. I ain't doing all that hot there. And I'm supposed to go to summer school to make up some stuff. It seems like a giant waste of time somehow. I had to get away from there for a few hours so's I could think straight."

"You didn't exactly look like you were doin' any serious contemplatin' last night. But you sure had a belly full of beer, dude!" shouted Red. "Hey, why don't you crash at my place for a couple weeks. You can just lay back and set yourself free, man!"

Somehow, the impulsiveness of the invitation seemed natural. He and Red, by virtue of alcohol, screaming guitars and raw knuckles, had bonded. "I'll think about it," Wes scratched his head. "First, let's get out of here."

Red's place was a dump. Meager, but not dirty. Somehow, Wes liked it. Compared to his disciplined school life, it was fun. It was obvious Red didn't observe any rules, except for his protectionist policy regarding his beer. Red's real name was Stanley Kriskie. He was the son of a baker and had lived all of his life in St. Louis. He fled his family, sick of being reproached for breaking tradition by his experimental lifestyle. He worked rat jobs for a living and had recently been cast off by his long-time girlfriend.

"Well, I need to decide," Wes told Red on Sunday night. "I ain't sure what I wanna do, but I'm thinkin' that studyin' may not be it." He was earnestly tossing around the notion of not going back to the campus Monday.

"Okay, then, blow off the school thing. Like I said, you can crash here for a while," suggested Red. "That'd be cool with me."

Wes hesitated and then agreed. It seemed so simple. No big discussion, no weighing out pros and cons.

He nodded his okay, adding, "God, my old man will have a freakin' shit fit."

He wondered if his roommate at school would box up his clothes and stuff so he could pick it up.

Red had no problem with the new arrangement. He seemed to be happy being totally spontaneous. He called it freedom, which was a concept Weston Day still needed to define for himself. Freedom for Red was not at all perplexing. It meant just hanging out. Every day for Red was an opportunity to experience life.

"I like to get in there and see stuff up close," he partially explained his philosophy. "Up close. Don't hang back. Get up close."

"I have no idea what I want to do," said Wes.

"This is no real dilemma," Red counseled him, "so you don't wanna go back to school? Okay? You don't wanna tell your pop? Okay? Just don't do nothin.' *Nothin.*' And that'll be your decision."

The first few days proved to be a daily routine of sleeping late and cruising the city at night. Looking for action, Red called it.

"You have had such a boring-ass life," announced the self-appointed urban guide, "College for God's sake! Oh, we gonna show you some sights!"

Wes was politely silent, but smiled to himself. His life had been anything but boring. *Boring ain't the problem.*

"You got any more money?" Red asked on Thursday. "If not, we need to get some so we can eat."

"I spent $13 at that Salvation Army store for my one and only change of clothes. I got about forty bucks left. What do you do for money, anyway?" Wes was curious.

Red explained he was an independent businessman, an entrepreneur.

"Sometimes I work for this private investigator dude, you know, just sitting in my 'Vair watching somebody and making notes. That's the best job, but he's in Florida until August, so I been kinda hustling other jobs. I know where they are tearing down this old building and you can get all the bricks you want. And I know this one contractor who says he will pay pretty good for old bricks, all in one piece."

The two spent the next three days loading bricks in Red's Corvair, tapping the crumbling mortar off them and delivering them to the contractor. They made $30 apiece on ten loads. Red was disappointed.

"Cheap sonofabitch," he swore. "He told me he'd pay a hundred. No matter, tonight we'll steal 'em back and sell 'em to a landscaper I know across the river."

"No way I'm loading all those bricks again. There's got to be an easier way than this to make money!" By this time, Wes was developing doubts about Red's talents as a businessman.

***

Wes Day's roommate at school was a chemistry major known campus-wide as "All Night Dwight White." During the summer, White took extra courses and hoped to graduate early. Wes had been toying with the idea of phoning him.

"All Night Dwight White, eh?" Red was impressed.

"It's not what you think," Wes was quick to explain. "We call him that because he studies all night. In fact, the asshole's *always* studying."

On Tuesday, he walked down the block to a nearby pay phone. Dwight, cramming for a test, was at the dorm room and promptly picked up.

"Where in the hell are you? Are you out of your mind? You can't just drop out," said the All Night Man. "What if your dad comes up here looking for you? What am I supposed to say? Oh, man. You have really put me on the spot."

"Dwight, you're a pain in the butt," Wes rolled his eyes. "Just say I left school for a day or two, and I'm staying with a friend in St. Louis."

Dwight protested, but finally agreed. And he would pack up Wes' stuff and keep it in his closet.

"I'll need a few clothes. And I need all my books. I'm going to take them to a bookstore and sell 'em," Wes explained. "And I need for you to get my truck keys back from Susan."

"Oh, sure! Do you know how pissed she is, man?" Dwight moaned. "You are in some deep shit with her."

Red offered Wes the 'Vair to sneak up to school and retrieve his belongings. The next evening, Wes gassed it up. They arrived about dusk and parked in the dormitory parking lot. As they pulled in, a well-built, blond-haired man in his early forties left the building. He wore a denim shirt and Wranglers, long and stacked in folds around the top of his boots. He stepped into a white GMC dually pickup truck, backed out and pulled slowly away.

Wes sucked in his breath and ducked down in the seat like he was under fire.

"Holy shit!" he screeched in a loud whisper.

Red looked up and observed carefully as the truck cruised by, not ten feet away. "You sure look like your old man," he snickered.

This drew a scowl from Wes, prompting Red to add, "which ain't all bad. I thought he would be some old fart. He looks like some Hollywood type. Tall, blond and look out, ladies!"

Cautiously, Wes sat up. Two sets of eyes followed the taillights of the white truck.

Red looked at his friend. Wes' face mirrored that of his perfect cheekboned dad, but somehow, the classic comeliness that imparted pomposity to Jeff's countenance was absent in the son. Perhaps it was the freckles, honest eyes, or the younger Day's artless hair. Red grinned. "So what's your old man's name? Lance? Brad? Bruce?"

"His name is Jeff. He's a real asswipe sometimes, but not totally a bad guy." Wes surprised himself with his concise but accurate description of his father.

After the truck was safely gone, the two entered the building and took the back stairs to the second floor, reserved for second year students. Dwight's door was open. When he saw them, he launched into an attack.

"God! Your father was just here! Just minutes ago! I couldn't tell him the truth. I told him you were on a five-day biology trip with the Science Chapter," he groaned.

"The Science Chapter? He knows better than that." Wes was incredulous at Dwight's lack of invention. "Why didn't you just say I was at a Glee Club competition?"

"Screw you, man. I couldn't think. He said he was in Kirksville for some business. He brought you an envelope with some money. Said he sold one of your old saddles or something like that."

Wes pursed his lips. "Business, my lily white ass. He was probably checking on me. See if I was screwing up. Give me the envelope and my truck keys, I'm outta here. I'll call you every once in a while to check on stuff."

He and Red took the boxes he needed and wasted no time in goodbyes.

Dwight stood in the hall yelling at him as he headed down the back stairs. "Your truck is parked in the lot by the girls' gym!"

It was an '87 Ford 250, black and silver. Wes was relieved to have his truck back and Red could see why. In a pretty good imitation of Cheech Marin, the redhead whistled and shouted "charp, man, charp," when he saw it.

By the time they got back to the apartment, Red was ready to party.

"If we blow my money now, how are we supposed to pay your crummy rent? Do you ever think ahead?" Wes asked the self-proclaimed Party Animal.

"Man! You amaze me. Do you know anything about how it comes and goes?" Red shouted, looking through the CDs he had recently bought out of some guy's trunk. "If you do an honest job like selling bricks, busting your goddamn ass, then you have like major karma in the bank and it means some good windfall money is sure to come your way. Soon. Do you know what karma is?"

"Hell, yeah, I do," said Wes. Then he abruptly laughed out loud and turned to Red. "My Uncle Frank once had a mare named Carma. Carmelita something-or-other. Carma was the first mare I ever took in the show pen. I was seven and got a second place ribbon."

"What? You're a damned cowboy!" screamed Red, hopping up and down.

"Nah. Far from it. Anyway, it ain't important now," Wes said and turned away. In his mind, he was thinking of that ride and how proud he had been of his new saddle. He had outgrown it and no doubt, it was the one Jeff had sold.

But Red persisted. He had never known anyone who could ride a horse and was fascinated by this unique side of Wes. This was, for Red, up close.

"I grew up on the farm. We raise horses," Wes told him, first intending to be brief but soon found himself talking about New Winston, his parents and his little sister.

"Little sister?" questioned Red, sucking on a cigarette. "I have a sister named Hanna. She's a psychotic beast."

"Chris is a sweet kid. A little crazy. She's Dad's pride and joy," Wes smiled. "He always thought I was a loser. Mom's cool, though. I miss her. Right now they are probably counting the days 'til old Stella foals."

Red opened a cold beer. He wanted to hear all about it. Wes, encouraged, began to ramble.

"We have this great mare named Stella Dora," he began.

Red was really enjoying the story. Horses were very cool.

"And she is supposed to be due to foal this month," Wes went on. "She's carrying a foal by our young stud. Man, we had a hell of time getting her to settle."

"Settle? Hold on! Talk in English," Red interrupted, puzzled.

"Well, she wouldn't get pregnant, okay?"

Red motioned for him to continue.

"This was our young stud's first year breeding, so we bred Stella and three other of our own mares." Wes looked at Red, thinking he had rambled too much, but Red was on his feet. He was really interested in the breeding thing.

"So your stud jumps the mares!" He wanted to hear more of this. "Do you get to watch him do it?"

"Man, you are such a pervert," Wes laughed. "No, we don't do it that way anymore. We collect from the stud and do it artificially. Our new stud is worth too much and we don't want him to get kicked in the nuts while he is up there doing it. He probably would never want to breed again."

"Oh wow man. Good thinkin'. Not much fun for him, though. So, you just lined up the old girls and zapped 'em?" Red was trying to get the picture.

"Well, it wasn't quite that simple," Wes answered. "The other mares settled easy enough, but Stella had some problems. We finally got her in foal but it took a couple of months."

"Man, you really know this shit! You could be a damned veterinarian!" Red plied him for graphic details, but Wes put him off with an amused snort.

Red ordered, "I can see right now this horse business is more about sex than folks realize and therefore, I must investigate. Go on, and don't leave out any details."

"No, it ain't about sex … and yet, it sort of is." Wes opened a beer for himself. "Well, really, everything human or animal is about sex. When you're a country kid, growing up on a farm or ranch, you learn all about sex from the animals. We see what happens and somehow, there just ain't no questions."

"Exactly what do you mean, you 'see what happens'?" pressed Red, "I want specifics."

"Okay, before our young horse, Dad had this old stallion," Wes began. "I learned all about sex by watching the stallion. We didn't do the artificial insemination thing then. We let the stud cover the mares. Dad would bring him out, and the stud would tease the mare we thought was ready to breed. That means he, the stud, would talk to the old girl. Talk big time. He didn't touch her, though. Not until she said okay. You should have seen our stud. God, he thought he was a freakin' Romeo."

Red loved this story. He begged for more.

"Now if the mare squealed and gave him dirty looks like she could kill him, then she was likely saying she wasn't in heat." Wes was playing with Red now, narrating the tale in his best sleazy voice. "Now if she was ready, but not real sure about the whole thing, he would keep making noises at her and dancin' around. So she'd watch him, thinking about changin' her mind. Dad would let the stud have more rope. The old boy put on a show, givin' it all he was worth. Finally, she'd give in, squeal a little, and back right up to him."

"Wow," Red exhaled. "That's *exactly* like real life."

"Pretty much."

They laughed.

"So, what are your folks gonna do when they find out you ditched school?" said Red, genuinely interested in Wes' life. "They don't even know where you are."

"Once they find out, it's best it stay that way for a while, until the old man cools off." A wave of guilt had made an unexpected attack and Wes collapsed on the old stained sofa and threw his head back. Red was sympathetic.

"Don't sweat it, man," he said. "My pop is always pissed at me."

"My folks have spent a ton of bucks on sending me to college," Wes lamented. "They sure had high hopes for me, like in business or somethin'"

"Parents are all alike that way. Like 'we're gonna make you miserable and you'll thank us later.' It's just too freakin' much pressure." Red shook his head, feeling a common frustration. "Prob'ly never asked what you wanted to do. 'Cause it don't matter what you want. 'Cause you're too stupid to know what you want!"

That night, Wes couldn't sleep. He lay in the dark thinking. Oddly, he thought about barns. The new barn on the Day place was only ten years old. Wes walked through it in his mind. It was very functional. Nice. It was built to replace the tired old barn.

In height, the old barn dwarfed every outbuilding on the Day farm. It was built nearly a century ago. Classic shape, stone foundation, dark and quiet, it was Wes' secret place. It was now owned by yellow and black spiders, orb weavers, whose work somehow Wes dared not disturb.

Sometimes he felt like an intruder there. He and Chris visited the old barn when they thought about it, as if it were an elderly relative. She said she felt sorry for the old barn somehow, because it had been so many years since it had experienced children playing and laughing or horses nickering or roosters crowing.

He finally fell asleep, dreaming of two young children playing in the old barn and spiders weaving huge silky webs.

CHAPTER FOUR

"How can I talk to Mike with you hanging on my shoulder?" Joanna dialed McGraw's office with Chris hanging over her back in the classic overgrown-daughter-drape. She was anxious to hear every word.

"Jeff already called," the vet greeted Joanna. Despite the day's ordeal at the university, Jeff had showered, drank three cups of coffee and headed to work.

"I'm really sorry about Stella." Mike hated to lose a patient and his voice was apologetic, as if it were his fault. "Jeff said she had a uterine artery rupture." He was silent for a moment and then asked. "How 'bout the colt? Jeff didn't mention him."

"That's what I called about. I just got off the phone with the university and it looks like he's going to be okay. His heart rate is about 96 beats per minute and respiratory rate is where it should be. Temperature was 102 this morning. For a newborn, that's really not high, is it?"

"Nah. It'll come down a bit in a day or two. Does he seem to be healthy? I mean, is anything wrong with him?" Doc asked.

"Actually, he's doing fine. They do want to keep him for a week."

"That's not unusual," Mike assured her. "I'm sure they want to do a blood work-up on him, monitor him and so on. The regular stuff."

"They said they've got him off the IV and started him on milk replacer and want to see if they can get him drinking from a bucket. Maybe in a few days."

"It'll sure be easier for you if they can. Know anyone who's got a nurse mare?"

"No, I don't think so. This is pretty new to us. We've never raised an orphan. We did have one mare reject her foal for the first few days."

"Similar, but nothing close to what you are about to take on. Hand-raising a foal is a hell of a demanding task," he sympathized. "Make sure you have plenty of milk replacer on hand. You'll need to feed him every two hours for several weeks and then see how he's doing. After that, you can ease up a little on the milk if he's eating any solids. At the end of three months he should be eating well enough to take him off the milk. Have Jeff call me and I'll go down with him to pick up the colt."

When the colt was ready to be released, Jeff and Mike made the trip while Chris was at school. They had returned from Columbia and were standing by the barn when the girl drove in. She sprang from the truck and hurried inside and down to the stall she had prepared. Uncle Frank was already on duty, as he had promised.

Seeing her colt all alone in the big stall, she was suddenly struck by his pathetic predicament. She looked closely at his face, marked with a tiny crescent-shaped white spot. He looked quite different from the wobbly infant she had left in Columbia. His legs were long and straight. His neck was elegant and his head was exquisitely shaped for a young foal. Inside the stall, she stroked his back and curled her fingers in his wispy black mane. Accustomed to being handled by the vet students, he seemed to have no fear of her.

"He's really beautiful!" She appraised him from head to toe. "Do you think this muddy color will turn black?"

"That's what I'd guess." Frank leaned on the stall door. "Betcha he'll be black as coal. Look at him finish off that pail of milk. He doesn't know to sip from on top of the milk. He sticks half his head in and gulps, then backs out gasping and blowing for air. Funny, huh? By the way, the pail and all need to be sterilized and the powder mixed for the next feeding. Are you ready for this, Chris?"

"I think so!" She took a deep breath. "I've got to feed him every two hours, eh? So, I'll do my homework, then feed at six. Then eight, then ten, midnight ... then two, four and again at six ... " She stopped, thinking about the task confronting her. "I guess I'll set my alarm in between feedings."

"Then Lil and I will take turns during the day," Frank said gamely, patting the colt on the rump. "Somehow, we'll make it."

Chris found the first few feedings exhilarating, but as the week progressed, her job as night nurse drained her and the rigorous schedule quickly began to take its toll.

The colt was getting stronger and at the sound of her footsteps, he bounced around wildly, nickering and crowding her when she stepped inside the stall.

"Get off! Don't you make me spill this!" she shouted at him. "Get back!"

Each night, she finished her ten o'clock feeding and lay across her bed. Fully clothed, her boots at her bedside, she set the alarm. By the time she sterilized the pail and mixed the milk and fed him, she was getting about forty-five minutes of rest in between feedings. She found herself in an inescapable state of weariness, perpetuated by the endless cycle of feedings.

"What a nightmare! And he doesn't even appreciate it. In fact, he's a little monster," she confessed to Joanna. "Every time I step inside the stall, he jumps all over me. I push him back, but he still does it."

"As big as he is, you need to get him halter broke, Chris," said her mother. "He already weighs more than you and you've got to get a handle on him."

"I've *been* working on it! I can put one hand on his butt and one on his chest and guide him around, and I can lead him with the hip rope pulling him along. But when I try to just lead him with the halter on his head, he goes nuts!" she said in a defeated voice. "It's like he's scared to death. He goes crazy when you pull on his head. I've never had a colt do that. He acts like a brainless idiot!"

"He's not an idiot. He's an orphan," Joanna said, placing both hands on her daughter's shoulders. "Behavioral problems like this are common in hand-raised foals. They have no sense of the natural order. Your father and I tried to warn you when Stella died."

Frank and Chris stepped up their efforts on the halter-breaking task. The colt, growing stronger daily, showed no signs of giving up the fight. She found she could talk him into anything, but forcing him was out of the question.

"You have to remember horses are bred to be herd animals," Dr. McGraw told her when he stopped to visit. "He is completely alone. His instincts are telling him to run to the herd. Run to momma. Run away. But he can't do any of those things. And he's fighting mad about it."

"But what's he fighting me for? I am the one responsible for his survival!" argued Chris.

"He's not really fighting you," Mike assured her. "I think he's just saying he doesn't have an identity at all. He's not a horse, he's a hot house plant. He depends on you for food and water. And he's confined to a stall."

"I *can't* turn him out with the others and still feed him 'round the clock! What am I supposed to do?" she begged for answers.

"I wish we could find him a nurse mare. Then, you could turn them out with the others in the pasture. The little guy's got to know where he fits in."

"You're talking 'bout the pecking order," she said.

He nodded. "Never forget that in the horse's world, all is relevant to that order. You know this, Chris, from watching your own horses in the pasture. You really know who's who when you throw a bale of hay out there in winter."

"I know. And when you take a horse away from the herd, there's still gotta be a pecking order."

"You got it. In the herd, he learns discipline and respect. And those two things he will have to know, with or without peers."

"Dad says orphans are screwed up," said Chris. "Mom says so, too."

He paused, searching for just the right word. "They're just, well, befuddled. Things are not the way they are supposed to be. He doesn't know how to act or react, and that's scary. Horses, young or old, are most dangerous when they're scared. Your folks are afraid you'll get hurt."

"Befuddled, huh?" she said, wrinkling her forehead and half ignoring the implied warning.

"Just make sure he understands the pecking order. It tells him how to act. And make sure he knows *you are the one in charge*, or he will sure enough try to be."

***

Frank called all over Missouri, Kansas and Iowa, looking for a nurse mare. Large, docile draft mares were best, McGraw told them. But each call was a dead end. No one seemed to have a fresh mare without her own baby to feed.

Day and night had no perimeters for Chris during those weeks. Other than school and her barn chores, she had no other activities, no other purpose than to feed her colt. She soon learned every expression, every breath, every movement of his ears, and like every new mother, she learned what each signal meant. When he was hungry, she was there to feed him. For him, just the sound of her voice set off a conditioned response. She represented food.

All the while he continued to grow stronger, and to Chris, he seemed to be in a perpetual state of total starvation. Following Mike's orders, she had started feeding him hay and just a sprinkle of milk pellets, increasing it just a bit every day. When she walked into the barn, she was met each time with a shrill whinny. Although he was anxious to be fed, he began to respond to her slap and backed off as she attached the pail to the snap on the wall. Chris rejoiced at this achievement. Maybe he would be able to understand discipline after all.

At four weeks, she mixed a handful of sweet feed with the milk pellets. He cleaned it up in minutes. But an hour later, Chris returned to the barn to find him standing in a watery brown mess splattered all over his tail, legs, and rear end.

"Okay, cut out the sweet feed. His digestive system can't handle it yet," the vet told her. "Keep up the hay and the milk pellets."

The diarrhea subsided within a day or two, but the problem was replaced by one of constipation. "Adjust the ratio of the powder and water," Doc advised.

Chris adjusted the mixture, but constipation returned. For two more days, she struggled to get the milk replacer liquid just right. At the end of the third day, the colt was beset with an explosive case of diarrhea. The vet returned to the farm and suggested taking the colt off solids and going back to the milk every two hours.

"Somebody just shoot me," groaned the girl and collapsed beside the stall.

When the colt was six weeks old, Doc examined him and ordered her to start increasing the solid food again. The colt seemed to tolerate this well and at last the vet told her she could adjust his milk ration to every four hours for a couple weeks, and then every six hours. Although Chris welcomed this break, it was still an exhaustive routine. She dragged herself home from school each afternoon to relieve Frank and Lil, who trudged home, glad to be off duty long enough for a night's rest.

One Saturday morning, the haggard girl left the barn after her early feeding. She had accumulated a sleep debt over the past month that would have made a prisoner of war confess to anything. Her body ached and her head hurt from the relentless schedule. On the road, she heard plodding hoofbeats approaching the farm and was surprised to see Aunt Lil astride her old gray mare. Chris smiled at the sight of Lil, in polyester slacks and hot pink canvas shoes, perched on the fat mare. Lil was riding Spider, named for a spider-shaped black mark on her hip. The elderly mare was twenty-plus years old and well known to the girl.

"Spider Woman!" Chris patted her affectionately. She flashed a smile at Aunt Lil. "What possessed you to drag this old grandma out of the pasture?"

"She's a gentle thing, but always was a firm hand to her young'uns. She can't milk, of course, but that poor little devil of yours needs some companionship from his own kind." Lil swung a leg over and dropped to the ground.

For the first few days, Spider was stalled beside the orphan. She nickered to him constantly and he began showing some interest. Soon, she was clearly attached and he didn't seem to object to her attention. Frank paraded her daily by the colt's stall. On the fifth day, the colt called to the mare as she clopped down the alleyway. Frank hesitated, then took Spider outside. The colt was furious, twisting his head and kicking out.

"Listen to him holler!" Lil was delighted. "He's madder than hell that you took her away!" It was a good sign.

After a week, Frank turned Spider into a small lot next to the barn. He tied her to a post and he and Chris guided the colt into the pen. The old mare looked at him affectionately and called to him. She allowed the colt to stand by her and touch her with his nose. When he began to nudge her and look for a place to suck, however, she squealed and stamped a hind foot, all the while careful not to hurt him.

Chris and Frank repeated this the next day. The mare was attentive as the colt grew bolder. He rubbed against her and chewed her tail a bit. She stood patiently.

"What do you think?" said Frank, shifting his eyes to Chris. "Shall we turn them loose together?"

"Let's do it," she sighed. They watched for an hour as he dashed about and made defiant little gumming motions with his mouth at the mare. She was now following him around the pen.

"Spider could care less," laughed Chris, watching him. "I hope this works."

"Well, it looks like she's tolerating him," said Frank. "But it's got to be more than that. She has to decide to take him on as a responsibility."

Every day, he put the two in the small pen together and watched. After several days, he saw a glimmer of a protective relationship forming on the mare's part when Joanna rode up to the pen to watch. Spider lunged at the rail where Joanna and her horse stood on the other side. She snorted and glared, pinning her ears flat. She nickered at the colt and he skittered to the back of her, peeking around her swishing tail.

Frank grunted approvingly.

"It looks like maybe she's adopted the little turkey." Joanna respectfully backed her horse away. "This'll solve one problem, but Christine is still the one that's got to keep him fed."

Soon Chris would graduate from high school, but the girl was too spent to even care about the pomp and the circumstance of senior activities. She sat through classes like a zombie and on returning home, headed dutifully to the kitchen to prepare the pail of milk.

In the following days, Spider and the colt spent hours together in the pen. The old mare developed a fierce motherly attitude toward her new ward, gently nipping at him when he playfully climbed on her or tried to nurse. When he tired and flopped on the ground for a nap in the sun, she stood over him, head lowered, tail swatting flies.

From Spider, the colt was learning respect, and the lesson was transcending to his interactions with humans. As he began to show respectful deference to Chris, the halter breaking became easier. Although he remained rambunctious, he did not fight her as much. Occasionally, she rewarded this with a pat of approval on the rump. Even though she had grown to love him deeply, Chris remembered what the Doc had told her about the pecking order and she tried to refrain from spoiling him.

"Firm, fair, and consistent," preached Frank, "and don't ever forget it."

By the end of May, Frank was still feeding him milk twice during the day and Chris fed him twice during the night. Jeff headed downstairs one morning and found her asleep fully dressed on the stairway at 5:30 a.m.

"Are you coming or going?" he leaned over her as she awoke.

"I don't know, Dad, I'm too tired to think," she said, looking at her wristwatch. "I guess I never made it upstairs."

"Just remember, kiddo, you wanted this. You promised Stella when she died. And now, this colt is totally dependent on you." He started on down the stairs, then glanced back at his daughter and softened. "I know it's hell, baby, but you're going to make it. I haven't told you this, but I'm really proud of you."

He kissed her and left for the office.

The graduation she had anticipated all year became nothing more than an inconvenience. After the evening ceremony, the family returned home. Joanna walked down to check the horses as Chris changed her clothes.

"He's got diarrhea again," Joanna announced when she returned to the house. "You need to clean the stall and scrub his rear end."

After the scrub down, Chris returned to the house and washed up. Forcing her unwilling body to climb the stairs, she fell in a drained, coma-like sleep across her bed, jeans and boots still on. *Sleep ... just one full night of sleep,* she thought as she closed her eyes. The radio alarm woke her an hour later, music slowly bringing her to consciousness. It was a country western song, pretty popular, about a guy and a dog. She became aware of the words as she lay there, convinced she couldn't move. "If I should die before I wake, feed Jake." The lyrics floated in her head and suddenly it seemed as if the words were meant for her.

That's what I'll call him, she thought. *Jake.*

CHAPTER FIVE

It was shortly before midnight when the phone rang. Jeff had just fallen asleep. It rang ten times before he made it downstairs to the kitchen to answer. The voice on the other end was familiar.

"Jeff. It's Claudia. Did I wake you?"

"Yeah, ah … Claudia?" He began to squirm at the sound of her voice. He couldn't imagine why she called. "Mmm. Claudia. What's up? How's the family? Still living in Kansas City?"

"Yes, as a matter of fact, we are." Her voice was breathy, with a hint of theatrics. "I'm sure you must be surprised to hear from me after all this time. I … have a … situation. I know it's late, but I need to talk. I'm afraid it's not gone well for me lately. Vic is gone. He has been gone about three months."

She began to sniffle. Jeff sighed, bored already. "So he took off, eh?"

"No! Jeff, he passed away! We were on vacation in Arizona and he had a heart attack. He was on the golf course and he died on the way to the hospital," she whimpered. "I'm a widow. It's just been, well, a nightmare, of course. How is Joanna?"

"She's fine. Still working at the junior high during the school year, working her butt off at the farm," he replied, unable to bring himself to console her.

"Are you still a foreman at that trucking outfit?" she inquired.

"Vice president of operations," he corrected.

"Oh? Wonderful. And Chris? I guess she just graduated from high school. My Jenna is in college, of course. I can't believe she is no longer a child. It makes me feel soooo old."

"She must be quite a girl now," Jeff recited, his words measured. He was still waiting for the reason Claudia called.

"Yes. But we are having some problems. The last three months have been really tough on Jenna." She took a deep breath and continued. "We are both seeing a counselor but nothing seems to help. She seems terribly unhappy with her life. Depression is such a mysterious disease. It is a disease, you know, Jeff."

"Yes, I know. What about yourself?" He wasn't really interested. "Last time we saw you, you were doing pretty well. Let's see, it was a football game, wasn't it? The Chiefs played the Raiders at home … has to be at least six years ago."

"No doubt. No doubt it was." She dropped the mournful display and laughed, pleased that he remembered. "Anyway, I am so happy you and Joanna are successful. Two lovely children, big horse farm. We went to the American Royal show last year and I saw your name in the program as an exhibitor. How fun! It's exactly what you and Jo both wanted. You are so suited to each other!"

"We don't do too bad." He became suspicious, as she was speaking too kindly of his marriage to Joanna. Claudia and Jo were college friends and sorority sisters, but during the unfolding of certain events during those years, the bond between them suffered damages.

The women were alike in their collegiate interests, perhaps, but thoroughly dissimilar in personal ethics. Joanna was pretty, smart and likeable. Graceful without trying. Claudia was beautiful, witty. Cagey to the core. Joanna wanted to fall in love with a normal man who would be a loving husband and good father to her children. Claudia had loftier requirements. She fancied a man with money. Packing school lunches and hauling kids to little league games? Her last wish.

"Anyway, I adored Vic, of course, and the loss has just … well, it's devastated me," Claudia was saying. She began to sniffle again. "We had such a wonderful marriage!"

Jeff wasn't really listening. *How old was she now, anyway?* Probably about 42, a year older than his wife. Her drinking habits, he recollected, were almost as vicious as her sexual appetite. She was, however, memorable to distraction. Brilliant blue eyes, dark hair. Loved the lusty passion of classic old movies. She was a woman who could get away with anything.

"Enough small talk here. I need a huge favor from you and Jo and don't say no to me, Jeffrey." Claudia would not shut up. "I need a long vacation from this mess. And my baby is simply too troubled to stay here alone in this house full of memories of her step-daddy. Jenna needs a change in scenery. Surely it would be no great burden if she spent the summer on the farm with you all?"

"Well, I have to talk this over with Joanna …" began Jeff. He needed to get involved with Claudia's problems like he needed a hole in the head.

"Oh puh-lease! Don't give me that crap. Jo and I are sorority sisters," she hissed. "I was her big sister! Do you know what that means? We have an unconditional loyalty to each other! And you *do* realize my daughter was named for you and Jo, don't you? I'll make arrangements and Jenna will be there Saturday morning. She has her own car and checking account, of course. She needs this, Jeff. Don't let me down!"

"Claudia, wait, you can't just ..." he attempted to cut her off. *What the hell was she up to?*

"Stop! Don't say a word. I know you'll do this. If I can't rely on beloved old friends like you and Jo, who can I rely on?"

After she hung up, Jeff sat down at the kitchen table and lit a cigarette. He cursed Claudia and tried to imagine what Joanna would say. He realized with an awful, inadequate twinge that he was clueless to how she would react. *Which Joanna would step forward and respond?* Living with her was like being a contestant on some kind of "Faces of Eve" game show, he thought. *Sweet, sweet Joanna.* All these years together and he still wasn't sure what really made her happy. On the other hand, he could read Claudia the shrew, like a book.

Christine's senior picture on the refrigerator made him think of Joanna in college. Blonde, long tanned legs. Odd, he couldn't conjure up the image of Joanna as a co-ed without seeing Claudia. What an unholy pair they had been, he recalled. He smiled as he remembered how inseparable they had been.

His thoughts could not block out darker recollections. His impulsive fling with Claudia prior to meeting Jo. The memories provoked an involuntary shudder.

He lit another cigarette and sat there, thinking about Joanna at age twenty. She quit college to marry him and a little over a year later, Wes was born. Jeff soon had a degree in business management and a new job as an entry-level manager with a trucking company. The company operated a main terminal near New Winston. It wasn't long before Joanna was pregnant again with Chris.

Meanwhile, Claudia had abruptly attached herself to a faculty member named Warren St. James. When he accepted a position at another college in Ohio, she transferred there and wrote a terse note to Jeff and Jo, informing them she was married. Joanna heard she had given birth to Jenna after becoming the bride of Professor St. James, but the story was a little vague. By that time, their college friendship was strained.

Jeff had developed a real animosity toward Claudia and ordered his wife to stay away from her. Claudia remained unruffled and kept in touch from time to time, thoroughly enjoying Jeff's discomfort. Jeff and Joanna were invited to her second wedding and to her third. They didn't go, but heard each was an elaborate affair.

After Warren, Claudia was married briefly to a golf pro. After that fell apart, she married a stockbroker from Omaha. When Claudia divorced him and claimed half of his money, she rushed to Mexico to "ease the pain." There, she met Vic Gambiano. He had just moved to Kansas City to supervise a long-term commercial construction project. Within a year, Vic found himself building a large house and pool for his new wife and her young daughter.

Jeff wondered what Jenna would look like. *Would she be as striking as her mother? Perfect throat, tiny waist?* His thoughts were interrupted by the click of a switch and the kitchen overhead flooded the room with light. Joanna leaned over his shoulders and took the cigarette out of his fingers. She took a drag and returned it to him.

"Who was that calling at this hour? Is Wes all right?" she said, cinching up the tie belting her long, loose robe.

"You better sit down. It was Claudia." He didn't look at her face. "Vic's dead. Had the big one three months ago. Claudia needs a vacation. Her daughter has become a nutcase and since you are sorority sisters, she wants the girl to stay here for the summer for some old-fashioned country peace and quiet."

It came out all in one breath. He waited for the explosion, but Joanna's reaction was one he could have never predicted.

She raised her eyebrows, pulled on one ear and murmured, "Poor old Vic. He was so good to Claudia. Well, it's okay, I guess. When is she coming? I'll get the guestroom ready. This will be good for Chris. Since the neighbor girls moved away, she's been kind of a loner."

It was true that Chris seemed to drop out of the small town's social circle when her two best friends moved out of state. And following the birth of Jake, she seemed to have no life at all outside the barn. Jeff thought about this and nodded his weak approval.

The next morning at breakfast, he informed Chris that a friend's daughter would be coming to stay with them for a while.

"Keep in mind this girl has been through a lot," he advised.

"Don't worry, Dad!" Chris seemed satisfied with his brief explanation. "She's gonna love it here. She can help me with my colt. God knows I could use some help! And we can take her to the horse shows with us."

"Christine!" Jeff shook his head incredulously. "For most people, a three or four-day horse show in 98 degree heat is an endurance event, not fun! I certainly would not drag her to a show unless she was up for it. She may not be a glutton for pain."

Jeff thought about how different his family's lifestyle would appear to an outsider. A life of mixing work and school with horse shows. Ordinary people would likely pass on giving up weekends and holidays to attend out-of-town horse shows. All to compete in a couple of events.

Chris and Wes grew up being horse show kids and for them, this kind of life was normal. Chris was her father's number one fan and was a familiar sight in the stands yelling "Good ride, Daddy!" when she was too young to even know the difference in a good or bad go. Wes started competing at age seven. Chris didn't make her show ring debut until she was a little older. A "kid" horse is one special horse. Until Chris got Leroy from Uncle Frank, Jeff and Joanna didn't have a horse safe enough to trust with their young daughter.

Wes' first horse, Carma, was pretty respectable. Her most valuable attribute was that she was virtually bombproof. Nothing scared her. Carma was quiet, but she was also cranky and hated everyone, including kids. While she would listen to Wes some, she had no respect at all for Chris and refused to do anything on cue. Carma acted so sour in the show ring, it was clear Chris needed her own walk-trot horse. Uncle Frank solved the problem by dragging Leroy out of the pasture.

"He's been a pasture bum for too long," Frank told Jeff. "We'll put him on a diet, slap some shoes on and see what he can do."

"Retirement is over," Frank informed the old horse and snatched him out of the field, grass still hanging out of the sides of his mouth. "Your lazy ass is going back to work."

Leroy turned out to be a fine walk-trot horse. The main reason for this is he didn't have to lope in this particular competition – just walk and trot. Leroy, fat and content in the pasture, hadn't moved any faster than a trot in years. Uncle Frank said anything requiring energy was against Leroy's religion. Leroy was virtually incapable of bucking, kicking out, rearing up or running off. He was perfect for Chris' first riding horse.

Quarter horses were a way of life at the Day farm and it was more than a hobby. It was a lifestyle commitment. Raising horses and taking the best into competition was a challenge for each member of the family. Jeff thought about this as he sat on the front porch waiting for a stranger's car to come down the road. People who raise horses pledge themselves to a daily routine of feeding and caring for them that affords no days off, no vacations. He wondered how Jenna, destined to join the household for the summer, would adapt. This was not the idyllic dude ranch. This wasn't life with Dale and Roy.

Jeff tried to picture Claudia's daughter. He envisioned an aluminum-and-wire-fanged mall rat, raised poolside and dutifully enduring ballet and piano lessons. Likely, she was just as comfortable at a Las Vegas casino as she was at home. Probably knew every classic romance movie made and wore chartreuse iridescent toenail polish. Her mother reincarnated. Jeff began to sweat.

How troubled was she, anyway? How would Joanna treat her? More significantly, however, he puzzled over the real reason Claudia was sending her to New Winston.

The family gathered on the porch as Jenna St. James drove up to the farm in a dark green Jeep Cherokee. She stepped out of the Jeep and waved gaily. Jeff blinked in disbelief while Chris bounced out to greet her. Tall and slim as a runway model, Jenna did not favor her mother at all. Jeff found himself staring at a clear-eyed beauty with a sweet face and long brown curly hair. There was not a trace of "come hither," and he couldn't imagine her painting her toenails while watching a rerun of Lancaster and Kerr in the pounding surf. She was dressed in very short cut-off jeans and a red plaid blouse. The city mouse was ready for the country. On her head was a straw hat straight from hillbilly heaven.

"Good God, is that Daisy Duke?" said Aunt Lil, standing beside her husband, the perfect impersonation of the American Gothic wife.

"Nope. Too scrawny," Frank said.

CHAPTER SIX

They sat in the darkness with a growing awareness of a budding friendship. It was late, but the two young women settled comfortably in the big wicker porch swing, each pursuing a fact-finding mission about the other's life. Jenna told Chris how much she had come to respect and depend on her stepfather and his mature and kind ways. The younger girl sat with a somber face as Jenna told of his death. She didn't have much to say about her mother. Jenna was straightforward, but Chris sensed she was not without secrets.

At daybreak, Chris rousted her out of bed to help feed Jake and the others. As they walked down the concrete alleyway of the barn, the whole structure came alive with the sound of the hungry horses rattling their feed buckets, like prisoners clanking tin cups against iron bars. Chris pushed a green feed cart ahead of her and measured out scoops of oats. The sounds of munching and oats rattling around in the feed boxes awakened an untouched territory in Jenna's head. Although she was a non-morning person, it felt good.

"This is Zan. He's six." Chris introduced each horse and recited its prescribed ration. "He's a power house, so Dad shows him, but we all ride him at home. He gets two scoops and one big flake of hay."

Christine approached another stall and spoke to a pretty sorrel. The mare pleasantly stepped up so the girl could touch her.

"Hey, baby!" Chris spoke as she dumped the feed. "This is Sheila. She's my brother's mare and I ride her while he's at college."

The next stall was home for a tall colt. He was pacing anxiously for his feed.

"This is Zip," she said simply. "He's going to be shown in western pleasure when he's broke enough. He's a two-year-old and Dad has been riding him since December. He's a gorgeous thing and real sweet. You'll love him."

She moved on. "This is Cherry. She's the same age as Zip and we'll show her in pleasure, too. She's a little high strung, so Mom is going slow with her."

Cherry's navy stable sheet was awry, so Chris stepped in the stall to straighten it up. As she fiddled with the sheet, a yet unseen creature in the next stall was raising a mighty ruckus that resounded throughout the barn. Jenna looked at Chris with a baffled look.

"Who is that?" Jenna asked, peering in the direction of the pandemonium.

"That's my orphan baby I told you about last night. He does this at feeding time and every other time anyone walks in the barn," the younger girl explained. "Come on! I'll introduce you."

The colt bounced madly around inside his stall. When Chris slid the door open, he laid his ears back and whirled, throwing his rear end toward them and threatening to kick.

"Whoa, now!" she shouted, taking a lead rope in with her. The colt kicked out one back leg in a test. The girl smacked him on the shoulder with the flat of her hand. "Meet Jake."

"Oh! Don't hit him, he's so cute," pleaded Jenna, although Chris' action was far from severe.

"Cute, my butt. He's a brat," said Chris between clenched teeth. "One little smack doesn't really hurt him. But if he double barrels you with those hind feet, you'll know some pain. He's a baby, but he can hurt you."

The colt refused to face her and Chris moved from side to side in an attempt to get close to his shoulder so she could use the lead rope to restrain him. Finally he looked backward and turned to face her. He stood quietly while she slipped a tiny halter on his head, buckled it and snapped on a lead rope. This was an accomplishment and Chris began to praise him, but as soon as she started to lead him from the stall, he suddenly stood straight up on his hind legs and pulled back. She released the lead and let him fall into the deep bed of wood shavings.

"Oh, my God!" cried Jenna. "What's he doing?"

"Bein' an asshole," Chris sighed, a bit peeved. "His manners need a lot of work."

He scrambled to his feet and stood still. She patiently picked up the lead again and led him out of the stall. She ran her hands over him and picked up each foot. He accepted it. It was a ritual she did four or five times a day and eventually, she knew he would get the picture. Jenna reached out to pet him but thought about his tantrum and changed her mind.

He stood impatiently as Chris rubbed his muzzle and pulled on his ears. Finally, he couldn't stop himself and nipped at her sleeve. With the flat of her hand, she slapped his shoulder.

"No, Jake!" she shouted at him, jerking the lead a bit to emphasize her displeasure with the nipping.

"It is a constant deal with me and him. I can never let him act up, not once, without a reprimand," she explained to Jenna, who was frowning. "If I let him nip me once, I am telling him it's okay, so next time he'll chomp me good. I only smack him when he's acting up. Never when he's scared. You gotta know the difference. While I hold him, you get the bucket of milk we mixed up and hook it on that bull snap in the corner."

"So this is mare's milk substitute?" asked the novice as she followed orders. "And you don't have to bottle-feed him?"

"No, after his mom died, he learned to drink from a bucket," explained Chris as she put Jake back in the stall. He moved to the pail and began gulping.

"Poor little guy," Jenna lamented. "It's awful coming into the world and not having a mother to take care of you."

"Yeah, he's our first orphan colt. It's probably awful for him, but it ain't no picnic for me either. Uncle Frank and I have had one heck of a time. He's not ornery, but his playful stuff ain't always funny. Last week, he tried to jump on Uncle Frank. His front hooves scraped right down old Frank's back. Now, he has started this rarin' straight up stuff."

"Would he be any better if he still had his mom? Is it because he's mad?" This situation fascinated Jenna.

"Well, some mares really discipline their babies," said Chris, "I mean, they teach them to mind. They don't let their babies waller all over or bite or kick."

"How do they make them mind?" Jenna asked. She could not imagine a docile old mare controlling this wild baby.

"If the colt jumps on 'em or bites or whatever, the old mare'll nip their fannies. Or if the baby runs off too far, she'll holler and carry on and teach them to run right back to her side. I just know Stella would have been a good mom. I wish she were here. But Aunt Lil has an old mare named Spider who's taught him a lot. He's not nearly as bad as before we got him a babysitter, but still, I wish he would respect me more. As far as he's concerned, I'm little more than room service."

Jake splashed his nose into the milk pail and began banging it against the wall. Stimulated by the clanging noise, he kept it up, sloshing milk everywhere.

"He really is a goof," Jenna observed, making Chris laugh out loud.

The orphan finished the milk and was banging on the bucket. Chris stepped in and retrieved the empty pail. She then removed the halter, explaining it was a pain in the neck to put it on and take it off so much, but it was good training for the colt.

"Besides," she added, "if I left it on, he could get in trouble and maybe even get a foot caught in it."

Jenna started to ask how he could possibly do that when Jake picked up a hind foot and deftly began to scratch his jaw with it. She watched him, mesmerized.

"Come on," Chris said as she pulled Jenna away. "We need to feed the stud before he tears the barn down."

At the end of the barn was a special stall, larger than the others and separate. It was built of stained oak lumber like the rest, but Jenna noticed the door had two safety latches instead of one. Moving closer, she beheld the most stunning horse she had ever seen. Blue-black in color, he was distinctively marked with a large white crescent in the middle of his forehead. His splendid coat shone under the lights and his huge, round eyes glittered below an exquisitely arched brow.

His handsome head was different than the other horses, thought Jenna. It was the shape of it, she decided. His muzzle squared off neatly around the large nostrils, his lips were straight and tight and his jaws were extraordinarily large and round. He tossed his head and a silky black forelock fell beguilingly over one eye. Jenna was speechless. He was the essence of masculinity and power. She had never in her life been in the presence of a living creature comparable to this black horse. Her throat tightened.

Chris dumped the feed through the small window cut in the bars above the stallion's feed bucket and tossed a giant flake of hay over the top of the stall. The stud shot her a defiant look while stepping up to his feed. Every other bite, he repeated that same look. Jenna still had not been able to take her eyes off him.

"Jenna, meet 'the King.' This is the guy who really calls the shots around here. He's Dad's whole life and our whole future. His name is JJ Invincible. We call him Vince."

Chris pushed her closer to the stud's stall.

"It seems like yesterday when Dad bought him as a weanling and brought him home," she continued, smiling wistfully as she recalled how the entire family had been swept up in the whirlwind years of Vince's show career.

Jenna settled on a bale of hay beside Vince's stall, anxious to learn more. As a child, she had loved horse stories and was mesmerized by classic horse heroes like Anna Sewell's "Black Beauty."

"I was a freshman in high school," Chris began, "and I spent every evening in the barn, helping Dad get Vince ready to show."

As Jenna sat smitten, Chris recalled those victorious days – clearly the most glorious she had ever known. While Jeff Day had a fair reputation for his accomplishments with performance horses, his competence was undeniable when it came to fitting a halter horse. He liked the pure, visual directness of this event, where the horses are lined up by their exhibitors and judged on the balance of their conformation and degree of muscling.

Jeff knew he lacked the national notoriety of the big-name trainers and breeders, but he was confident in his ability to successfully show the colt. By picking the right shows and picking judges who would like this type of individual, Jeff and Vince accumulated some impressive wins.

When the quarter horse industry gathered for the World Championships in Oklahoma City in the fall of 1991, Jeff's yearling stallion had earned enough points to qualify for the competition.

"The whole family loaded up the trailer and took off to Oklahoma City," Chris went on. "Leading the colt into the show ring with the top yearlings in the nation was among my father's greatest moments."

Jenna pulled her knees up under her chin and listened as Chris described the scene. Invincible showed to perfection, posing motionless as each judge inspected him. Jeff stood proudly beside his horse, waiting for the judges' individual placings. After it was over, the Day family went home with a prestigious third place in the World.

"Mom was shaking in absolute disbelief! Third in the world! Us, the Day family from Nowheresville, Missouri. But Dad was disappointed. In his eyes, he had walked in with the best colt, and he had wholly expected to win it."

At Jenna's urging, Chris continued with Vince's story.

By December of that year, the fast-growing black colt was nearing his two-year-old birthday, which for all horses is January 1, no matter when they were actually born. Jeff's firm hand and miles on the show circuit had yielded more than points and notoriety. Although the young stallion's hormones were beginning to make themselves known, the constant handling had instilled impressive manners in the horse.

"If there was ever any doubt Vince might be a stud prospect, those doubts were gone by the time he turned two. But before Dad made the decision to use him for a breeding horse, he had to make a big choice.

Would Vince make the big time based on his good looks, or would it be his ability to ride? Performance or halter? What would it be?"

The girl remembered her father's long phone conversations with Texas trainer, Larry Wayne – discussions that left Jeff perplexed. Wayne, a close friend of Jeff's, was of the opinion the colt was growing too tall and lanky for the halter competition. He was long necked, short backed and balanced. His hip was muscular and chest well developed but still, he did not have as much power as the judges would like to see.

Larry thought Vince was looking more and more like a rail horse. He visited the Day farm at Christmas and suggested Jeff cut back his feed, slim him down and try him under saddle.

"I begged Dad to let Wes help by doing the ground work. My brother's a pretty good rider, but Dad wouldn't even consider it," Chris told Jenna.

In Jeff's opinion, which ruled the household, his son was better suited to hauling hay, building stalls, fixing fence, painting and other chores. Jeff always said it kept Wes out of trouble.

Chris couldn't argue her brother had a mind of his own, but she never understood why he had to constantly prove his worth.

"In January of '92, Vince left home," Chris continued. "This time, at Larry's suggestion, he joined a stable of two-year-old pleasure prospects at a training center in Oklahoma. Brock Howard, one of Larry's friends, is really sharp at showing young horses. His job was to evaluate Vince's potential and tell us if he had any talent."

Chris was obviously impressed with this young trainer. Her concise profile on him fascinated Jenna.

Brock was not a cowboy type and didn't try to be one. He was a Texas college grad with an equine management degree. He did not trail ride, round up cows or rope. He took young horses, studied them and then developed them like professional athletes. Each stall had a clipboard where Brock and his staff made notations on each young horse's progress. He was extremely patient and started each one with plenty of groundwork. Every day, his equine students were saddled, exercised and then drilled with the basics of western pleasure. When each lesson was learned, it was on to the next.

"Well, Vince became Brock's favorite two-year-old," Chris continued. "Sometime before July, Brock approached Dad with show plans for the stud. He agreed Vince was really good minded and a drop-dead mover. Brock said he had a tremendous frame and slow legs. He thought he was good enough to go to the Congress. Hearing that from Brock, Dad was all for it and from there on out, it was all he could think about. Vince's accomplishments were Dad's purpose in life."

The All-American Congress, she explained, was held in Columbus, Ohio, in the fall. Winning the two-year-old open class was a level of achievement attained only by the best. Brock was convinced the black colt could do it. Those convictions became a driving force that consumed Jeff Day.

Brock Howard chose the best of his pleasure horses for competition. When he showed, he was dressed flawlessly in starched Wranglers, starched long-sleeved designer shirt, chaps and perfectly shaped hat. Everything he wore and every piece of tack on his horse was in consummate sync with the quarter horse trends. With his tanned face and calm blue eyes, Brock knew how to present himself, and he knew how to present a young pleasure horse. In the show ring, paired with a talented colt like Vince, he was a deadly competitor.

"So, in October, there we were in Ohio at the Congress!" Chris savored telling the story as much as Jenna enjoyed hearing it. She described in detail how Invincible and Brock swept through the elimination classes, entering the final go-round riding on a fearsome reputation.

"Vince had no problem meeting Dad's expectations. He simply could not be beat. The judges were all eyes for him. We couldn't wait for the final go-round."

The details of this day were permanently recorded in Chris' memory. "Brock rode Vince toward the covered warm-up arena, walking real slow to relax him. You should have seen him, Jenna. He never looked better." She glowed with pride as she recalled how the stallion's black hair glinted in the sunlight and his long, black tail nearly touched the ground. He was moments from victory.

"Wes and I stood with Mom and Dad at the pen. Mom looked like she had been hypnotized. Dad was a nervous wreck."

Jenna smiled and nodded, easily imagining how it would feel, anticipating the moment that would catapult one's horse to such a level in the quarter horse world. She looked up at Chris expectantly for the rest of the story.

"Before the class was called inside, Vince was standing with other competitors, ready to file into the arena. Then, without warning, a skittish two-year-old mare standing several feet in front of him squealed and kicked out. From where I stood at the rail, I could hear the thud as the filly's hoof connected with his front knee. Vince reeled back, dropping halfway to the ground."

Jenna, engrossed in the story, caught her breath. "Oh, no!"

"As quick as Brock was out of the saddle, Dad was at his side. Blood was running down our stud's leg. He couldn't even stand on it. The whole scene was awful! The mare's rider was hysterical, apologizing for her horse's behavior. Mom was screaming for a vet. And, in the middle of all this confusion, the ring steward called for the horses to enter the arena."

Chris opened Vince's stall door a few feet and beckoned for Jenna to come closer. "See that scar on his leg? He was hurt pretty bad. It got him right on the kneecap. So he was stitched up, wrapped and sent home with Brock. Every day, Dad talked to Brock on the phone. After several weeks and a dozen x-rays, we knew he'd never completely recover."

"Mom tried to pacify my dad, but he was out of his mind. We all realized any performance career was out of the question, but at least we knew Vince wouldn't be *permanently* lame. So Dad decided to go ahead and start using him for breeding."

Chris closed the door to the stud's stall and secured both slide bolts. "Dad and Uncle Frank drove to Oklahoma and brought Vince home. And even though those glory days are over, he's still the king. This entire place, this operation, all the mares, everything. It's all for him."

CHAPTER SEVEN

"I want you to go someplace with me today," Chris announced to Jenna. "Lil says she'll take care of Jake, and I thought we'd take a little trip. I want you to meet my brother."

Wes hadn't called in weeks and Joanna was deeply concerned. Jeff was clearly peeved. Somehow, during most of his adult life, Weston Day had managed to be a constant source of vexation to his father.

Jeff and Uncle Frank had taken Zan to a three-day show in Iowa and Joanna was certain if her husband returned and there was still no word from Wes, he would be more than just annoyed.

"Your dad is going to lose it," Jo told Chris. "Wes knows better than to let two months go by without calling. We haven't even given him a check for his summer tuition."

Everyone knew Wes was impulsive and at times, rebellious, but he was devoted to his family and the horses were very much a part of his life. Joanna had called the dorm numerous times, but her son's roommate, Dwight, reported with some evasion Wes was not around.

"I know he needs money, so I'm sure he'll call any day now," Joanna told the girls. "I don't know why you want to drive all the way up there."

"Really, Mom, we just want to take a little road trip. I haven't been off this farm in weeks," said Chris cheerfully, revealing not a trace of her real reason for driving up to Kirksville. "Ray is here if you need anything."

Ray Slankard had been working part-time for Day Quarter Horses for several weeks. Jeff hired him to clean stalls, exercise horses and for general chores. Three days a week, Ray showed up early in the morning and worked until feeding time at four.

Slankard was a tall, wiry man. He was not yet fifty years old but had a deeply creased face. His large head was topped with a scraggly shock of greasy hair. He was originally from somewhere in Kansas. He said he had worked at the stockyards for a couple of years and had moved to New Winston to live with his brother. He owned no more than two shirts and both had snaps down the front and sleeves torn out, showing a suggestively tattooed arm.

In the weeks he worked for the Days, the family had never seen him without an old beat-up sweat-stained felt hat, four-inch brim rolled up all around. Jeff suggested tactfully Ray buy himself a new straw hat, but Slankard protested, defending his old hat. He bragged it had taken years to get it to look the way it did. His boots were dark brown with very pointed toes and high underslung heels, made to look ridiculous by skin-tight blue jeans inches too short.

Joanna could not stand the sight of Ray from the beginning. He knew this and kept away from her. He really didn't care much whether she liked him or not. During his brief employment, she had been at work most of the time and he liked this cushy job.

He hurried through his chores and then parked himself in the air-conditioned office at the new barn, watching television. The hired man was sloppy in his job and beer cans were often found in the trash, sodden cigarette butts stuffed inside. But it was hard to find barn help and Ray was tolerated.

***

Joanna was privately relieved Chris was driving to Kirksville. She, too, wondered if there was something wrong, but had kept her concerns to herself. She didn't want to bring it to Jeff's attention.

It had been her son's habit to put off regular calls to home for a number of reasons. He did it when he got kicked off the wrestling team for drinking. He did it when he flunked two courses. He did it when he was experimenting with his life path. Joanna smiled and remembered when he was dating the girl from back East. Jeff and Joanna went up to the school to have dinner with their son and his new girlfriend. Mirah, who was very mature for her age, told them she had kicked a bad cocaine habit to return to college. Jo laughed aloud when she remembered those months, but nonetheless, Wes' relationship with Mirah had been sorely disconcerting to two Missouri farm parents.

Jo pulled on her boots and headed to the barn to see if Ray had finished cleaning the stalls. She needed to discuss the day's work schedule with him. Jenna and Chris, ready to go, walked toward the barn with her.

"Are you gonna ride Cherry today?" asked Chris.

Joanna had been riding the filly and Jeff had been working with Zip. Both two-year-olds were on their way to becoming pleasure horses, but far from finished. Cherry was a nervous sort, distracted by every noise, every movement. Zip could jog alongside a freight train.

"If you'll wait until we get back to saddle her up, I'll take care of Jake and then I'll ride with you," volunteered Chris. "I'll ride Zip. Dad won't care, I've been on him a few times."

"We'll see," Joanna laughed as the three walked through the big barn door. She had promised her friend, Rita, she'd go shopping with her and didn't plan to ride until late afternoon. "We'll talk about it when you two get back."

Chris began to speak but was interrupted as Ray blundered out of the office, surprised by the voices.

"I was just ... putting a new light bulb in there," he covered, his eyes darting. "Have you heard from Jeff and Frank? Hope they're kickin' ass at the Ioway show!" He knew he had been caught loafing and quickly brought up a subject he calculated would distract Jo. She didn't answer him but recited the instructions for the day.

"Turn Zan out for a couple of hours in the dry lot behind the barn. Fly spray him good. Turn Zip and Cherry out for 30 minutes each," she ordered. "Early so they don't sunfade. Put Chris' colt out in the small pen with Spider. And Vince needs some exercise. Just turn him loose in the indoor arena and keep an eye on him."

"Yes sir! I mean, ma'am!" mocked Ray as Joanna turned and went into the office. "Everything is under control with old Ray here."

He stood leering at Chris and Jenna, both irresistibly fresh in their tucked-in pastel blouses and form-fitting jeans. He could smell the light summer scent of Jenna's cologne. With her long fluffy ponytail pulled through the back of her navy blue Nike cap, designer sunglasses and pretty pink lipstick, he couldn't take his eyes off her. Her waist must be no more than 18 inches, he thought to himself. As he turned his gaze at Chris, he found himself looking straight into venomous eyes.

"You better keep those looks to yourself," she spit the words at him and escorted Jenna out of the barn. Ray ignored her and continued to inspect Jenna's slender body.

"Really nice little ass," he muttered low as the girls turned and walked out.

When the two young women were outside, Chris shot a look back at the barn. "I can't stand that guy," she said to Jenna. "I almost hate to leave Mom here alone with him. Man! He's such a *cockroach*."

"You heard her say Rita will be here in an hour. Don't worry about it, he's just a goon. Come on, let's take my Jeep. You can drive," said Jenna. "I'm really anxious to meet Wes."

"You may not meet Wes today," Chris said mysteriously as they drove off. Jenna turned, waiting for an explanation.

"I know he's up to something." Chris smiled, gripping the steering wheel. Jenna lifted an eyebrow. "He wouldn't go this long without calling me. He doesn't even know about Jake."

"Oh, don't get bent over it," said Jenna. "He's probably not calling because he's got some new big tattoo. Maybe he shaved his head or embraced some weird religion that forbids him to use the phone."

"It's got to be more than that," said Chris, reaching into her blouse pocket and pulling out an envelope. "Stella has been dead almost two months. I've called for him a dozen times. I know his roommate is lying for him. So I mailed him this letter last week and yesterday it came back. He's not there and left no forwarding address."

"That's why you have been the first one to the mail box all week!" said Jenna. The two young women drove on in silence. "Has your brother done stuff like this all his life?"

"Yes, sort of. He's kind of unpredictable," Chris shrugged. "Once he and Dad had a fight on the way home from a horse show. When we stopped for gas, Wes got out of the truck and walked to the highway. We couldn't stop him, so Dad just left him there and we drove on. Mom was carryin' on. It was a mess."

"What happened to your brother?" Jenna asked.

"He hitchhiked home. He's done it before."

On the way, Chris tried to call Wes' room at school again on the cell phone. Dwight answered.

"What's the deal, man?" Chris grilled him. "Where in the hell is my brother? I'm on my way to the school and I'll be there in a half an hour. I want to see Wes!"

Dwight was evasive, but finally told her he was gone and had left school some time ago. Chris, convincing him she was near tears, demanded more information.

"I'll meet you in front of the dorm in 30 minutes," he said, exasperated. "I'm tired of this bullshit. I'm out of it." When Chris and Jenna pulled up, All Night Dwight White slid in the back seat of the Jeep where he slouched, avoiding eye contact.

"This is our friend, Jenna. She is staying with us this summer," Chris explained. "Jenna, this is Dwight White."

"I can't believe he hasn't called you." He cut the polite introductions short. "But don't worry, he's okay. He did leave school, however, and he's staying with some weird redheaded hippie friend in St. Louis. He calls once a week, just to check on stuff, but I don't think he has a phone."

"Damn him!" Chris screamed dramatically and Jenna could see she was tuning up for something big. "Why does he do this shit? You tell him the next time he calls, his sister is dying of a terrible disease and he better come home!"

Jenna looked at her in shocked silence. Dwight was frantic.

"Oh, no, God, no! I am so sorry!" he stuttered.

Jenna rolled her eyes and leaned back in the front passenger seat.

"I have this terrible, incurable condition," Chris cried. By now, she was unstoppable. "I am taking all kinds of treatment and they might do surgery, too. Tell him if he wants to see me before I die, he better get his ass home. Now get out!"

Dwight sprang from the back seat, looked back at her, then hurried into the dorm. Jenna turned to Chris, astounded. The younger girl pounded the steering wheel with a maniacal grin.

"That bastard! This will get him home," she said with clenched teeth.

"Somebody in your family is going to die, all right, and it ain't gonna be you," hissed Jenna. "It's gonna be Wes, because your father is going to kill him."

"Maybe Dad won't know he wasn't in school," muttered Chris. "Weston Day is going to owe me for the rest of his life."

Chris started the Jeep and they roared out of the parking lot. Jenna shook her head and began to smile. The smile exploded into laughter.

On Sunday night, Jeff and Frank returned from the Iowa run in high spirits. Jeff was always in a good mood when he did well. He showed Zan in senior pleasure and earned several points on the horse. The family demanded a detailed account of the show and begged for any new quarter horse gossip. To Chris' relief, Jeff was too preoccupied to ask if Joanna had heard from Wes.

"Brandon Penny was there with his new four-year-old pleasure horse," Jeff reported to Chris. "He walked by our stalls eight or nine times a day just looking for you. Finally Frank talked to him a little bit and let him know you had stayed home. He seemed disappointed. Well, devastated would be more like it, wouldn't you say, Frank?"

"Oh, Dad! You're making all that up," Chris said, cheeks flaming. "I like Brandon, but we're just friends."

"Well, your friend's father has a mare for sale and I want to go look at her." Jeff became serious. "You want to ride to Clayton with me Tuesday evening?"

He knew she would. Although Brandon Penny was popular among other young women and an outrageous flirt, the good-looking kid ardently assured Chris she was his preferred companion at the horse shows.

Brandon's parents spent plenty of money making sure he was mounted on a horse capable of winning. He didn't always take first place, but he was consistently in the top five. Chris looked forward to riding to Clayton with Jeff. She had never been to Brandon's home and was curious to see what the place looked like.

On Tuesday, the pair drove off in the truck. Wes' blue merle dog perched between them, happy to be going along. As they wheeled out of the driveway, Joanna heard the truck radio blasting the familiar music of a nearly worn-out Eagles' tape. Jeff's voice belted out the words of the song. Chris chimed in. "I'm standin' on the corner in Winslow, Arizona!" The tune was their traveling song. Jo smiled and shook her head. *Why couldn't she and Jeff be like that again?*

She returned to the house, rummaged for a hidden pack of cigarettes and lit one. Later, Jenna heard her talking and laughing on the phone with Rita. Jenna was surprised how differently Jo acted when her husband was gone.

They sat down to a late supper alone. Between bites, Jenna rambled on with stories of her first riding lesson under the tutorship of Uncle Frank.

"In one hour, he had shattered all my girlhood fantasies about riding horses! I thought when you wanted the horse to go you just said 'giddy up!' When did they change *that*?"

Jo laughed loudly.

Later in the evening, Jo announced she was going to wash her hair and headed toward the bathroom, glancing at the clock.

"It *can't* be after ten already," she said. "When I get done here, we'll have a bowl of ice cream. But I'll need to run down to the barn and check the horses first."

"Sounds good," Jenna called back. "You know, I could go do that while you're washing your hair." Jo didn't hear. She'd already turned the faucet on full blast.

Jenna wandered onto the sprawling porch in her nightgown and bare feet. It was a beautiful, perfect evening. A breeze ruffled the white cotton gown as Jenna reached back and pulled her ponytail loose, shaking her hair out. She loved this big old farm that roosted on the bluffs of the river. She loved the trees, corrals and barns. No street lights, no sounds of traffic, no sirens.

The barn lights had already snapped off, controlled by the electric timer. She smiled, thinking of Jeff for a moment and how Chris teased him about doing his ten o'clock barn checks in boxer shorts and boots. Tonight, she would do it, dressed only in her nightgown. She stepped off the porch and padded barefoot down the path, still marveling at the rural isolation of the place and the freedom it afforded the family.

As she stepped through the wide-open portal, she heard noises that seemed to come from inside the office. She approached the closed door curiously and stood for a few seconds listening. *Had a cat accidentally been shut inside?* She reached up, flipped a wall switch, and a shaft of light slithered across the concrete from under the closed office door. It suddenly swung open and she stood face to face with Ray Slankard. He had an armful of show halters and bridles.

"What the hell are you doing with those?" she growled, raising her face to his vacuous gape. "Just borrowing these, huh, Ray?" She snatched at the expensive tack, but he tightened his grip.

"Actually, I *was* just borrowing them," he lied, eyes flicking back and forth debating his next move. "If I put them back, we could keep this our little secret."

"Well, let me tell you a little secret!" Jenna stepped away from him. "When Jeff finds out ..."

A strong, large hand grabbed her behind the neck and she reacted with a fierce slap, straining to grab on to the valuable equipment. The slap amused him and he managed a wide grin showing neglected, stubby yellow teeth. There was no saving his job now and he knew it.

"You're a purty little miss," he grunted, still holding her by the neck. He leered at her for a moment, then pulled her closer to his face, roughly covering her lips with his mouth. She kicked at him and dropped the halters and bridles, fingers clawing at his face. He backed off for a split second then quickly lunged at her, wrapping both arms around her and crushing her to his chest. She gagged at his breath and his tongue in her mouth and tried to free her arms to push him away.

"God, you smell good! Makes me want to get to know you better," he hissed. He tightened his grip and slammed her against the feed box. "I can see you feel the same way!"

As she fought back, he reached down and pulled her nightgown up. Kicking violently, she wrenched away from him and screamed. He brutally slapped her face hard and closed his calloused hands around her throat.

"Nobody here but Joanna, and I would like to have a piece of that bitch, too," he snarled as he clamped his fingers over her mouth, "I really like your little nightie. Wanna take it off?"

He jerked at her gown and as it ripped, there was a sudden movement behind him. Out of the darkness, a tall figure leapt toward them and wrenched the attacker loose from Jenna's half-naked body. A fury of brutal punches sent Ray to the ground and in the light, the shaking girl could see him struggling to get up. His face was greasy with blood and foul epithets trickled from his mouth. Jenna heard herself cry out as another unsparing blow sent Ray hurtling backwards through the barn door and onto the gravel. He hit the ground with such force, his right arm snapped. He howled.

"Get in your truck and get down the road," a low voice snarled. "Don't show your sorry ass around here again. You're damned lucky you ain't dead."

Ray was dragging himself toward his truck.

Jenna had collapsed, sobbing, on the floor. With one hand she held her torn gown around her exposed body as she huddled against the feed box. The other hand covered her face. The same powerful fists that had so viciously punished Ray were now perfectly civilized hands that tenderly gripped her shoulders. The stranger knelt beside her in the dim light.

"Y'okay? Are you hurt?" her defender mumbled softly, pulling her close and rocking her. She tried to cover herself and he took off his shirt and wrapped it around her. "Let's get you to the house. Want me to carry you?"

"I can make it," she sniffled, wiping tears from her face.

"Come here," he muttered and gently scooped her up despite her flimsy protest. Outside the barn, he paused with Jenna in his arms and looked down the road. She clung to his neck, bare legs dangling in the moonlight. They watched the retreating taillights of Ray Slankard's old truck weave slowly into the distance.

"Who are you, anyway?" Jenna said in a whisper, although she knew.

"I'm Wes," he said.

CHAPTER EIGHT

Long after the police chief had departed and Jenna was dozing fitfully on the couch, Joanna sat at the kitchen table. Seated across from her, Wes finished confessing the details of the past months in St. Louis. At any other time, she would have been infuriated by his reckless actions, but any anger aroused in her had been numbed by this evening's incident.

Joanna stood and moved to the back of her son's chair, leaned down and encircled his broad, bare shoulders with a meaningful embrace. He reached up and took her hand. He made no attempt to push her away, as was his nature, but allowed her to bury her face in his neck.

Wes was trying to put the events of the last week in order. He had talked to Dwight and immediately headed home to see what kind of terminal disease his sister was raving about. He suspected all along that Chris had set him up.

Joanna told him about Stella's death and Christine's daily challenges raising the orphan. Jo also told him more about Jenna and spoke briefly about Claudia.

"Supposedly, Jenna was having some emotional problems following her stepfather's death," Joanna told him. "Truthfully, she's been here for weeks and we have seen no sign of it. Really, it's been good. She's nothing like her mother."

"Well, she really held up pretty well tonight, considering what happened to her." Wes scratched his head. "So, she was supposed to stay here all summer?"

"That was the plan. In the fall, she goes home and back to UMKC. Third year. She wants to teach English."

"Hmmm. Isn't that what you wanted to do?" mused her son. "You wanted to be a school teacher, but you quit college to marry Dad."

"If you don't want to go back to school, what do you want to do, honey?" Joanna probed, ignoring his observations. "Talk to me."

"I don't really know," he began. "Some people know what they want to do with their life from the git-go. I'm not one of those people. Why do I have to decide? What if I decide wrong?"

Joanna began to answer, but was interrupted by the sound of Jeff's pickup truck coming up the road. Wes stood quickly and walked out to the porch. As they pulled up to the house, Chris had already spotted her brother's truck parked down by the stud pen and was waving out the window. Wes' dog jumped from the truck and together, Josie and Chris raced to the porch.

"Sshh. Jenna's on the couch asleep," said Wes with finger to his lips. Joanna, behind him, recounted the incident with Ray.

Jeff listened to the whole story, blinking in disbelief. His only response was to pick up Wes' right wrist and hold it up to the porch light. He looked at the swollen, raw knuckles and then into the face of his son.

"Jo, get me a beer," he said with one hand on Wes' shoulder. "And get one for my son. We're gonna sit out here on the porch for a while. Chris, go inside and keep an eye on Jenna."

Chris started to argue with him, but thought better of it and went inside. The two men sat on the front porch steps as the sounds of crickets and frogs filled in the silence.

After a while, Jeff asked, "Well, did you beat the dog shit out of the sonofabitch?"

Wes looked straight ahead and answered. "Yeah."

After a bit, Jeff took a deep breath and stood up. "C'mon, let's go on in. Chris will want to show you Stella's colt in the morning. Quite a deal. She and Frank are nearly dead from hand-raising him. And I'd like for you to look at Zip. I think he's gonna have kind of a nice way of going. I want to see what you think." It was a blunt acknowledgment, but for Wes, it was enough.

***

The morning after the incident with Ray, Jeff left early for the office. He liked his job, though he often worked long days. He had been with this company since graduating from college and had helped build it into one of the major trucking companies in the Midwest. Three years ago, he had been named vice president of operations. The promotion meant a welcome increase in salary, and it guaranteed his weekends off. This was critical to his expanding horse business. Joanna had worked at the junior high school as secretary for years. She liked her job, too, especially the time off in the summer.

"This is my last week at work, so I'm glad you're home," said Joanna when she heard her son's boots clomping down the stairs. Breakfast was nearly ready. "You *are* home, aren't you?"

He nodded. "I'm not going back. School is not my scene."

"You'll have to tell your Dad, but it can wait," Joanna said simply. "When the time is right, let me talk to him."

"What? And let him chew your butt for my screw-ups?" He started to protest, but she held a hand up and stopped him.

"It's not a screw-up, honey. It's just a change in the grand design." She flashed a big motherly smile and placed a platter of biscuits on the table.

"Where's the girls?" he said.

"Doing chores."

"Do you think she ... Jenna ... will be all right?" He moved to the refrigerator, scanned the door shelf and retrieved a jar of blackberry jam. "Do you suppose she'll call her mom and want to go home?"

"Not a chance," Jenna answered for herself as she and Chris entered the kitchen through the screen door. "I was pretty freaked out last night, but I'm better now. Fine enough to thank you for what you did, Wes. And for giving me your shirt."

He nodded and thought of how she looked in the obscure light of the barn, nightgown torn, legs bare, breasts exposed. He felt a bit guilty thinking of this, but the sight of loose hair and naked thighs had haunted him all night.

Jo inspected Jenna's bruised face. "Let me see you!" She peered at Jenna close up. "Does it hurt?"

"What happened last night," Jenna began, gently ignoring her, "I want to forget about it. I hope you all understand, but I don't want to talk about it. I've been so happy here. I don't want anything to spoil it."

"We understand perfectly," said Joanna.

"What about Ray the Cockroach?" said Chris as she washed her hands in the sink.

"The state police will be looking for him," answered Jo. "But no doubt he's high-tailed it. Attempted rape, assault, theft. Those are pretty serious charges. It's my guess we'll never hear of him again."

"So, are you a farm boy again, or what?" Chris obligingly changed the subject, sat down at the table and leveled her eyes at Wes.

Jenna's head swiveled, waiting for his answer.

"I guess so. I need to take care of some things in St. Louis and get my stuff," he replied. "I'll go back this weekend and do that."

He glared at his sister, who seemed in perfect health, shaking his head with a grin as the girl assumed an innocent expression, revealing her ruse.

***

Wes spent the better part of the next two weeks helping with Chris' colt. He surmised immediately that Jake liked playing games with his handler and needed some firm attention. Soon, the orphan would be able to use his size and strength to gain the upper hand.

"He's messin' with you, Chrissy."

"I know!" Chris defended herself. "We've been doing pretty good but just lately, he's got it in his head he's going to be a jerk and start testing me again."

"Listen up," Wes told her. "This is the ongoing game of who's the wimp, and it will go on until Jake gets it 'in his head' that it's not you. When you are leading him and he decides to go left when you want to go right, if you don't fix it that second, you're a goner."

Jenna smiled. Uncle Frank had explained this fundamental to her in her first riding lesson.

"If you let the horse ignore you when you say 'whoa' then it is your fault when he doesn't stop," Frank had told her. "When you say 'whoa' three times and that old horse, who knows better, just keeps right on going, I am going to be yellin' like a maniac. You can't allow it. You have got to get your point across, okay?"

Frank was a good teacher, but a strict disciplinarian from the old school. Jenna learned that rail horses, racehorses, eventers and working stock were simply not backyard ponies.

"Any horse that carries a rider into competition is not a pet," Frank stressed. "A spoiled horse doesn't know the meaning of the word 'obey' and therefore, can't cut the mustard on the course or in the pen. Horses get spoiled because some rider lets them develop bad habits and didn't fix 'em."

Horses learn bad habits just as fast as they learn good ones, Frank told her. It was an old horseman's dictum she'd hear many times.

Jenna had long discussions with Frank over the mysterious intelligence of horses, a topic he enjoyed immensely.

"Contrary to what most folks think, horses have a medium, if not a low intellect in comparison to some animals," he said. "Combined with the fact he can't come right out and tell you what's going on his head, it takes a bit of savvy to figure a horse out. Make no mistake, the books may say they may have a low IQ, but they are amazingly sensitive to stuff. You got to watch, learn and read the horse. You gotta get inside his head." Jenna learned he didn't think most horses were stupid, but sometimes their riders were. It was another horseman's mantra.

Frank taught Jenna that taking care of a horse correctly applies to handling him and also taking care of his health.

"It's a whole lot more than mental. A horse carries a lot of weight, so his legs and feet need a lot of attention. The horse depends on you for exercise, water, food and shelter," Frank told her.

"Why are they always in the stall?" was one of Jenna's first questions. "Aren't horses herd animals? Wouldn't they be happier just out in the pasture?"

"All good questions. Yes, they are herd animals and they do need time in the pasture with others. Our colts all run in the pasture before we bring 'em in. But a show horse has to be in optimum condition and unfortunately, he don't get that way out in the pasture," Frank said. "If you put him with other horses, he could get kicked, nicked up, or his tail chewed off by another one."

Jenna quickly learned the significance of "optimum condition." She learned how to bathe and groom a horse. She also learned how to work a horse in a large circle on a long rope called a longe line. She liked this work and it made her feel like part of the crew when Jeff or Frank would pull a horse out of the stall and turn it over to her for grooming.

In the alleyway, two strong cables were attached at the same height on opposite sides of the wall. Each cable had a snap on the end and when not in use, hung down. Jenna learned to lead the horse out, position it in the middle of the alley in between these crossties and snap each cable to the side of the halter.

She learned to lift each foot and pick out dirt, leaving a clean sole, protected by the iron shoe. This was daily routine, along with brushing and polishing the horse's hair. The tails on show horses were kept braided and stuffed into a tail pouch or sock and tied up until they went into the show ring. Sometimes Jenna would carefully take the tail sock off, unbraid the tail and carefully pick it out with her fingers so not to lose any precious hair. Once a week, she would wash and condition the tail.

Early one morning Jenna took a longe line and a whip and led Zip out to the arena. Joanna sat on the porch and watched her. Holding the end of the cotton rope, Jenna gradually let him move away from her, guiding him with the position of the whip. Soon she had him trotting around her in a large circle. Standing in the center, she let him play a little, then popped the long whip at his heels, getting down to business. He settled down and began to trot out, long and smooth steps that would build muscle and ligaments, and discipline as well. Aunt Lil joined Joanna on the porch.

"She sure has taken to the horses," Lil commented. "That malarkey about her being a little wacky? What a crock!"

During the next month, Jenna helped exercise the horses and had taken over much of the grooming. Her first show was approaching and she fretted over each horse as if it were going to compete in an international beauty contest. She wrote to Claudia about it. The letter was brief but detailed, and intentionally upbeat.

Dear Mom,

I am going to my first horse show. It's a real big show, and we're taking the two-year-olds, Cherry and Zip. It's their first show, too. Jeff will ride Zip and Joanna will ride Cherry. My job is to make sure the horses look like a million bucks. Chris is teaching me to band manes and I've been practicing every day. Chris is like a sister. Do you know Uncle Frank and Aunt Lil? Frank is teaching me to ride. The horse I'm riding now is Frank's old horse, an older red roan gelding they call Pink Floyd.

She signed it and before sealing it, dropped in a photo of herself in the wash rack with Cherry, both covered with soapsuds. Chris had taken it. She walked down the drive to the large mailbox, deposited the letter and flipped the red flag on the side of the box into an upright position.

CHAPTER NINE

Jeff stood looking at his one-ton dually with pride, cursing the spitting rain threatening to deface its polished perfection. The customized truck never left for a show without being washed and waxed. The trailer, a four-horse Sooner, was show-ready, too, with aluminum gleaming, doors open and red running lights glowing. The words "Day Quarter Horses" were lettered high on the side of the trailer. Frank thought it nonsense to spend so much money customizing a rig like this and so much time keeping it immaculate. When the judges started handing out ribbons for trucks and horse trailers, he said, it might be a worthy project.

The back of the trailer was bedded down with clean pine shavings, and Wes was stuffing hay into two woven nets with drawstrings. He would tie these inside the trailer for the horses to eat on the way to the show. In the front part of the trailer was a fully equipped dressing room with adjoining tack compartment for saddles. Inside the dressing room, Joanna was hanging up the clothes she and Jeff would wear in the show ring. Chris was loading various pieces of equipment, going over a carefully prepared checklist.

In the barn, Jenna worked on Zip and Cherry. Both were bathed and brushed until their coats glistened. She had been standing on a milk crate beside Cherry for nearly an hour, twisting tiny rubber bands into the mare's short, evenly trimmed mane. Zip was already banded.

Frank grinned and winked at her. "Damn rain! God knows we need it though. It looks like it's gonna clear up later!" He kneeled to wrap the horses' legs. "Nice job on the manes."

Down the way, Jake romped inside his stall, excited by the early morning activity. The round-the-clock feedings had finally been modified, and he seemed to be thriving on sweet feed and brome hay. He spent most of his day turned out with Spider in the outdoor arena.

"Well, soon he'll graduate to the pasture in back of the house," Chris sighed. "It's only ten acres, but the fence is good."

"Can't you just turn him and Spy out in the big pasture with the other mares and foals?" Jenna asked, wiping off the toe of one spanking new boot.

"Nah. It would be a battle to single him out to feed," Chris said. "They'll be okay in the little pasture."

The girl had barely left the colt's side for two and a half months, and although she was a bit worried about turning him out, she knew it was a necessary sacrifice.

"I'd rather keep them up at the barn where I know he's safe, but he's got to be a real horse for a while," she explained to Jenna. "About six weeks before the Fair, I'll bring him back in, wean him off Spy and start working on his hair. I want him looking good for the weanling class."

The sun was trying to make an appearance when Wes and Jeff came for the horses and led them down the concrete alley, out of the barn and up to the back of the trailer. Jenna felt her heart thumping with excitement as she watched them load.

The aluminum trailer was partitioned for four horses and padded on the sides. The movable partitions were positioned at a slant so each horse faced the wall, where they would be tied. Each had its own rectangular drop window. Zip jumped into the back as if he'd done it a hundred times, Cherry hesitated but finally stepped inside. Wes swung the big door closed as Chris shut the drop windows. Everybody piled into the extended-cab pickup, waving goodbye to Frank, who shouted a token "good luck" and retreated inside the barn to finish morning chores.

The competition was a four-day quarter horse show, held each year at Columbia over the Fourth of July holiday. The list of events, or classes, was the same for each day. Jenna, sitting in the back seat with Chris and Joanna, studied a show bill featuring every type of class imaginable from hunter under saddle to trail classes.

"Here's a class called 'two-year-old western pleasure.' Is that your class?" she asked.

"That's it," Joanna replied. "I figure we won't show until about three or four o'clock. I'll have time to ride her this morning. And they'll give the two-year-olds a fifteen-minute warm up before the class."

She explained to Jenna this show would be the first time western pleasure horses of this age were shown under saddle.

"It's the official debut for two-year-old riders," she explained. "The association doesn't sanction this class before July 1 as the horses are too young and they don't want to encourage pushing them too hard. I hope Cherry holds together for me. She's never been anywhere before."

"I'm not real worried about Zip," Jeff boasted. Despite the sprinkling rain, he was in a good mood. "He'll be just fine. Any bets on me and Zip?"

Chris laughed. "Don't count Mom out. Cherry's been going pretty good all week." She was pleased her mother was going to show the filly.

Joanna had been riding since she was a teenager and during the first ten years of her marriage made regular appearances in the show ring. Chris remembered Joanna riding in western pleasure, trail and leading colts into halter classes. When Chris was twelve, Jo bought a big, leggy brown mare called Reba and began to compete primarily in English classes. By showing English, she isolated herself from competing with Jeff. Chris could never understand why he was touchy about this, but it was clear that instead of feeling pride at his wife's accomplishments, the possibility of her placing higher than him was a real threat to Jeff's ego. The English competition was Joanna's haven. She knew Jeff would never go in a show ring anywhere wearing jodhpurs and a helmet.

It had been two seasons since Chris had seen her mother compete in western pleasure. The good mare Reba became arthritic in her older years and after her retirement, Joanna relegated herself to the job of family show manager. Her new behind-the-scene position meant she was responsible for everything from cleaning out the trailer to making sure the entries were made and horses were ready to show. While this job allowed her to show only occasionally, it seemed to suit her, as it kept her from personally having to endure Jeff's harsh coaching style.

"The Pennys will probably be there," Jeff mused aloud. "When Chris and I were in Clayton, Brad mentioned he planned to come over to the show with Brandon's new mare. She's a nice trotter and real looker, but Brad says her lope needs some work. They expect her to bring home plenty of wins, though."

"Bullshit," said Wes. "Brandon needs to learn to ride first. All he has ever had were 'made' horses, trained to death and ready to win. All he has ever had to do is sit up there and look pretty. He couldn't ride if he was in a wagon."

"That's it, shut your mouth!" shouted Chris.

"I'm just calling it the way I see it," he continued. "Did you ever notice how Brandon's great high-dollar horses just get worse after he starts showing them? Eventually, his old man sells that one and buys him a new one. Your boyfriend's butt never hits the saddle for more than five minutes of warm up. Watch him work his horse in the morning. He just sits up there. He don't have a clue."

Chris silently fumed as she stared out the truck window. Every guy she had been fond of failed what Lil called the "Wes Test." It didn't take much to be tagged a loser by her brother. Chris wondered if he realized how much he was like Jeff in that way. In the back seat with the girls, Joanna laughed and put her arm around her daughter.

"Christine, don't let him get to you! You know this is his favorite game."

By seven o'clock, they had arrived at the show grounds just west of Columbia. Jenna was amazed to see so many trucks and trailers, people and horses. Joanna had reserved three stalls in one of the barns. One for Zip, one for Cherry and one for saddles, bridles and arm loads of other necessities. As Jeff and Wes unloaded the horses, Chris and Jenna helped Joanna carry in water buckets, feed, hay, grooming tools, and more. Soon the tack stall was neatly organized and with the addition of five fold-up director's chairs in front of the stalls, they were settled in for the duration.

While Joanna took her tooled notebook of registration papers and health documents to the office to enter the horses, the girls walked around the show grounds. The main arena was indoors with a large warm-up pen nearby. Parked trailers surrounded the stall barns. Jenna looked at the lettering on the sides of the trailers and observed numerous out-of-state license plates.

"Texas, Oklahoma, Arkansas, Tennessee, Iowa, Kansas," she read out loud as Chris waved hello to almost everybody they passed.

"Do you know most of these people?" Jenna was astonished.

"Well, a lot of them, yes," said Chris. "We've been doing this for a long time, and you see these people over and over again. Pretty soon they get to be a part of your life." She spotted two young women walking toward them.

"Hey! What's up, you two fools?" she shouted. Dana and Desiree Jordan were sisters. Also known as the Terrible Twins from Topeka, they had known Chris for years. She never missed an opportunity to have a little fun with the fact they were born on April Fool's Day.

"Know who's here?" said Dana, smiling. "Old Bob Vaughan from Little Rock! And you have *got* to see his trailer. You know his white trailer that used to say 'Bob and Brenda Vaughan Quarter Horses' on it? Well, the word 'Brenda' has been painted out and it now says 'Bob and Terenda' Vaughan. And sure enough, Brenda's gone and he has a new wife named Terenda. You can see he just changed the first two letters of her name."

"Well, it costs a lot to have your trailer custom lettered!" Desiree laughed, "and he always was a cheap ass. But you ought to see the new wife!"

"She is at least fifteen years younger than him," added Dana. "And Rod Rollins is here, too. He's training for Genesis Ranch now, in Texas. Doing pretty well, I guess."

"Hey, we gotta go help Dad with his halter horses!" Dana pulled her sister away. "Tell Joanna that Mom wants to talk to her, I think it's about the bake sale tomorrow. See you later?" The girls hurried off to another barn.

Desiree yelled back at Chris and Jenna, "Let's go shopping at the big mall tomorrow!"

The show had begun and tall athletic horses with neatly braided manes and English saddles were everywhere. Jenna loved the way the English riders looked in their breeches, tall boots, blazers and black velvet-covered helmets.

"I want to watch a few English classes," said Chris as they walked inside the main building housing the show ring, bleachers, office, concessions and more. She loved the jumping events and was thrilled by the skill of the riders.

After a bit, Chris looked at her watch. "Mom and Dad are probably riding. Let's go look for them."

Jeff and Joanna were already aboard their horses and in the large outside pen, letting the colt and the filly walk slowly around the inside of the fence, looking around. Zip acted like he had seen it all before, but Cherry was jumpy and had a tough time paying attention to Joanna.

"There's Cherry! And she looks like she's scared to death," Jenna groaned.

Chris nodded in agreement, but her attention had shifted to another rider. Coming up the left side on a pert mare with a perfect head and long, sweeping tail was an extremely handsome young man. As he approached the end of the pen where the girls stood, he reined up and stopped.

"Well, it's about time you got here, Chris. You must be Jenna! So, what do you think, ladies, here's my new mare." It was Brandon Penny. "Wait until you see her go."

He jogged off neatly and in ten feet or so, he asked the new mare to lope.

"The western pleasure lope is what we call the money gait," Chris said, eyes on Brandon. "It's what gets you on the judge's card. When it's done right, it's a very cadenced, precise gait. When it's wrong, it's funky."

Brandon's mare lifted up slightly and came down with too much of her weight on the front end of her body, or forehand. From there, as long as she was in full motion, she was unable to shift it back to the rear end, so the longer she loped, the worse it looked.

Jenna watched and finally said to Chris, "Well, I don't know much, but that looks awful to me. She looks like she is dipping and plunging, dipping and plunging, way too much."

Chris nodded in agreement. "She's kind of a deep loper," she muttered, eyes still fixed on Brandon. "He probably needs to stop her, get her rear end under her and start off lighter, picking up on her if he has to, to keep her lighter on the front."

"Lighter on the front," Jenna said, paying stricter attention.

Brandon circled and came back to Chris, who was standing outside the fence. "Well, what do you think?"

She could tell the mare had the potential of being a really nice pleasure horse, but it was apparent Brandon couldn't get it out of her. Chris held her tongue and grinned sweetly.

He started off again, and Jenna noticed he made no effort whatsoever to try to fix anything. He seemed completely unaware of the problem, and the mare churned on with her artificial canter. It was slow enough and the mare's hooves drummed an even 1-2-3, 1-2-3 rhythm as they hit the soft dirt, but the look of it was awful. Oblivious, Brandon patted her on the neck, rode out of the pen and dismounted.

"That's good! I'll finish on that note," he said, pleased with himself. "Hey, you two, wanna duck out of here for some lunch?"

Chris lit up. Jenna could see she wanted to go with him and so she whispered to her friend, "Hey, why don't you go and I'll stay here and watch Zip and Cherry? Go on!"

Jenna watched them walk away. Brandon was tanned, muscular and a little on the short side. He did have a great face. His skin was flawless. He had a strong jaw, nice mouth and big brown spaniel eyes. His teeth were perfect and a little too dazzling. The pair moved out of sight and Jenna was still thinking about Brandon's teeth and wondering if they glowed in the dark. A low, strong voice, just inches from her shoulder, interrupted her thoughts.

"Cherry looks a little tense," Wes said, not looking at her, but scanning the warm-up pen. Joanna was really struggling with Cherry now. "You know her real name ain't Cherry. It's just a nickname and it's short for Cherry Bomb."

"Is that true?" Jenna didn't look at him either.

He smiled, and she couldn't tell if he was kidding or not.

"Have you ever been to Worlds of Fun in Kansas City?" He seemed to change the subject unexpectedly. Jenna nodded and he went on.

"You know when you wait in line at that giant roller coaster and you finally get up front and realize you are too scared to get into that little car?" Jenna was puzzled, but tried to follow.

"You know there's that little door up there going back downstairs and the sign above it says 'Chicken Exit?'" he continued. She nodded.

He draped an arm around her and whispered in her ear. "Well, old Cherry Bomb is looking for the Chicken Exit right now."

Wes' lips so close to her ear and his arm so casually pulling her close ignited a reaction in Jenna that made her cheeks pink. She looked uncomfortable, so he gave her a long, slow smile and let her go. Jenna began to speak but changed her mind. She stood motionless, watching Joanna's war for Cherry's attention.

"I'm going to unhitch the truck and then go to town and get a taco or something, you wanna go?" Wes looked down at the dust and spoke to her. Finally, she took a little breath and turned to him.

"Aren't you going to stay and make sure your mom is all right?" she said.

"No. She's fine. Hell, she'll be in there for the next hour or two. Mom won't ride out of there until she gets the mare right."

Jenna declined the invitation, explaining she wanted to stay and watch.

"Maybe I'll learn something," she said as he shrugged and turned to walk off.

She watched him, half hoping he would turn around and ask her again. But Wes walked on, sensing her eyes on his back. He was preoccupied with his own Lord-have-mercy thoughts of loose hair and a white cotton gown.

Later in the afternoon, Chris and Jenna brushed the horses, painted their hooves shiny black and oiled their muzzles. As Jeff and Joanna were changing clothes, Wes saddled Zip and Cherry and pinned the competition numbers on the rear corners of the show pads. Jeff's show saddle was a light, natural color with an abundance of silver trim. Joanna's was an older saddle, pecan colored leather with less silver, but acceptable. Both horses were nearly ready when Jeff returned from the trailer. Jenna shook her head in admiration. He wore a long-sleeved tan shirt with tan and black plaid sleeves, heavily starched. A light tan silk scarf was tied neatly under the collar, showing only two short tails and a knot. His creamy white straw hat was shaped perfectly.

As he was zipping up his tan leather chaps, Joanna arrived in full battle array. She was smartly dressed in black jeans, white tuxedo shirt and a fitted scoop-necked red and black vest. She was not usually a heavy user of makeup, but her lips were now expertly outlined and filled in with a dark red. A touch of color on her cheeks accented her tanned face. She looked remarkable.

"Will somebody help me pull my hair back?" she asked, blushing a little at her staring family but thoroughly loving the attention. Chris grabbed the hairbrush and went to work. She pulled Joanna's loose blonde hair back into a fluffy ponytail, pinning a large black bow above it so it would lie just under the brim of the hat. It was the style. Jo pulled her hair back off her forehead as Chris positioned the new straw hat on her mother and straightened the horsehair and sterling silver bolo around her collar. She sighed and threw a hopeful glance at her husband, remembering how he used to whistle and slap her on the butt when she dressed up. He looked back at her, casually lit a cigarette and walked down to the end of the barn to smoke outside. She might as well have been standing there in a flannel housecoat.

"Fantastic," Jenna said, astounded by this transformation.

Jo smiled, took out a pair of sterling silver disks she called her lucky earrings and put them on.

"I need your black chaps, Chrissy. They're a little long, but they'll be okay," she said. The girl nodded and retrieved the fringed chaps from the tack stall. Jenna, glad to be a part of it, helped zip Joanna into them.

Wes had both horses completely ready and Jeff was already mounted on Zip. Chris gave her mother a leg up, pulling the bottom of the chaps down and dusting off her boots.

"It's show time. You two go on, Jenna and I'll come along behind with the fly spray and stuff," said Chris as she patted first Cherry and then Zip on the neck and stepped back to let them pass.

Outside the gate, a handful of young horses waited for the class. Jeff kept Zip moving, cramming in every minute of schooling he could. But Jo reined up on the far side and sat quietly aboard Cherry. Another rider sat on his horse nearby, watching. After a minute, he stepped off his young gelding and moved to Cherry's rear end, smiling as he shook out the filly's tail. Chris had looped it into a single knot to keep it from getting dirty on the way to the ring.

"Someone forgot to take the mud-knot out of her tail," he said. Jo turned and looked down at him in surprise. It was Rod Rollins. He ran his fingers carefully through Cherry's tail. He took a step backwards and gave the tail an approving nod. Jo thanked him and as he swung back into the saddle, Jeff and Zip lined up beside her. Jeff motioned for Chris to administer a last minute brushing and to fly spray his colt's legs. In a few minutes, the woman at the gate called for the class.

Thirteen horses were entered in the class for two-year-olds. Most were ridden by trainers or experienced owners. Only four of the riders were women. It was a tough competition by any standards. Because of the inexperience and tender age of the horses, the announcer asked the spectators to step back away from the rail.

The crowd was silent as each young horse came through the gate and for the first time in its life, competed under saddle. For most of these equine juveniles, it was a moment for which they were destined from birth. But it was a baptism that passed without fanfare as riders concentrated on making the most of the allowed warm-up period. Some riders simply walked their horses around the rail. Others loped small circles. At last, the ring steward signaled to take the horses to the rail to be judged.

Chris sat high on the bleachers for the best possible view. Jenna sat beside her, motionless and intensely trying to watch Zip and Cherry both. The horses began jogging counterclockwise, all trying to space out along the rail for good position. The judge studied each one. Zip was calm and moving very well, but his long legs were covering too much ground, making him appear to be moving slightly faster than the others. Jeff frowned as he was forced to go around several other riders.

Chris winced. "Man, Zip's too strong. And he has his head too low!"

Joanna rode by where the girls were seated, looking straight ahead, shoulders back, appearing very confident. Cherry seemed to be nervous at first, but soon relaxed and was jogging along with perfect cadence. The ringmaster called for the walk and then the lope. Jenna's fingernails dug into her hands.

Joanna responded to the call for the lope as if she were in slow motion. She calmly gave the cue to her filly, who moved out and cruised down the rail, her large eyes looking brightly ahead. The judge was standing close and examined the perfect pair for several seconds.

"Nice pass, Mom!" Chris whispered to herself.

Zip had changed gaits, as well, to a nice rocking, slow-legged lope. Jenna gave a quizzical look at Chris, who was studying the colt's movements, which seemed to look fine. But Chris was frowning.

"It's slow, but his head should be vertical, like his forehead was against the wall. His head's behind vertical a bit, see? It looks like he's staring at the dirt!" Chris chewed a fingernail and shook her head. "Dad needs to let him have a little more rein. Judge won't like that headset."

Horses and riders loped another full circle and then were called down to a walk. When the ring steward ordered the horses to reverse at the walk and continue clockwise, several young horses had already been eliminated in the judge's mind for their coltish mistakes. The judge studied them long and hard, making notes. After working horse and riders to the right, or clockwise, he had picked his favorites. The announcer told the riders to "bring 'em in and line 'em up facing the ring steward." The judge walked in front of each horse, paying careful attention to the bits and bosals, and asked each to back up. Several more of the horses lost points for backing badly.

"We have the results of the two-year-old snaffle bit western pleasure," drawled the announcer, after what seemed forever.

He began to read off the top eight places. In the ring, Cherry had become agitated by the delay and Joanna was walking her in small circles. The blue ribbon went to a well-known trainer from Indiana. The applause was considerate, as the horses were young and the crowd knew better than to scare them.

When second place was announced and Joanna Day's name rang out, more applause erupted from around the arena. Jo had many friends. She smiled graciously, then leaned down and patted Cherry as she rode to collect the red ribbon. Wes was at the gate and took the mare as Joanna slid from the saddle, surrounded by friends. The reading of the places continued. Seventh place was awarded to Jeff and Zip. Jenna started to clap her hands, but was silenced by a look from Chris.

Back at the stalls, an exuberant Joanna sank into a chair while her son unsaddled Cherry and put the little mare away.

"I knew I was getting a great ride," Joanna laughed, mopping the sweat from her face. "I wasn't worried about anything but the lope, but she felt so solid, I just pitched the reins to her and let her cruise."

Jenna watched and listened as Joanna savored the achievement.

Jeff and Zip didn't return to the stalls for nearly an hour. Chris knew he was off schooling the colt somewhere until his temper cooled. When they returned, Jeff wordlessly handed the hot, tired horse over to Wes. He fished a beer out of the cooler and sat down beside his wife.

She touched his hand and said, 'Tomorrow's another day."

He scowled and got up. "Yeah, right, Scarlett," he muttered in a surly voice and headed out of the barn. "Larry is here, I'm gonna go look at his new trailer."

Wes watched him exit the barn door. "If Larry Wayne is here, Dad won't be back for while. Let's go ahead and rinse 'em off and then why don't we all ride into town and eat? Afterwards, I'll drop you girls off at the motel while I feed."

Joanna nodded approval of this plan. She and the girls had a room at the nearby motel. Jeff and Wes planned to sleep in the trailer, which was equipped with a foldout cot and a double bed over the gooseneck.

"I'll come and get you in the morning," Wes finished, "and we'll go for breakfast."

On the second and third days of the show, the weather turned miserably hot. The barns were quiet. The crackle of the loud speaker calling for classes periodically interrupted the low hum of box fans hung on the front of each stall. The days were long and sundown was a welcome sight. The classes were nonstop and Jenna spent hours watching the various events, more enjoyable as she was now recognizing familiar horses and rooting for her favorite riders. She and Chris became a foursome with Dana and Desiree, and they shopped at the big Columbia mall and swam at the motel pool.

Jenna took dozens of pictures to send Claudia, including a photo of the Days' trailer, Jeff and Zip, Joanna and Cherry. Wes took one of Jenna, Chris and the Jordans posing on the tailgate of the truck, arms interlocked. Brandon followed Chris around like a stalker. Jenna snapped photos of Chris and Brandon riding double.

Joanna and Cherry placed second again on Saturday. Jeff and Zip managed to land a fifth.

"He's getting worse," Jeff confided in Larry after his ride. "His head ain't right, and at the lope, he gets to doing something really funky after he gets tired. Maybe I'm riding him too much before the class."

On Sunday, Joanna earned a respectable third place. Jeff and Zip failed to place at all. As he rode out, he growled at his wife, who had waited for him.

"Go scratch me for tomorrow's class. No way I'm going back in there and look like a fool."

Later that evening, Chris and Jenna walked out to the trailer to inspect the fireworks Wes had bought for the following night. Discussing Cherry's impressive debut, Chris paused abruptly and leaned forward, eyes bugged.

"Did you realize Cherry could be the circuit champion for the two-year-old class?"

Noticing Jenna's puzzled expression, she explained. "To be the circuit champ, Cherry has to have the most overall points and she has to compete all four days."

The girls were trying to figure if any other horse and rider could beat two seconds and third, when Wes sat down with them and grinned.

"You know the trainer who beat Mom on Friday and got second on Sunday?" He leaned toward them and confided. "He's loading up to leave right now 'cause he's got to be back in Indiana by tomorrow. So guess what that means?"

Chris thought about it for a second and jumped to her feet, shouting "Slam dunk! Let's go tell Mom."

The three hurried back to the stalls where Joanna was wrestling her big show saddle out of the tack stall, heading to the trailer with it. Chris saw her mother had been crying. Joanna's face was a mess.

"What's going on here?" Chris shouted as she tried to grasp the meaning of the tears. *Why was Joanna putting her saddle away?*

"What are you doing! All you have to do is ride tomorrow and Cherry's got the circuit championship!" Wes howled, face ignited. He stormed past the stalls to look for Jeff, but Joanna ran after him and grabbed his shoulders.

"Your dad's going to ride Cherry tomorrow. He's gonna scratch Zip. Please don't say anything to him. This has caused enough trouble already," she begged, eyes swollen.

"Why is he taking over?" Chris shouted. Joanna shrugged off an answer, wiped her face and turned back to her hot-tempered son, who had kicked over the two water buckets and scattered them.

"You were doing great!" He was seething.

"Weston, I am asking you, please don't make a scene. Let it go." Her voice was desperate.

"So Cherry's circuit championship buckle will be his, huh? That selfish bastard," he raged, brushing past her and heading toward the door. "Why won't you stand up to him?"

Jenna, silent until now, called out, "Wes! Don't do anything to make this worse!"

Wes stopped and looked at her, jolted by her intervention.

"You don't want your own actions to cause your mom more pain, do you?" Jenna walked to his side. "I know how you feel." Her face was ripe with a secret understanding and it commanded his attention.

He paused for a long while, looking back at Jo with anguish. Then he backed slowly away from the stalls as if looking for a safe way to detonate the fury inside him.

Jenna took his hand and led him out of the barn and across the lot to a grassy hillside. She sat down and pulled him down beside her. Sitting close, she leaned into his shoulder and began to speak softly to him. He wasn't really listening to what she was saying, but it was soothing and he didn't want her to stop. He closed his eyes and let the sound of her voice guide him to a place where he could leave the anger.

The next day, Jeff won first place and the circuit championship on Cherry.

CHAPTER TEN

Downstream from New Winston, the Missouri River surges past the landings and terminals, under giant bridges and through the rural, quiet villages of the Missouri River Valley. The great wide channel bends itself through venerable towns like Lexington, Waverly and Prairie Rock, a sparse, modest little town, isolated from urban sprawl and unnoticed by most of the world.

Gabriel Judd lived alone above Charlie Edwards' old farm supply store in Prairie Rock. Narrow stairs led up the back to his unrefined apartment, an angular attic area with planked walls and raftered ceiling. A crude lodging by most standards, it nevertheless had become his home.

The young man liked the old paned windows and alcoves of his refuge. He liked the rough wooden floor, scrubbed and painted dark green with surplus paint. The place, however simple, was not austere. A large iron bed, an estate sale treasure, sprawled in the corner under a patchwork quilt. A primitive cupboard, an old rocker, a small painted table, and other simple pieces filled the place.

There was a small bathroom, but no kitchen. Every morning, Gabe ate breakfast at the town's only restaurant. Most evenings, he returned to Vicki's Cafe for a corn dog or cheeseburger. Sometimes he had supper with Charlie and Edith Edwards. Charlie was a tall, imposing man with an amiable, weathered face and thick graying hair. His plump wife was of German descent, as were many of the town's inhabitants. She was typically fair-haired and blue-eyed.

Gabe had worked for Charlie at the feed store since he was sixteen. Charlie and his wife had no children of their own and had grown to consider Gabe part of the family. They had known Cynthia Judd for years. After the funeral, her son lived alone at the farm outside of town for a month. When fire destroyed the small rented house and barn, Gabe went to Charlie seeking a job. Edith begged the boy to come and live with them in the big house on River Street. Gabe politely declined, but accepted instead, the attic room above the store.

"I worry about Gabriel," Edith Edwards told her husband often. "He works so hard. That's all he does!"

"Workin' keeps him straight with the world. Too bad more young people don't realize that. This country wouldn't have so many screwed-up kids."

"He doesn't run with the other lads in town much and as far as I can tell, hasn't much interest in the girls."

"Don't fret about the kid, he'll be fine," her amused husband replied, "he's saving all his money for a down payment on a pickup truck. And don't worry about the girls, for God's sake. They come in the store from all over the county just to look at him. Ferd Meier said his daughters fight over which one gets to come to town for feed."

"Maybe one of these days, some nice girl will catch his eye."

"I suspect that will sure 'nuff happen."

"But it's not normal for a boy his age to spend all his time working," Edith persisted. "He acts so, well, so old. I think he lost his childhood way too soon. Remember how skinny and tall he was when he first came to us, needing for a job and a place to stay?"

Charlie smiled. "Yep. He's a fine strappin' lad now. He's a little on the quiet side, but there ain't nothin' wrong with a fella who don't flap his jaws when there's nothin' to say."

On Gabe's seventeenth birthday, he bought himself a used pickup. Charlie looked approvingly at the new purchase and offered to let Gabe park it in the old tin-roofed concrete block garage in back of the store. The two spent one whole Saturday cleaning out this shed. Observing Gabe's satisfaction as he discovered the structure was substantially sound and larger than it looked, Charlie concluded it had been claimed in the same way Gabe claimed the attic. Soon it had new light bulbs, several old chairs, and a radio.

Although Edith was hopeful the truck would lead to a change in Gabe's social life, he continued to fill his daylight hours with his after-school chores at the store and odd jobs around town. One of his regular jobs was helping the Widow Kochendorfer with yard work. The Widow K. owned a large, old house on a hillside at the end of town. Her son, Gilbert, was a slim young man with long pale hair. He was a year younger, but there was something about Gilbert that penetrated Gabe's silent shell. After the mowing was done, the two frequently sat on the porch steps, gulped lemonade, talked and laughed. Gilbert K. had been blind since an accident at age nine, but he belonged to a CD club and enjoyed the reputation of being the hippest guy in town.

"I heard Charlie caught a good mess of catfeesh last week," Gil said one Saturday night. "Man! I sure would like to go fishin'. My old man used to take me before he died. And there ain't no better eatin' than catfeesh."

"I ain't fished the river for a while myself," said Gabe. "I didn't want to have anything to do with the river for a couple years, but I'm over that now."

"Are you sure you're okay with it?"

"Yeah. It's funny, but the river don't bother me now ... bridges do, but the river don't."

"We got an old johnboat, ain't but about a twelve footer, but it's got a little outboard," said Gil, thumbing his Ray-Bans back on his nose. "It's out behind the old chicken house. We could load it in your truck and set some limb lines on the point and then run 'em about midnight."

"And then we could run 'em again in the morning, early," said Gabe, interested. "We gotta have some good skeeter shit, though."

"Got some."

"I can get the bait then. Charlie keeps some jars of stink bait in the old icebox at the store. It's supposed to be killer stuff. Rotten chunks of shad soaked in some other God-awful secret shit."

"Good stuff, eh?"

"Good? It's foul. You gotta wash your hands with ketchup to get it off. I'll grab a few jars. Pick you up after supper."

Despite Gil's handicap, Gabe found him to be a good fishing companion. They put the boat in at the end of the levee, baited their hooks with chunks of putrid shad and tied the lines to tree limbs protruding from the point. It was nearly eleven when they headed back to check the lines.

After dark, the river became an ominous place. The night air was filled with the resonant drone of insects and frogs, and the sound of the murky water slapping at the mud along the banks fused with the rushing sound of the great channel.

It became their Saturday night routine, to tug the flat-bottomed boat into the truck bed and head for the riverbank. Guided only by a large flashlight, Gabe maneuvered the johnboat from line to line. The river was alive and occasionally a heavy splash in the water near the boat broke the eerie solitude, never failing to startle the fishermen. Each time Gabe pulled up a heavy line, both held their breath, anticipating what might be on the end of the hook. Maybe a snapping turtle, maybe a big carp. Maybe

Gabe would flash his light into the menacing jaws of an angry gar, one of the most repulsive creatures of the deep. If they were lucky, they might pull up a fine channel cat.

"What would you do if you pulled up somebody's leg? Half ate up by fish?" Gil whispered. "You know, up in Kansas City, they kill people and throw their murdered bodies in the river to be found by folks fishin' …"

"God! I don't know! I hope we never find nothin' like that!"

"I guess that would be one time I'd be *glad* I'm blind," said Gil.

Gabe's favorite time on the river was before dawn. He liked to watch the sun come up on the rolling brown water, and Gil enjoyed his friend's narration of the event. Each time, it was different.

"What do you see up river?" Gil asked one morning.

"Oh, lots of stuff. More river I guess."

"Can you see very far up there?"

"No, there's a bend. But I know the river goes all the way to the headwaters in Montana."

"You ever been downstream?"

"A ways. I know it winds down through Jeff City, then Charlie says it joins the Mississippi just below St. Charles."

"Man! I woulda like to have been Lewis and Clark when they were discoverin' it. Don't you know this river blew their everlovin' minds? Not knowing what was around every bend. Come to think of it, they musta been sort of like me … Not bein' able to see what was out there."

"I don't really think it makes any difference if you can see or not. A person never knows what's around the bend until he gets there." Gabe jerked the rope starter on the small outboard. It coughed a plume of gaseous smoke and purred into action.

"Let's go see if we caught anything."

CHAPTER ELEVEN

Under Frank's scrutinizing eye, Jenna saddled the red roan. Floyd, a patient sort, stood quietly, eyes half closed. Although Jenna admired the youthful show quality of the Days' horses, she was content to call the old roan "her horse." He had been a fine show gelding, and Jenna was thankful Frank saw no reason to sell him after the old horse's glory days were over.

Both Frank and Lil enjoyed riding, and the couple kept a few older broke geldings and several over-the-hill mares. Frank had a no-nonsense attitude regarding proper basics, and his well-broke and kind-mannered horses made commendable teachers for kids and novices. Weston and Chris had learned to ride on Frank's old horses and now Floyd, it seemed, was on the job, teaching Jenna.

"If you measured this roan horse's brain activity, you'd see a flat line, but that's what I like for western pleasure," he said. "Easygoing, compliant. See, a laid-back horse just says okay, and does what ever you want. A shrewd horse will try to outthink you and maybe outmuscle you. A wily horse will always demand you prove you are the boss. Now, a really crafty horse will let you think you *are* the boss until you ask him to do something he doesn't really want to do."

"So are you saying Floyd's a retard?" asked Jenna.

"No. He just doesn't give a shit. He's perfect for you," Frank told her. "In fact, he's lazy. I'd have you ride with spurs, but you need more experience first. Today, I want you to work on your hands. You're jiggling 'em too much. You haven't developed a rider's seat yet, and eventually, you'll learn to ride more with your legs. For now, all the control you have is through the reins. So you gotta keep your hands soft and quiet."

She finished adjusting the saddle and gave the horse an affectionate pinch on the neck. Frank checked her work and cinched up Floyd a bit more.

"All right, young lady, here's a little test. Go into the tack room and get the grazing bit in the split ear head stall."

She returned with the wrong bridle.

"That's a grazer all right, but I said split ear head stall. Go back and try again." Soon she returned with the correct headstall. This had become a game with them.

"Let's ride, Clyde," he said when Floyd was thoroughly fly-sprayed.

"Are you riding with me today?" she asked, brows lifting in surprise. Usually, he stood in the middle of the arena and coached her. But outside, tied to the corner rail of a turnout pen, was a large bay horse.

"Yep. We call this tub of lard Sweet Jesus. He was so big and ugly when he was born, me and Lil just stood there and said 'sweet Jesus!'" He patted the fat horse on the rump so hard that a puff of dust rose from the sunburned hair. "I got him up today 'cause he needs the exercise."

The big bay snorted and shook his head.

"Instead of working in the arena, let's just walk down the road a piece," suggested Frank, replacing the bay's halter and lead rope with a bridle. "We'll ride down by my place."

As they clopped down the road, Jenna learned that Frank's brother, John, originally owned the little place. For thirty years, Frank and John operated a small hardware store in town. The brothers had assumed ownership from their father and worked hard to build it into a flourishing business. Years ago, John's wife left the farm and divorced him. No one knew where she went, but she left behind their fourteen-year-old daughter.

"And John's girl was, of course, Joanna," Frank explained. "Lil and I were living in town and we couldn't stand the thought of my brother and Jo living out on the farm alone, so we went out and stayed with them. That same year, my brother passed away of a massive heart attack." He thumped on the lethargic gelding with his heels to keep alongside Jenna and Floyd.

"We sold the hardware store and moved permanently to the farm," he continued. "Our next-door neighbors were the Days. They were fine old people. Both gone now. Jeff was their only grandson. Jeff's father died years ago in an accident. His mom remarried and moved to California."

Joanna didn't know Jeff, as he grew up in Lexington, Frank told her, settling back in the saddle and giving the horse his head. "When they later met at college, both of 'em were pretty shocked to find they were purt'near neighbors. Well, you know the rest of the story. She quit college to marry him."

Frank scowled. "He sort of inherited the farm and when he graduated from college, they moved in."

"Somewhere along the line, Jeff met my mom," Jenna offered, trying to fill in the facts.

Frank scratched his jaw and raised one eyebrow. "So your mom ran with Jeff a little before he started goin' with Joanna? You mean they dated some?" he rambled, testing her for information.

"Yes, but I think it was more than just a dating thing. She was *insane* for him. Mom's told me about him. I think they went together a long time. Does anybody know that?"

Frank shook his head. "I reckon just Jeff and Joanna," he said, a bit troubled. "And it probably ought to stay that way."

He guided the conversation back to the comfort zone, chatting more about Joanna's childhood. "She's always been the finest kind of competitor. Even when she was young, she would always congratulate those kids who placed higher than she did. And she meant it, too."

"If competing is so important to her, why did she let Jeff hog all the glory for Cherry's big win?" Jenna never had to play a cautious role with Frank. "And the part I don't get, Joanna was doing great. She would have won it for Day Quarter Horses! I know she's still pissed about it, 'though she doesn't say."

Frank knew it was true that Joanna remained unsettled by Jeff's actions. After the show, she had distanced herself from the daily horse operations and had not saddled Cherry for a full week.

"Who knows why he does stuff like that? But, he's always been full of himself," Frank confessed. "Mr. Super Ego."

"Do they fight a lot?" Jenna asked bluntly, pushing for more.

Frank shrugged. He enjoyed theorizing on any subject. "They always get into it at horse shows. Mostly, she gives in. You know, Jeff doesn't do any outside training now. He just trains his own horses. He's the type of trainer who is a control freak. He shows the young horse the deal right off the bat, 'we do it my way, and you and I will have no problems.' The problem is, he takes it a step further and can't help trying to control everyone around him, including his wife."

"What you're saying is he treats his wife like he treats a filly in his show string," Jenna looked him straight in the eye.

"Yep, pretty much. She does whatever he says and sometimes I don't believe she even thinks for herself anymore." He stopped. Listening to his own words, he decided he was talking too much. He settled back in the saddle and closed the subject.

***

The early July days were torrid and the air thick with humidity. Thriving cornfields baked in the sun and tall thistles grew flush with the fence line. Early one morning, Jenna accompanied Frank and Chris as they took Spider and her adopted son to a small fenced-off grassy area behind the old barn. By this time, anywhere Spider went Jake followed obediently.

"I guarantee you can catch this mare anytime, anywhere. Just call her and she'll come to you, and that little demon will be right behind her," Frank told Chris.

"So what's the plan here?" Jenna, the novice, was inquisitive. "I'm still not getting the big picture. I thought you were going to turn them out in the pasture."

"We are, but we need to let 'em out here for just an hour at a time for a few days so he can get used to fresh green grass. Else it'll make him sick. Then, we can turn him out in a bigger pasture and let him run with Spy for a few weeks. We can go out there and feed him twice a day, and he can get all the green grass he can eat."

They watched as Spy and Jake explored the small pen and eventually began grazing. "All young horses need pasture time, but Jake especially needs it," said Chris. "I want him to be as normal as possible. He needs to run and play and develop his legs, tendons, muscle, all that. Wish it could be longer."

"Won't he get sunburned and look awful for the Fair?" Jenna was wising up and her comment forced an amused smile from Frank.

"Good point, but he'll be all right," answered Chris. "He's still got his baby fuzz. That will come off and he'll have a new coat of hair by the Fair, and then we'll know what color he is going to be. Uncle Frank still says he's going to be black."

"Like a black cat in a coal bin at midnight," stated Frank, and the girls smiled appreciatively.

After supper on Saturday night, Frank and Chris decided it was time to take Spy and Jake to the bigger pasture. The horses had adjusted to the change in diet and Jake was ready, at last, for his first real taste of freedom.

Jenna joined them as they walked down the path in back of the house. "I wouldn't miss this for the world."

Ten acres had been fenced off separately and used as a small hayfield. It had recently been mowed and was level and cleared of brush and trees, with the exception of three large elms near the gate. A common fence separated the area from the thirty acres of pasture, ponds and trees where the Days' brood mares raised their foals. This larger pasture extended north to Frank and Lil's property line.

Chris swung the big gate open and Spider raised her head and called out to the other mares in the adjoining pasture. For years, the old mare had shared a common fence with them, and therefore was no stranger. As the fat, glossy mares and their foals looked up from the grassy waves of green, Frank released Spy and she trotted off. Chris took a deep breath, unbuckled the halter from Jake's head and stepped back. He stood for an instant, then wheeled around and plunged away, nickering for Spider. As his long legs stretched out and he sped into the free world, he seemed to flash airborne across the ground.

"Only the wind dare give chase," Jenna whispered, remembering an old quotation from a horse book.

"That's for damn sure," Frank said softly. He glanced at Chris, intent on her colt's first interaction with the others across the fence.

"You all can go back to the house," she said, squinting, focusing only on Jake. "I have to stay here and watch for a while."

Jenna hesitated, wanting to stay, but Frank motioned to her. They headed back down the path. "Let's leave her alone for a bit," he said. "She's been through it with this colt. The letting-go process will likely be tough on her."

Jenna was awakened at next daybreak by the sound of footsteps hurrying down the stairs. She heard the back door slam, rose from the bed and stepped to her window. Her room was on the back of the big house and faced the east pasture. Below, she saw Chris walking down the path and up to the big gate. The sun's first rays bathed the green expanse and the landscape glistened with morning dew. Near the back of the pasture, Jenna spotted the gray mare grazing peacefully. Several yards away, nestled in the grass, Jake was motionless, save an occasional flick of his short tail.

Chris placed the red feed can on the ground and stepped inside the gate, calling to them. The colt stretched out his long front legs and scrambled to his feet, looking toward Spider for a brief moment. The old mare heard the call and had begun a slow, lumbering walk toward the girl. Jake raced ahead, making big circles.

Chris approached the mare and slipped the halter on her. Then, grabbing a handful of mane, she swung up on her broad back, holding the lead rope as a single rein. Jenna watched as the girl rode back to the main gate, Jake trotting brightly along beside them, skittering about in the purity of the day's first sunshine. Watching them from her window, Jenna envied the girl's uncomplicated and joyful relationship with the horses.

Her thoughts were interrupted by the sound of voices inside the house. The large bedroom at the end of the hall belonged to Jeff and Joanna and as Jenna peeked out of her room, she saw the door was closed. In the still morning air, the angry conversation was clearly audible.

"When are you going to get your ass back on that filly? Do you think she's so good now you don't have to ride her every day?" Jeff was ragging at his wife.

"I think she needs a rest. I've been riding her hard since February, and I …" Jo began to make excuses, but then stopped and thought better of it. "No, actually, I'm the one who needs a break. You didn't think I was good enough to ride her the last day at Columbia. Now we're home, she's mine again, huh?"

Jeff exploded. "Oh, here we go again on that crap! We've got a lot invested in that filly. Time and money! But I guess you never think about that, do you? What's with you, anyway? I've given you everything you've ever wanted!"

The conversation continued, but it was muffled and Jenna couldn't make out the words. Suddenly, Jeff screamed, "Hell, I don't care. Send the filly down the road for dog food! I don't give a shit!" The door opened and he stormed out, slamming it behind him with a force that rattled the upstairs walls.

***

By the end of July, Joanna was spending more time at the house and rarely even came to the barn. Chris finally cornered her one morning in the kitchen.

"Mom, are you ever going to start riding again? I miss you at the barn." She placed her arms around her mother's waist and hung her chin over Joanna's shoulder.

Jo wiped her hands on a dishrag. "I don't want you to worry about me, but I don't know what I want to do, honey. I do know I don't want to ride Cherry anymore. I don't want to ride at all."

She turned toward her daughter and embraced her. "Why don't you take over riding her? That would make me happy, really. It's not her fault, and she's too good to waste. How about it?"

Reluctantly, Chris agreed, feeling a jab of pain for her mother's distress. Joanna was genuinely relieved, knowing another dreaded confrontation with Jeff could be avoided if Christine took over. She was hoping Jeff would be pleased if the pretty little chestnut mare became Chris' responsibility.

Chris began riding daily, often with Jenna. They rode in the arena, and sometimes down the road and through the woods. Frequently, Wes saddled his mare Sheila and joined them. Jenna liked to watch Wes ride. He didn't sit the saddle like Chris did. Chris unconsciously rode like she was in the show ring. Wes was totally relaxed. He hadn't shown a pleasure horse since he was in walk-trot. Instead, he liked to haul his mare over to the next town where he and some friends drank a few beers and took turns throwing their loops at a practice cow.

He liked to tease Chris and rode close to her, taking his foot out of the stirrup nearest her and nudging Cherry with his boot toe. Threats from his sister simply egged him on and he enjoyed trotting Sheila by Cherry's head, teasing and threatening.

"I wonder if I reached out and just took this filly's bridle off, what she'd do."

"Leave me alone, you jerk!" Chris yelled.

One evening, in the big outdoor arena, Wes loped Sheila in large fast circles, deftly flipping a rope around in front and behind her. Her ears were pinned but the mare endured it.

"Old Sheila's gonna make a pretty good rope horse," he said, playing with the loop. "I bet little Cherry Bomb would be scared to death if I tossed this at her." He headed toward Chris and the filly.

"Don't you even think about it!" Chris screamed. "Don't you dare scare this filly while I'm riding her, or I'll just get off and put her away!"

"Ain't that just like you! So what are you going to do if something really spooks her? Get off? How are you gonna teach her to accept surprises?" Wes was serious. "It looks to me like she's training you."

Chris scowled at him, grumbling a denial.

"She's training you, little sister, and you don't even realize it." He kept it up. "If she doesn't like something, you avoid it so you don't upset her." He was trying to make a point, but Chris continued to glare.

"Shut up and leave me alone, dipshit!" she growled. Wes feigned disappointment and backed off, joining Jenna and Floyd on the other side of the arena.

"Jenna," Chris called out, "don't let him mess with you!"

"I'm not worried," said Jenna.

Wes' point was evident to her and made perfect sense. Confident in Floyd's bombproof nature, she circled the gelding around the mare, came in close and looked at him defiantly, corners of her mouth crinkling in a teasing way.

"You can mess with me all you want. I can handle it."

"Can you now?" He shook his head wickedly, pretending to read a second meaning into her words. He smiled, coiled the rope up and dropped it over the rail.

***

The two young women climbed the fence and walked across the pasture.

"This is it, Jen. It's time to wean Jake away from Spider and bring him to the barn full time." Chris heaved a sigh of finality. "He ain't gonna like it, but he doesn't need her anymore." Jake spotted her and, as was his habit, called out with a coltish whinny. He dashed forward and met them, wheeling and kicking.

"You pest! Get back!" shouted Chris. She caught the mare and swung up on her back. She extended a hand to Jenna. "Come on, we'll ride double. It's safer up here."

Frank came in the afternoon with Aunt Lil, who took the old mare and headed out of the barn with her. The old gray nickered to Jake as she realized she was going home. Down the road, Chris heard her calling to him again and again. Having been separated from her frequently, Jake wasn't particularly upset.

"Will he throw a fit when he realizes she's really gone?" Jenna asked.

"Probably." Frank shrugged. "But we'll move Cherry to the stall on the other side of him and he'll probably take up a little with her. Which is good, since we'll be hauling them together to the Fair."

Although Chris enjoyed riding Cherry, the focal point of her day was working with Jake. He was now four months old and the mousy gray baby hair was shedding, revealing patches of glistening black color. She brushed him until his hide was tender, plucking the fuzz a bit at a time until his entire coat looked like black patent leather. The crescent marking on his face was snowy white. He was the image of his sire.

Wes liked to watch her working with Jake. He particularly enjoyed coaching and crabbing from the sidelines.

"He's not a pet!" he barked at every opportunity. "Don't treat him like one. Getting him ready for this weanling halter class at the Fair is going to require a total commitment from you, little sister."

Chris looked back at him in shock. "Total commitment? I wrote the book on total commitment!" she glared.

Jenna laughed, loving them both. She noticed he was wearing the same shirt he was wearing that night in the barn, the first night she had met him. The sight of him in that shirt forced wistful, half-formed feelings to tumble out. For weeks she had caught herself thinking about Wes and had tried to ignore those signals. She tried to remember how Wes' arms felt around her, but she had exorcised that awful night from her mind and all sensations of it had been banished.

She wondered if he even realized this was the same shirt he had wrapped around her.

***

Along with the daily schedule of feeding, exercising horses and cleaning stalls, working with Jake consumed much of Chris' time. Each day, she reserved time to teach Jake halter horse etiquette. She entered the indoor arena as if she were presenting him to the judge, and walked briskly down the center of the pen with Jake beside her. Jenna impersonated the judge, walking around the colt and feigning great interest. After weeks of practice, Jake trotted alongside keeping pace with Chris' steps. Then she moved him into an imaginary line of colts and set him up in the model position standard to quarter horses – all four legs perfectly straight, feet precisely in place, long, slim neck extended and nose tipped out.

She taught him to stand motionless while she relaxed the lead and walked around him, straightening his hocks by hand and at times lifting a tiny hoof that was slightly forward and placing it down again. By tugging on the lead, rocking him back and forth and tapping on a hoof with her boot, she taught him to automatically assume this stance.

By mid-August, he had learned this lesson well, and Chris could set him up quickly and then return to the left side of his head and position herself for Jenna's inspection. Jenna, with hands folded in back of her and looking sternly down her nose, would saunter around him, pretending to look him over in the most critical manner she could muster.

"Hey, Christine! I'll give you fifty bucks for him!" Uncle Frank would yell from the doorway where he watched.

"He is special, isn't he?" Jenna asked Frank one afternoon as Chris trotted Jake up and down the arena. Frank reached in his back pocket for his tobacco can.

"Let me put it this way. He's gonna be every bit as good as Vince. But, he's gonna be taller. Look at the legs on him."

Each evening after supper, Chris buckled protective splint boots on Jake's front legs and turned him into the outdoor arena to play. He loved this freedom and streaked around the large pen like a speeding bullet, exhibiting long, sliding stops. Chris and Jenna never failed to appreciate this show and often flipped on the arena's outdoor lights so they wouldn't miss anything. Oblivious to his amused audience, the black colt would trot down the center of the arena, swinging his pretty head from side to side, snorting and blowing like a full-grown stallion. They held their breath as he would charge recklessly across the arena and straight for the fence. Just before he slammed into it full force, he would gather himself up and as quick as a thought, swap directions.

As summer drew to an end, the sweltering heat ruled the work schedule. They sat in lawn chairs in the shade on the east side of the barn, watching the shadows lengthen and waiting for sundown. Late evenings at the barn became a routine. After Chris put Jake away, it was often several hours before the temperatures were tolerable for riding. Afterwards, they took turns rinsing the hot horses in the wash rack and would tie them outside at a long hitching rail.

Chris had her own hitching rail beside the barn wall. Posted above it was a big plastic red sign reading, "Christine's parking: all others will be towed." It was a present Jeff had brought back to her from a big show in Springfield, Illinois. Family and friends honored the sign, and the space became Chris' private parking spot for both her vehicle and her mount.

After the barn chores were done, they sat and talked until late, lounging back in the chairs and watching the bug zapper. Often, Frank and Lil joined them, along with other horse people in the area who dropped in to visit. Mike McGraw stopped by frequently. Sometimes, after a long day shoeing horses, their farrier Al George came by before heading home.

The conversation was guaranteed entertainment and never failed to be stimulating. The topics addressed were sometimes intensely serious in nature, at other times amusing. While the main menu always offered up horses and horse people, the dialogue moved effortlessly from music groups to UFOs and on to endless personal anecdotes.

These breezy conversations proved to be learning experiences for Jenna. She was developing an understanding of horse people, and more significantly, she was becoming one.

"Once the telling of horse stories begins, a terrible thing happens," Chris explained one night as Frank began one of his tales. "It's sort of like the ninety-nine bottles of beer song!"

Jenna sat for the next two hours, bombarded by stories of near-fatal riding accidents and dozens of grisly accounts of injury. As soon as Jeff finished telling the details of the compound fracture he suffered when he and his horse slipped and fell, Lil took the lead.

"Why, you miserable cream puff! One time my thoroughbred mare fell on me, broke both my legs and it was six hours before anyone found me."

"That's nothin'!" Frank jumped right in. "I was riding Leroy when he was two, barely broke to ride and he decided he was gonna play with me a little. That goofball bastard suddenly reared straight up and fell over backwards with me and landed right on me. Saddle horn drove through my chest, broke three ribs. I was coughin' up blood and nearly unconscious – didn't even know where I was."

Chris began to tell Jenna a story about Leroy going down with her as they were crossing the creek.

"Let *me* tell this story," offered Wes, loudly interrupting her. "Chris had this super bad wreck down at the creek when a horsefly landed on old Leroy and he fell ... well, she says he fell, but I think he just lay down in the water and rolled to get the fly off ..."

By now, his sister was out of her lawn chair, trying to choke him, but Wes fought her off and continued the story. "Anyway, not only did she get a little mud on her, she broke a fingernail to boot. It was one *hell* of a wreck!"

"That's it, no more beer for you tonight!" Chris retaliated, giggling through her feigned aggravation.

Later that night, Jenna lay on her bed, trying to write a note to her mother. Earlier in the week, Claudia had called and announced she had made arrangements for her daughter's return to school. But Jenna didn't really want to think about school. It had been a particularly good day and she sifted through its events. There was so much she wanted to share with Claudia.

Mother,

I can't begin to tell you how much I love this place. Hard to believe the summer is almost over and it's time to go back to school. Chris and I are getting Jake ready to show at the Missouri State Fair, and I have promised to be there when he shows. Plus, Chris is riding Cherry and she needs me to help. Hey, thanks for going along with me on this dorm thing. I really wanted to live on campus this year. Talk to you soon.

Jenna signed it with love and added a P.S. - *Here's a photo I took of Invincible and Jeff.*

It was nearly one o'clock when she turned out the light to go to bed. At her bedroom window, she thought she heard a noise. She tiptoed lightly across the dark room and pulled the curtain back. Sitting on the roof outside the window was Wes.

"Hey, wanna come out?"

"I'm not dressed!" she slid the screened window up and leaned out. She was wearing only a long pink tee shirt and her underpants.

"Is this what you sleep in?" He boldly touched the sleeve. His hand moved to her face. He slid his fingers along her cheek then stopped.

"What are you doing out there?" She clutched her shirt to her body. The feel of his hand on her face sent a tremor through her belly.

"Well, I wanted to see you and I can't very well just go knockin' on the door." He spoke softly, a brazen smile tugging at his lips. "So I climbed up the tree to the roof. C'mon. Get out here."

Jenna hesitated, then pushed up the window screen and stepped through. Her bare feet and legs in the moonlight made his heart race. The tee shirt hung nearly to her knees and she demurely tugged it close to her as she sat down next to him on the roof. The asphalt shingles were still warm from the heat of the day.

He leaned towards her. Before she could decide what she should do next, he pulled her body around and wrapped both arms around her. He felt hot against her cool skin.

"Wish you didn't have to leave, Jen," The words spilled out. His lips were boldly brushing against her hair. "Know what I mean?"

He lifted her and sat her on his lap. Jenna had known from the beginning how many personalities lived inside Wes' head. She had seen most of them. She knew he was recklessly impulsive and while this knowledge should have served as caution, she succumbed to the truth that for some time, she had longed for this intimacy.

His hands dropped around her waist and she felt his breath on her neck.

"If you want me to stop, just say so. You want me to stop? Say it," he whispered, lips pressed against her cheek. She hesitated and he held her tighter. "Say it."

"No, don't stop." Her voice surprised her.

"Kiss me or I'll throw myself off this roof," he said. She hesitated, amused, then abruptly surrendered and turned her face into his. He smiled at this and lightly touched her mouth with his lips, treasuring the texture and the taste. He continued to kiss her face, teasing, until she dug her fingers on the back of his neck. Her response abruptly unleashed an intensity in him that both shocked and aroused her. He clutched a handful of her hair and kissed her with unbridled urgency. One hand slid along her silky bare thigh toward the edge of the pink tee shirt and then stopped, restraining a backdraft of desire. He lifted her and sat her aside.

"Ride with me tomorrow," he said breathlessly, cupping her face with both hands. "We'll go up to the hayfield. It'll be our last chance to be alone before you go back to Kansas City."

She felt a tearing in her chest at his words and closed her eyes. He leaned over and pressed one more long kiss on her lips. And then he was gone. Jenna refused to move, afraid the slightest movement would erase the feelings still vibrating within her. She finally rose to her feet and climbed back inside. In her bed, she lay quietly, feeling her own pulse in her fingertips.

When she awoke, it was a bright, steamy morning. Although the sun had erased the night, remnants of its dark heat lingered within Jenna. She dressed and went downstairs.

"Wes has already had breakfast, well, if you call aspirin any kind of breakfast," said Chris. "He's a little hung over. He left with Al George, our farrier. Wes rides with him sometimes to help him shoe horses. I think Al wants Wes to go to work for him."

It was nearly four o'clock when Wes returned. Jenna finally heard Al's truck leave and walked to the barn where she found Cherry and Sheila already standing in crossties.

Imitating Uncle Frank, Wes gave her an order. "All right, here's a test you won't be taking at the university. Go in the tack room and, for Cherry, get out the single-piece headstall with the O-ring snaffle, the one with the latigo reins. Also, get a running martingale. For Sheila, get the D-ring snaffle, I guess."

She laughed and easily retrieved the correct equipment.

"I noticed when you work Sheila with this snaffle bit, you use draw reins. Want me to get 'em?" She faced him, hands on her hips. An even smile spread across his face.

"Not this time, I'm not in the mood for schooling today. Let's just have some fun."

They rode out side by side. Wes glanced at her sideways, satisfied how confident Jenna looked astride his mare.

"Let's ride down in back of the barn, cut across the creek and up to the west hay field," he suggested. She nodded her assent, pleased at being alone with him.

"Do you like her?" he said, after they had ridden about a half-mile. "I mean, the mare. Do you like her?"

Jenna laughed. "Of course, I like her. It's like having power steering and cruise control after riding Floyd!"

It was a humid evening and they stopped at the creek and allowed the horses several swallows.

"Tomorrow morning," he said, suddenly distant.

She caught the meaning, looked away and stared down at her reflection in the water without a word.

"Tomorrow morning you'll head back to school," he continued, "and in a month, you'll forget all about us."

Without seeing his eyes, she was unable to discern if he was serious or teasing. He pulled Cherry's head up out of the water and urged her across the shallow creek. Jenna gave the mare her head and Sheila willingly moved out, splashing along behind. At the top of the bank, she squeezed Sheila and moved up beside Wes again.

"I'm not going to be staying at home. Mom doesn't like it, but I'm living at one of the dorms this year," she said, looking straight ahead as she spoke. "So you could come up anytime, you know." She wrestled with words that needed to be said.

"Maybe," he said, pulling his cap down. She knew he would be elusive. His personality was consistently one of practiced indifference. "You'll probably meet some guy up there and then you won't want …"

She interrupted him. "Stop it!" His words had disappointed her.

He paused and then moved Cherry forward as he spoke.

"I don't know. I might come and see you. But the truth is, after you leave here, I'll probably never see you again." He placed as much nonchalance as he could muster into the word "never."

He looked around in the saddle to gauge the effect, but Jenna had wheeled the mare around and was headed back. He watched her as she crossed the creek and cantered down the road toward the barn.

"Jenna! Damn it!" he yelled at her, really agitated. He took a deep breath and pounded the saddle horn, mumbling to himself. "It took me two months to teach that mare not to run back to the barn!"

CHAPTER TWELVE

The only light in the room glimmered from a small brass lamp topped by an antique stained glass shade. Perhaps years ago, the colors of the glass were brilliant, but now they were dull and bathed the room with a shadowy, seductive light. Refreshed from her shower, Jenna turned the lamp off, pulled on her pink tee shirt and went to the window. Outside, the panorama of cornrows and hayfields were illuminated by a full August moon. After some hesitation, she opened the window and stepped out.

She sat quietly on the gently sloped roof and listened intently to the bullfrogs and to the incessant babble of thousands of night insects. She concentrated on Wes' face, and willed him to think of her. With all of the power of her unified body and mind, she summoned him to come to her, to climb the tree to the roof. It was nearly two o'clock when finally she stepped back inside her room.

She lay face down on the bed and let her tears soak the pillow. *Perhaps revealing herself to him, showing she cared, had been a grievous mistake. Riding off on Sheila. Why did she do that?* This was not the way it was supposed to end. And she was sure it was over. Over before it really began.

She practiced a ritual she had taught herself as a little girl. Whenever Claudia came home with too much to drink or stayed in bed for weeks floundering in self-induced depression, Jenna would pretend she had a small control room in her brain where there were hundreds of switches and buttons. She could visualize herself going to this control room and turning a switch that would eliminate bad or hurtful thoughts from her mind. It was useless. The image of his face set off a neon sign in her head that flashed "danger!" in large, glowing red letters and there was no switch that could turn this off. It was nearly daybreak before she drifted off into a fitful slumber.

When she roused from that unsettled sleep, she realized there was a body flopped across the bottom of the bed. It was Chris, already dressed to do morning chores.

"Wes left with Al George a while ago. He left you a note," she said with a sly grin and dropped a sealed envelope onto the pillow beside Jenna's head.

Chris slid off the bed and left the room.

"I'll go feed and meet you downstairs for breakfast," she called over her shoulder. "And then I'll help you load your stuff."

Jenna sat up in the bed looking at the envelope, her pulse on the rise. She slowly opened it and unfolded a piece of paper and read: *If you take the chicken exit, you'll never know how good the ride can be.*

She read it three or four times and lay back on the pillow, clutching it. *Damn him!* It wasn't much, but it was enough. She was suddenly exhilarated and bounded from the bed. *This was far from over. In fact,* she thought as she dressed, *it's just beginning.*

Downstairs, Jeff was flipping pancakes and making an attempt to appear helpful in the kitchen.

"Chris should be done with chores anytime," he said brightly. "When Frank and Lil get here, we'll eat."

Jeff could be a jackass at times, but he certainly was charming, thought Jenna. Joanna fussed over the table, straightening the red gingham tablecloth and placing a large vase of fresh flowers in the middle.

"Looks like a breakfast table fit for a king." It was Frank. He and Lil came in through the back porch door.

"When do we eat?" he said, producing a small wrapped box that he shoved toward Jenna. "It's from all of us. Here comes Chris, so you can go ahead and open it."

Jenna's eyes moved from face to face around the large kitchen table, savoring the feeling of being surrounded by family. It was a new sensation for her and she treasured it.

Opening the box, she found a splendid pair of sterling silver spurs with brass rowels and leather spur straps, tooled in a basket weave pattern.

"Oh my gosh," she stammered. "Does this mean I have graduated from the School of Floyd and I'll be moving on to another horse?" Her eyes were wet and her smile was out of control.

"Yes, indeed it does, my dear," said Lil patting her hand. "And it means you are very much a part of our world here. We want you to know this and never to forget it."

"What it means is next summer you'll be in the show ring with Chris and me," said Jeff. "I'll probably be on Zip and Christine on Cherry. We'll fit you out with Zan, maybe. Whatever. We'll work on it this winter. Meanwhile, this is your first piece of equipment."

After breakfast, Jenna walked to the barn with Chris.

"I need to say goodbye to Floyd, Vince and the others. Especially Jake," she whispered, "but I'm not going to say goodbye to you or anyone else here. This is not a goodbye thing. You know what I mean?"

Chris acknowledged this and shrugged. "You're just going to school, for God's sake, not to China."

"And I'll be back so often, you won't know I am gone!" Jenna wrapped her arms around Chris. "And I'll do all I can to be in Sedalia for the Fair, I promise."

Chris returned the sisterly embrace and they walked hand in hand from the barn. She returned to the porch to wave as the Jeep pulled away from the farm.

***

Each highway mile to Kansas City served as a memory marker as Jenna St. James recounted the weeks she had spent in New Winston. Before now, she had not used the years of her life to any purpose. She was twenty-one and had no hobbies, no interests, and no skills. No boyfriends. No stories to tell.

She thought of Chris and her face eased into a smile. Christine Day was an outrageously vibrant young woman, full of heart and spilling over with soul. The girl moved through every hour of her existence with spirit and vitality that might have made Jenna envious but instead evoked a deep sense of esteem. Chris had a bright, appealing face and was strong-willed, like Jeff, and yet she was blessed with Joanna's generosity and grace.

Jenna did not remember her own father, who was a college professor, and wondered if she carried any of his qualities. He was supposedly in Canada or someplace. She thought about him often and occasionally considered trying to find him. She could not think there was much likeness between Claudia and herself. Perhaps her eyes, nose. Maybe her skin. Claudia's temperament was of such a difficult nature, Jenna was thankful there was no resemblance there. She knew better than anyone that her mother's intimidating manner was not driven by true power but had been created to mask many failed attempts to control the people in her life.

As Jenna drove along the interstate toward home, she realized that although she had been away from Claudia all summer, she was going home with a better understanding of her mother than she had ever thought possible. It was like suddenly being moved to a room with a view.

"Poor Mom. Too much booze, too much money, too many men," she said aloud as her mind pushed into the new territory. Having said it, it became no big deal. Claudia's problems would no longer be her daughter's punishment. Jenna had a new plan, a new design, and a blueprint in her head to guide her. No more free falling.

The summer in New Winston had been pivotal and as she approached the city, she knew what she wanted for the first time in her life. She had discovered a world where she belonged and she knew precisely the moment her life took on a new direction. It was at the Fourth of July show when Joanna returned from the trailer that first day, prepared to show. Jo was calm, beautiful, and ready to take on the world. Brave enough to hang it all over the edge and expert enough to know she could. She remembered Joanna's smoldering eyes as she made her entrance into the show pen. As Jenna looked in the rearview mirror, she saw some of that fire in her own eyes. It was a new look and it pleased her.

The front door was locked. Vexed, Jenna rang the doorbell. A Hispanic-looking young man answered the door in a scant black swimsuit. He was thirtyish, good looking. He had a towel draped over his shoulders and had obviously been swimming.

"You must be Jenna. Welcome home," he said politely, in perfect English. "Claudia is on the patio by the pool. She's expecting you."

She eyed him with some disdain. *New house boy and poolside companion for mother?* He introduced himself as Miguel and said he was an actor. He had met Claudia in Las Vegas. Jenna tossed her purse on the glass dining room table and stepped outside to the white-tiled patio. Claudia rose smiling from her lounging chair, and threw her arms around Jenna and held her slightly puckered mouth up to be kissed.

"Didn't I tell you a little country air would suit you?" Claudia chattered. "Miguel, isn't she as lovely as I told you?"

He nodded, a little too emphatically, thought Jenna. Claudia looked sensational, as usual, and a sudden rush of emotion reminded Jenna that despite everything, she was glad to see her mother. Claudia returned to her chair.

"Miguel, get me a ciggie! I need to hear all about it. Tell me about Jeff. And his family, of course. Let's hear it. And don't leave out a single thing," she directed Jenna. "From your letters, I gather you have practically become one of the clan."

"They really are great people, Mother. I already miss them, and I plan to spend a lot of weekends down there, so I'll see them soon," Jenna began, pleased her mother wanted to hear so much. "Chris is like a little sister to me. And Wes and I ... well, we get along, too."

"What about Joanna?" Claudia pressed for more information. "How does she look?"

"She looks good," shrugged Jenna, amused. "Very pretty, actually."

"She's probably had a face lift. How's Jeff?" Claudia continued. "Still God's gift?"

"Oh, I don't know about that," laughed Jenna. "He's really nice looking and basically an okay guy, but he can be a major jerk sometimes."

Claudia jumped up and hugged her daughter, throwing her head back and shaking her dark hair.

"Sweetheart! The guy has a jerk-streak eight miles wide. Believe me, I know. Oh, well. So, is he rich?"

"I don't think they are rich, but he has a good job. I think the farm and the horses must be worth a lot. You know those pictures I sent you of Invincible? The stud? He's probably the most valuable thing on the farm. In the spring, mares are coming from all over the country to be bred to him. We call him Vince. He is *so* cool."

"Really? Mares from all over the country?" Claudia was interested. "I am absolutely thrilled for my friend Joanna. And Jeff, too, of course. Jo has been competing with her horses for as long as I have known her, so I am certain she is on top of the world. I mean, with this kind of success and all."

"It's pretty neat." Jenna didn't want to go into much detail about Joanna. "Jeff is the one enjoying it the most, I guess. Although Jeff and Jo own the stud together, Vince is Jeff's prized possession. He goes down to the barn every single night to check the horses one more time and look at Invincible before he goes to bed. It's like he can't sleep until he does this final check."

"It all sounds wonderful. Are you ready to go back to the university?" Claudia crushed out her cigarette and reached for her wine cooler. "As long as you have decided you don't want to live at home, I have an idea. Instead of living in the dorm, why don't we get you a cute little apartment?"

"Mother! That's a great idea! I'd love it!" Jenna was surprised and genuinely thrilled. Claudia, always a domineering mother, had always refused to discuss the possibility of her daughter living in her own place. Now that Claudia was a widow, Jenna had expected it to be possible only after a full-scale war of words.

"Actually, I happen to know of a small one bedroom apartment on the top floor of a positively divine carriage house near the campus." Claudia continued. "Remember the couple who used to live next door to us? They own some lovely rental property and I called them. It's still available if you want to go look at it."

By the end of the week, Jenna had canceled her plans to live in the dorm and was partially moved in to her new apartment. She longed to go shopping for a few pieces of furniture, but instead, she spent hours standing in long lines to enroll in the classes she had selected. Classes were scheduled to begin on Monday and she needed to hit the bookstores to find the prescribed study material and course manuals.

"There aren't enough hours in the day!" she wailed to Claudia. "Thanks for taking care of the phone and utilities. After classes start, I want to get my boxes unpacked and start fixing the place up."

"I'm sending Miguel over this afternoon with a few basic things you'll need, like kitchen stuff," said Claudia lovingly, "and as a moving present, we've bought you a new bed. I'll send some bedding, too. Then you can really get moved in."

Jenna gave her a quick hug and sprinted up the stairs to pack more boxes. Miguel sprawled on the couch in the large front room, surfing through the channels with the remote.

"I thought you never wanted her to leave home." He looked sideways at Claudia. "You sure seem to be involved in this apartment thing." She kicked off her high-heeled sandals and curled up beside him.

"Sometimes I think you are an idiot. This is not about any damned apartment. Truthfully, I was sick of hearing all about the Day farm and all those stupid horses."

She stretched out with her foot, tickling his leg with her bare toes.

"I know my daughter best. And I know what she needs and what she doesn't," she chirped. "Perhaps you haven't noticed, but since we leased the apartment, she seems to have forgotten all about New Winston."

Miguel was still puzzled. "I thought you wanted her to fit in there, to have a nice summer."

"I just wanted them to get to know her. I never expected her to come back wearing cowboy boots, for God's sake." She pulled him close and faced him. "I have much higher goals for her."

She flicked her tongue along his lower lip and then suddenly, bit him. He drew back and then responded to her call for rough play by clutching a handful of hair.

"Don't you like the idea of her having her own apartment, babe?" She fondled his thigh. "With her gone, we'll be alone again ... and I think a grieving widow needs privacy."

"Why did you send her there in the first place?" he whispered as he sucked on her ear. "So you could go to Las Vegas and find someone like me?"

"Jeff and Joanna are two of my oldest and very best friends," she hissed back at him as she pulled him to his feet and pressed against him. "Jenna is my prized possession and I told you, I wanted him ... I mean both of them, to see how smart and lovely she is."

Early Monday, Jenna headed to the campus for her first class. Claudia was still in bed. When the phone rang, she picked it up. A young female voice asked for Jenna.

"She had an early morning class," Claudia replied. "Can I take a message?"

"This is Christine Day," said the voice, a little frustrated. "She said she would call me ... and I'm getting ready to go to the State Fair. I wanted to know if she could make it. I am leaving Wednesday night."

"Oh, Chris! She *tried* to call you!" Claudia was always quick on her feet with a lie. "I'm afraid she won't be able to make it to your show. Now that she's home, she's so busy with other things. School and all. She feels terrible about it, but I know you understand. Will you be showing your colt? I've heard all about him."

Chris hesitated, puzzled and disappointed. "Yes, I'm showing him. I thought she was going to be there. Can you have her call me?"

Claudia assured her Jenna would call as soon as she found the time.

"Good luck at the show, sweetie, we wish you all the luck in the world!" She hung up and smiled to herself. Reaching for the phone book, she flipped hurriedly through the Yellow Pages and picked up the phone again.

"This is Claudia Gambiano. I was in your store the other day to pick out some furniture," she said. "I would like to make arrangements to have those things delivered to my daughter's apartment late Wednesday. If you can't do it late Wednesday, I don't want it."

Miguel, who was sleeping next to her, stirred when she hung up the phone.

"I thought Jenna said she had to go to the Fair," he yawned. "What's the deal now?"

Claudia slithered from the bed and slipped on a fluffy white bathrobe.

"Summer is over and there is no need for her to continue hanging out with cowboys. I told you, I didn't intend for her to make it her whole life. She'll be so involved with moving into her apartment that she won't possibly be able to get away for any damned horse show."

Later in the afternoon, Jenna walked in, arms full of books. "My new English lit professor wants us to read ten novels and evaluate them."

Claudia was lounging on the couch, absorbed in a Lana Turner movie.

"I know you are going to be swamped, darling," she said nonchalantly, "but I have picked out a few new things for the apartment and they are delivering them Wednesday night. And the painter called and he will be painting your apartment Friday. You should be all moved in this weekend!"

Jenna paused, dumbstruck. "What things? What painter? I can't do it this weekend. I have to go to the State Fair!"

"I meant to tell you, Christine Day called and I explained what was going on. What a doll she is! She said to tell you not to worry about it as she had plenty of help and she would try to call you Monday or Tuesday and let you know how the show went. What a sweet girl! She is very excited about your new apartment." Claudia was masterful.

Jenna walked slowly up the stairs to her room, replaying the conversation in her mind.

Claudia called to her from the hallway downstairs.

"Don't forget, we have to meet the delivery people at the apartment Wednesday night! I bought some really cute things to surprise you. And you didn't think you could move in without having the place completely painted, did you?"

The weekend rushed by and on Monday evening, Jenna was ready to move into her newly furnished, freshly painted apartment. She was upstairs, gathering one last carload of clothes from her walk-in closet, when she heard the doorbell ring. Miguel would probably get it. Minutes later, Claudia stormed into the room, visibly agitated.

"There is a very rude cowboy standing in my foyer and refuses to leave until you see him," she fumed, hands on her hips. "I presume he is just someone you met this summer at a rodeo."

Jenna darted to the window and saw a familiar truck parked in the circle drive. Pushing Claudia aside, she bolted down the stairs.

She heard Miguel's voice. "Her mother doesn't think she wants to see you, whoever you are."

In faded Wranglers and dusty boots, his shirttail out, Wes stood in the foyer. He was ignoring Miguel.

"Hey! I just thought you'd like to hear how we did at the Fair," he said loudly as Jenna landed breathlessly at the bottom of the stairs.

Claudia was behind her now, sizing him up. Wes' eyes never left Jenna.

"Too bad you couldn't be there for Jake's first show, but that's okay," he said, trying to be loose and friendly.

"I'm sorry I couldn't come. How did it go? How'd Jake do?" Jenna was scarlet. Reporting on the Fair wasn't the real reason he was there and she knew it.

"He kicked ass. He was first under every judge we showed him to. Chris will never be the same." Wes suddenly became conscious of Miguel and Claudia. "Is this your mother?"

Jenna, eyes wide, nodded to him.

"I'm Weston Day." He introduced himself to Claudia and turned abruptly to Jenna again.

"Let's go sit in my truck. We need to talk."

He guided her out the door and gave one last look at Claudia, who was circling him like a cat. "See you again soon," he whispered to her and smiled, not the least bit threatened.

As the heavy front door closed, Claudia unleashed an agonized scream and snatched a small vase from a hall table. Cursing, she heaved it against a mirrored wall, smashing it. Grabbing a nearby lamp, she raised her arm and clenched her teeth, preparing to demolish the twin ficus trees that flanked the front door.

"What the hell are you doing?" Miguel's fingers closed around her wrist. "Are you nuts?"

"Don't you know who that was? It was Jeff's son!" she screeched. "And did you see how they looked at each other? How could she fall for him?" she stopped herself. Old feelings for Jeff Day still raged in her and she knew exactly how it happened.

She threw herself on the large overstuffed couch and cried out in torment, "God! What have I done?"

Outside, sitting in the truck, Wes leaned out the window and tried to be casual.

"Your mom is a piece of work. I guess that guy is her new squeeze, eh?"

Jenna nodded, embarrassed. They sat in silence for several minutes. Wes shoved Aerosmith in the tape player and turned it up. She turned it down.

"Dad and I had it out over me going back to school," he told her. "I told him all about last semester, St. Louis, and all. Anyway, to make it short, I got a job. You know Al George, the guy who shoes our horses? I'm working for him. Matter of fact, we had to come to Kansas City today to reset shoes on a half-dozen head in a big hunter-jumper barn. He's having lunch with some gal he knows and I gotta pick him up in a while."

She announced her own news.

"I'm moving into my own apartment. I'll give you the phone number."

He smiled and looked at her. The excitement that came from her touch seemed different, deeper, and more reverent than it had been with other women. This elusive sensation preyed on him, roused him, and he longed to feel it again. He leaned forward on the steering wheel, turned his head and gazed at her.

Her composure was capsizing under the weight of the sweet expression in his eyes.

"Do you think you might want to go on with this horseshoer thing?" She found her voice.

"Maybe. I could go to school in Oklahoma and take a course. It wouldn't be a bad career for me right now." He rested his head back on the seat. He was such an expert being suddenly aloof. "Al and I go all over Missouri and even over to Kansas to shoe horses. It's likely I'll get up this way some. And Al's the official farrier for the American Royal Quarter Horse Show here at the end of October. So I'll be up here a week with him then. We'll be pretty busy. But I could get away, probably late in the evenings. Real late."

She pulled her ponytail loose and shook out her hair. Wes felt a stab in the pit of his stomach. *That's it,* he thought to himself. *That ponytail thing.* How this movement affected him was both cruel and wondrous. She reached out and slowly laced his fingers in her left hand.

"What do you mean, real late? What are you getting at?"

"What am I getting at?" he repeated.

She moved closer and he suddenly felt as if her very presence was inflicting an all-out assault on his male senses. She turned her head to face him. The fingers of her right hand, now kneading his thigh, were paralyzing him.

His nonchalance disappeared. "Are you messing with me or what?"

Her pretty face softened and her eyes flashed him an unmistakable signal.

"You know how I feel about you, Jenna," he heard himself confess. "I can't stop thinking about it. Damn it! What else do I have to say?"

She closed her eyes and tipped her head slightly. "I don't know … I'm not sure."

"Bullshit!" he muttered, cutting her off. "This ain't one of those things that needs a lot of figuring out. Either you want me or you don't. Which is it?"

She leaned toward his face with a look that delivered an electric shock to every nerve. Her finger traced the outline of his mouth and touched the beads of sweat on his upper lip. She kissed him.

"I've missed you so much," she breathed in his ear, "I think you know how I feel. After I got home, I wasn't really sure about you. I'm still not sure." Her fingertips now tracked the inseam of his jeans and she loved the feeling of power it gave her. "Promise me you'll be back soon."

He took both of her hands and pressed them to his lips, closed his eyes and murmured, "I promise."

He knew it was more than a pledge of passion he was giving her. It was a commitment of the heart and to his surprise, it was more exhilarating than he could have ever imagined.

CHAPTER THIRTEEN

When Jenna returned to the house, Miguel was sweeping the marble tiled floor in the foyer.

"What's all this glass?" She knew instantly it was the aftermath of a Claudia tantrum. Jenna clamped her eyes closed and exhaled. Arms folded, growling, she reminded Miguel of Claudia. He looked at her with an odd smile.

"Where is she?" she demanded.

"She went upstairs to get something to settle her nerves," he said, trying not to talk too loud.

"What set her off? Wes? She didn't seem to like him much." Jenna shook her head, disgusted. Miguel didn't really want to say more, but he glanced up the stairs quickly and motioned to the girl.

"You better try to keep him away from here. And the less you say about him, the better," he muttered in a hushed tone, "I think the last thing your mom had in mind was for you to get hooked up with her friends' son."

Jenna stuck her chin out and raised her eyebrows. Miguel shuddered. She was so much like Claudia and yet so different.

"It's too late … " she began.

A rustle from above made them both look up. Claudia stood swaying at the top of the stairs. Her eyes were sullen and voice raspy.

"Too late for what? Do you have something to tell me about Jeff's son? Have you been in New Winston all summer screwing the son of my good friends? Whoring around with Jeff Day's son, for God's sake?" she yelled, tottering a bit as she tried to come down the stairs. "I have never been so humiliated in my life and I forbid you to ever see him or speak to any of them again!"

"You *forbid* me? You are really deranged, Mother," Jenna said calmly. "And the truth is, I have never screwed anyone in my life. Thanks to you, I've never even had any boyfriends."

"Don't talk to me like that!" Claudia steadied herself on the handrail. "Miguel! Help me down the stairs. I need a drink."

"You need more than a drink," her daughter suggested, unusually collected. "You need to get it through your head that I'm twenty-one, I'm leaving home and I can have a relationship if I choose. I don't need you, Mother. And thanks to Vic, I don't need your money."

Claudia gasped at these words and clawed at her forehead. It was radically unlike Jenna to be insolent.

"How dare you? If I had not married Vic, he would have never left you a dime! Now you think you've got it all, don't you? After everything I've done for you!"

Jenna, purse and car keys in hand, was sidling out the door. She figured Claudia would rage on for an hour or two until she was too stoned to recall what she was raving about.

"I'm outta here, Miguel," Jenna called to him. Then as a last minute thought, she turned and added, "When she mixes narcotics and alcohol, she always gets real sick, so watch her, okay?"

As she drove to her new apartment, Jenna organized her thoughts as if she were sorting through piles of laundry, some soiled, some freshly washed. Her life's direction was changing so fast she needed time to think. She was on her own for the first time, leaving Claudia and years of conflict behind. *So perhaps it was not the most pleasant of partings, but so be it.* She preferred not to dwell on this and chose to think about Wes instead. To savor, over and over, his touch, his words. She tried to imagine a rerun of their conversation in the truck and his voice whispering. *This ain't one of them things that needs a lot of figuring out ...* She was electrified with the implications of his words.

What would her life be like with Wes? Jenna spent the evening unpacking boxes, arranging her apartment and thinking how it would be, the two of them, together. It was nearly nine when she picked up the phone and called Chris.

"I missed it! I can't believe I missed the Fair and Jake put it on 'em!" She spilled out her apology and begged for the details.

"It was so cool, Jen, I was a nervous wreck!" Chris was shouting in the phone. "On the way there, Jake got a little stupid in the trailer and banged his front knee up. So Dad and I spent all night with ice packs on it to get the swelling down. But it was okay by Friday and he showed like a pro."

Jenna was desperately full of regret at her absence. "Did Jeff show him in the futurities?"

"Yeah, Dad got along with him great. Jake was the biggest colt in the class and you should have seen him trot in there with Dad." Chris' voice glowed. Jenna could picture her face as the girl babbled. "Some of the younger colts had just been weaned and were carrying on a little. Hell, not my colt. He's always had to be a big guy. I almost felt like crying. He looked like a million bucks, ears up the whole time!" She would have gone on forever.

"Was Brandon there?"

"You bet! After Jake showed, Brandon and I led him back to our stalls. On the way, some guy from Nebraska offered to buy him! But I said he wasn't for sale."

"Of course not. You could never part with him. Besides, he was a gift from your father. And Stella's last foal. Oh God! I wish I would have been there!" Jenna truly ached, missing the excitement of it.

"Uncle Frank and Lil came down on Friday morning and videotaped the whole thing, so when you come, you can see how good he looked," chattered Chris. "We didn't show Cherry. She got sick and was coughing her head off and running a temperature, so we scratched her and Dad took her home Saturday afternoon. Hey! Mom wants to say hi!"

Joanna's voice on the phone line was warm and reassuring.

"Hi, hon. Everything okay up there with you? I was worried when you didn't come to the Fair. Did you see Wes? He said he was going to see you. I gave him Claudia's address."

"Yes, I saw him earlier today," Jenna replied. "I was at the house gathering the last of my things and he found me. I'm afraid he got a taste of Mom in one of her moods. But, I'm here at the apartment now. I'm on my own, Jo!"

"I know it's been tough for you, honey. And remember Claudia is going through a rough time, too." When it came to sincerity, Joanna was gifted.

"You know my mom," Jenna sighed. "Vic left too much money for her to be grief-stricken. I think the only thing she's grieving about is the fact my stepfather left half his estate to me. She's got a new live-in boyfriend already. Mom's such a schizo. It was her idea for me to get this apartment, but right now she's pissed at me. I don't know, I just can't worry about it."

"Listen, as soon as you can, come down for the weekend," Joanna urged, "Wes has been gone every day. He's either off shoeing or roping. But I'll try to get him to take a few days off. We'll do something fun. Maybe we'll have a big barbecue!"

Jenna felt good after talking with Chris and Joanna. She set up her little stereo system, plopped in a CD, and unpacked boxes until midnight while singing uninhibited duets with Lyle Lovett. The last box contained old photos and scrapbooks. Some of them were ones Claudia had passed on to her. She sifted through them, smiling at her own baby pictures. Inside the last box was a large brown envelope she had not seen. Inside were some old papers, photos, Claudia's birth certificate and piles of letters. These must have been packed in the box by mistake, she thought, as she leafed through the envelopes and old bank statements.

Sandwiched between some brittle pages were two faded color photos. One photo depicted a slim young Joanna with long straight hair, arm-in-arm with Claudia. Jenna smiled at their bell-bottom pants and skimpy halter tops. On the back was scrawled, "The Stones' concert, me and J." The other photo was of Claudia, in faded blue jeans and tie-dyed tee shirt, massive lengths of dark hair, clinging seductively to a nice-looking man in slacks and dress shirt. On the back was written, "Warren and me. 1974."

Jenna squinted and held the photo to the light, trying to see the face of Warren St. James. He looked nice. Older than Claudia. Dignified. She wondered if he was still in Canada and if he had to run that far to stop thinking about his marriage to Claudia. *Did he ever wonder about his daughter?* Suddenly, a thought seized her. *Did he ever pay child support?* If so, her mother must have known precisely where he was all these years. Excitedly, she sorted through the papers. On the bottom she found what she was looking for – a torn empty envelope, postmarked Aug. 12, 1991. The return address read "W. S. J., 16 Rue Charles, Montreal, Quebec."

Jenna instinctively clutched the envelope and the photograph to her breast. *What if she wrote to him? Would he reject her? Was he so wounded by Claudia, he didn't want any part of his daughter?* Maybe someday, she would try to find him. She placed the address and photo back in the box and headed toward the shower, thinking about his face.

Two weeks passed and Jenna came to relish living alone. There had been no word from Claudia, but Miguel had called and let her know they were going to Cabo San Lucas for a week.

Jenna spent her days in class and in the evenings, she studied. Wes called frequently and she existed for these conversations.

"We're working seven days a week," he complained with an exaggerated whine, seeking her sympathy. "Al is killing me. But you wouldn't believe how much money I'm saving. I'll take some time off someday soon and come see you. Either that or just go crazy."

One Friday afternoon, she returned from class to find an urgent-sounding phone message from Wes with instructions to meet him at the farm. She stuffed some clothes in a small denim backpack and headed the Jeep toward New Winston. As she turned off the state highway and drove down Old Pike Road toward the farm, it was like going home. Ahead she spotted the white rail fence that fronted the Day farm on both sides and her hands tightened on the steering wheel in anticipation.

She pulled through the open gate and rolled down the window. The house overflowed with warm light and the hickory aroma of meat cooked on the grill wafted on the evening air. Wes' truck was down by the barn, so she parked and headed there to find him. The inside arena lights were on, its skylights sending pale beams into the twilight. Josie bounded to greet her as she stepped inside the big door. Immediately, Jenna recognized a low whistle. She turned and felt a stiff loop of rope settle about her shoulders. Wes was on the other end, pulling the loop tighter. Jenna laughed as he reeled her in close.

"I always wanted to do this to some city girl who might be impressed." He lifted the rope over her head and sneaked a kiss. "I missed you bad."

"What's going on?"

"You'll find out soon enough. Wanna see Jake the Snake? He's outside in the big pen."

They walked together toward the pen in the darkness. The screen door slammed at the house and Chris appeared, waving wildly. She headed toward them.

"Hey! Wait a minute and I'll flip on the outside arena lights and you can see Jake."

Jenna could hear hoofbeats on the other side of the fence. At the sound of Chris' voice, the colt began to nicker. Despite her firm handling and the spankings he had endured at her hand for biting and kicking, the colt had an unmistakable relationship with his owner. Even Uncle Frank admitted it. The orphan colt recognized her on a different level than other humans.

Light flooded the outdoor arena and Jake came flying across the smooth dirt to the fence. Jenna was shocked at how much he had changed in a month.

"Incredible," she murmured, as Chris climbed over the fence and approached him with a lead rope.

"Whoa, now, twerp!" Chris spoke to him fondly as she snapped him up and led him to the gate.

"He's looking pretty good," said a male voice behind her. "Don't you think?"

Jenna turned at the familiar voice and smiled as Jeff stepped up to join them.

"Come on up to the house," he said with a wide grin. "Joanna and Lil have got supper just about ready."

He put his arm firmly around her shoulders.

"It's good to have you home."

The simple message, with emphasis on the word "home" impacted Jenna in a surprising way. Jeff Day was masterful in his controlling actions. She knew it, but it somehow felt all right. She was surprised to find herself sliding her arm around his waist submissively.

It was an evening of good food, laughter and warm feelings. Wes was openly affectionate and Jenna occasionally thought she caught an amused exchange of knowing smiles between other family members. After she dried the supper dishes for Joanna, Jeff sauntered in and pulled her into the front room.

"Let's go sit on the porch. We need to discuss something," he whispered in her ear.

As the family gathered on the large porch, Jeff sat down on the front steps and lit a cigarette.

"We've been talking about a horse for you. Something you can show," he said casually. "We don't think Zan is what you need. You need something with more experience. More rail time."

"To get to the point, we know this guy from Illinois who's got a really nice pleasure mare." Frank took over the conversation. "She's seven years old, bay. Pretty mover. Nice-looking. She belongs to this guy's wife, who is now pregnant, so they want to sell the mare."

Jenna's heart stopped. The prospect of a horse of her own made her feel like an excited child.

"Tell me more! Where is she? How much do they want?"

Chris moved over to crouch beside her on the step, eyes devilish.

"We'll talk about money later. It'll be a good deal, though, 'cause they want to work it out so they can bring two other mares to Vince," continued Frank. Jenna looked baffled.

"To cut to the chase, I would like to breed these two mares. They are both top producers, and the people want to trade out breeding fees in part for this pleasure mare," explained Jeff. "We don't need her, but we think she'd be perfect for you."

"She's really lovely, Jenna. Her owners told us she was trained by a woman here in Missouri," Joanna interjected. "She did a nice job."

"Cynthia Judd was her name," added Frank. "She's dead now. But she lived somewhere over by Prairie Rock and, at one time, was a damned good trainer. The mare is show-ready, right now. In fact, she's been showing all summer in Illinois and has done pretty well."

"If you start working with Frank and come down every weekend between now and mid-October, you might be able to show her at this big open show we want to go to over in Kansas." Chris' eyes were aglow. "It's the weekend before the American Royal. It's a good show and we want to take Cherry, kinda like a warm up for the Royal."

"Oh my God! I can't show! I've never ... I don't know, I mean, I want to more than anything, but I don't know if I can do it!" Jenna gasped at the challenge.

"No pressure. First we need to try this mare out." Frank stood up and stretched his legs. "So, do you want to look at her?"

Jenna took a deep breath. "Where is she?"

"They brought her over from Peoria last night. She's in the barn," said Wes, grabbing her by the hand.

The bay mare was elegant, long necked with fine features – large, kind eyes and short, pert ears. As Frank led her from the stall, Jenna's heart raced. She ran her hand down the mare's back and over her round, muscled rump.

"I'll work her on the longe line a bit so you can see her move," said Joanna, saddling the mare and leading her into the indoor arena. "Doc McGraw was here last night and looked her over, said she was sound."

The mare trotted flawlessly around the circle, head perfectly level. When Joanna asked her to lope off, she stepped into the gait change instantly. Her fluid movements were exquisite. Jo stopped her, gathered up the longe line and traded it for a bridle. Joanna began to step up on the mare, when Jeff shoved her aside.

"I'll do this," he said and swung into the saddle.

The mare stood quietly. "She has a very soft mouth, so you don't need your hands, just leg. Stay off her mouth," said Jeff, moving off at a very controlled walk. "If you want to trot, cluck to her." He trotted circles. "Pick up slightly, sit back and lay your outside leg on her, then smooch to her a little to go lope," he continued, slipping off into the lope.

"She's got a nice stop on her, and you don't have to touch the reins to back her. Just squeeze your legs and tell her to back," he said, demonstrating.

"She also side passes, trots diagonals, pivots, and all kinds of other nice things," said Chris. "She's really broke, Jenna. Are you ready to ride?"

Jenna adjusted the stirrups and stepped up into the saddle as Frank had taught her, sitting quietly as she made sure the slack in her reins were perfectly even. For the next forty-five minutes, Frank coached her through small circles, large circles, rail work and more.

"Drop your hands! Sit up straight! Look where you're going!" He drilled her from the center of the arena. "Use your body. Let her feel which way you want to go. This mare ain't like old fat Floyd. Shoulders back, weight on your stirrups. Heels down! Don't hurry through your transitions. Slow motion!"

Jenna's head was spinning. There was so much to learn. But the bay felt good under her and as she loped the mare by the gate and caught Jeff's satisfied grin, she knew she was doing all right. She glanced at Wes, standing beside him.

"Don't watch the spectators!" snapped Frank. "Ride your horse. Think about it every second. Now walk. Slower! When you hit that corner, set her up for the lope. Think about it. Be ready for it. Pick up a little … bring her to you. Can you feel that? When her weight shifts to the rear end, she's ready. Use your outside leg, smooch. Now! Give her more rein … let her go! Not bad, but you need a lot of work!"

By Sunday night, the details had been resolved. The bay mare known as Tess belonged to Jenna.

She spent the next three weeks juggling her schoolwork with weekends at the farm riding her mare. Uncle Frank was a relentless taskmaster and this kind of riding was far from the basics she had learned for fun on Floyd. Several times, she finished her ride near tears, overwhelmed by the requirement to learn so much and Frank's hard, fast rules. Eventually, the rides started getting better.

"The mare is so detached," she confided to Frank. "I'm a stranger to her. She doesn't seem to have any personality. I mean, she's wonderful, but she seems so remote."

"Riding is like, well, ice dancing," he told her. "It's a partnership that comes from experience. It's not an instant thing. It comes from lots of wet saddle blankets. Give it a chance."

She spent hours in the arena riding with Chris on Cherry, and Jeff on Zan, learning what riders called "rail etiquette." She learned to pass slower horses, stay away from trouble and to block out distractions and pay attention to her horse at all times. She learned to rate the speed of the mare's walk, in order to improve her position on the rail and help create space in front of her to go into the lope.

She missed Wes, but he was working with Al on the weekends and although they talked on the phone, it had been almost three weeks since she last saw him.

"Al and I are goin' over to Lawrence for the show," he assured her. "He's got some clients who are going and they want some work done. We figure we can do about six head and watch some classes, too."

As the show approached, she tried on shirts and jackets of every color and design. She was amazed at the collection of show clothes appearing from the upstairs closets and was delighted Joanna's black Stetson and Chris' black chaps fit her perfectly.

"Don't worry about the rest, we can decide later what looks best," Jo told her.

"Normally, we'd just drive up early Saturday morning, but they've got a limited number of stalls and if we get there Friday evening, the horses won't have to stand tied to the trailer all day," Jeff announced the weekend before the show. "It's just a one day show, but it's one of the biggest open shows in the Midwest and there's good payback. Chris will show Cherry. You'll ride Saturday afternoon."

Jeff's words haunted her as she drove back to Kansas City. *You'll ride Saturday afternoon.* The thought of her first competition suddenly turned from joyous anticipation to the deepest fear she had ever known.

On the phone, she confessed her terror to Wes, who chuckled sympathetically.

"You'll be fine. It's just a show. It ain't like trying out for the Olympic Team!"

On Thursday morning, she called Claudia. It was the first time they had talked since Jenna left the house.

"I just wanted you to know I bought a horse," she announced cautiously, "and I'm going to ride her Saturday at an open show in Lawrence."

"I knew you were spending your weekends in New Winston," Claudia snapped. "Miguel told me. I guess you two talk every once in a while?"

"Yeah. Miguel's kind of an okay guy," Jenna answered. "I can't imagine how he puts up with you, but he actually seems to have a deep affection for you."

This made Claudia smile. Perhaps her daughter was not as gutless as she had seemed all these years.

"I'm impressed with your smart mouth," she sniffed, "but I'll have you know Miguel could have a great number of women and chooses to stay with me. Are you still seeing Jeff's son?"

"Yes," Jenna answered simply. This was met by silence on the other end. Claudia finally cleared her throat and calmly asked if school was going okay. Jenna was surprised that her mother so quickly dismissed the subject of Weston Day, but chalked it off to denial.

"Fine, school is good. I aced my last two tests."

"So, will you call me and let me know how your horse show goes? After all, I am your mother." Claudia was an excellent martyr.

"I'll call Sunday evening." Jenna hung up the phone.

On Friday afternoon, she sat in class, waiting to be dismissed so she could head to Kansas. She scribbled down the assignment, but the nervous stream of reservations filling her head obliterated the professor's detailed instructions. After class, she hit the interstate and in minutes had left Missouri behind. She drove west toward the town of Lawrence and easily found the show grounds, feeling a little more assured when she spotted the Days' big aluminum trailer. Jeff waved her down and pointed toward a row of stall barns.

"You and Chris need to saddle up and let the horses see the place. Work 'em on the longe line first."

Although she wanted to find Wes, she followed orders. When you are at a horse show, the horse comes first. She repeated Frank's words to herself. Hours later, she traced the clanging sound of iron to a barn where Al's truck was parked and found the farrier bent over, fitting a shoe on a gray gelding. Wes was holding the horse and talking with the gelding's owners. He listened to them, biting his lip and rocking on his heels.

"Jenna! Get Dad!" he called out sharply when he spotted her. "Tell him to get up here. *Now!*"

Within minutes, she had retrieved Jeff. As they approached, Wes was still talking to the people who owned the gray.

"This is my dad, Jeff Day." His jaw twitching, Wes introduced the couple. "Dad, this is John and Ruth Shaw, two of Al's longtime customers. They live near Fort Scott and have two teenage daughters who show."

"Oh, sure," Jeff responded, extending his hand to John. "I've seen your girls ride. Both have gray horses, right? Do western and English?"

"That's right," Ruth Shaw replied. "We were telling Al and Wes that we have a new barn manager. In fact, he's here with us this weekend. Wes says you all know him. His name is Ray Slankard."

"Damn!" Jeff spit out the curse. "Ray, eh? I might have known his slimy ass would show up somewhere around another horse barn."

Seeing Jenna recoil, Wes gave the lead rope to John and stepped over to slide his arm around her.

"Ray's here? Should we call the police?" Jenna's eyes welled with tears. Ruth shot her husband an alarmed look. Jeff recounted how Ray had been caught stealing equipment and told them of the crude assault on Jenna.

"My son, here, happened along or who knows … " Jeff began, but Ruth Shaw, her hand to her mouth, cut him off with a muffled cry.

"Oh! I knew he was a low-life snake!" She was furious. "I told you it wasn't safe to have someone like that around our girls. Christ, John! He hasn't been able to take his eyes off either one since we hired him." She glared at her husband. He was already on the move.

"He's at our stalls right now," growled John and stalked toward the barn, flanked by Jeff and Wes.

"Stay here, Jenna," ordered Al, who had stopped his work and was holding the horse. "Hold this horse. I saw a couple of town cops a few minutes ago drinking coffee over at the office. I think I better get 'em."

As John Shaw approached, Ray was inside one stall picking manure. He straightened up and turned to find the three men blocking his exit.

"Guess there's no need for introductions," Shaw snarled as Ray backed into a corner. "Jeff says you worked for him and frankly, he ain't giving you too good of a recommendation."

"Bull crap! It's all lies," hissed Ray, blinking in surprise.

"Shut up!" Jeff snapped, "Stealing my equipment is one thing, but what you did to Jenna makes me want to cave your face in! What did you have in mind for the Shaw girls? Same thing? You sick sonofabitch!"

Al appeared, followed by two deputies. One patted the radio on his belt, and pointed toward Ray.

"Is this Raymond Slankard? Dispatch says there's a warrant for his arrest in Missouri."

"I didn't do nothin' to the girl," Ray insisted as they rotely conducted the proper procedures and checked him for a concealed weapon. "I got a good job now. I don't need this shit!"

"I think you can consider the job at Shaw's place history." Jeff's eyes narrowed, boring holes into Ray's twitching face. "I can guarantee you one more thing. You'll never work in this business again. I'll make damned sure of it."

Ray swore as the officers pushed him toward the parking lot.

"You're gonna be one sorry bastard," he called over his shoulder, curling his lip and leveling deadly eyes at Jeff.

John stood silent as the police car drove away. Ruth clutched Jeff's arm and muttered her sincere thanks.

"I knew he would show up," Jeff told Wes. "Just a matter of time."

Wes nodded, running his fingers through his hair and replacing his ball cap. "I hope we've seen the last of him."

CHAPTER FOURTEEN

Inside the trailer's small dressing room, Jenna sat nervously on a tack box and looked up at Chris with a tense, pale face. *Why had she wanted to do this so badly?* Watching Chris get ready for her class, Jenna was suddenly frantic at the thought of riding Tess in front of all those people.

"I was so sure this is what I wanted to do!" She swallowed hard. "I don't know if I can do this, Chris, really, I think I'm gonna be sick."

"Anxiety attack," said Chris sympathetically, as she buckled her belt. Her class was coming up and she was nearly ready. "You'll make it."

Jenna's eyelids collapsed. "I really ought to scratch. I know it's going to be awful and I'll embarrass everyone."

"The waiting is tough, but once you're on the horse, it'll be better."

"Chris! You don't understand! I'm *flat-lining*!"

"Take it easy! After I ride, I'll help you get dressed." Chris seemed so relaxed. "After my go, we'll have about 45 minutes or so until your class."

A knock on the trailer door was the signal from Jeff that Cherry was ready to go.

"Let's rock and roll, Christine!" he yelled.

"Come on and watch, don't just sit here and stew, for God's sake!" Chris stepped confidently from the trailer. In tawny chaps and a celery green sweater, she looked exquisite. Jeff gave her a leg up and she settled in the saddle as he dusted off the toes of her boots.

"It's show time," she said with a grin.

It was a sunny Kansas afternoon, full of blue October sky and dramatic cloud formations. The temperature hovered at 60 degrees, requiring Chris to ride Cherry a little longer before the class. She allowed herself an hour that morning, a break, and then a 20-minute warm up just before the class.

"Pull a little sweat on her before the class," Jeff directed. "It's a cool day and the little rip will be full of herself."

Jenna joined Jo in the bleachers around the indoor arena and they waited for Chris' class. Christine had signed up for junior western pleasure, as the class schedule had no competition specifically for two-year-olds.

"Most of these horses are three and four-year-olds," Joanna told her. "Cherry's probably the youngest one in there."

Ten horses were entered in the class. Jenna felt a rush of pride as she watched the pair make their entrance. Cherry seemed a little agitated, but her rider appeared to be oblivious to it. Jenna knew, however, that Chris was acutely aware of every move the mare made. Wes and Jeff joined them and the four sat motionless as the gate closed and the judging commenced.

Suddenly, music blasted from the speaker. It was not unusual to have music, but the recording was scratchy and loud and threw harsh echoes off the walls of the arena. Cherry threw her head up and jumped sideways three feet off the rail toward the middle. Chris snatched the slack out of the reins and drove her heel into her left flank. Cherry dropped her head and moved back to the rail, wringing her tail.

"I can't watch!" Wes pounded his knee. "Damn the music. You'd think she'd be used to that. We play the radio night and day at home."

Jeff was calm, eyes straight ahead. "It's different, she's nervous and she's never been here before. Her adrenaline has kicked into high gear."

After the jog and walk, the announcer called for the lope. Although Cherry stepped obediently into the change of gait, she was moving faster with every step. Within seconds she was passing other slower horses on the rail and Jenna could read Chris' lips. *Easy, girl, easy.* But Cherry would have no part of anything easy.

Jeff muttered under his breath. "Forget the class, baby, she's blown it. Talk to her. Let's get through this."

As if she had heard Jeff's instructions, Chris moved her off the rail, lifted her hands and seesawed on each rein, trying to bring her back into control. As the ring man signaled for the jog trot, the girl maneuvered the young mare back to the rail, talking to her quietly. The horses on the rail reversed and began to work clockwise. Jenna held her breath. After a brief walk, the announcer called for the lope again. Chris held the mare back firmly and tried to ease her into it, but Cherry gave her head an angry shake and plunged forward. Chris checked her and brought her back to the walk. The girl waited until she was clear of other horses passing and attempted to lope off again. This time, Cherry stepped into the gait. It was a little more controlled, but the motion still too strong.

As the ring steward signaled for the walk and finally gestured to the riders to line up, Chris stayed on the rail walking the full length of the arena. She stopped Cherry at the end and guided her to the middle to join the line. After the judge turned in his card, she circled the mare slowly, keeping her moving until the winners were announced and the class dismissed.

Chris reined up outside the arena after the class.

"Whoa! You little tramp!" she barked to Cherry as Jeff and Jenna met her at the gate. "Sorry, Dad. What a disaster."

She twisted her face into a goofy exaggerated frown and laughed.

"Jenna, I need to ride this silly sow outside for a while before we go back to the stalls. Is it okay if Mom helps you get ready?"

Jenna was amazed at how cool Chris appeared and how forgiving Jeff seemed to be. She nodded and headed to the trailer with Jo, realizing as they walked that her stomach felt much better.

"I'll grab Dad's show saddle out of the trailer and finish saddling Tess," offered Wes. Jeff had donated the use of a new wool saddle pad, a red and black Navajo design. He also loaned Jenna his show saddle and a trendy bridle, trimmed with sterling silver.

In the trailer, Jenna dressed herself in the short-waisted black wool jacket and black hat so carefully selected earlier. The double-breasted jacket sported rows of sterling silver buttons and was trimmed in red braid, military style. She slipped it over her white tuxedo shirt. She buckled the snug black chaps and zipped them down as far as she could manage.

Joanna brushed Jenna's long, curly hair back into a low ponytail and adjusted the black Stetson until it was just right.

"Here, wear my lucky silver earrings." Jo's motherly voice had a calming effect. "And put on a little more makeup. You need more color."

Jenna shuddered. This was it. She felt a bit jittery, but ready to do it. A knock on the trailer door set her heart to pounding.

"I know," she forced a laugh and called, "let's rock and roll!"

Opening the door, she stepped to the ground. Jeff whistled in appreciation.

"How 'bout a kiss for luck?" Wes smiled and leaned close.

She obliged, brushing her colored lips on his tanned cheek.

"Let me finish zippin' these chaps down for you." He bent down and zipped the last six inches on each side of the black suede chaps.

After she was in the saddle, he pulled the bottoms of the chaps down and brushed out Tess's tail one last time. Chris was unsaddling Cherry and called out, "Go on, I'll catch up."

"Good luck, babe. Just head to the warm-up pen and keep her moving." Wes patted Jenna's knee and stepped away as she walked the mare toward the arena, Joanna alongside. He dropped back to walk with Jeff.

"She looked pretty nervous earlier, but I think she's got it together now." He wiped the lipstick mark off his face.

Jeff placed a hand briefly on the shoulder of his son as they walked. "Yeah, I think so. It surprises me that the deal last night with Ray didn't freak her out more."

Inside the arena, the previous class had lined up. Joanna gave a wave from the door to Jeff, who motioned for Jenna to get ready to go. Tess was relaxed and responsive, instilling a confidence in Jenna that she needed. The gate man checked her number with his entries and thumbed her to the entry gate.

"Senior pleasure horses going in," he said into his two-way radio. "Got fourteen head."

Jenna clenched her fingers on the reins and stiffened. She thought of the Fourth of July show, of Joanna's first ride on Cherry and that fierce, bold look in Joanna's eyes.

"What the hell," she muttered to herself, tucking a stray wisp of hair under the hatband. "Let's do it."

She evened the reins, grasped them in her left hand and dropped her right hand slightly, elbows close to her body. With head up, shoulders back and chin forward, she clucked to the mare and moved her through the gate. Across the arena, she saw Wes on the bleachers as Tess hit the jog trot. Jenna never looked at him again.

She glanced around quickly to check her rail position. *Walk your horses, please.* Tess dropped to a precise, pert walk, opening up several lengths in front of her. Jenna would guard that space, needing it to fully show the judge how pretty Tess' transitions could be. In seconds, the ring man's hand would go up and the announcer would ask the class to go lope. Jenna headed into the corner of the rectangular pen. *Good,* she thought. This would help her get the correct lead.

Out of the corner of her eye, she saw the ring man raise his hand. She sat back slightly, her right hipbone putting pressure on the saddle and her outside leg against the mare. As he called for lope, she slowly lifted the top of her rein hand an inch, sending the softest signal to the mare's mouth. The mare was ready, waiting for her cue. As Jenna made a light kissing sound to her and touched her with her outside leg, the mare slipped into the loping gait like a feather to the ground. *Everything in slow motion.* Jenna forced herself to breathe, Uncle Frank's lessons ringing in her head.

The judge was a tall, broad shouldered man in palomino-colored boots and navy blue jacket. He scanned the horses from his vantage point in the center of the arena. He had already eliminated half the class from possible placings for mistakes or moving badly. The three he was now eyeballing would probably go one, two, three, unless one blew it as he was watching.

He scrutinized his favorites. The slim man on the stocking-legged sorrel was super flashy and up to this point, had been perfectly consistent. The girl in the black and red jacket on the elegant bay certainly had the crowd's attention. She was probably the most appealing of the class and the mare seemed to move well. The gray horse was plain, but good and steady.

The judge wanted to see them lope to the right, and he knew it was here that he would likely make his choice. He nodded to the ring steward who raised his hand, signaling the announcer. The gray was a good loper, as was the bay. The flashy sorrel was superb. As the man rode by, perfect cadence, his number seemed to tug at the judge's pencil. But in his peripheral vision, the judge saw a sudden movement and turned to watch the sorrel speed up at the far end. The rider held the reins up hard, at the same time driving the horse forward with a spurring motion. He reached up and took the outside rein in his left hand and jerked the horse's head down. All the while, the judge watched this schooling like an eavesdropper, sighed and promptly scratched the sorrel from the top of the list.

He surveyed the class and noted the gray gelding and the bay mare both cruising down the rail. He hesitated, then made his choice. He gestured he was through and the steward signaled for the riders to line up.

He inspected each horse, feigning interest, but his decision had been made. He walked casually behind each horse as one by one the riders cued them to take several steps backward. The young woman on the bay backed five perfect steps. He marked his card, gave it to the ring steward and sauntered to the side of the arena to take a sip of his coffee. For him, it was like another day at the office.

He could not, of course, have had any thought of how his decision would impact the slim young woman on her brand new horse who sat mounted, knees shaking, as it was announced she and Tess had won the class.

Lips trembling, pulse exploding, Jenna rode forward to accept a large blue ribbon with a huge rosette. At the gate, Jeff was waiting with a satisfied grin.

"Nice go," he proclaimed. His pairing of Jenna and Tess had just proved to be a success and he spoke loudly in an approving voice intended to let everyone know the two were under his tutelage.

She dismounted outside the arena and dropped to the ground into Wes' arms.

"Mighty fine trip there, girl," he crowed, removing his straw Resistol hat in a courtly but natural gesture that moved her.

Jenna stroked the mare's neck.

"It was Tess's win. She's a real pro," she said, surprised at a new, deep feeling of affection for Tess.

As she unzipped her chaps and draped them over the saddle horn, the girl on the gray gelding rode by with her second place ribbon. She leaned down and extended her hand.

"Hi! I'm Becki Shaw. Congratulations!" She offered a handshake as genuine as church apple butter.

Jenna touched the gelding's shoulder, moved by the girl's graciousness.

"Thanks! I'm Jenna St. James. You really have a nice horse."

"I'm pretty happy with him. Why don't you come over to our stalls after while and meet my sister, Kathy? She usually rides but her horse has a sore back."

Jenna assured her she would come by later. She turned a flushed face to Chris and Joanna, standing nearby. As her eyes met Joanna's, a gratifying message was exchanged. Jenna pressed the blue ribbon into Jo's hands.

"This is for you. I thought of you before I went in and I wanted to look just like you."

Jo interrupted her with a quick hug. "You take it home for a while. It's your first blue ribbon. Later, we'll put it on our fireplace. Why don't we go unsaddle Tess and put her up?"

"I want to do it myself." Jenna took the reins from Jeff. She unsaddled the mare, took the bands from her mane and led her into the stall. Jenna patted her rump, longing for some kind of response, but Tess turned away indifferently and moved to her water bucket for a drink. Jenna sighed and latched the stall. After she changed from her show clothes, she and Chris looked for Wes, but he was working with Al. They decided to find the Shaw girls.

Becki and her older sister, Kathy, were as different as thunder and lightning. Becki was funny and talkative, and Jenna was soon at ease in her company. Kathy was somber and thoughtful. They spoke briefly of Ray and the incident of the previous evening. Sensing Jenna's discomfort, Chris guided the conversation to horses.

"Your mare is super, Jenna," Becki chirped, catching the drift from Chris. "I love the way she moves. My horse, Chester, is such a lug. He used to travel better when he was younger, but he's almost fifteen now. But I love him to death. If I asked him to run right straight into a wall, he'd do it!"

Jenna was amused. "I just bought Tess, so I don't know her very well."

"It won't be long before you know what it means every time she flicks an ear," Kathy spoke up. "It's a good feeling. And soon, she'll share that with you."

It was nearly six when Chris and Jenna returned to their stalls. Wes had finished up his work with Al and would ride back to New Winston with the Days. Jenna felt a stab of isolation as she watched them load the horses and prepare to leave together. Familiar feelings flooded her brain. She remembered spending birthdays alone while Claudia was in New Orleans, or Reno. Or somewhere. She stood by her Jeep, clutching her blue ribbon.

Wes slammed the back of the trailer and looked at her standing there alone. He paused for a moment, then approached the Jeep's passenger side and opened the door.

"Get in," he said. She looked puzzled. "You ain't going home alone. We can follow the folks to the farm," he said, signaling Jeff to go on without him. "You can go back to Kansas City tomorrow night."

"You don't have to do this." She touched his arm. "I guess it would just be best if I went on home by myself. And I need to report in to my mom."

"You can call the Queen Mother from the house." She climbed in beside him. "What we really need to do is celebrate." He started the engine and pulled the Jeep out on the road, falling in line behind the trailer.

CHAPTER FIFTEEN

A week before Gabe Judd's twentieth birthday, Charlie gave him his first raise.

"For a guy who don't spend much money on anything," Edith told her husband, "he sure seemed excited about the extra twenty bucks on his paycheck."

"He's stashing it. He's got nearly $500 saved up. Says it's for a rainy day." Charlie told his wife about the boy's savings. He was proud of Gabe's prudence when it came to money.

"He sure is a sensible boy."

"I wonder how much he thinks about his mother. And the horses."

She patted her husband's arm. "I wonder about that myself. I'm glad you're taking him with you to the American Royal next week."

"I can't take off and see any of the horse shows, but we're gonna do some business and see the sights."

"That's probably better anyway. I'm not sure how he would feel about a horse show," Edith frowned. "The boy is a great help to you and the fact you trust him is a comfort to me. I think Gabe could handle a few more business responsibilities if you would give him a chance."

"I plan to do just that," Charlie told her.

***

The American Royal presides over horse and livestock shows as one of the oldest and largest in the Midwest. Along with rodeos, livestock classes, parades and exhibitions from various breeds of horses, the Royal includes a sanctioned quarter horse show. As official farrier for the show, Al George needed to go early to set up shop. He and Wes arrived in Kansas City on Thursday and prepared for exhibitors who would be pouring in from all over the nation for the show.

"The Amer-i-can Royal!" said Al. "This is usually a good show for me and there's plenty of work. There's some good places to eat around here and a couple of good bars, but believe me, Weston, my man, you'll be ready to skip that and hit the sack after resetting and shoeing horses all day. I got a room reserved at a motel not far from here with two great big double beds. I guarantee all you'll want to party with is that pillow!"

Wes laughed. Horse shoeing *was* damnable hard work.

"My folks are coming in tonight. Dad left Cherry home, but he's showing Jake tomorrow."

"I thought Cherry was supposed to show."

"Dad didn't want to take the chance of her freakin' out and embarrassing him in front of all his pals."

"Embarrassing him? Chris is the one riding her."

"Same thing."

"What about Jenna and Tess?" Al continued. "They looked great last weekend at Lawrence, from what I saw."

"Naw. They need a few more rides before they take on this kind of show."

He and Al worked until after ten, stopped for burgers and headed to the room. He called Jenna late that night from the motel.

"I have classes all day tomorrow and I have a test at 3:30," she said, "I'll miss Jake's class!"

"Can't be helped," he sighed, too tired to think about it. "After your test, come and meet me. The show's in Hale Arena. Just south of there is a long building full of stalls. I'll be at the end of that building near the entrance. Look for Al's truck."

It was nearly five when he saw her walking toward him. She wore a lightweight burgundy-colored jacket, collar up. Fitted at the waist, it bloused a little, making her legs look even longer. Her starched Rockies were stacked neatly over thick-soled burgundy ropers and she walked with a confident swing. She took off her sunglasses and shook her loose hair back. *Christ,* he thought. *She's a knockout.*

"How's the show going? How'd Jake do?" She offered a familiar wave to Al.

"Well, Mom and Dad haven't had a fight yet and we snagged another big win for Jake the Snake." Wes smiled, still staring at her. "We've got a horse coming over in a few minutes with a loose shoe, but I can take you over to our stalls."

"Go on, bud," Al spoke up. "I can handle it for a minute."

They walked down the middle of the building, stalls on each side, amongst the crowd of riders and horses. Many stalls were decorated with the barn colors of the exhibitors and furnished with tables, chairs and even potted plants. Large signs identified horse farms from Texas, Oklahoma, Iowa, and dozens of other states. Larry Wayne's operation dominated one whole double row of stalls, all decked in royal blue and white.

"Hey! Jenna!" a voice shouted. It was Dana Jordan and her sister, Desiree, leading wet, freshly bathed horses. They spoke briefly and walked on. At the far end of the building, she saw John and Ruth Shaw, followed by Becki, who offered a friendly wave. It felt good to see familiar faces.

At the Days' stalls, Chris was feeding Jake. A huge blue ribbon with long streamers hung from the front of the tack stall.

"Jen! We won weanling stallions!" she shouted, then lowered her voice to a whisper. "Brandon said a few people have asked him how much the stud fee is on Vince!"

"Hmmm. Brandon's here." Jenna observed. "Everybody's here. It's like a big family reunion."

"Yeah, I need to go find him and say goodbye," she said. "We're going to head on home. Mom and Dad went to get something to eat and then I think we're going to load up."

Wes headed back to join Al. Jenna perched on a tack box and leafed through the printed program of events.

"Would you stay here and watch Jake while I go find Brandon?" Chris asked her. "I'll be back in a while!"

Chris felt good about the show. Her colt was gaining a reputation and she glowed when Brandon told her he thought Jake was the best stud colt in the Midwest. She walked down the narrow alley on the outside of the stall rows. Brandon wasn't at his parents' stalls. She walked on, glancing down each row of stalls. At the end of the building, she called to Al.

"Hey, have you seen Brandon?"

"He walked out toward the trailers just a while ago." Al nodded and thumbed toward the parking lot.

She headed toward the large parking area full of horse trailers and scanned it for the large white trailer with copper brown trim with "Penny" in huge letters. She spotted it. The trailer was a four-horse slant with a tack room and a large, plush living area with beds, kitchenette, the works. She walked to the door, and hearing voices, paused. The door of the living quarters was closed, but it wasn't a solid door. The top part was a screened window and it was open. She heard Brandon speak, low and teasing, following by a cooing female response. Chris recognized it as the voice of a girl they both knew.

"Brandon, stop it!" The girl giggled and whispered something.

Chris froze, blood pounding in her head. She heard Brandon laugh. The sound of the girl's silly chirping nauseated her. Stepping closer, she laid her hand on the closed door and her eyes focused on two entwined figures on the other side of the screened window. Neither saw her peek in.

Face burning, she backed up and walked away. She rushed inside the building and hurried down the crowded alleyway. By the time she got back to Jenna, hot tears were streaming. As Jenna pieced together what had transpired, she instantly thought of Wes.

"Chris! You've got to get it together!" she pleaded. "If your brother sees you like this over Brandon, you'll be crying your face off at that shit bird's *funeral*! You know that don't you?"

"God! I hate him," the slighted one sobbed.

"Listen to me!" Jenna held her tight. "If he is that much of a worm, you don't need him! He just proved he's not good enough for you!"

Chris was making half an attempt to control the sobs.

Jenna gripped the girl's shoulders.

"Somewhere in this world there is someone for you. And he's going to be a helluva guy! You don't need that pretty boy!"

The girl was sniffling and trying to find a mirror to look at her eyes.

"Get some ice and put it on your face," ordered Jenna, guiding her toward the cooler.

"I've got to get Jake's legs wrapped." Chris was still struggling to get words out.

"Sit here and calm down, I'll do it. You want his hood and blanket on now?"

"Just the blanket," she hiccuped. "The leg wraps are in the tack box."

As Jenna finished getting Jake ready for the ride home, Chris joined her in the stall. She draped her arm over the tall colt's back and leaned her head against him, sniffling.

"You know, no matter what happens, I'll always have Jake," she murmured, sighing as she closed her eyes and patted him. He nickered.

"See there, he says no matter what, he'll always love you," offered Jenna, trying to console her.

"Jenna! He didn't say that at all. What he's really saying is that I forgot to throw him a flake of hay," she sniffled and a nasal laugh escaped her. "I'll be all right. I just want to go home."

It was nearly 8:30 when Jeff and Joanna returned from supper. They loaded up the equipment, chairs, tables and lastly, Jake. Chris climbed in the back seat of the truck, sliding one last sulky look at her confidante. When they were gone, Jenna returned to the end of the building to find Wes and Al.

"Can you take a break for some supper?" she asked.

"Probably not." He was holding up the foot of a sorrel horse and rasping the edges of the hoof. "I'll be done here in a while though. I need to run by the motel and shower. Then, let's go over to your place. I want to see it."

It was late when they arrived at the apartment. She threw her purse and keys on the table and turned on the light as Wes inspected the place. She took him by both hands and led him inside.

"What do you think?" She studied his face.

"Nice. Private." He liked being completely alone with her at last. She slipped off her burgundy jacket and stood smiling before him, hands on her hips.

"Can I fix you something to eat? I know you're hungry." She walked to the kitchen area, his eyes following her. He sat at the small table as she prepared a ham and cheese sandwich. He was dead tired and didn't have much of an appetite, but he finished it off and drank a glass of milk to please her.

"Did you and Al work on a lot of horses?" she asked, washing and drying the single plate and glass.

"Yeah. All day long. I'm worn out ... and my back's killing me." He walked to the window and looked out, casing the neighborhood.

"Want me to rub it for you?" She stepped up behind him, massaging his lower back and then slipping her arms around his waist. "Come and lay down on my bed and I'll rub on it more."

"Jenna, do you know what would happen if I lay down on your bed?" he spoke slowly.

"You'd fall asleep?" She was smiling modestly, but her eyes were playful.

He turned around and looked down at her uplifted face. "I don't think so." He stared at her, trying to read her thoughts.

"I need to ask you a question," he murmured, kissing her head and wrapping his arms around her securely. "Do you love me?"

She lifted her eyes, surprised, then leaned against his body.

"I think you already know the answer."

He was silent for a moment, taking in the feel of her and the smell of her hair. "Say it."

She backed up a half step and tipped her face up. Her lips were parted and nearly touching his.

"I love you."

Unexpectedly, the sound of the words and how much he wanted to hear them jolted him. Her face delivered a shy but willing signal. She walked to the bedroom and turned on her bedside lamp, calling to him. He followed her, unbuttoning his shirt. Her arms encircled his neck and pulled him down on the bed. For Jenna, it was Independence Day.

Afterwards, she lay across his chest, eyes closed, smiling. Her damp, tangled hair touched his face and eventually, he realized she was sleeping. His senses were charged with an aching need to wake her and tell her he loved her, too. He closed his eyes.

The gray light broke through the bedroom window like a curious intruder, finding Jenna propped up on one elbow, already awake and intently watching him sleep. She reveled in this new level of intimacy with him. With her eyes, she explored his face, strong and handsome in repose. His rumpled hair sharply outlined against her pillow somehow made him seem so vulnerable.

Thoughts rambled through her head, leaving a trail of images. Wes crashing to the ground with Ray that night at the barn. Sitting beside him on the hillside after the Fourth of July show, trying to calm him down. The first night she kissed him on the roof.

She touched her lips to his shoulder and he stirred. He gathered her body in his arms and lay still. After a while he yawned and stretched.

"I need to get dressed and you gotta take me back to meet Al. Got coffee?"

"Yeah, Al will probably be wondering what happened to you last night." She flounced out of bed and began rummaging through a drawer.

Wes rolled his eyes and shook his head. "It's not like he had to rack his brain to figure it out."

She slipped on a pair of old jeans with worn knees and a faded red plaid flannel shirt and headed to the kitchen. He pulled on his Wranglers and sat bare-chested on the edge of the bed, watching her through the bedroom door.

"Hey, you. Come here," he finally said.

She looked up from the sink and smiled, returning to the bedside, where he motioned for her to sit on his lap. She curled up against his chest and he held her tight, chin on her shoulder. Eyes closed, he began to rock back and forth just slightly, savoring the feeling. Pure joy. Zen level joy.

"I love you," he told her.

CHAPTER SIXTEEN

The first snow fell on the Missouri River Valley the week before Christmas. Work with Al had dropped off some and Wes spent more time at the farm helping with the horses.

Chris exercised Jake daily and kept the colt in winter blankets, planning to show him in February.

Jeff had brought the other three weanlings in from the pasture and stalled them on the south side of the barn where incoming brood mares would be kept. Two were fillies, sizey and pretty-headed.

The other was a chestnut stud colt, tall and muscular. He was a quality colt and Jeff was pleased with him, but the Day show string had no need for a second stud colt. He would only have to compete with Jake, who was by far the most exceptional of the coming yearlings. The week before the holiday, Doc McGraw came to remedy this matter.

"I saw your ad in the *Journal*," said the vet. "How many mares have you got booked to Vince?"

"Enough to keep us pretty busy," Jeff told him. "I won't take any more than twenty outside mares. We just don't have the facility or the help. We've got six mares of our own to breed. Plus, we donated a couple of fees to futurities."

"I heard you sold your pleasure gelding," he made conversation as he got the chestnut colt out and sedated him for the castration.

"Zip? Yeah, he's gone," Jeff said. "Larry Wayne found a buyer in Texas who wanted him."

"Your orphan's sure making a nice horse. Hell, he's almost big enough to saddle right now. You're not going to leave him a stud, are you?"

"Only for another year. I want to leave him a stud long enough to show him in yearling stallions. So far, he's been no problem for Chris, and she's the one who works with him here at the farm. And you'd never know he was an orphan."

"What's Wild Wild Wes up to these days?" Doc asked as the anesthetized colt went to the ground. "Still shoeing with Al?"

"Oh yeah. It's an okay job. He likes it. I know he's been socking away some pretty good cash," said Jeff. "Jo thinks he's gonna buy a saddle for his girlfriend."

"I guess she's really teamed up with Tess."

"Yeah. Seems so. She fits in here like a glove. If I were to pick out a wife for him, I couldn't do much better than her." Jeff squatted and watched the surgery. "Only one thing bothers me. Her mother. You know I told you her mom was an old friend of ours, one of Joanna's sorority sisters."

"I remember you mentioned that."

"Well, I used to go with her. Before Joanna. I've tried not to think about this, but it would be kind of strange to have her as my son's mother-in-law." Jeff gave a nervous laugh.

The vet gave a cock-eyed look at his friend. "Like bad blood in the family, eh?"

"Something like that," Jeff answered, looking away. "I was only with her a few months, maybe longer. Just long enough to find out what a little bitch she was. She hated my guts after I dumped her for Joanna."

"Whatever, if I know Wes, he can handle it. And if he can, you can," said Mike.

"Hell. It *was* twenty years ago. It's probably no big deal."

Mike asked, "Is she married?"

"The guy she was married to died and left her a bundle. Her and a new boyfriend have been in Las Vegas or someplace for weeks. The boyfriend calls Jenna every once in a while. I don't know what's up with that. Don't care. I think he's just checking on her for Claudia. Jenna and her mom are on the outs right now. Anyway, Jenna's coming here for Christmas."

"It'll work out," Mike said, finishing up his job.

"Probably. Although you never know about Claudia. She's a little unbalanced."

The groggy colt was on his feet, and Jeff guided him back to his stall. "She sure doesn't think much of Wes. She probably had hopes of Jenna hooking up with somebody a little more high-falutin'."

As Mike pulled away in his truck, Jeff stood by the barn door and watched the vet's white dually churn through the snow and out of sight. It was nearly dark. The sputtering sound of a poorly tuned engine caught his attention and his eyes fixed on a deserted lane between the entrance to the Day farm and Frank's place. Puzzled, he watched red taillights pull from the lane and turn onto the Old Pike Road. He walked slowly to the porch, thinking about this. *Who was parked on that lane? Young lovers? Not likely in this snow. What, then? Hunters?*

Inside the kitchen, he paused, then pulled on his insulated boots, grabbed a flashlight and slipped out the back door. Jeff was suspicious of anybody trespassing on his property.

He circled the house and took a snowy path toward the road. When he reached the dead-end lane intersecting with the road, he saw several sets of tire tracks, footprints, and cigarette butts. The footprints led to a nearby tree on a rise overlooking the Day farm. More cigarette butts were on the ground there, crushed out in the frozen mud. Jeff squatted and looked at the tracks. He spotted an old, yellowed butt. Whoever it was, had he been here more than once? He returned to the house and called Frank.

"You know that dead-end lane between my house and yours? Ever see anybody parked there? You know, kids, lovers, or whatever?" Jeff tried to sound nonchalant.

"Matter of fact, last month Lil said she saw a car parked there one night. It was nearly dark. All she could see is that it was an older model car. She saw it pulling out and as it passed the house, she said it looked like a longhaired fella driving. I told her to keep an eye out," said Frank. "Why?"

"You say it was just one guy in the car? By himself?" Jeff quizzed him.

"Yeah. Just one guy. Why? Did you see him, too?" Frank demanded to know. He didn't like trespassers, either.

"Only the lights. I hadn't noticed it before, but somebody was there tonight. I walked down there just now and there's tracks in the snow, cigarette butts like he's been there a couple times lately."

"Hmm. We might ought to call old Ken," suggested Frank.

The police chief of New Winston was named Purvis Thompson, but everybody called him Ken. He had known Jeff since they were childhood chums in Lexington. Ken listened carefully and then spoke.

"Don't go back out there and don't disturb anything. I want to look at it myself. It might be nothing, it might be something. I'll be there in forty-five minutes."

It was late when the two men returned to the lane. With flashlights, they inspected the tire tracks.

"These are my footprints," Jeff said, fitting his boot into one track. "The others are somebody else's."

Ken studied the footprints and the tracks to the tree. "Couldn't have been a hunter. The prints never leave here. Too many cigarette butts.

Somebody drove in here. Backed in, and sat parked here for a while. He must have got out of the car several times and stood, watching your house. See how the toe prints face the house? Then, look here. He smoked a couple of cigarettes here by the car and then walked to the tree, watched, smoked, came back."

"Sonofabitch!" Jeff swore, "Somebody's watching my place! And see over here, more of the same tire tracks. This guy's been here twice since it snowed."

"Looks like it," Ken said in a terse voice. He flashed the light over by a nearby fence post. "And you're right about it being a guy. See this yellow snow? Probably had to piss. So, have you heard any noises from the guy who assaulted the girl here last summer? The guy arrested in Kansas?"

"Nothing since we saw him in Lawrence," Jeff replied. Ken had pulled on a latex glove and was picking up cigarette butts. He dropped them methodically into a plastic bag.

"Any reason why anybody would be watching you, or Jo, or anybody in your family?" The lawman was studying the cigarette butts with the flashlight. Jeff shook his head.

"Nobody except Ray Slankard, and I thought he would be serving some time. Whoever it is, I wonder what the hell he wants?"

Ken didn't want to say this. "Where's your wife and daughter? And the girl, the one Slankard assaulted, is she around?"

"Joanna and the kids went over to Rita Randall's Christmas party. Jenna's home in Kansas City. She's down here a lot though."

"Yeah, well, I'll check on Slankard. You call Doc and see if he saw anything when he left. Meanwhile, I'm going to send a deputy up this way a couple times a day, just to keep an eye on the place," Ken said. "Let's go back to the house and talk a bit."

Back in the kitchen, the men warmed themselves with big mugs of coffee.

"I don't want you to be worried, but I don't think you ought to leave the place unattended for a while. I don't know if you want to tell your family about this or not. It's up to you. Just be careful … at least until we see what's going on here." Ken turned to go. "Try to have a nice holiday."

**

In Kansas City, Jenna finished wrapping her Christmas gifts. She surveyed her work then picked up the new denim shirt folded carefully on her bed. It was a birthday present. On January 1, Chris would be nineteen and Jenna had bought her a denim shirt the girl had admired in a western catalog. It was embroidered with little black horses.

She loaded the Jeep with the gifts, clothes and cupcakes she had baked herself and drove east, leaving the city behind. She was consumed with a holiday spirit she had not known since she was a child. Turning the car radio up, she sang loudly until she saw the bluffs south of the river town. Turning onto the Old Pike Road, her Jeep's headlights lit up the trees. The bare limbs sparkled as if trimmed in shining crystal and up the hill, she saw red and green lights crisscrossing the front of the farmhouse. A perfect calendar shot.

Inside, the Day family awaited her arrival. Wes perched on a stool in the kitchen and watched his mother bake cookies. This room was the core of the old house's lower level. The area was Joanna's special domain and as much a part of her as the barn.

The aroma of glazed ham and apple pie filled the house. The spirit of the family's sense of togetherness had an unprecedented sentimental effect on Wes. An awareness in the back of his mind seemed to tell him these fading moments of his youth were already a memory. He found the worry-free exuberance of his sister assuring, almost infectious, and every time Jo turned away, he and Chris took turns sneaking a bite of the cookie dough.

In the front room, Jeff sat quietly in a huge leather chair, head back, eyes closed. He favored this large room, warmed by ceiling beams, ginger-tinted hardwood floors and large braided rugs. At the end of the room was a massive rock fireplace with a heavy mantle showcasing rows of trophies. The walls were adorned with framed photographs of family, favorite horses and prestigious show ring victories. While more or less neglected in the summer, the room was a favorite gathering place during winter months and especially Christmas, when it was dominated by an elaborately decorated tree.

Jeff listened to the laughter coming from the kitchen, then stood up and walked to the front window. He hadn't told them about the incident in the lane. The day before he had received a call at his office from Ken and it wasn't the news he wanted to hear. Ray had served sixty days and had been released. His whereabouts was unknown. Jeff knew he would have to tell his family, but he thought he'd wait just a day or two.

He watched the road. As he saw the dark green Jeep approaching, he smiled to himself.

"Jenna's here!" he announced loudly.

Wes ducked out of the kitchen and glanced nervously at his father before he stepped out the front door. They exchanged a private nod.

Jeff stood at the window and watched as Jenna, in a heavy white sweater, jeans and goose down vest stepped out and threw her arms around Wes' neck. Jeff watched as they kissed enthusiastically and Jenna turned to retrieve an armload of gifts. He heard a rustle at his shoulder and Joanna joined him, whispering.

"Move over, I want to see this, too."

They watched as Wes reached in his coat pocket for a little velvet-covered box and they saw Jenna's face freeze in utter surprise. Jeff and Jo observed as their son opened the box and the flash of diamond sent his intended into uncontrollable spasms of tears. The wrapped gifts had dropped to the ground. She leaned into him, box in her fist, joyfully kissing his face.

Behind the sheer curtain, the observers were silent. Chris, slipping up behind them, noticed Jeff had placed his hand on his wife's shoulder and was caressing her neck. Joanna stiffened and made no effort to respond.

CHAPTER SEVENTEEN

After Christmas, Jenna drove back to her Kansas City apartment. As she unpacked her clothes, she casually tapped the blinking light on her phone to listen to her recorded messages. The last one was from Claudia. She and Miguel had spent the holidays in Las Vegas.

"Hello, Jenna. We're home. I suppose you spent Christmas break in New Winston with Wes. Oh well. Call me."

The voice was clipped and more than a little frosty. Jenna fingered her new engagement ring and picked up the phone. It was late, but she dialed the number. *No need to put this off.*

"Mom? It's me. How was Vegas?" Jenna waded in cautiously.

"Okay, but our flight back was horrible. The plane was jammed full of people. We sat in Denver for two hours to catch our connecting flight, and I had to walk a half a mile to get up to the damned smoking lounge." Claudia was not in an indulgent mood. "Jenna, I came home right after Christmas just to see you and as you know, you were unavailable and with absolutely no message letting me know where you were. I can't believe the way you treat me."

"Sorry." Jenna had no desire to provoke her.

"Well, then." After a moment of silence, Claudia seemed to switch personalities. "You *are* going back to school, I hope. God! I can't believe you have only one more semester and you'll graduate. It seems like you've been in school forever. Your best years are in front of you, Jenna Louise. I would hate to see you do something incredibly witless and quit to run off to this new life you have found so fascinating."

"School is going well and I'm right on schedule for graduation," Jenna said, masking her irritation.

"After graduation, what are your plans?" Claudia asked briskly and Jenna heard her take a drag off a cigarette. "Or are they a secret, like your social life for the past month has been?"

"It's no secret," Jenna hesitated, then dropped the bomb. "I'm gonna get married."

After several seconds of utter stillness on the other end of the line, she heard a quick, forced breath from Claudia and the click of the phone as her mother hung up. Jenna sat quietly, trying to compose herself, then redialed the house. Miguel answered.

"She just stormed out the door, headed for your place," he told her, "and you better be ready for Hurricane Claudia. She's beside herself. What did you say to her, for Chrissakes?"

"I told her I was going to get married," said Jenna and hung up.

Twenty minutes later, she heard her mother's car screech to a stop and in seconds, Claudia was pounding on the door. Jenna opened it, expecting a dramatic entrance. She was surprised. Claudia stood, calm and cool, with a sly half smile on her face. She sauntered in and sat on the edge of a chair, crossing her legs, shapely in snug black leggings.

"You can't marry Weston Day and that's that." She took out her cigarette case. "I'm shocked, frankly, that Jeff has allowed this fiasco of a relationship to go this far. Surely, you have to know why this thing can never, ever be."

Jenna began to feel weak in the knees and sat down on a footstool near her mother.

"I'm going to do it, Mother. And don't start with the Jeff thing. I know you used to date him. That was a long time ago."

"Date him?" Claudia touched her slim throat, threw her head back and laughed. "We were insane for each other. And, Jenna, we did what people do when they are madly in love. And that's why you can't marry Wes."

"Because you slept with Jeff? That's crazy. I don't care. Nobody cares!" Jenna was on her feet. "I'm going to be Wes' wife and you can't say anything to stop me. You're just going to have to deal with the fact Jeff's his father."

"Perhaps then, there is something else you should know," Claudia puffed on the long, slim cigarette. Her large eyes blinked a few times before she said the words. "Jeff Day is your father, too."

The words jabbed Jenna like a snakebite, paralyzing her. When her voice came, the words erupted as a scream.

"You're a liar! You can't stand to see me as part of this family when you never could be! Why has Jeff never said a word? He would have stopped it! Because *you* are a liar. You've seen too many daytime soaps, Mother!"

Claudia was unruffled.

"Just get out!" Jenna hissed. "Don't say another ..."

"Dear, sweet, stupid Jeff," Claudia continued. "He probably hasn't figured it out. I never told him, you know. And then I left him and went to Ohio and married Warren. Poor Warren."

"I said get out! You're way over the edge." Jenna frantically pushed her toward the door. "Don't call me. And don't try to see me."

Claudia, unperturbed, smiled as she stood up and blew a kiss.

"I truly am sorry, baby. It's cruel how the past comes back to haunt us." She slipped her designer purse over her shoulder and left.

Jenna slumped against the door, slid to the floor and beat the wall with her fists.

"Liar!" she screamed, answered by the sound of Claudia's car speeding away. Suddenly the anger died and something else took over. Something worse. Shaking too badly to stand, she crawled to the bathroom and hung over the stool, vomiting. Fighting hysteria, she staggered to the bedroom and threw herself on the bed. It was nearly four a.m. when she sat up and turned on the bedside lamp. She felt as though a stake had been driven through her heart.

Rummaging furiously through her closet, she clawed her way through shoes and books. Under the magazines, she found the box containing the photo of Warren St. James. She sat on the floor in front of the closet for a long time and studied it, then reached for the envelope with the Quebec address. The colorless light of morning found her sitting at the kitchen table, staring at the envelope and watching the clock.

At seven o'clock, she picked up the phone.

"Can I have an area code for Montreal, Quebec?"

She prayed he would still be living in Montreal. Minutes later, she was writing down the phone number. Her hands were still quivering and she had to dial three times before she completed the number. It seemed to ring forever, when suddenly, a sleepy female voice answered.

"I need to speak with Warren St. James," Jenna blurted, sucking in her breath.

"He's not here. Who is this?"

"This is Jenna. Jenna St. James. I need to talk to him." Her brain was numb and the words sounded like they were coming from someone else. "Please let me talk to him."

"Jenna? He's not here, dear. This is Suzetta, his wife. I'm sorry, I'm just so surprised to hear from you. You'll have to forgive me. He's out of town. But he's on the way home and should be here by noon. Can I give him a message?"

Frustrated, Jenna pressed her lips against the phone, words sticking in her throat. But the way Suzetta used the word "dear" encouraged her.

"Yes. Tell him I need to talk to him. I'll call."

She hung up. Walking to the window, she rocked back and forth, arms across her chest. She crossed the room to her dresser and leaning close, she studied herself in the mirror. The reflection surprised her. She looked awful, but her eyes were bright and determined.

She walked to the closet, pulled out a small suitcase and began stuffing it with a few things. An hour later, she was flipping through the Yellow Pages. Courageously, she dialed the phone.

"When is your next scheduled flight to Montreal?" she said in a collected voice. "Ten? That's two hours. I can make it."

Montreal! No matter. She didn't care how far it was. She would have stepped aboard a jet plane for Nepal for just one shred of truth. She tore through her drawers. No need for a visa or passport. *Birth certificate, where was it? Photo ID, driver's license.* Jenna stuffed them into her purse, grabbed the small bag and pulled on her coat.

***

The jet lifted off the ground destined first for St. Paul. Jenna sat back, buckled into her seat and closed her eyes. Unable to erase the image of her mother's face, she took out the photograph of Claudia and Warren. In the photo, Claudia's eyes were sly, her lips pursed, almost mocking. How well Jenna knew *that* look.

The bright afternoon sun had succumbed to a heavy cover of bluish gray clouds by the time her connecting flight to Montreal took to the air. It was not a long flight. Arriving at Mirabel airport, she impatiently endured the customs' check, and exchanged her U.S. money. She wondered how well her high school courses would serve her in this French-speaking city. The man at the rental car booth was friendly and spoke English. He gave her a map and outlined a route to the Ville de Montreal.

"Look here. See this long avenue along the edge of the city? Follow this route and you should find it," he explained. "It's about an hour's drive."

Jenna cruised slowly through the heavy traffic and although preoccupied with her mission, found herself marveling at the European flavor of the city. It was a gray, snowy afternoon and the street signs were difficult to read through the huge flakes, but at last she found the address – 16 Rue Charles. It was a large, brownstone house with small windows and huge front door. Heart pounding, she parked on the street and walked up the short brick sidewalk to the house.

She clanged the brass knocker. The heavy door swung partially open and a round-faced woman peeked out at her. Jenna shifted her weight and nervously asked to see Mr. St. James.

"Votre nomme, mademoiselle?" the woman politely inquired, curiously appraising the tired-faced young woman standing before her. Jenna pushed back an uncombed lock of hair from her forehead and gave her an imploring look.

"Jenna St. James." She cleared her throat and tried to compose herself. The woman, appearing to be some kind of housekeeper, looked at her with a merciful smile.

"St. James? Come in, dear, please!" She ushered Jenna into a long hallway, and gently prodded her to remove her coat.

Presently, Jenna heard a strong male voice and turned to face a tall, pleasant-looking man with gold wire-rimmed glasses. He wore a large, baggy pullover sweater precisely the same gray hue as his hair.

"It's Jenna? My God! Jenna! What is it, are you all right?"

Her sudden appearance both shocked and alarmed him. His unsettled eyes were fixed on her, as if searching frantically for some vestige of the child's face he once cherished. Recovering, he pulled her inside the large comfortable room that was his study.

"What! What in the world are you doing here?" he stammered. "Suzetta said you called. How did you know where to find me?"

"I don't know where to start. I found an address … I had to know … everything."

She took a step closer to him. He smelled nice and had a wonderful face. He was now looking at her adoringly, not at all apologetic for not seeking her after he and Claudia divorced.

"Why?" she blurted out, her carefully rehearsed lines forgotten. "Why didn't you ever come to see me? All those years?"

He paused strangely, head slightly tilted, puzzled at her forthright question. After taking a deep breath, he attempted to tackle an explanation.

"She took you away when you were two years old! I tried to see you! I called, I wrote. I even flew to Omaha twice to be turned away by your mother. She refused to let me even see a photograph of you!"

Jenna's knees began to shake and she looked around helplessly. Warren guided her to the center of the room toward two overstuffed chairs. Sinking into one of them, she listened while he talked.

"She later notified me she was in Kansas City, married again. About that time, I contacted an attorney who pressed Claudia for my visitation rights. I was, after all, paying child support. She was really difficult to deal with."

He paused, not knowing how far he should go. The incredulous expression on her face told him to go on.

"I thought she had done all the damage she could do to me and then, she called me. She said no matter what, I could never see you again."

"And you let her bluff you!" Jenna challenged, face twisted, eyes pleading for answers.

He stopped and drew a breath, weighing his words. "She told me, Jenna, I had no right. She told me – you were not my daughter. It wrecked me."

Warren was now on the edge of his chair, hand on Jenna's knee. His last words had proved to be utterly destructive. She was whimpering grievously and helplessly wringing her hands.

"Honey, don't. Listen to me! Your mother is seriously psychotic, do you know that?"

He tried to talk but Jenna was sobbing loudly. He was surprised at how easy it was to call her "honey." She dropped her head in her hands and he noticed the engagement ring on her finger.

"Your mother told me that a previous lover was your father."

This provoked excruciating wails. He desperately knelt on the floor and put both arms around the girl he had not seen for twenty years.

"But, sweetheart, that's not true. She lied."

Jenna swallowed hard.

"I know this now. She lied. You, my dear, are my blood daughter. Look at you. Look at me." He cupped her wet swollen face. "No wonder she never would let me see you or send me a photo. You're the image of my mother. Same face, same nose, same eyes. And my sisters? Same slender legs. Come here. I want to show you something."

He helped her to her feet. They walked slowly into the hallway.

"Come, come over here!" He was excited now and pulled her to a wall covered with framed photographs. He pointed to a large oval portrait of a young woman with curly brown hair, strong cheekbones, full lips, and heart-shaped chin. Jenna stared in disbelief, soothed by the image.

"This is your grandmother when she was your age." He gauged her reaction and broke into a hesitant smile. As hope crept over her, she wiped her face.

"And see here," he said gently, "just look at these other family pictures! Brown curly hair? We all have it. Mine was, too, until it turned gray."

At last, she felt she could speak without choking.

"I want to believe this so bad. You don't know!" She looked at her engagement ring and held it to her lips. "I'm engaged to be married to Jeff Day's son. And Mother just told me last night Jeff was my father."

"Christ Almighty!" Disgust and anger filled his eyes and he clenched his fists and lowered his head. "She wishes he was your father is more like it."

Warren looked at her with a pained expression.

"I really loved Claudia. I want you to know I did. She, however, never recovered from her obsession with Jeff. I actually believed you were not my child. God forgive my foolish soul. All these years she has deprived me of a daughter. I am so sorry she made your poor little heart a pawn in her one-sided game."

Jenna felt a strange stirring inside her as she watched him and listened to him talk. His manner of speaking was precise, perfect. Professor-like. He made her feel very safe. Pacified, she moved timorously toward him. Warren bent slightly and wrapped his arms around his daughter, buried his face in her hair and they stood there for several minutes, neither wanting to separate.

Then he spoke, "Let's go sit again and we'll have some tea and straighten this out."

The housekeeper, whose eyes were wide and fearful, having heard the young woman's hysterical wailing, served tea. Warren reclaimed his big chair and began to talk.

"When I first met your mother, she was one of my students. She was failing my class and I requested a counseling session. She told me the boy she had been in love with had broken it off with her and had taken up with her best friend, Joanna. It seems Jeff and Joanna were to be married. Claudia was extremely distraught."

He rubbed his forehead and bravely continued. "We began to spend time together. We sat up many nights talking about her problems. Then one evening, out of the clear blue sky, she said she wanted to … have a relationship with me. I was crazy about her. I knew it wasn't good, but she was so beautiful. She stayed with me that night. When school was out, she came back to the campus to visit me and we spent a week together."

Warren reached for his pipe, lit it and proceeded.

"At the end of the week, I told her I had taken a new position teaching in Ohio in the fall and had resigned from the university staff. She was totally upset I was leaving and we argued. She left and I never heard from her all summer. In the fall, I began teaching at the University of Ohio. One day she just showed up. I was in shock. She told me she was five months pregnant. We were married shortly after that. She told me the due date was in January. You were born in February. Claudia convinced me you were a late baby."

"So when she came to Ohio, she was probably only four months pregnant," Jenna said, counting on her fingers. "Which means she got pregnant when she came back to the college to visit you. And Jeff was already out of her life."

"Absolutely. In fact, he was already married. Poor wretched, delusional Claudia! She's convinced herself, somehow, you were his daughter, not mine. Lord! How she must have hated it when you grew up to be the image of a St. James." He plowed his fingers through his thick curly silver hair.

"She tried to get me to bleach my hair blonde a dozen times," Jenna recalled. She told Warren how Claudia had called Jeff and arranged for her to spend the summer with his family. "Poor sick Mom."

"Before you go home, dear, we will settle this once and for all. You and I will simply have one of those blood tests."

"Can we do that without Mom's blood?"

"We certainly can. I'll send you the results. Should there be a continuing problem for you at home, you'll have proof I'm your father. And should you need anything else, you just call me."

Warren took both of her hands, his eyes signaling a lasting promise.

The two heard the front door open and the housekeeper hurried toward the hall. It was Warren's wife, Suzetta, carrying in shopping bags. She was a plump, attractive woman with a poised, easy smile, and short, neatly cropped hairstyle.

"Suzetta, come in here," he said to her and she peeked in the door of the study. "I want you to meet my daughter, Jenna Louise." He gave his wife a meaningful look.

Suzetta hesitated, then eased the packages to the floor, beaming. She turned tenderly to her husband and in an emotional voice, whispered, "At last, Warren, at last." She rushed to Jenna and kissed her soundly.

"I know you and your father will want to stay up late and talk privately, so I'll have our guestroom prepared for your stay and tomorrow, we'll have a wonderful day," she spoke affectionately, still grasping

Jenna's hand. She turned to Warren. "Please show her around the house and instruct Marie. I want Jenna to feel at home."

After she gathered her packages, she disappeared up the stairs.

"I like her," Jenna voiced her first impression and it was one that caused a large smile to spread across Warren's face. "Is she from here?"

"She is from Arizona. Phoenix, actually. We both teach at a small university here." He was still in wonder at the sudden appearance of his daughter and dazed that while minutes ago, she seemed near traumatized, she now actually appeared composed. He admired her courage. There was so much about her he longed to know.

Marie brought a tray of sandwiches and cookies, poked at the embers in the huge fireplace, and turned on another lamp in the study. Jenna sat across from Warren and for hours, they exchanged stories. She told him about school, Vic's death, and her summer with the Day family. He thoroughly enjoyed her account of the first competition with her new horse. He was moved as she spoke of Wes and her stories of him brought a warm, approving glow to his face.

He settled back in his big chair. "So you two are getting married in the spring?"

Jenna was elated at the obvious pleasure he shared in this event. She slipped from her chair and impulsively stood before him. Looking into his eyes, indescribable warmth filled her and she collapsed impulsively into his lap. He sighed and rested his chin on top of her head, as she marveled in the recognition of the thing called unconditional love.

He picked up her left hand and admired the ring.

"Would it be acceptable for the father to give the bride in marriage?"

CHAPTER EIGHTEEN

Fearing she might falter in a face-to-face encounter, Jenna clutched the results of the paternity test from Warren and picked up the phone. Although convinced she was ready for a dramatic battle, nothing could have prepared her for the napalm temper unleashed by Claudia when confronted with the truth. Jenna hung up, shaky, and wrote to Warren.

Dad,

I got the test results and really had it out on the phone tonight with Mom. No matter what, she really seems to be convinced I'm Jeff's daughter. She ranted and raved, saying Jeff took her dream away and now he was taking me away from her, too. She's so screwed up!

I thought you might like this photo of Tess and me. I've been riding her as much as I can, but it's hard to get to New Winston every weekend with so much schoolwork. Wes has been in Oklahoma at a school for farriers (that's a horseshoer) for nearly two weeks. He'll soon be done with the course. We plan to get married the week before my graduation and I'd like to do an outdoor wedding in the orchard at the farm. After the graduation, I think we are going to live here at my apartment for a while. Wes' partner, Al, has dozens of customers in this area and he thinks it would be a great idea if Wes could take them over. Joanna wants me to tell you she is planning on you and Suzetta staying at the farm when you come.

She signed it with love from "Jenna Louise" and sealed the envelope.

***

By the end of January, Wes was home. During the week, he stayed in Kansas City with Jenna, handling Al's customers who lived in the Kansas City area. While shocked at his lover's sudden trip to Quebec, he accepted the fact she had suddenly just decided to find her father. He was proud of her for showing such spirit and never suspected any other reason.

On the weekends, he left Jenna to her studies and returned to New Winston to help with breeding season. February had brought a stream of outside mares to be bred to Invincible. Dr. McGraw, nearly a permanent fixture during the breeding months, was pleased with the conception rate. Most of the outside mares would be sent home after 60 days, checked safe in foal.

Jeff had purchased a new mare and she had foaled in late January, rewarding his investment with an exceptional filly. Like several other mares he had acquired during the winter, her bloodlines were selected specifically to cross back with Invincible. Convinced by the quality he saw in Jake, he intentionally sought mares equal to the caliber of Stella.

Although Joanna was fretful over the investment, Jeff was building a superb band of brood mares and was positive their offspring would guarantee the success of his business. Joanna tuned out her own conservative instincts and wrote checks inflicting serious reductions to their savings. As always, she dutifully supported her husband's choices.

Two more of the family's own foals by Invincible arrived the last week of February and more were due. Chris shared her father's goals, and while he was at work, she virtually lived at the barn during those months. While Jeff, Frank and Mike McGraw handled the breeding operation, she became the self-appointed foaling manager. As each foal opened its eyes and took its first breath, Chris' heart spilled over with a sense of accomplishment. To her, nothing on earth was as joyful as the live birth of a young horse, pure with innocence, full of promise. To Jeff, each healthy foal was money in the bank.

In mid-March, Chris and Jeff took Jake and one yearling filly to a show in southern Missouri. Jake, now officially a yearling, was the tallest and most handsome colt in the class and remained undefeated. Jeff's filly lacked the heavy muscle some of the young mares displayed, but she was tall, elegant and very fit. He was not disappointed in the judging of either entry.

The show was small and although the halter classes were sizey, the western competition was thin and Chris was thankful when she noticed Brandon Penny was not there.

He had called numerous times since the American Royal, but she had refused his calls.

"What's the deal?" Joanna had inquired finally.

"Wes was right," Chris had told her flatly.

Jo was satisfied to drop the subject, but Jeff reminded Chris the Pennys had brought a mare to New Winston to be bred and ordered his daughter to be civil, as Brandon's father was a paying customer.

When the Pennys' mare was checked in foal in April, Brandon drove over from Clayton with his father.

"We've been watching the flooding in these parts on the local news. We were kind of worried about you guys," said Brad Penny.

"The town had some damage, but not as bad as '93. And up on this hill? Well, we've never been underwater," replied Jeff. "I would have let you know if there was any danger to your mare."

As Jeff and Brad walked to the barn office to retrieve the paperwork, Brandon cornered Chris alone.

"What's going on with you, anyway? I thought we had some kind of fun little thing going on."

Chris smiled, remembering her father's orders. But caustic memories of the American Royal washed over her and she impulsively turned on him.

"Brandon, do you know the story of Peter Pan and Wendy?"

Brandon paused, thoroughly confused, but nodded yes.

"Well, Peter was a swell guy and good lookin', but he had this big problem. He didn't want to grow up," she explained. "Wendy thought he was very cool at first."

"So?" He shook his head. "I don't get it."

She faked a sugary smile. "So, after a while, she got sick of Peter and dumped his sorry ass."

Brandon stared, trying to comprehend this odd dialogue. He would think about it all the way home to Clayton. He sensed a maturity in Chris that was beginning to reveal itself and he found this intensely appealing, despite her latest rejection. Chris waved sweetly as the Pennys' big trailer turned around and headed through the gate. He leaned out the window and gave her one more imploring gaze. She laughed out loud. He really did have a great face.

John and Ruth Shaw also had sent an excellent mare to be bred. When they were notified the mare was ready to go home, they drove over from Kansas at the end of the month with their daughters. They were anxious to see the Days' new foals by Vince and accompanied Chris to the pasture, where the babies romped and showed off for the visitors. John was particularly impressed with one filly and by the time they left, had negotiated with Jeff to buy her.

"I'll be back to pick her up when she's weaned," John said, pleased with his purchase. "Becki and Kathy have been wanting a black Invincible baby ever since they laid eyes on Chris' orphan. I guarantee she'll have a good home."

By May, all of the mares had foaled except Joanna's old mare, Reba. Jo scrubbed the foaling stall, bedded it down with clean straw, and brought Reba in from the pasture. She and Chris hovered over the mare, fretting over every ponderous sigh, but the old mare showed no signs of delivering her foal.

"What's the old saying? A watched pot never boils?" Aunt Lil said. "I say leave her alone and let's tear into the spring cleaning. The house needs it and the barn needs it. And we've got to get ready for a wedding."

***

On the morning of June 1, Jenna stood before the full-length mirror in her bedroom at the farm. Joanna sat at her feet and finished adjusting the hem of the softly flowing slip her son's bride would wear under her wedding dress.

Chris flittered around the room, decked out in the pink flowered dress she would wear in the ceremony. She slipped on her heels and practiced walking. Posturing and fluttering her eyes, she pushed her blonde hair up on her head and gazed into the mirror.

"You're like a butterfly in a cabbage patch," Jo laughed. "Why don't you just light somewhere?" The girl kicked off the heels and flopped on the bed, surveying various gifts and tokens of tradition that had been lovingly lavished on the bride-to-be.

Her favorite was a heavy photo album with a leather cover, Wes' gift to Jenna. The leather was a light oak finish and custom hand-tooled in a basket-weave pattern, edged in tooled roses. It was an exquisite piece of workmanship befitting the finest show saddle. Chris held it to her face and breathed in the pungent smell of the new leather.

On the inside cover, finely scripted in the leather, was Wes' message. Chris had read it over and over, memorizing the words. "Let this be filled with the story of our lives - one marriage certificate, tons of photographs, a few birth certificates and a picture of us on our 50th anniversary."

Her brother's sensitivity moved her in an extraordinary way. It was a perfect gift for new beginnings.

"Something old, something new," she murmured in envy, "and something in leather."

Wes and Jenna were married in a small private ceremony at the Day farm. A white lattice gazebo had been erected in the apple orchard and was decorated with white ribbon and pink potted azaleas.

Wes, balking at a tux, wore starched jeans and a starched white shirt. His best man, Al, was similarly attired. They stood waiting for the bride, proudly escorted to the orchard by Warren St. James. She was dressed in a soft white crepe dress with a beaded bodice. A short veil framed her face. Walking toward Wes on the grass, her white satin heels caused her to falter slightly on the spongy turf. She paused, smiled and blithely kicked off her shoes, and then clinging to her father's arm, she walked barefoot toward her husband-to-be.

As she took her place beside him, she gave Warren an enthusiastic embrace, released him and whispered to Wes, "Let's rock and roll." He smiled, suddenly easier with the ceremony thing, and took her hand.

After the uncomplicated ritual, the wedding party gathered on the front porch for cake and champagne.

Warren joined Suzetta and Jo in the kitchen, where the women were arranging the table with sandwiches. Outside, Jeff proposed a toast.

"I want to wish the best of luck to my son and his bride," he began, "and I ... "

He was interrupted by the sudden screech of wheels and a small silver car careened into the drive. Claudia emerged from the car, smartly attired in a bright blue suit and floppy hat, and walked briskly toward the porch, carrying a large wrapped gift.

Jenna paled and rushed toward her, fearing a scene, but Claudia was perfectly serene and greeted her lovingly, gushing over the dress and planting a motherly kiss on her cheek. With the poise of an accomplished actress, she acknowledged Wes and approached Jeff.

"Did I miss the ceremony? Oh, Jeffrey! I did, didn't I?" She squeezed his arm and eyed him with a saucy grin. "Sorry, darling, you know I'm always late. What a great day for a wedding."

Jenna, composing herself, stepped in and pulled her mother away from Jeff. "What are you doing here? How did you know?"

"I make it my business to know what my daughter is doing, dear," she purred, "And truly, I thought I owed it to you to be here. I am, after all, the mother of the bride. And it's only right you know you have the support of your mother – and your father."

She glanced at Jeff, who received her sly look as if it were a poison dart from a blowgun. Frank, sensing an impending panic, leaned forward and took control of the situation.

"It's nice of you to come. I'm Joanna's Uncle Frank and this is my wife, Lil. I don't believe you know Dr. McGraw, our veterinarian and friend ... and this is Al George, a friend of Wes' ... "

Claudia extended her hand graciously to Al and moved swiftly to Wes, wrapping her arms around him.

"I'm afraid we got off to a bad start, Weston," she cooed, "but we have to put that behind us now."

The screen door opened and Warren stepped out with a tray of sandwiches. His face darkened as his eyes met Claudia's. She was, for an instant, paralyzed, caught off guard by his unlikely presence. When she finally spoke, her voice trembled slightly and a single word fell out of her painted mouth.

"Warren!"

He calmly placed the tray on a table and turned to her, "Hello, Claudia. How have you been?"

She stared at him, then finally spoke. "I just drove down to bring Jenna a gift ... but I can't stay. I must be going." She whirled on one spike heel and hurried down the steps to the car, mumbling frantically to herself.

"I see how it's going to be. I spent my whole life protecting her, giving her anything she wanted," she hissed audibly, "and she cuts me out of her life like I was nothing." And she was gone.

***

Jenna's graduation from UMKC was scheduled for the following Saturday afternoon. Afterwards, the family would take her and Wes to the airport, as the newlyweds planned to fly to Montreal for a two-week stay with Warren and Suzetta.

As Joanna was dressing to leave for Kansas City, Jeff returned from the barn and informed her that Reba, now past due, was showing signs of labor.

"It's Frank's Law," he told Joanna, who was struggling with her nylon hosiery. "You know what he always says. It's the golden rule that a brood mare shall wait for any kind of momentous occasion to begin labor."

She said nothing but peeled her pantyhose back off and slipped into her faded jeans.

"I guess that means you want to be the one to stay home and watch her," Jeff was hesitant, recalling Ken Thompson's advice. But it had been months since the car had been spotted on the dead-end lane. "I could get Frank and Lil to do it."

"No, they're really looking forward to going to the graduation. You all go on. I'll stay with my mare."

"We'll be home by midnight," he told her.

As the family left for Kansas City, Joanna walked alone to the barn to check Reba. The old mare was arthritic and the extra weight on her legs was painful. Joanna ran her hands over Reba's back ankles and noted the dripping milk from her udders.

She returned to the house, fixed a sandwich, and threw in a load of laundry. Between trips to the barn, she piddled with her housework, swearing that the next spring the foaling stalls would be equipped with a camera surveillance system allowing them to monitor the mares from the house.

Evening found her camped outside the stall, sitting quietly in the shadows. In the privacy of the darkness, Reba's water broke and the mare soon was stretched out in the clean straw in full labor. Ten minutes later, she delivered her foal. The birth was easy and Jo peeked inside the stall to watch. Reba needed no assistance, and soon the foal was nestled quietly in the straw. Joanna backed off and waited another fifteen minutes before checking on them again. After a bit, Joanna opened the stall door, armed with iodine for the foal's navel.

The unexpected crunch of gravel startled her and she heard a car pull in the drive and park outside the barn. *Why had there been no headlights?* Josephine, who had been dozing near the tack room, leapt from her spot and raced through the crack in the barn door. Joanna paused, listening to the opening and closing of car doors, then voices. The conversation was muffled and she strained to make out the words. Outside, Josie was on the job, and her threatening growls signaled strangers on her property.

The sliding door being pushed open at the end of the alleyway made a slow grinding sound and the glare of a single flashlight shot a beam of light inside the shadowy barn. Alarmed now, Joanna crouched against the stall door and pressed her body into the wall. As a single cautious footstep on the concrete alleyway invaded the tranquility of the barn, a rush of authority washed over her.

"Who's there?" she demanded loudly.

A defiant Josephine was now barking savagely. Jo heard a sharp yelp from her, then silence. The barn door slid closed and soon she heard the car's engine start up. The car backed up and peeled out. Still no headlights.

After several minutes, Joanna crept from the stall and hurried down the alleyway. In the bright moonlight, she could see Josephine, lying motionless on the ground several feet from the door. With an angry cry, she clasped the shepherd in her arms and rushed back inside the barn. A trickle of blood dripped onto her sleeve from the dog's ear. Desperately, she tried to find a pulse, a heartbeat, any sign of life. She closed her eyes tight and rocked Josie in her arms, her wrath mixed with grief. Tenderly placing the dog on a pile of horse blankets, she stepped inside the office and furiously flipped through the card file for the police chief's home phone number.

Ken Thompson's wife answered the phone. She listened carefully to Jo's agitated words and quickly called to her husband. Ken was on the couch in front of the television engrossed in "Walker, Texas Ranger." It was his favorite show. It was almost over and Walker was just about to kick some butt.

"Ken! That was Joanna Day on the phone. She's at the farm alone and someone was there. She's so upset, I couldn't quite get it, but whoever it was apparently killed the dog."

Ken was on his feet and out the door in minutes. When he arrived at the farm, Joanna was standing in the barn door waiting.

"You all right, Jo?" Ken saw the dog on the blankets. "What are you doing here alone? What the hell is going on?"

She clutched her throat nervously and tried to recount the evening's events. "My old mare, Reba, had her foal and everything was going fine, then I heard a car pull up, but no headlights."

He looked inside the mare's stall and the foal was standing on unsteady legs, nursing. "Did you see who it was?"

"No. Josephine was going crazy and, well, someone started to come in. With a flashlight. I hid in the stall. I called out. Then I heard the car leave. When I found Josie, she was dead!"

He examined the dog carefully and surmised she had been struck in the head.

"I think I'll step outside and look for some kind of weapon or something. If the guy dropkicked her, I don't think it would have killed her."

"I already looked," said Joanna, nervously twisting a lock of hair, "I didn't find anything. Poor Josie. She was trying to protect me!"

"Did your husband tell you anything about seeing a car parked down there watching the house … a while back?" he pointed toward the dead-end lane. He was aggravated Jeff had left her alone at the farm. "Did you know anything about that?"

"Well, he mentioned it after Christmas. He said not to worry. It was probably no big deal." She gave him a baffled look.

"I'm gonna stay here with you until Jeff gets home," he assured her, stepping outside the barn door. "I'm not sure what is going on here. I don't have the manpower to have somebody patrolling up here all the time, but we'd better get to the bottom of this. From now on, I don't want you or your daughter here alone at night."

Although Ken's job of police chief was an elected one, he was a frontline lawman. He had spent twenty years in law enforcement and was a good cop. And what made him good at his job was his innate ability to know when there was trouble, and as he stood in the moonlight and scouted the dark trees lining the road, a nagging signal in the back of his mind was sounding a very real alarm.

CHAPTER NINETEEN

It had been raining since March. As the heavy snows up north melted and saturated the tributaries of the Missouri, Prairie Rock and nearby towns suspended themselves in a perpetual state of flood watch. Upstream, the river surged from its banks, silently converging over acres, towns and homes. By mid-April, Charlie Edwards had become a nervous wreck.

"I got a real bad feeling," he fretted to Gabe as they watched the news on television. "It's gonna do it again. I just know it. This spooky old river can be a wicked stream. *Wicked*."

He rambled on a bit, repeating stories his father had passed down to him.

"I remember plenty of stories from my pappy about the Missouri," he told Gabe in a low, fearful voice. "He was working on a crew toting barges. Folks back then called fellas like him river rats. It seems that one night – now this was about 1915 – he and his mates were making the turn into the Camden Bend and the water seemed to be all of a sudden moving upstream. They heard this deep, rushing boom like the river was crashing off the Wellington bluffs. After hundreds of years, the Missouri was changing its course! They say it formed miles of new channel that very night! My dad was a young man, but it shocked him so, from that night on, he had gray hair. It's the God's truth!"

Gabe knew it was a true story. He had heard it before. Both he and Charlie, along with other townspeople had a healthy reverence for the Missouri.

The Army Corps of Engineers warned the inhabitants of Prairie Rock that the agricultural levies were not expected to hold. Although some had been repaired, many were still damaged from the flood of '93. As area creeks began to slowly flood the flat cropland, the edgy townspeople began 'round the clock sandbagging. A week later, most of the town was under water.

Although Charlie and Edith's house on River Street remained on dry land, the lower streets in town filled up with the brown water. Gabe had worked day and night to move the bags of feed and the store's entire stock of farm supplies to a safer building in back of Charlie's home. Edith's prayers to spare the business were useless in the path of the relentless water, and it eventually flooded the feed store.

When the water receded, it left the store a dangerously filthy slime pit of mud, silt, clouds of mosquitoes, rotten carp carcasses and snakes. With the assistance of the Red Cross and National Guardsmen, the townspeople returned to their devastation to rebuild one more time.

Throughout the summer, Gabe worked ten to twelve hours a day for Charlie and in the evening did odd jobs for people trying to recuperate. He missed the tepid nights on the river with Gil, but there was no time for catfishing and their favorite point was now a stinking sea of mud, sand, and dead fish.

The early July heat was cruelly humid, but the rural inhabitants accepted it as they accepted the unpredictability of the river. Up and down the wide channel, in tiny towns like Prairie Rock, folks moved slow, sat on the porch and fanned themselves. Even those residents with air-conditioned homes often chose to forego that luxury in the evenings, opening up the house and heading to the porch, denying their neighbors a claim to more than their fair share of the misery.

Gabe didn't mind the heat so much. He and his mother had never enjoyed the comforts of air conditioning and he grew up accustomed to not having it. The Widow Kochendorfer, however, knowing the rooms above the feed store were insufferably hot, gave Gabe a large oscillating fan. On torrid nights, he opened the windows and turned his big fan on high. He aimed it directly toward the bed, and lay there as it whirred and moved a man-made breeze over his long legs, across his bare chest and shoulders and then back the other way again. The fan was soothing and the movement of the air through the darkness kept his mind off the reality of his utter seclusion in this lonely attic.

***

"I don't care if the river is up again. I'm taking Jake to the Fourth of July show," Chris told Joanna, who was standing in the bedroom door. The girl surveyed her clothes closet, selected several shirts and jackets and placed them on the bed with a stack of starched jeans. Joanna, arms crossed, watched the drizzling rain beat against the window, as it had for days.

"It's out of the question. It's supposed to rain more this weekend and the main road's almost covered with water now. I'm worried enough about Frank and Lil being able to make it back from Branson."

"I'm so sick of the flood water! Why do we have to live in this God-awful place where every other year the river ruins everything? Practically the whole valley has been flooded for months. The place stinks to high heaven. I hate it."

"It's no paradise for any of us, honey. But you put the horse show out of your mind. Anyway, you know your dad's got to stay here and watch the farm. After what happened to Josie, he's not going to leave the place unattended, even if it stops raining. So, forget it."

Chris continued to fold her jeans. "I can go by myself."

"No way. Your father's *not* going to let you take his truck and trailer and go alone."

"Then, *you* go with me!" Chris stopped packing and challenged her mother. Joanna had not been to a horse show since the American Royal. "Dad can stay and take care of things by himself."

Joanna leaned against the doorframe, frustrated. "I'm not going to tangle with him over it. I'm out of it."

Chris walked to the window, strategizing. The dormer window with its cozy alcove and upholstered window seat had been her favorite spot in the house since she was a small child. As she peered out at the black churning clouds, lightning slashed and a low rumble of thunder rolled. She snorted. "I'll find a way."

"I guess you could talk to him again, but I can't guarantee anything." Joanna turned and headed downstairs.

Minutes later, Chris heard Jeff's truck pull in and splash to a stop. Bolting down the stairs, she met him on the porch.

"We need to talk," she said in a stern voice demanding his attention. "We need to get Jake to this show, Dad. We've almost got him qualified for the World!"

Jeff shook his head and began to speak, but she was in his face.

"We're running out of time. I'm going to take him and Mom'll go with me."

"Your mom said she'd go, huh?" Perched on the porch swing, he pulled off his muddy boots. "That's a joke. She don't even care about the horses anymore."

Through the open kitchen window, Jo listened to their discussion with mixed feelings. She did care about the horses and desperately missed the horse shows, but at the same time, she had found staying home a welcome break from the incessant friction. It was simply a relief when her husband was gone for a few days.

Jeff entered the house, Chris on his heels.

"Larry Wayne will probably be there. Why don't you call him and see if he'll show Jake in the open class?" The girl was still at it, anticipating every argument. "You know he'll do it if he doesn't have another yearling stud to show."

Later that evening, Jeff called Larry. After they talked for a few minutes, Chris headed upstairs to pack her show clothes. Joanna smiled to herself.

Larry had agreed to show Jake in the open competition. He was coming in from Texas with two yearlings needing points. Rod Rollins, hauling a junior pleasure horse, would accompany him. The Genesis Ranch was close to Larry's place and the two men frequently hauled together. They would meet Jo and Chris in Columbia.

***

When Jeff Day's truck and trailer pulled on to the show grounds, the two men were waiting. Joanna and Chris waved as Larry approached the truck.

"I was worried about you two! I thought you'd be here hours ago."

"We've got a lot of flooded roads, so we had to take a detour to the interstate. And then we had a flat tire on the truck!" Joanna was exasperated. "Chris and I got it changed, though. Sorry we're late."

"You know Rod, don't you, Joanna?" Larry dispensed with the introductions. She and Chris were very aware of Rod's reputation. He was originally from Missouri and had campaigned many good western pleasure colts in the state before moving to Texas. Rod nodded to her. He remembered seeing her.

"You rode here last year," he acknowledged Joanna, "in the two-year-old snaffle bit class. You forgot to take the knot out of your horse's tail and I did it for you." She smiled appreciatively, remembering.

"Larry says you have a topnotch yearling stallion," he continued.

"Actually, he belongs to my daughter, Chris," Jo replied. "He was an orphan and she hand-raised him. We think he's pretty nice."

The black was now more than fifteen hands tall. He was a good-legged colt, with a long, elegantly shaped neck, and muscular hip. He was glorious to look at and Larry enjoyed showing him, but on the first day, he placed only fourth out of seven. First place went to a heavier sorrel stud from Iowa.

Larry was disappointed with the upset. "Jake's a lot like his sire. He's going through a growing spurt and getting a bit out of balance, so that might have hurt him some."

Chris, now too old for youth competition, had graduated into the amateur classes. Competing in the amateur division requires the exhibitor both own and show the horse. No trainers allowed. Although showing a halter horse was new for her, she knew exactly what to do from years of watching her father. But it was Chris' first time in the show ring with Jake and Joanna was surprised to find her daughter pacing nervously before she took the lead from Larry.

"Relax, get him set up and watch your judge," Larry coached her. "Don't think about how he placed Jake and me."

Absent the professionals, the amateur stallion class was not quite as tough as the open division, and the scrutinizing judge used Jake second out of four in his class. Chris led Jake from the arena, red ribbon in hand. She passed Brandon Penny, who was watching from the rail. Brandon and his mare had been schooling all winter with a trainer in St. Louis and he was enjoying a record season, leading Missouri in amateur western pleasure.

"Your colt's better than ever, Christine," he patronized. "He looks big enough to ride right now."

"Yeah, and when I get him under saddle next year, I'm coming after you," she snarled. He drew back, intimidated by the sincerity of her threat.

The second morning of the four-day event, Rod met Joanna early at Jake's stall.

"Bad news, Joanna. I had to take Larry to the damned hospital! Late last night, he wanted to take his horses into the pen and lead them around a bit, let 'em check out the scenery, etc. Well, the yearling filly went nutty. She went straight up on her hind legs and fell over on him. They think he has a bad concussion, and the hospital wanted to keep him until the swelling goes down."

"Oh, Lord! This has turned out to be the horse show from hell!" Joanna sat down in a folding chair outside Jake's stall and closed her eyes.

"I think he's okay, but she laid him out with a good one, up side of his head," Rod continued. "I'm not all that great showing halter horses, but I told Larry I'd lead his in. I'll help you out with Jake if you want. I know you need the open points."

Joanna felt a jolt of apprehension, but tried to appear calm. Larry would not be able to show Jake in open, the division in which the colt was nearly World qualified.

"Don't worry about Jake. I'll show him myself," she announced briskly, paying little attention to the shocked expression on her daughter's face.

It had been years since Joanna competed in a halter class. Even then, Jeff had only allowed her to lead in a second string weanling. It was not her territory. *You get 'em ready, I'll show 'em,* Jeff had told her.

She picked up the longe line and headed for the black colt's stall. An hour later, she retreated to the trailer dressing room, leaving Chris, already dressed to show, with Rod.

"Your mom is a trouper," he said as they put the last minute touches on the show-ready horses. Chris bit a fingernail.

"She doesn't show halter, does she?" he spoke in a low secretive voice. Chris smiled and shook her head no.

When Joanna returned, she had traded her faded jeans and tee shirt for a fitted pair of black jeans and starched white shirt. She slipped into a black and butter-yellow checked jacket, adjusted her light straw Stetson and stepped inside the tack stall to apply lipstick.

"Are you ready?" Chris looked at her lovingly.

"Wait! I need my lucky earrings!" Joanna ducked into the dressing room and came out with them. *If she placed dead last, what would Jeff say?* But she smiled at Chris, showing not one vestige of the jitters she was feeling, and whispered, "Let's rock and roll."

The open classes were first, and the sight of Joanna leading Jake into the show ring did not go unnoticed. Interested friends and acquaintances moved closer to the rail to watch. Jo looked straight ahead and at the signal from the ring steward, she presented the black colt to the judge. He arched his neck and Jo gave the lead shank a warning jerk. He trotted in beside her, ears forward and eyes wide. She set him up perfectly in the line of colts and walked to his head, where she assumed a pert, business-like stance provoking a rush of admiration from her daughter. *She's such a pro,* thought Chris.

The day before, the class winner was a sorrel yearling stud. He was now lined up in front of Joanna and Jake. As Jo stood, ready for the judge's inspection, the sorrel became unruly and reared up, nearly running over Jo and causing Jake to jump backwards. She calmly gathered the black colt's lead and set him up again as the patient judge watched. Chris saw the pink flush of Joanna's cheeks turned scarlet and sensed her anxiety, but Jo's actions were steady. The judge, a slim young woman in light starched jeans and teal blazer, walked up and down the line of horses, making her final decisions. She then returned briskly and motioned for Joanna and Jake to step up to the first place hole.

"Looks like it'll be a better day, Chris," Rod congratulated her as the places were announced and Joanna collected the blue ribbon. "I know how this judge operates and she's always extremely consistent in her picks. She might not use Jake as Grand Champion, but this means you'll probably cop a first in your class."

Rod was right. When it was Chris' turn to show Jake, the judge was true to her opinion, placing Jake and Chris first in amateur yearling stallions.

The next two days of the show began with pre-dawn rain showers replaced by soaring temperatures. Chris' attempts to brush Jake to a shine were useless as the humidity prevailed.

"Look at his hair coat," she lamented as she tried to make him look his best. "It's fluffing. It's so hot and sticky, I can't keep him from sweating! He looks like crap." But by the third day, Joanna and Jake had accumulated enough open points to go to the World Show.

Rod's efforts at halter were respectable, as well, and he was pleased with himself.

"Well, I don't have the clout you do, but your customers shouldn't be disappointed," he told Larry, who had been released by the hospital nursing a killer headache.

The junior pleasure horse Rod had brought to ride was an exceptional young gelding but had been injured in the spring. Rod confided to Chris he wasn't hoping to bring down the house with the colt, but would be happy just to get him shown.

"He's owned by the ranch. I'm not expecting to make a killin' at this show, but if he'll go a couple classes and stay sound, I'd call it a big deal," he said. "I really like this horse, and I've worked my butt off to get him solid again. My boss's got cancer. I'd like to give him a good report."

Rod had more than good looks. He was a sensitive trainer and Chris admired his down-to-earth attitude. And she didn't mind at all the envious looks she noticed coming from the Jordan girls and Becki and Kathy Shaw.

"Mmm-mmm," Dana Jordan mumbled to her as they watched Rod win junior pleasure. "He is *so* easy to look at. Bet he knows it, too."

"Heck, no, he's a really good guy, and fun!" She laughed at Dana's infatuation.

Rod was slim, long-legged with square, wide shoulders. He had perfected a controlled, yet relaxed look when he was riding that put the judges on notice. He was all business and was always a contender.

"His jeans and shirts are always perfectly starched. He never gets dirty, have you noticed?" Dana observed. "The guy never even sweats."

Rod rode out of the class with the blue ribbon and dismounted. Chris met him at the gate and held the reins as he unzipped his chaps. He fingered the ribbon.

"I didn't expect that." He spoke to her in a private, familiar manner that made Dana lift her eyebrows slightly.

"Gotta go," Chris took advantage of the moment and tossed the words over her shoulder. "See you later."

"I'd say we're having some luck," Rod proclaimed on Saturday night. "Aside from old Larry's aching head. He wants to go to the motel for a while, but what do you say we go to town for prime rib?"

He had a good sense of humor and Chris was pleased as she noticed with each day, the old spirit she knew in her mother was making a revival.

Supper was fun and the conversation was amusing. He must be in his mid-thirties, thought Chris, watching him as he talked. She liked his face. It was tanned and perfectly symmetrical. His eyes were very blue and his hair dark, an unusual, but striking combination. The conversation naturally turned to horses, and Joanna asked how he liked working for the Genesis Ranch.

"Hard work, but it's great. The ranch is nice. The owner is a super guy, but like I told Chris, he's real sick and all last year he went through radiation therapy and chemo … He's determined to make it, though." He then smiled and changed the subject. "I miss Missouri sometimes, but I sure like Texas. I'm even sorta gettin' to be a Cowboys fan."

By the last day of the show, Larry seemed to be recovering and although the headache was subsiding, his left eye was sporting a horrendous shiner. As Rod and Joanna were packing up the tack and preparing the trailers to roll out, Chris helped Larry wrap his horses' legs.

"I'm glad you're feeling better," she told him as they worked. "Because this has been the most fun Mom and I have had for a really long time. Rod's great."

"Yeah, Rod's a helluva guy. This show's been good for him, too," he spoke casually. "He's been a little bummed out lately, both with John Wyatt being sick and his girlfriend running off to England."

Chris dropped the leg wrap and quickly picked it up again, brushing off the dirt. "He told us about Mr. Wyatt, but we didn't know about any girlfriend. What happened?"

"Oh, I don't know. They just broke up, I guess." Larry began gathering water buckets. "She was pretty good lookin', but a total dipshit. Actually, she could have cared less about living in Texas and she hated horses. I've never really understood it, but Rod has really crappy luck with women."

CHAPTER TWENTY

The mailbox was stuffed full and a brown-wrapped package was placed outside the door of the apartment. It had arrived express mail from St. Louis and Wes knew immediately it was from his friend, Red. He had spoken to him several times and even invited him to the wedding, but the Party Animal's car was broke down and he couldn't make it. Inside the box was an old brick, caked with crumbling mortar and a note that said, "Always remember the good times; never forget the tough times."

"What a guy," Wes mumbled, placing the brick with pride on the coffee table. "What a *guy!*"

He continued to prowl through the mail as Jenna called Claudia's house. She waited impatiently as the phone rang five or six times, nervously playing with the phone cord. Miguel finally answered.

"Jenna! How was the honeymoon?" He always seemed genuinely pleased to hear from her.

"Great. Montreal is an amazing place," she told him. "It was wonderful, getting to really know my dad. Is Mom there?"

"No, she went out for a while. Shopping, I think. I hope she didn't ruin your wedding day. She told me she crashed the party."

"She did," said Jenna. "That's my Mommy Dear."

"She was really upset that she didn't get invited. But what really freaked her out is that Warren was there."

"I can't believe she found out about it," Jenna said.

"Well, you know how she is. She called New Winston a few months ago and subscribed to that little newspaper there. She gets it every week and reads the whole damn thing, word for word," he confessed. "I couldn't imagine why she did that, but I guess I should have known. She showed me your engagement announcement. Soon after that, she ran right out and bought a new outfit, wedding gift and all."

"She subscribed to the newspaper? God!"

Miguel sighed. "Sometimes she does some crazy shit. But, don't worry about her, all right?"

"Right," Jenna replied doubtfully. "So how have you been?"

"Fine. I got a job at a little dinner theater here in Kansas City. I like it a lot. The show I'm in runs through August and then Claudia wants to go someplace where there's decent weather. If you want, I'll call you every once in a while and keep you posted on what she's up to."

"I guess that would be all right." She chewed her bottom lip. "Miguel … there are things between my mother and me, things she's done and said, that I can't forgive her for right now. Maybe someday, but not now. Take care of her, okay?"

He assured her he would and hung up. Jenna slid into the corner of the couch and propped her feet on Wes' lap, giving him a baleful look.

"Like I always say, your mom is a piece of work," he said and pulled her closer. It pained him to see the misery in her face. She had been so happy in Montreal.

"Tomorrow morning, let's get up early and head to the farm for a week or so," he suggested. "You can ride Tess and I can help Chris and Dad at the barn. When I called Mom last week, she said they're stripping stalls and painting and stuff. Dad's moved Vince to the other side of the barn, and he and Frank are repairing the stud stall. There's a lot to do and they need me there."

He rubbed his jaw and continued. "Besides, Mom said Reba's colt was real nice and I want to see him. She also said something had happened that night the colt was born. She acted funny. Real funny. Said she needed to tell me in person."

"I remember you mentioned she was a little weird. Wonder what that's about … " Jenna hung around his neck. "Hey! Why don't we just go tonight? We're not unpacked yet. I really want to spend some time with Tess."

It was nearly eleven o'clock when their truck turned onto the Old Pike Road. As they approached the main gate, Wes' face blanched as he saw a squad car parked at the barn. He braked hard as an ambulance pulled past him and hit the road, its red lights illuminating the night. He frantically shook Jenna, who was dozing.

"What's happened?" she exclaimed with a start.

Wes slammed the truck to a stop and jumped out as he spotted the police chief standing in the barn door. As Ken walked in his direction, Joanna raced past, throwing herself in her son's arms.

"Oh, God! Wes! Someone came in tonight and took Jake! We were in the house and Chris went down to the barn to turn the fans off and when she didn't come back, Jeff went down and found her." Jo was breathless, eyes brimming with sheer panic. "She was lying in the gravel in front of the barn door."

Jenna began to wail and Ken spoke up quickly. "She's all right. She took a pretty hard knock on the back of the head, but the medics think it's just a concussion. We're taking her to the hospital. Jeff's with her."

"What do you mean, they took Jake? Are you saying someone just stole him? Right out of our damned barn?" Wes exploded. "Where the hell's my dog? No one ever comes in without my dog throwing a fit!"

Joanna broke in. "I wanted to tell you on the phone. About Josephine. The night you and Jenna left for Montreal? The night Reba foaled?"

She was still clinging to her son. He drew back and stared at her as she finished the story.

"Josie? They killed my dog?" He was numb. "What the shit is going on here?" He narrowed his eyes in disbelief and with clenched fists, demanded an answer. Ken shook his head.

"Wes, I don't really know. We know someone has been watching the house for months. You know that. Your Dad told you. We've been tryin' to patrol up here every once in a while, but we haven't seen anything. There was nothing we could do."

It sounded lame, and Ken looked at the ground.

"I've got to get to the hospital," Joanna spoke up. "Jenna, come with me and Lil. Frank and Wes can stay here."

"I need to ask some questions," Ken continued, as Jenna took the keys and motioned for Lil to help Jo into Wes' truck. "As far as I can figure, they had a truck and trailer parked down the road and led the horse out. When I got here, Chris was conscious, but so hysterical I couldn't get much out of her. She had dragged herself out of the barn and collapsed, but she saw the taillights."

The chief walked back inside the barn and carefully inspected the alleyway, followed by Wes and Frank.

"Did he have any kind of tattoo or a brand?" Ken asked. "One of those embedded micro chips, maybe?"

"No, I supposed we should have done that, but we've never thought about it." Wes shook his head.

"We'll put out a bulletin with his description and in the morning, we'll check with sale barns in this area. I'll call the Missouri and Kansas Highway Patrol."

"What can we do to help?" Wes was sick with anger. "I can't just sit here, I'll go nuts."

"You can notify veterinarians here in the state. Doc is likely to be helpful on that. You ought to make up a flyer and plaster it everywhere horse people go," suggested Ken. "And you can help out by contacting other farriers."

"I know the chances of us getting him back are slim," Frank interrupted, "but we've got to find this horse. We've qualified him to show at the World show in November. He's worth a buttload of money, Ken. We've got to find him."

"I don't care how much he's worth," Wes muttered, peeved at Frank's concern with the monetary loss. "It ain't the money! Who would take him? Why?" He sat down on the concrete in front of Jake's empty stall and rested his face on his knees. "My little sister is going to lose her freakin' mind!"

"What kind of criminal offense is this, Ken? Does the state police really care when a horse is stolen?" Frank asked.

"If the horse is worth more than $150, it's a felony in Missouri," said the chief. "With no identifying marks, recovery isn't as likely, but we will work this as aggressively as we can, I promise."

The next morning, Chris was released from the hospital. Jeff drove her home, followed by Jenna with Jo and Lil. They had sat up all night, trying to calm her, but there were no words, no actions that could soothe her. As the x-rays showed no concussion, the doctor finally ordered her sedated and suggested they keep her quiet for several days, until the initial trauma subsided.

She sat in the front seat beside Jeff with a dull, medicated expression as they turned in the main gate. Jenna parked and ran to help Jeff get Chris out of the truck.

"Christine, listen to me, we'll get him back. We'll do whatever we have to do, but we'll get him back," she declared. The grief in Chris' dilated eyes made Jenna look away.

**

During the following weeks, Jenna and Chris drove more than a thousand miles, visiting every sale barn in both Missouri and Kansas. Wes made endless phone calls and distributed flyers with Jake's photo to every farrier in the Midwest. The state horse associations and councils were alerted and as the word spread like wildfire among the quarter horse people, friends called with promises to help find Jake. Horse people who were complete strangers to the Days called with offers of support.

Mike McGraw contacted veterinarians and every clinic and university facility in the four-state area. No one had seen a black colt. Most people in the Missouri River Valley were more concerned with ravaged crops, exposed by the receding water. Many folks had lost stock, including horses and pets, but Ken Thompson reported to Jeff every day or so, with updates of his postings. The chief prudently checked slaughterhouses in bordering states, praying for no news there.

The investigation bureaus of neighboring states, versed in livestock theft, released information to every agent. State highway patrols had been notified, but after the first week, it was not likely they would be helpful. After twenty-four hours, Thompson told Jeff, the chances of stopping a horse trailer on the run with a stolen horse were not good. Local jurisdictions were notified, but after weeks passed, most of the bulletins became buried under stacks of other routine notices. The chief doggedly exhausted each trail, and his fruitless efforts left him pounding his desk in frustration.

Frank and Lil drove from town to town with flyers, handing them out to farmers, saddle clubs and feed store owners. One day in late August, Frank made a trip to Prairie Rock. He parked beside Charlie Edwards' store and walked to the front of the old building. A slight young man with sunglasses sat on the porch by the Coke machine, whittling on a stick of wood.

"Is the owner here?" Frank inquired.

"No, but Gabe's here. He's out back unloading fertilizer. What do you need?" The whittler seemed to be looking straight ahead through his Ray-Bans.

"Well, I want to leave this flyer with him." Frank produced a piece of paper and handed it to the young man. "We had a horse stolen in July. Do you think y'all could keep an eye out for him?"

Gil chuckled. "Sure thing, mister. I'll keep an eye out. What's the horse look like?"

"Well, his picture is on that flyer. If you see anything, the phone number is on there, too."

"You bet. If I see anything, I'll call you." Gil smiled, folded up the flyer and tucked it in his shirt pocket.

***

"By now, this horse could be anywhere," Ken confided to Frank as they shared morning coffee at the town's cafe.

"We can't give up, Ken. Christine is a mess. She's making herself sick."

"I know, we've done everything but put the freakin' horse's picture on milk cartons." Ken sipped his coffee and added more sugar. "But the bitter truth is, my friend, chances of getting him back are less every day. If I were you, I'd give her another colt and hope she gets attached to it like she did the black."

"You don't know Chris," Frank rose to leave. "She'll never give up looking for him. At every sale, every parade, every rodeo. In every pasture, every feed lot."

The chief looked up, forehead wrinkled. "I'm sorry, Frank. She's a good kid. I know it's tough."

"Last Thursday we drove to Mound City and I helped her pass out some flyers to some 4-H kids there," Frank groaned. "Along the way we saw a field full of horses. One was black. Tall, pretty, shiny. I stopped on the road and she jumped from the truck and was over the fence before I could stop her. When the black horse turned and she saw he had no white crescent on his forehead, she dropped in the grass like she'd been shot. I don't know how much more she can take. I don't know how much more *we* can take."

CHAPTER TWENTY-ONE

Despite the flood damage, Charlie Edwards' feed and farm supply store was back in business and thriving. Through the years, it had become the most successful store in town, which was no famous accomplishment, as there were only three other businesses in the tiny river community. Rural villages like Prairie Rock were hard-pressed economically, but the small store managed to stay alive. Although the town's population boasted no more than 300 folks, Charlie's store stayed in business due to the fact it was the only feed and farm supply in that part of the county. With good service and fair prices, he continued to enjoy the support of his customers.

Gabe worked six days a week at the store. After closing time, he sometimes went out back to the concrete block garage and passed the time by polishing the truck. He occasionally cruised the back roads in his pickup with Gil, sharing a six-pack of beer or sitting on the porch, listening to one of his friend's new CDs. His life was uneventful, but Gabe didn't mind. He was waiting to see what was around the bend.

For several years, he had experienced a recurring dream at night and was convinced this dream had some kind of special meaning. In these dreams, Gabe was traveling. Traveling alone. Suddenly, people are crowding up around some gates and there are animals and shouting and the smell of cattle. And he would wake up abruptly with the crushing sensation he had been pushed to the back of the crowd and the very purpose of his life, his destiny, was hopelessly bungled. A near hit. A clear miss. *What was beyond those gates?* Gabe experienced this same dream over and over.

In late October, Charlie traded in his well-worn stock trailer for a new one manufactured in Arkansas. He planned on going to pick it up himself, but his wife protested, reminding him of the family reunion scheduled for that weekend. At her insistence, he delegated the responsibility to Gabe, who accepted without hesitation.

"The truck's hooked to the old trailer. Here is some money for food and gas and here's my paperwork," Charlie said, "and, Gabe, there'll be an extra $100 on your paycheck this time. Now get goin'."

Gabe arrived at the dealership late on Saturday morning, and after the new trailer was wired for lights and brakes, he headed back home. He pulled through a small town called Mintonville shortly after one o'clock and stopped for lunch at the Crossroads Cafe. He had seen a billboard twenty miles back touting the Crossroads' Big Porkie tenderloin sandwich as "the biggest in the Ozarks." The billboard didn't lie.

From the booth where he sat, he looked out the window at the activity across the road as he tackled the monstrous sandwich. He could see a multitude of trucks and cars parked around the local sale barn. Some people were hawking goods off their tailgates, and there were cages of puppies and boxes of baby ducks, baskets of garden vegetables and more, all for sale.

Detached, he watched a throng of people crowding against a large gate leading inside the barn. It struck him mid-bite, this scene was oddly familiar. Suddenly, Gabe recognized this place. He dropped the uneaten portion of the Big Porkie on his plate, paid the waitress and hurried across the road. An auctioneer was shouting and he heard horses nickering. It was a perfect enactment of his recurring dream.

He joined the crowd and pushed his way to the gate. Inside, he could see the area around the sale ring teeming with people. With an unknown but driving sense of purpose, he walked quickly to the window and got a number. *Was he playing out his dream?* He tried to sort it out.

The crowd outside the gate swelled, pushing him to the back. Gabe looked around for an alternative way to get inside. He saw a flight of stairs leading up to a second story door and through that door, light and noise. *This way*, a familiar voice seemed to call to him.

He stepped inside and found himself looking down at the sale ring. The auctioneer and his assistants were running several saddled horses through. The same guy rode each one into the ring, pulling the creature around, whooping it up and hopping on and off to show the horse was "broke to death."

The fourth had no saddle and the man leading him turned the horse loose and shooed him around the ring, all the while waving madly. The horse was tall and pathetically thin with dark, sunburned hair, scorched mane and chewed-up tail. His unshod feet had not been trimmed in months and were cracked, split and badly chipped. The auctioneer introduced the unnerved sale victim as a three-year-old stallion.

"Been pasture breeding all summer," called out the man in the ring.

Gabe sized up the horse. *Sick and probably wormy.* He had old summer sores all over his chest and flies had chewed around his eyes and made them runny. Some bidding began and someone yelled, "How's he bred?"

The man in the ring answered, "He's a full-blooded quarter horse, but the papers, they were … uh … lost."

Bidding slowed down and languished at $325.

"He's green broke to ride, folks!" shouted the man in a voice like a carnival barker. The auctioneer picked up on that and bidding went up to $400.

A voice in the crowd yelled for the man to swing up on him bareback.

"Show us how broke he is!" called out another. The man hesitated, but approached the horse. He was thinking about it when the scared animal suddenly reared up and struck out a ragged hoof, barely missing the man's shoulder. He ducked back, regarding the defiant horse. The bidding died at $425. The auctioneer continued to harass contending bidders for more, but most were declining with a nod.

"Who'll give me $450?" pleaded the auctioneer.

Gabe scanned the crowd for a responsive face, but the horse's rebellious behavior had squelched their interest. *Raise your hand*, the familiar voice in his head seemed to guide him. Gabe slowly rose to his feet and obediently raised a finger, pointing to the horse. He barely heard the rest of the auctioneer's song, concluding with "Sold!" He was staring at the sickly, terrorized stallion, standing frozen, eyes rolling. Gabe walked down the steps and vaulted the fence into the ring.

"This your horse, mister?" Gabe took the lead rope from the withered hands of the handler and eyed the horse. The stud stood in the middle of the ring, every muscle tense.

"Nah, some guys brought him to my place and said they'd pay me to keep him for a few weeks," the scrawny man replied. "They never came back to get him, never paid me and it's been months. So here he is. They said he had papers."

"Easy, son. Whoa now," Gabe crooned as he walked cautiously to the young stallion's side, watching intently for any aggression. There was none, only a piteous defensive snort as Gabe ran the short chain on the end of the lead through one side ring on the halter, over the stud's nose and through the ring on the other side.

"You know a little about handling studs, boy?"

"Some," Gabe answered tersely and walked out of the ring with the apprehensive young horse. Outside, Gabe looked at the horse's teeth. The stud respected the chain over his nose so easily and looking at his teeth was so uncomplicated, Gabe knew he had been handled plenty.

"Heck, this is just a big old colt. He's not as scared as he is mad!" he thought to himself. "Who in the hell would have a stud this young out with mares? And with the papers lost, at that?"

"Yep, it don't make sense," Charlie agreed when Gabe called him from a gas station in Mintonville. "You think he's worth the trouble, eh? Well, you oughta know. Bring him on home, son."

Charlie and his wife were waiting at the store when Gabe pulled in with the stallion. As Gabe unloaded the horse, Edith scurried to a safe distance.

"He's all right," he assured her. He stroked the horse's sweating shoulder. Gabe tied him to the side of the livestock trailer and went for a bucket of water.

"Charlie, got any feed around here?" said Gabe with a half smile and throwing a glance at the feed store. Edith and Charlie hesitated for a second and laughed out loud.

"I don't know what he's been fed." Gabe held the bucket before the colt and watched him drink. "So I'll start him out on a scoop of oats. Do you think it would be okay to move my truck out of the shed there, bed the floor down good and put him in there?"

"Poor thing!" Edith, gaining confidence, stepped a little closer. "Maybe you and Charlie can build a stall inside. That big door is about to fall off. Why don't you tear it down and put a double door there so he can see out. We've got some wire hog panels over there we could use."

"Yeah, that would be fine," her husband agreed, returning with a sack of oats. "Honey, while we are feeding him, go call your brother and have him bring over a couple of bales of brome hay."

Hours later, Charlie and Gabe stood outside the shed, looking in at the starved horse snatching mouthfuls of the good brome.

Gabe scratched his head. "He's supposed to be broke to ride, but I doubt it. They said he was three but that's bull crap, too. He's big, but from the looks of his teeth, he ain't even two yet."

"Maybe in a week or so, you oughta give him some worm medicine. He's too poor right now," Charlie observed. "Man, even his feet are a mess!"

"I'll try to rasp 'em off and shape 'em up a little tomorrow. First, I'll just let him settle in and try to get some ointment on those sores and cuts."

"Still a stud, eh?" said Charlie. "You better wait to have him gelded. He ain't healthy enough to handle that. He might really get down. Mercy, he's a ratty lookin' thing. E-maciated! What ever possessed you to buy him?"

Gabe shrugged. He really wasn't sure. Charlie continued to look the stud over.

"You know, he ain't bad lookin', Gabe. Nice neck, purty head. Big sucker. His hair's so sunburned, what color do you think he is? Buckskin?"

"Maybe. I don't know." Gabe studied the horse. "I like his head, too. He won't be too bad when we get him in shape. That white spot on his forehead is kinda different."

"Yeah," said Charlie, "it sorta looks like a half moon."

CHAPTER TWENTY-TWO

Joanna watched her daughter withdraw into a dull, emotionless world like a budding flower suddenly blighted by an early freeze. The season changed, transforming the Missouri River Valley into a fiery palette of color. But even the blustery sky and swirling leaves Chris usually loved so much had a melancholy effect on her.

Months idled by in tedious succession and the bleak onset of winter plunged her deeper into despair. The holidays had little meaning for her and although Joanna persuaded her to participate in the Christmas shopping and decorating the house, she played the role with no enthusiasm. Every day since Jake's disappearance, Chris finished up her chores by smoothing the shavings in his empty stall with her rake. When she fed and watered the other horses, she always dumped out Jake's bucket and filled it again. On Christmas Day she placed a wreath on his stall door.

The months of January and February were busy, and mares arrived almost daily in preparation for breeding. Some had brand new foals on their side. By March, the barn was full. Jeff needed Jake's empty stall bad, and it surprised Joanna that it remained empty. Jeff and Wes built five new stalls on the south side of the barn to accommodate the family's own growing show string.

In Chris' opinion, Reba's colt was the best of this lot. He was smooth made and very pretty, with a fine, willing disposition. But he was born late and was immature in appearance. He was a leggy bay with plenty of height but narrow in the chest and slight in the hip. He would never halter. He was a born rider like his dam, and would likely be a good English prospect.

He was unusually affectionate and he held a special place in Joanna's heart. Since his arrival, she had laid exclusive claim to his handling. She called him Lester. Showing Jake at the Fourth of July show had restored much of Joanna's confidence, but since that show was Jake's last, it was not one the family talked about much.

"What would you think if I showed Lester in the yearling longe line class," she asked Chris one day. "I think he'd be good. He's a righteous little mover. Maybe he'll be my next English horse."

"That would be fun," said her daughter with little expression, watching Jo longe the colt in the indoor arena.

"Would you help me?" Joanna probed for approval.

"Sure. Jenna wants me to go to Carthage with her and Tess in April. We could take your colt and just get him used to riding in the trailer and all."

"Wes and Jeff both have to work. Maybe you, Jenna and I could go. Just us three," Joanna continued, hoping for a reaction.

She finished working Lester and snapped him in the crossties.

Chris thought about this idea and finally nodded her assent. Actually, she was glad to see her mother striking out in her own direction. It was clear to Chris that Joanna didn't share Jeff's dream of showing halter and western pleasure horses. Chris knew Jo was still seeking her own niche.

The April show was held near Carthage and was often a cold, rainy event. The unpredictable Missouri weather, however, blessed them with bright sunshine. It was Jenna's first registered show and although she was nervous, she was somewhat excited about the competition and the opportunity to wear her new show clothes. For Christmas, Wes had bought her brand new chaps and several trendy blouses.

Tess was not herself on the first day and a bit strong at the lope. It was not a performance that impressed the judge. But the second day told a different story. Joanna suggested a different bit and longer warm up. When Jenna entered the show ring, she flashed a confident look at Jo on the rail that made her mother-in-law smile.

"I hate it that Wes can't be here," Joanna told Chris.

It was a good ride and competitive enough to earn Jenna a second place. When it was announced, she patted Tess and rode forward. *Ridden by Jenna Day.* It sounded good.

"Nice go!" Chris congratulated her.

"How'd she look loping to the right?" Jenna was breathless as she slid to the ground outside the gate. "It felt like she was getting a little quick down on the far end, but I picked up on her a little when the judge wasn't looking."

"It looked great!" Joanna was amused at Jenna's fluent quarter horse chatter. They returned to the stall, analyzing every part of the ride.

On Sunday morning, the three drove over to Joplin for breakfast. Jenna ordered scrambled eggs and bacon, but when the waitress placed the hot plate of steaming food in front of her, she suddenly became pale and excused herself to the restroom. Minutes later, she returned.

"I don't feel so good," she murmured weakly. "I think I'm coming down with something."

Although she seemed to feel a bit better later in the morning, Jo was concerned.

"I think we better just scratch our classes, load the horses and head on home. We've got a long drive, but we can be home for supper."

On the way home, Jenna slept in the back seat of the truck.

"I hope she doesn't have the flu," said Chris, looking back at Jenna sleeping. Joanna pursed her lips, looking straight ahead at the road as she drove.

"I don't think Jenna has the flu, honey. Remember last Tuesday when she was feeling queasy? I think it's morning sickness."

***

On the following Friday afternoon, Joanna returned from the doctor's office with Jenna. Wes was waiting in the kitchen, pacing.

"Well?" He demanded a report. Jenna patted her stomach with an anxious half-smile. He grasped the meaning immediately, embraced her then held her at arm's length.

"I guess Tess will be taking a vacation," she whispered as he looked down at her. "I hope you're not disappointed, 'cause there ain't no chicken exit here."

He suddenly threw his head back and let out a cowboy whoop that could be heard a mile. Then unpredictably, he began to flap his elbows, dancing like a chicken around the kitchen table and crowing like a rooster. For the first time in many months, Chris laughed out loud.

"Let's celebrate, let's go out. All of us," Wes suggested, grabbing up the phone to call Frank and Lil. Then, he promptly hung up. "I forgot, Uncle Frank had to go to Victor City to judge some little open show tonight. Aunt Lil went with him."

"Let's wait until Dad gets home, then let's all go down to Victor City. We can watch the show and harass Uncle Frank!" said Chris, with a sparkle in her eyes that did not go unnoticed by her family.

The open show was held inside at the new facility near Victor City. It was an all-breed competition and the warm up arena was filled with quarter, paint, and appaloosa horses. The halter classes were over by the time the Days arrived. Lil, sitting alone on the bleachers, spotted them.

"What on earth are you all doing here?" She was genuinely surprised and pleased. As Joanna shared the good news, the expectant mother accepted an excited hug from Lil. Cheeks pink with excitement, Jenna sat down by Chris and noticed her sister-in-law was wearing the birthday shirt embroidered with little black horses. Chris hadn't worn it since Jake was stolen.

Jenna scanned the arena and saw Uncle Frank, in starched Wranglers, sharp khaki shirt and tie and perfectly shaped Stetson. He was standing in the center of the arena, hands behind his back, studying the youth pleasure class that had just entered the arena.

"Frank looks like a million bucks!" she exclaimed approvingly.

"He used to do this quite a bit. Now he just does a few shows," Chris told her. "He's a really good judge."

They had barely settled in their seats when Jenna spoke. "You know, I would die for some nachos and cheese from the concession stand. How 'bout you?"

Amused at Jenna's sudden whim, Chris slung her purse over her shoulder and set off to the concession stand. The line was long and while she waited, she stood watching the class file out of the arena.

The next class entering the ring was a snaffle bit class. The show bill in her pocket told her it was limited to two and three-year-olds. She casually sized up the class. Six horses in the pen. She ordered the nachos and bought two large soft drinks. The woman placed them in a cardboard tray and counted out the change. As Chris turned to walk back to the bleachers, she glanced into the ring and abruptly froze. Uttering a strangled cry, she dropped the tray, scattering chips and ice over the concrete floor. In the show pen, a tall young man was jogging down the rail on a black colt. The mark on his forehead was a perfect crescent. She knew in an instant it was Jake.

Her eyes blurred, filled with tears and before she could move, Wes was by her side.

"We saw him, too." He guided her away from the line, where people were staring. She couldn't feel her legs, but Wes held her up until she found the end of the bleachers and sat down. In a heartbeat, her father's arms were around her.

"I'm calling the sheriff! Stay here. Don't do anything," he ordered and hurried to find a phone.

Inside the show pen, Frank stood, stunned by what he saw. He looked quickly toward Lil, who was on her feet wringing her hands, and tried desperately to concentrate on judging the class. The young man on the black colt rode an old saddle. He wore a simple plaid shirt and straw hat. He had no chaps. The colt was more peevish than nervous and broke from the lope several times. Composing himself, Frank finished working the horses and then signaled to "bring 'em in and line 'em up." He approached the black horse and looked him over. There was no doubt in his mind.

"What's your horse's name, son?" He cleared his throat and spoke.

The rider replied, "I just call him Buck."

"Is he a two-year-old?"

"Yep. I've only been riding him about 90 days. He's green, but not scared of much."

Of course not, thought Frank. *Not as many times as he's been in the show ring.*

"I didn't use him today, but when you get him broke, he's ... going to be pretty nice. What's your name?" Frank stumbled on the words.

The rider answered, "Gabriel Judd. I live over in Prairie Rock."

Frank turned away, his eyes furtively searching the bleachers for his niece. Outside the ring, he spotted Chris, now on her feet and racing recklessly along the side of the rail toward the far arena gate.

After the placings were read, the horses filed out one by one. Outside the gate, the black colt's rider dismounted and started to lead his horse away when he was broadsided by a screaming bombshell of blonde hair and clawing fingers. He stepped back in shock as Chris slammed past him, flinging herself at the black colt.

"You sonofabitch, you've got my horse!" She screamed as she reached up and wrapped her arms around Jake's long neck. She pressed her cheek against his shoulder.

"Don't you remember me? Jake?" Her tears were beyond control and she alternately wept and cried out with joy.

The colt shifted his weight apprehensively, his eyes on Gabe, who stood shocked and bewildered at the girl's delirium.

An abrasive voice exploded behind him and Gabe spun around to face Jeff Day.

"This horse belongs to my daughter. He was stolen from our barn last July."

Wes arrived, menacing, ready for battle. "I don't know who you are and how you got this horse, but we're taking him home."

Gabe Judd's jaw dropped.

"I'm sorry, you got to be wrong," he stammered, astonished by the sight of the girl hanging hysterically on his horse's neck. He stared at the murderous expressions on the faces of the hostile strangers surrounding him.

Jeff took another step forward. "I've called the sheriff and he's on his way."

As shock turned to anger, Gabe's voice rose above the din of Chris' wailing. "I bought this horse," he declared. "And I got the receipt from the sale!"

A crowd had gathered and a tall, heavy man in a uniform pushed to the front.

"I'm Sheriff Edwards. What's the problem here?" After curtly introducing himself, he nodded a familiar greeting to Gabe Judd.

Jeff began to explain the situation, as the sheriff bobbed his head in disbelief.

"And you are sure this is your horse?" He glanced at Chris, who had stepped away from the horse and was standing tearful and defiant at her father's side.

"I know this guy," said the sheriff. "He works for my brother at the feed store over in Prairie Rock, and he wouldn't steal anything. He bought this horse and I remember when he brought him home. I thought he was a buckskin … he looked like hammered dog shit and was poor as a snake."

Jeff snorted and shook his head. "There's a reward for his recovery and we'll make sure he gets the money."

"I don't want no money," Gabe said loudly as his fingernails cut into the palms of his hands. He gripped the reins. "This is my horse."

With balled fists in the air, Chris broke from her father's grip. The colt, startled, jumped sideways. Instantly, Gabe laid a quieting hand on the black's shoulder and whispered to him with a sureness that sabotaged Chris' intent.

"Just hold it right there, everybody." The sheriff licked his lips and gestured. "Gabe, step over here."

He pulled Gabe aside, horse following obediently. After they had talked for a few moments, the sheriff's large hand closed over the colt's muzzle and he pulled the lip back, looking for a tattoo.

Turning back to Jeff, Sheriff Edwards hooked a thumb in his belt.

"Here's what we're going to do. As I said, I know Gabe Judd and I'm going to send him home with this horse. I know where he keeps him and he's promised me that's where he'll be. I guarantee his word is good. You need to go home and have your local authorities call me and we'll work this out. Seein' as how there are no identifying tattoos or brand, we'll likely ask that you request a blood test."

"He's a registered quarter horse and we do DNA testing from hair samples now, not blood," Jeff corrected Edwards, who didn't appreciate this stranger's expertise all that much. Ignoring the lawman's scowl, Jeff added, "We own the stud and his DNA is on record, so there'll be no problem."

Grievously disappointed, Chris collapsed against the horse. Gabe gathered the reins and stared uncomfortably at the ground. Then, Joanna was there, arms around her daughter, pulling her away. Chris painfully retreated, fingers trailing gently down the colt's shoulder.

"What did you say your name is?" Somehow compelled to address her, Gabe spoke.

"Chris. Christine Day," she answered, wiping her wet cheeks.

"I'm sorry, miss. I know you think this is your horse, but it has to be a mistake." He draped an arm over the long black neck. The colt, beginning to fret, was instantly submissive. "He's my horse and he knows it. He don't know you from Adam."

Gabe turned and led the colt from the barn. Behind him, he could hear the girl crying out in protest, muffled by the voices of her family trying to pacify her.

As Gabe and the horse crossed the lot and moved into the shadows of the parking area, he heard one last desperate scream from the girl. A single hysterical word pierced the night air.

"Jake!"

In the dark, the black colt stopped dead in his tracks, eyes suddenly alert. He pulled roughly away from Gabe, twisted his head and instinctively looked back toward the now familiar voice. Then, from deep in his chest, he responded with a rumbling nicker that ripped through Gabe Judd's heart.

CHAPTER TWENTY-THREE

Charlie Edwards left his brother's office feeling more than a little distraught. It was much like the fearful apprehension he sensed when the river approached flood stage. He and Edith had watched the black colt bring new life to Gabe, and they had encouraged him to take the stock trailer and drive over to Victor City for the open show. Charlie felt responsible for this threatening turn of events, and he was powerless to stop it from reaching disastrous proportions.

"My brother says the Days have a lot of show horses and this black colt is worth a ton of money," Charlie lamented to his wife. "A person sure wouldn't have thought it if they'd seen him when Gabe brought him home."

"We can't let them just take Gabe's horse, Charlie!" Edith wrung her hands. "There must be something we can do. That horse is the most important thing in his life!"

"Well, it seems Jeff Day owns the sire of Gabe's horse and all they've got to do is some kind of parentage verification deal with the quarter horse association." Charlie patted her. "I don't think there's much we can do."

But that afternoon, after much discussion, Charlie and Edith Edwards left the store in Gabe's hands and told him they had some business to take care of in Jefferson City. They drove instead to New Winston, where they met with Ken Thompson. As Ken had promised, Jeff Day was there, too, and his daughter, Chris.

"I'm not going to beat around the bush," said Charlie. "Edith and I, well, we have some savings. And we'd like to know if you'd sell us the black horse."

Jeff's jaw dropped and Chris clamped her eyes closed. It was not what they had expected to hear. Ken was just as surprised and scratched his head. He doubted that whatever the couple had stashed away, it would not be adequate to even negotiate a purchase. Charlie waited hopefully for a response.

"I'm really sorry, Mr. Edwards, but I don't think there is any amount of money that could buy him from my daughter," Jeff spoke simply. "And the papers are in her name. The colt's mother died when he was born and Chris hand-raised him. Until he was taken from our barn, they were inseparable."

"Now I've found him, I can't let him go," said Chris kindly. "There's just no way."

"I'm sorry to hear that," Charlie said as he placed his arm around his fretful wife. "We think the world of Gabe, and he and the horse have quite a relationship, too. The colt was in pretty bad shape when Gabe bought him at a sale down south. His hair was so sunburned and scorched. We didn't know he was black until just recently, when he started sheddin' off. The boy don't have much, miss, and this horse is more than a horse to him. I guess, since you know how special he is to you, how Gabe must feel about him, too."

Chris lowered her head and rocked on her heels. "I guess so," she murmured. She looked helplessly at Jeff.

"What you don't realize, is that the horse went through a lot," Edith spoke for the first time. "And we've watched this colt come back to health, in mind and body, and grow very attached to Gabe."

Chris sat down in the police chief's chair and placed both hands over her face. After a moment of silence, she spoke.

"I'm sorry. You know I gotta have him back," she said softly. "I don't think there's any more to talk about."

Charlie hesitated, then addressed the police chief. "Well, then, I guess we'll be going. I'd appreciate it if you wouldn't let Gabe know we came."

After they left the office, Jeff turned to Chris. "Okay, here's the deal. We'll go over to Prairie Rock, pull some mane hairs from Jake. That should settle it."

"I'll handle it myself," his daughter said in a subdued voice. Edith Edwards' words had deeply affected her and she pictured Jake, abused, going through a strange sale barn. She knew the colt was no doubt attached to his rescuer by now, and she was confused by an unlikely compassion for Gabriel Judd. She thought about it all day. That evening she asked Wes to walk with her to the old barn.

"Don't get sappy," her brother told her as they sat alone on the stairs leading to the timbered old loft. "Get the DNA testing done and we'll go over there with Ken and bring him home. That's all there is to it."

"You know what? You are just exactly like Dad!" she exploded, suddenly seeing more pieces of a lifelong puzzle. "I saw that the other night at Victor City. You can go from nice guy to jackass in 60 seconds flat. If the sheriff hadn't come when he did, you were ready to throw punches."

"And you weren't?" he shouted back at her.

"Sure I flipped out but I wasn't ready to knock somebody's head off before I found out what was going on! Even now, you don't want to look at the whole situation."

"I'm not like Dad, not even close!" Wes was disgusted with her. "And you're the one who doesn't get it. You feel sorry for this poor chump who bought Jake and was too dumb to even consider he might be a stolen horse. Nobody buys horses as good as Jake at a shitty little sale barn, no papers, unless there's something fishy goin' down."

"How was he supposed to know what a good horse Jake was?" she argued. "He had been turned out in a pasture and mares had beat the crap out of him. They said he looked like hell!"

"So what's the problem? You either want your horse back or not. What do you want?"

"Of course I want him back!" Frustrated, she put both fists to her forehead. "I'm just sorry for that guy. I guess I just know how Gabriel Judd must feel. That's all." She looked at the dusty floor.

"Okay, okay, I know you won't listen to anybody, but here's the story." Wes stood up and stepped toward the barn door. "We put up a reward on the horse, you know. The guy can have the reward and buy another horse. Then everything will be fine." He turned and left her alone in the still barn.

***

The April sky was turning dark. Gabe lay motionless on the bed in the stuffy attic as the light in the room diminished. Footsteps on the long staircase disrupted the stillness and a rap on the door made a hollow echo. He sat up on the side of the iron bed and flipped on his small lamp. Buttoning his shirt, he rose and walked to the door. He knew it would be Christine Day.

"Mrs. Edwards said I would find you here. Can I come in?" She nervously pushed a blonde strand of hair from her face. Standing close to him, she noticed he was well over six feet tall and although she figured they must be close to the same age, he seemed older.

"You live *here*?" She questioned, looking around with some incredulity. The lamp threw mysterious shadows in the corners and she almost regretted coming alone. Gabe motioned for her to come in. She gathered her self-confidence and when he moved over, she sidestepped into the attic.

She tried not to show her surprise at finding him in this strange place. Living alone, over this old feed store. *Who was he, anyway?* She looked at him in the lamplight but was unable to read his face. His expression was controlled from years of practice.

"I don't have many visitors," he said quietly. "Then, again, I guess you didn't just come to visit, did you?"

"No, of course not. I came here to tell you … " the speech she had prepared suddenly stuck in her throat and the threats she had intended to deliver seemed all wrong. She took a deep breath and walked around the room, winging it. "I came here to talk to you about my horse. Is he okay?"

Gabe snorted, disgusted.

"Of course he's okay." He shook his head in disbelief. "I knew you'd come, but I expected you to come with the sheriff, or a bunch of lawyers, or something."

"I could have done that," she said simply. "I think if we could just talk, you'll understand. I've been thinking about this and I know my colt has become attached to you. So for his sake, I just wanted you to know how bad I feel about this."

His eyes fixed on her. He knew she meant well, but the words sounded silly to him as they tumbled from her mouth.

"Oh, thanks a lot. That's so good of you," he sneered. "Let me ask you a question. How many horses does your family own? A couple dozen? To you, he's just another horse. To me, he's all I've got."

She cringed a little, not exactly expecting this to be his opening argument.

"You don't get it. He's my horse! He was led right out of my barn. And when those guys took him from me, it was like … it was like they cut out that part of me with a butcher knife."

Gabe was silent. This girl probably always had everything she wanted, nice house, good horses. How important could one colt be to her? She'd just take him home and put him back in the barn with all the rest.

"He was an orphan. The only reason he's is alive is because I begged for his life," Chris said as she faced him, hands on hips. "My dad was going to donate him to M.U. But I promised the mare when she died, I said I would take care of him."

"So what?" Gabe wasn't impressed. "No matter what you did, he'd probably still be dead if I had not bought him for a lousy $450 at the sale.

You should have seen your spoiled baby that day. Sores all over him, cuts, ragged feet. Wormy, skinny. He wasn't the same horse you raised and played around with. The colt you knew is dead."

"Stop it!" Her eyes were brimming with tears and her throat ached.

His cruel words stabbed at her logic, destroyed her fortitude, and she was almost afraid to look at him. She became acutely aware of the enveloping stillness of the room.

"You can have the reward for his recovery. It's $3,000. Did you know that?" She couldn't give up. "That's a lot of money."

"In case you haven't noticed," he said, "I don't care about money."

"I'm going to take some of his mane hairs for the DNA test. Where is he?"

"I want the sheriff here when you do it," he said calmly. She looked at him murderously.

"Why? I just need about 50 hairs." She was furious. It was a mistake to try to talk to him.

"I want the sheriff to seal the envelope and mail it. That way I'll know you just didn't pull some hair from one of those colts you got at home." He wasn't stupid and she realized he would fight any way he could to keep the black horse.

Hopelessly discouraged, she moved to the door and hurried down the dark stairs.

"I'll go find the sheriff, then," she said, refusing to look back. "I'll get the s.o.b. out of bed if I have to!"

She stepped out of the building and walked across the loading area in back of the store toward her truck. A strange anxiety began to form in the back of her mind, but she fought to resist it. She was stopped in her tracks at a sound emanating from an old concrete block garage nearby. In the darkness, she saw one of the front doors had been removed and through a large square window of wire, something moved. She stopped in her tracks and from the building came a low, familiar snort. *Jake!*

Rushing to the building, she fumbled with the latch and swung the door open. The black horse snaked his head out, pushing at her. Her heart exploding, she reached out to touch him. He snorted and nipped at her arm. She reacted with a quick slap, then stroked his neck.

"I'll be back for you," she whispered.

Chris looked up at the dim light in the second story window of the feed store. A tall, grim silhouette stood silently watching. As she closed the stall door and glanced back at the window, she saw him turn his face against the wall in a move of pure anguish. His unabashed agony consumed her in a sudden, unexpected rush. She hesitated, a feeling of unfinished business tugging hard at her.

Gabe heard her footsteps as she climbed back up the stairs. She didn't have to knock. He was waiting.

"I'm sorry, I … " He began to speak, then became frustrated and turned to the wall, pounding it loudly with his fist.

"I'm sorry, too," she murmured, "I'm sorry about this whole mess."

She walked inside and he closed the door, leaning against it. Glancing around the attic, she noticed a faded photograph tacked to the wall next to where he stood. In the picture, a pretty-faced woman sat proudly on a gray horse. Several people posed beside the horse smiling for the camera and a small boy stood there, too, holding the trophy.

"Is that you?" Chris asked, placing her finger on the image of the boy. He licked his lips nervously and looked away.

"Who is the woman on the horse?" she persisted.

He wouldn't look at the photograph. "It's my mom."

"Really? What is her name?" Chris was surprised.

"Cynthia."

Cynthia Judd? This was the woman who trained Tess. Didn't Uncle Frank say she was dead?

"I've heard of her," she said, handling it. "I remember my mom and Uncle Frank talking about her. My uncle said she was a good trainer."

"She gave it her best shot."

"What about your father, is he in this picture?"

"No. That guy owned the horse. I don't know anything about my father. My mom was never married. She raised me all by herself."

"Did you used to show?"

"Me? Hell, no. We didn't have enough money to buy me a foundered pony. But my mom was a good rider and other folks paid her to train for 'em." His hazel eyes were intense, but there was a sensitivity in them she'd not seen.

He walked over to an old chair, turned it around and straddled it. Leaning over the back, he faced Chris.

"Folks thought she was a little odd, maybe even crazy, but she was a good mother," Gabe said bluntly.

"Tell me about her." Chris' voice was steady. Gabe shot her a curious look. People didn't ask about his mother. Maybe it was the stigma of death, or maybe just the old guard politeness of the small town, but no one had mentioned her name to him in years.

"She could have been pretty successful," he said. He looked at the floor and then straight into Chris' face. "But she got real depressed sometimes."

"Did you grow up around here?" The sincerity of her voice surprised him.

"We lived on a little farm outside of town. The house wasn't much, pretty rundown. The barn was small, but she made it do. Folks brought her horses to train. None of 'em were ever ours. I learned to ride on other people's horses."

Chris pulled up a chair and sat close to him, hands cupped around her face, fixing on him with a look demanding more. She had a light, energetic presence that gripped him and his eyebrows pulled together for an instant. She thought she detected alarm. Then his face softened.

"Sometimes it was hard to pay the bills, but she was saving to buy me my own horse." He was succumbing to an unexpected and vague connection with his blonde adversary.

Chris chewed her bottom lip. "What happened to her?" she said softly, sensing the gentle prodding was somehow agreeable to him.

"She did a good job taking care of me. She never left me." He seemed now to be answering his own questions. "And then one day she stepped off of the bridge into the Missouri River." He threw the words at her.

Chris lowered her eyes to conceal her reaction, but he saw the compassion on her face. She spoke in a very small voice.

"I'm so sorry." There was a full minute of silence before she spoke again. "The colt's mother was named Stella Dora. She hemorrhaged after he was born and died on the way to Columbia. It was raining that morning. I had to fight Dad like a maniac, but he gave the colt to me. I raised him."

"What did you say his name was, anyway?" he said, although he knew it. His eyes were closed, his face very still.

"I call him Jake. I don't think you understand how much he is a part of me. And I don't know how to explain it. Do you know how it makes me feel when you tell me he's *your* horse?"

Her plea was simple and the torment in her voice fell heavily on him.

"What do you expect me to say?" Gabe propped himself up on one elbow, opened his eyes and looked straight at her. "When I saw him at the sale, I had no intention of buying him. I don't even know why I went in there."

He thought about telling her about the dream, but changed his mind. "A voice was in my head, I think," he heard himself saying. "I don't know. She told me to do it."

"Who told you to do it?" Her words cut through the heavy air. She knew what his answer would be.

"Mom. She had an eye for a good horse," he continued in a thick voice.

His words were so deeply personal, Chris was instantly uncomfortable.

"I have to go," she managed to say, "but you'll be seeing me again."

"I'm sure I will," he replied, locking eyes with her.

Driving home, she rolled down the window and let the cool night air rush around her. Her foot dropped on the accelerator, but she could not push the truck fast enough to escape the nagging stuffiness of the attic, its curious furnishings and the relentless hazel eyes of Gabe Judd.

CHAPTER TWENTY-FOUR

Lil sat straight up in bed, her sense of hearing instantly magnified. Maybe she'd dreamed it. The deadly quiet was abruptly fragmented by the sharp crack of a gunshot, then a minute or so later, another. She frantically reached for Frank and shook him hard.

"Wake up! Frank! I heard gunshots, down the road!"

He roused and swung his feet over the side of the bed, blinking. "Which way'd they come from?" he whispered, realizing what she'd said.

She scurried to the window and peered through the lace curtain toward the Day farmhouse.

"There!" she cried. They stood frozen in the bedroom for a full minute, listening, but the only sound was the sprinkling rain blowing against the window.

"Call the house," he commanded, climbing into his clothes and tugging on his boots. "Jo and Chris went to Prairie Rock tonight to meet with the sheriff and pull some mane hairs from Jake. They won't be home until late, but I think Jeff's home." He looked at his watch. It was nearly eleven.

"What about Wes?"

"He was taking Jenna back to Kansas City for a few days. They left this afternoon."

He pulled on his coat as she dialed the number. Letting it ring at least ten times, she fixed her eyes anxiously on her husband.

"Damn! No answer!" She hung up the phone and peeked out the kitchen window.

"There's lights on at the house ... and at the barn," she reported, then her voice became shrill. "Frank! There's headlights coming this way!"

They listened, and in seconds, a car sped by.

"How many shots did you hear?" he asked her, striding quickly to the hallway and lifting his shotgun from the corner of the closet.

"Two, I think. First one, then a minute or so later, one more. Does Jeff have a gun at the house?" She wrapped her chenille robe around her and trailed behind him nervously.

"Yes. And Wes' deer rifle's there." He opened the front door and stepped onto the porch.

"Stay here," he said firmly. "I'm going up there. I'll call you from the house."

Minutes later, Frank, on foot, slipped through the gate and cautiously surveyed the place. The east barn door was half open, and the bulbs hanging above the alleyway strafed the ground with a wide beam of light. He quietly approached the opening and hearing no sound, stepped inside. He noticed the horses in their stalls were agitated, causing him to quickly scan the long concrete alley. At the end of the barn, he saw something that made his heart skip a beat. Invincible's stall door was partially open.

He hurried toward the stall, a dark, hot rush of adrenaline sweeping over him. His eyes focused on the shadows inside and suddenly, his step faltered. The black stud lay on his side, motionless, head in full view through the slightly open stall door. Vince's eyes were wide open and a ragged, bloody hole behind his left ear oozed a sticky red drip pooling below his jaw. Frank dropped to his knees in horror and crawled slowly toward the opening.

"Mother of God!" he choked, "what's happened here!" He rocked back on his heels, supporting himself with the stock of the shotgun. Within seconds, an alarm sounded in the back of his mind. *Where was Jeff?*

He swallowed hard and struggled to his feet, leaning the gun against the oak wall. He pulled out a ragged bandana from his pocket and wiped the beads of cold sweat from his face, cursing and muttering under his breath. He blinked repeatedly, trying to block the dead horse's shocked expression from etching itself permanently in his memory. He stepped closer and swung the stall door all the way open. As a wide column of light streaked into the stall, a flash of color caught Frank's eye. Red. Red plaid flannel. In horror, he saw Jeff, lying crumpled in the far corner of the stall. He seemed to be almost in a sitting up position, head tipped back and twisted.

Frank called out to him, urgently, frantically. But as he looked closer, the words were smothered in the back of his throat. Blood, bone and hair splattered against the stained oak boards of the stall behind Jeff's head. Moving to the side, Frank half-gagged as he saw the extent of the gaping head wound. Jeff's eyes were open, fixed.

His senses convulsing, Frank backed away and prayed to his maker to restore his strength. The concrete floor seemed to be spinning and when it began to feel a bit solid again, he picked up the shotgun and walked to the barn phone. Lil picked up on the first ring.

"I'm in the barn ... Call Ken Thompson and get him over here." He tried to speak calmly for his wife's sake. "Lil? Tell Ken to send an ambulance. Jeff's been shot. You stay there and I'll come get you. Lock the doors."

He hung up and stared at the end of the alleyway. In minutes, he heard a truck wheel in the gate and the crunch of gravel as Lil, ignoring his orders, braked to a stop. He met her at the barn door.

"Don't you come in here, Lillian!" He grabbed her shoulders and she tried to push past.

"Oh Lord, Frank!" She strained to look inside the barn. "What happened?"

"Jeff's been shot. And the stud's dead, too." He held her shoulders, pushing her back from the door, as her stricken eyes met his and she reeled away from him with an anguished scream.

"Jeff! Dead? Are you sure? Did you ... ?" she cried out, refusing to believe him.

"He's dead, honey." He interrupted her, eyes clamped shut. Whimpering, she struggled and broke free. "Stop, Lil. You ain't goin' down there!" She took two uncertain steps toward the end of the barn and he reached out and seized her wrist. "Half of his head's been blown away."

She spun around and fell against his chest, heaving painful sobs. He patted her back and spoke with authority.

"When Ken gets here, I want you to stay close by. Chris and Jo will be back anytime and you gotta keep them from coming in here. My God, they'll both be insane!"

Frank heard the squad car speeding down the road and watched as the lights of the police chief's car splashed a dull red color on the trees. Deputy Howard Burns kicked the passenger door open, but remained slouched in the front seat, barking out a conversation over the car's two-way radio. Ken unfolded his lanky body out of driver's side of the car, walked briskly to the barn door and glanced around.

"The ambulance is on the way. They're about a half mile back," he said, fingering his belt. "Where's Jeff?"

Frank, his arm around Lil, pointed to the end of the barn. "No need for the medics to hurry, Ken," he said slowly, taking a hard swipe across his mouth with his hand. The chief gave him a comprehending look and dropped his head.

"Christ almighty," Ken muttered. His big fists were clenched and hung beside him. Jeff had been a friend since third grade. "Are you sure, Frank?"

Frank blinked hard and nodded.

"You say the family will be back soon? Well, we better get to work then. I'm gonna have to ask you to clear out of here, Frank. You, too, Lil. Did you touch anything?"

"Let me think. Yeah, I opened the stall door. And I used the phone."

Ken paused, then called out to the deputy. "It's bad, Howie. Get the county coroner's office to send somebody out here. Then run a check on the house, grounds, everything. We need to seal off the whole area."

When the ambulance arrived, Thompson spoke with the medics briefly and they hurried down the alleyway. One stepped inside the stall and minutes later, emerged and nodded to the chief.

"It looks like he was head shot, close range from the looks of it." The young paramedic paled as he gave his report. "We didn't touch him, but you can see the exit wound at the back right side of his skull is, well, it's massive."

A county sheriff's car pulled up and two men hurried inside the barn. Ken walked up the road to the dead-end lane where Jeff had showed him the tire tracks last Christmas. When he returned, Thompson confirmed to Frank that fresh tracks in the soft mud indicated a car had been there that evening.

Inside, the uniformed officer made copious notes and the plain-clothed detective from the county cautiously examined the entire length of the concrete alleyway. Someone announced that the county coroner had arrived and soon he hustled through, grim and silent and above all, careful not to disturb the crime scene before the photographer and detectives were finished.

It was after half past one when Lil saw headlights turn on the road and head toward the farm. She recognized the sound of the diesel engine.

"It's Joanna and Chris," she muttered in dread.

Chris' pickup turned in the gate and braked to a hard, sudden stop. The doors flung open and mother and daughter were out of the truck and running toward the barn. Frank and Lil moved in to block them.

"What's going on?" screamed Joanna, eyes wild. Lil grabbed her and pulled her back. "Let me go, Lil, what's the matter with you!"

"Joanna, I ... oh, my God, Frank! Help me!" Lil was struggling with Jo, who was becoming hysterical at the unexplained attempt to restrain her.

Frank stepped in. "Your aunt heard gunshots about eleven o'clock, and I came down and found Jeff ... "

"Is he hurt, what?" Joanna shrieked, shaking Lil. "Where is he?"

"I'm sorry, honey, there ain't no easy way ... " Frank began. Absolute denial in Joanna's mind crashed head-on with the meaning of his words. A long grievous scream escaped her lips. She turned and protectively clutched her daughter. Chris stood for a moment, dazed, then wrenched away and bolted for the barn.

"Daddy!" she shrieked over and over.

Jo cried out to her, but the girl had already rushed past the patrol cars, running headlong into Ken Thompson. The police chief, a large, broad-shouldered man, constrained her. He held her until she stopped screaming.

"I was one of your dad's oldest friends," he said gently. "Listen to me. There's nothing you can do for him, honey. We really don't want you in that barn right now. We've got officers scouring the place for trace evidence, other stuff that will help us find who did this. You do want that, don't you?"

She shook her head, strangling on the words she was trying to say. He put his arms around her and stroked her head.

"Sshhh, just take it slow. Try to get hold of yourself and help your mother through this," he said. "Your dad would have wanted you to be brave."

"What happened to him?" She wailed, still choking. The girl's face was petrified in fear of his answer, yet her eyes betrayed a desperation for the truth. Ken knew this look well and years of dealing with the families of victims had taught him how to handle it.

"Lil heard two shots," he began, "and woke Frank up. They heard a car speed up the road a few minutes later. We believe someone watched the house, thought everyone was gone, walked in the barn and shot the stallion. Jeff must have heard them and interrupted.

"Vince!" she howled in shock.

"We haven't figured out just what happened," he spoke firmly. "Frank found them both in the stall."

The horror in her eyes made Thompson suck in his breath. Pale and sick, she went limp in his arms and he knew she had lost consciousness.

"Get a paramedic over here for this girl!" he shouted. As a young man rushed to assist, Ken looked back toward the house for Joanna. She was sitting on the front porch steps, head in her hands, rocking back and forth. Lil sat close beside her.

He lit a cigarette. *God! How he hated this part of his job.*

Detective Tom Barnett, notepad in hand, strolled outside the barn and joined Thompson.

"Got a light?" he said, fishing out a pack of smokes.

"What's your take on this, Tom?" Thompson asked. He pushed his glasses back with his thumb.

"There's shavings all over the dead horse, which makes me think they must have dropped him first. Then it looks like maybe there was a scuffle in the stall. I'm sayin' maybe Jeff tried to stop 'em. They panicked and shot him, too. We sifted the shavings, found casings. There's a bullet lodged in the oak board behind his head. Howie's got it." he said, taking a drag off the cigarette. "Plenty of footprints. Looks like two guys."

"They've been watching the house," Thompson said. Barnett acknowledged with an affirmative nod. He, too, had examined the tire tracks and surmised the two fled the scene on foot. The car had been parked on the lane.

"I was out here at Christmas. Jeff called and had noticed a car parked there after Doc McGraw left." Ken crushed out the cigarette with his fingers and dropped the butt in his pocket. "McGraw never saw it, but I think Frank's wife had seen it on several occasions. We never got a make on it. Then in June, Joanna called me at home. Someone was here and killed the dog. It was after that when the colt was stolen."

"Somehow, it all must fit together," the detective said simply. When was the girl's black colt stolen?"

Thompson paused, scratching the back of his neck. "July. Why would they come back?"

"Maybe taking Chris' horse was a mistake," Barnett said intuitively.

"The stolen colt was definitely a ringer for the stud," Ken said slowly. "Maybe somebody meant to take the stallion, but screwed up. I was out here that night. Jeff had moved the stud to the other side of the barn so he could repair the stall."

"Strange stuff. One thing we know. They didn't intend to steal the stud tonight," said Barnett. "Or they would have had a truck and trailer. Those are car tracks."

"If they've been casing the house since Christmas, chances are somebody, neighbors or somebody, has seen a strange car cruising this road," Thompson mused, hopeful.

Barnett said, "I'll get on it in the morning."

Thompson shook his head approvingly. "And I want Ray Slankard picked up. Wherever he is, I'll find the sonofabitch. My guess is he knows more than a little about this."

The barn door slid open all the way and the two men looked up. The coroner and his assistant were removing Jeff's body on a gurney. Automatically, Ken turned toward the porch. The sound of the wheels in the darkness had brought Joanna to her feet, staring, clinging to Lil. Frank sat beside her, Chris' crumpled form clutched in his arms.

The chief took a deep breath. "Tell Howie to get somebody to move the dead horse in the morning. He needs to ask Frank what they want to do with him."

One of the medics approached, carrying a small white plastic cup full of steaming coffee. He extended it to Thompson and it was gratefully accepted. *It was going to be a hell of a long night.*

CHAPTER TWENTY-FIVE

Chris sat alone on the floor of the barn. A long sweeping set of fresh scrape marks on the concrete trailed down the alleyway toward the large, sliding door. The marks had been etched by Vince's iron shoes as the tractor dragged him out on the morning after the carnage. She reached and lightly laid her fingertips on the scrape marks. How her father had loved this horse!

"Chris. You need to change clothes. It's nearly time to go." Jenna's voice made her look up. She was dressed in a loose-fitting dark colored dress, black stockings and low heels. Her hair was knotted in a simple twist. Chris rose and automatically followed her to the house, thinking about the traces on the floor and wondering how long they would be there. Somehow those images kept her mind from confronting the afternoon's dreaded event.

Her father would have approved of the farewell to Vince. Aunt Lil's cousin had come with a truck and disposed of the stallion's remains. In the absence of a burial, Frank fashioned a simple white cross and drove it in the ground in the orchard where other family pets were memorialized. Wes hung Vince's halter on it. The traditional mourning ritual comforted Chris and she officiously hung Jeff's everyday spurs there, too.

Now, as she dressed for her father's funeral, she pondered if there was a heaven and if Vince was there with Jeff.

***

The First Baptist Church of New Winston was crowded with family, acquaintances and neighbors for the funeral of Jeff Day. Dozens of town folks milled around, seeking each other out, gathering in small hushed clusters. Old family friends and Jeff's co-workers recognized and greeted each other. Quarter horse people from the Midwest were well represented, shocked by the murder of their friend and deeply disturbed by the brutal killing of the stallion.

Jeff's mother, who had remarried after her husband's death, had arrived from California. Loretta Day Clifton had never developed a closeness with Joanna or her grandchildren. Tanned and still attractive for her age, she wore too much makeup and seemed a foreigner after all these years. Loretta feigned a warm greeting for Ken Thompson. She remembered him as a big, dull boy her son had grown up with in Lexington and was surprised he was serving his second successful term as the town's police chief.

Ken, while trying consciously to stroll respectfully through the crowd in an unofficial capacity, served as a bizarre reminder to mourners that there were yet no real leads on the murder. The evidence at the crime scene had failed to point solidly to Ray, but the chief placed great significance in what he called his "hunches," and had spent the last days and nights organizing a manhunt for the drifter.

Joanna sat numbly on the front pew, both hands tightly gripping her purse. She was wearing a two-piece dark gray suit she never liked and sat staring at her matching heels, troubled by the fact she couldn't even recall getting dressed. Wes sat stiffly at her right side. Chris, shredding a tissue, sat on her left, puffy eyes fixed on the carpet.

The eulogy and the sermon were lengthy and the words eventually became indistinguishable to Joanna. As Rev. Baker's toneless recitation droned on, she caught bits of words. "In my father's house there are many mansions. If it were not so I would have told you … " but she was thinking of something else. Joanna was trying to remember all the words to "Free Bird." It was Jeff's favorite Lynyrd Skynyrd song.

Following the service, the pallbearers filed in to move the casket outside to the hearse, and the family rose and fell into a procession behind. Jo's eyes wandered to the back of the church, fixing on a lone woman dressed in black. Her form fitting dress was impeccably styled. Her face was partially concealed by a smart, close-fitting hat and long, net veil shading her eyes. Joanna realized with a start, it was Claudia. Wes and Jenna were instantly on guard, and their eyes simultaneously darted in the direction of Jo's gaze. The appearance of the veiled woman confounded Wes and he stopped in mid-procession and stared.

"Mother!" Jenna gasped. Despite her embarrassment at the black widow outfit and veil, a private rush of sympathy flooded Jenna's brain. Poor Claudia had lost Jeff, too. Her love, her obsession. Claudia saw the charity in her daughter's face and dabbed a silk handkerchief to the corner of one eye. Wes turned to Jenna, perplexed, then dutifully guided his wife and mother out the side door.

Jenna stood waiting to be seated in the family limousine, her eyes frantically scanning the crowd pouring from the church's front doors. Claudia was nowhere in sight.

After the graveside service, Wes drove his family back to the farm. Frank and Lil followed, accompanied by Mike McGraw. At the house, Joanna, with Rita hovering at her side, made a valiant effort to visit with family and close friends. With the aid of the sedatives her friend had forced on her, she seemed a little faraway, but nevertheless gracious.

Several of Jeff's cousins came by with covered dishes. Lil and Jenna busied themselves in the kitchen, arranging a buffet supper while trusting Joanna to Rita. John and Ruth Shaw arrived, followed by the Jordans. Desiree Jordan asked about Chris.

"I think she's in her room. I know she's exhausted," said Jo, "Why don't you call her tomorrow? She'd like that."

Brandon Penny and his parents drove over from Clayton. Brandon glanced around for Chris, but not seeing her, returned to the living room and visited with Larry Wayne and Rod Rollins, who had flown in from Texas. Seeing Jenna, Brandon rose and attempted to inquire about Chris, but was met by steely silence and a deadly squint. Jenna turned and walked briskly back to the kitchen, ignoring him completely. He shrugged and returned to the other room.

"There must have been two hundred people at the service. I didn't know half of them," Rita whispered to Joanna in the kitchen. "Who in God's name was the wacky doll in the ridiculous widow garb?"

"That was Claudia. Jenna's mother. You saw her at the wedding," Joanna replied in a monotone. "She was always a bit unpredictable."

"I'll say!" Rita interjected. "She left after the service in some little silver car and followed us to the graveside. But I never saw her get out. But, then again, her skirt was so short, she probably couldn't have got out of her car without showing the world ... "

"I need to go out on the porch for some air," Jo interrupted, her voice weary. "I'll be all right."

She pushed the screen doors open and stepped outside. Rod Rollins joined her immediately and protectively guided her to the porch swing, where he sat down beside her. Rita looked through the door, checking on her friend. When Jo returned, Rita was curious.

"Are you okay? I saw you talking with that dark-haired guy on the porch, mid-thirties, starched jeans, sport coat."

"Um, that's Rod Rollins, a horse friend," Jo mumbled an answer. "He's a trainer from Texas. It was good of him to come. He said he was moving back to Missouri and offered to help out, if I needed him."

"You better think about it, honey," Rita advised. "You can't run this business by yourself."

Finally, the visitors thinned out. Finally, Jeff's mother and her husband left in their rental car for the airport. Lil sank into a large chair and thankfully watched them go. No one seemed to notice, Chris had disappeared.

***

She had changed her clothes and slipped through the woods and down the bluff's old road, walking all the way through town and back to the cemetery. Exhausted from two grim days and two sleepless nights, she sat in a semi-conscious state and watched the gloomy rays of the day's last light play with the shadowy tombstones. Later, the street lights in town blinked on. The dusky sky above the swaying treetops turned dark, but still, she couldn't leave.

A cold, misting rain began to fall gently on the freshly turned earth and dampened the mounds of floral arrangements. In blue jeans and barn coat, she sat on the grass. Strands of wet hair stuck to her face as she compulsively crumbled bits of dirt between her thumb and index finger.

A voice behind her broke the silence.

"What's a nice girl like you doing in a place like this?"

She looked up through red-rimmed eyes and was amazed to see Gabriel Judd. He hunkered down beside her, picked up a piece of dirt and let it sift through his fingers, watching it fall.

"You don't have to say goodbye to him, you know. I know it must seem pretty final to you right now," he spoke with experience. "But, your dad will be with you for the rest of your life."

She choked in a tearful breath at these words and put her hands to her face, leaving a smear of mud there. In an unseemly move that surprised her, he placed one lean, strong arm around her and drew her close. The deep-pitched resonance of his voice was warm, reassuring. She hesitated and gingerly leaned against his body with a newfound trust. An unanticipated serenity flooded over her, quieting and smoothing the frayed edges of her grief.

"I just can't deal with this," she whispered, her voice muffled against his faded jean jacket. "I don't even know how to begin."

"I know. It's a damnable deal." He pulled her gently away from the grave and walked her to his truck. He opened the door and she climbed inside.

Gabe sat quietly behind the wheel for a minute, listening to the sound of the light rain on the roof of the pickup.

"Charlie's brother came by and told me. I went by your house and your uncle said you were off somewhere, he didn't know where, but he figured you wanted to be alone. I sorta knew where you'd be."

She leaned her head back and sighed.

"Why are you doing this?" she finally asked.

"I don't know, maybe 'cause I wish somebody had done it for me. Somebody. Anybody." He answered honestly, turning the key in the ignition. She turned away from him and stared out the window, watching a large raindrop trying to chart its course down the glass.

"I know you must really hate me," she said, unable to look at him.

"I don't hate you, but there ain't no doubt in my mind you're big trouble." He gripped the steering wheel with both hands and stared ahead. *Why was he doing this?*

"I don't want to go home." Her words were barely discernible.

Agreeably, he turned off and drove out to the highway, heading east. His silence was not at all uncomfortable. After a bit, she lay down in the seat, her head resting on his knee, caving in to an unexplained connection to him. The darkness, the rain, and the motion of the truck lulled her and she dozed. When she awoke, she realized the truck had stopped, the engine was still and Gabe was lifting her from the seat.

"Where are we?" she murmured, still half asleep.

He didn't answer, but carried her up the long stairway to his softly lit attic. Pushing the door open with his boot, he stepped inside and walked to the bed. Bending over, he released her. She lay obediently in the middle of the large, soft feather bed and let him pull off her damp barn coat and wet boots.

"Listen to me," he whispered as he carefully tucked a quilt around her. "If any bad thoughts or feelings come at you, make them go away. Think, feel, hear nothing. When you get real close to an awful thought, don't go head on with it, just back off nice and easy, and get away from it."

He drew a chair close, leaned back in it and propped his feet up on the bottom of the bed. She willingly closed her eyes and tried to chase off her dark thoughts, desperately seeking relief from the jabbing hurt. His presence anchored her and soon she was drifting safely into complete nothingness.

Gabe sat motionless in the muted lamp light, watching her. He studied her face, her long dark eyelashes, the disheveled blonde hair in disarray on his pillow. Her lips were slightly parted, cheeks a little flushed. A slim hand clutched the quilt near her chin and he noticed the dirt under her short, trimmed fingernails. In his mind, she was graced with spirit and a spritely charm reserved for a social level of which he was not a part. He perceived her as a child of privilege, her boldness as arrogance. While that seemed repugnant to him, she captivated him. An instinctive voice inside his head flashed fervent warnings, but it was too late. He had been blindsided by a yearning that unleashed a torrent of first desire. The absolute futility of this longing stung him and made him ache.

***

Chris opened her eyes and lay very still. Her mind felt strong and clear and she studied her surroundings. As the morning sun filtered through the paned windows, the attic seemed to embrace her, and its modesty appeared friendly and almost protective. Gabe was nowhere in sight. She slid from the bed, pulled on her boots and coat and slipped down the narrow stairway to the back of the feed store. Jake's stall was empty and she instinctively caught her breath, fists clenched in apprehension.

The sound of steady hoofbeats on soft earth drew her attention to a large, graded lot behind the old building. Gabe had saddled Jake and was exercising him in small perfect circles. By the well-worn pattern in the dirt, Chris surmised this ground had seen plenty of these circles. Unseen, she leaned against the concrete block wall and watched.

The horse's fluid movement and effortless stride hypnotized her. Gabe, sitting easy in the old saddle, barely moved as the horse dropped into a slow-legged lope. Gabe's shoulders were motionless; both hands on the reins low and relaxed. The only cues she could see were from the pressure of his long legs. His hands never seemed to change position. She moved away from the building, seeking a full view. Her sudden appearance provoked an abrupt reaction from the black horse. He threw his head up and jumped sideways several feet, only to be swiftly booted back into position by his rider. Chris watched intently as Gabe's hands steadied the horse and with a heel, thumped his shoulder with a hard jab.

"You surprised him," Gabe called, never taking his eyes off the horse. Several minutes later, he reined to a halt, backed the horse and stopped. After sitting quietly for a moment, he dismounted and led the horse toward Chris. Jake acknowledged her with a low nicker.

"You know that's a bad habit. Him squawking every time he sees you," Gabe grumbled.

"I know. Dad says so, too." She bit her lip.

"Feelin' okay this morning?" he said, adjusting a stirrup. She started to answer then realized with a shock, he was shortening the stirrups … for her. When he finished, he handed her the reins.

"Need a leg up?" She declined and swung up into his saddle easily, blood pounding in her head.

"Easy with the hands, use your legs, not your heels," he instructed. "If he tries to play with you, you're gonna have to … "

"I know, let 'em know who's the boss," she finished it for him, remembering old lessons. She turned Jake and headed back to the soft dirt, her heart racing. She walked him in circles, moving her body to control him, guide him. He was nervous, but responsive. When she felt confident, she moved him into a jog trot. Suddenly, his huge body shot sideways without a warning and he bolted. Chris reacted, snatching his head with the reins and doubling his head back toward her knee. She thumped his shoulder hard with her outside bootheel and drove him into a small circle. After a few minutes she released his head, straightened out and asked for the jog again. Jake, ears up, body relaxed, took the first step and then every muscle coiled in a single instant and he exploded forward again. Chris was nearly unseated.

Feet out of the stirrups, she grabbed up the reins and doubled him to the left. Instead of responding by giving his head and slowing down, he began to plunge sideways. She was amazed at his strength and how hard it was to hold his head. In seconds, the plunging turned into a full crow hop and Chris, having lost her stirrups, was airborne.

As she hit the dirt, Jake stopped and trotted over to Gabe, snorting. Gabe checked the snaffle bit and without taking the time to adjust the stirrups, swung onto his back and backed him halfway across the lot. Chris was up, dusting herself off and frowning. Gabe was certain, with no small sense of satisfaction, she would be deeply embarrassed. He underestimated her.

"Get off there and let me back on!" she growled, "I'm not going to put up with this bullshit from that oversized sonofabitch!"

He ignored her, but found himself surprised at her nerve. Still, he refused to let her back in the saddle and instead, for the next half hour, she was forced to endure watching Gabe work the horse, his boots dangling over the saddle a full eight inches below the stirrup. Jake performed like a straight A student, never offering a sign of token misbehavior. Chris found a seat on an old sawhorse and perched, watching.

"Damn him," she muttered to herself. "Damn them both."

As he unsaddled the black horse and put him away, he quizzed her.

"Okay, what'd you do wrong? Have you figured it out yet?"

"The only thing I did wrong was not being ready when he cut up the second time. My feet were out of the stirrups." She put her hands on her hips and leaned her chin in, staring at him with lower lip slightly pursed.

"Nope," he said. "You'll never be able to ride this horse until you figure out what you did, because you did something he just can't tolerate." Gabe slung the saddle over the sawhorse and hung the headstall up. "It sets him off every time. He goes crazy when you do it."

"What? Do what? I didn't do anything and you know it! Tell me."

"Nope. I ain't telling you anything. You're supposed to know all there is to know about this horse." He stood and looked at her.

"I do. I know him like a book!"

"He's an orphan, right? Well, it should come as no surprise then, that he has some strange ways. You just found out about one of them. You got a long way to go, as far as figuring this horse out. And he's got some major secrets."

"He has no secrets from me, I raised him."

"That was a lifetime ago for him." Gabe was genuinely serious.

She looked at him, stunned, trying to figure out if he was leveling with her about Jake. *Was this some kind of ruse?* She studied his face. He was deadly earnest and his harsh expression showed none of the tenderness she had found there last night.

"I'd like for you to take me home," she finally spoke.

CHAPTER TWENTY-SIX

Ten days after the funeral, Ken sat in his office and dismally sifted through his notes on the Day murder. Efforts to locate Ray Slankard had failed so far and the evidence collected in the barn was scant. All Thompson had was a ballistics report and no weapon. The investigation on the case was going nowhere. Tuesday morning, however, he got a recorded message giving it new life.

Detective Tom Barnett's dogged persistence paid off. The message on the chief's phone was simple.

"Got a make and a plate on a car sighted near the Day farm. I'll follow up and report in."

A truck driver making a routine propane delivery had noticed the car frequently parked near the Day farm in the past months. The driver gave as much information as he could recall to the detective.

"I saw it there twice. Once in the spring, but I never paid attention. But I saw him again in mid-June," the driver recalled. "The guy was kinda heavy, longish hair. It was about sundown, but I could see him. He was standing by the car, smoking. He musta known I saw him, 'cause he got in the car and left. That made me a little suspicious, so I wrote down the make of the car. He drove right by me, kinda duckin' down, so I also wrote down the license. I don't know why, but I thought he might be meeting somebody way out there in the sticks, for a drug deal or something."

Barnett had been amazed. He had worked for years in St. Louis, where people saw nothing, heard nothing. This, to him, was thunderous. A routine check of the plates told Barnett the car was registered to a man named Huey Bates, last known address Warrensburg, Missouri. The plates were expired. Within hours, Barnett had a report for the chief.

"Age 41, white, single. Wanted for armed robbery in Clinton County, hasn't been seen in months," Barnett briefed Ken Thompson. "Used to live in a double wide near Warrensburg, but left seven months ago owing the landlord money. Has a brother, Duane, in Camdenton. The brother's wife says he left her, says she doesn't know where he is. One previous for the brother, an old poaching charge."

"Poaching! God! She say anything about the Bates brothers having anything to do with horses?" Thompson asked. Barnett's style was thorough and Ken knew he'd have an answer.

"No." Barnett flipped through his notes. "They grew up down around Gainesville, parents deceased. No other family."

"Wife have any photos of the brothers?" Ken picked up the phone to contact the state police as Barnett nodded.

"I'll drive down and get the pictures myself," the detective offered. "I want to question her more. She might be lyin' her ass off, with the s.o.b sitting right there."

The wife of Duane Bates was in her mid-forties, with badly bleached hair and a hollow face. She shared a small run-down house at the edge of town with a bug-eyed elderly poodle named Pootsie. She had been married for seven years to Duane, during which time she often saw his brother, Huey. It was obvious to Barnett she harbored a bitterness toward her estranged husband and a thorough dislike for her brother-in-law.

"I ain't seen Duane since spring," she declared simply, handing the detective several photographs. "The loser! I hope I nivver see him again. If I could afford it, I'd divorce 'em. I make a little money waitressin', but he never made shit. We was always broke. Him and Huey did all kinds of crummy jobs, like trash haulin', cleanin' up construction sites and such. It don't surprise me they're in trouble."

"What about the car? Huey's car?" Barnett asked.

"Some woman he ran 'round with bought it for him a couple years ago. They was gonna get married, but she got smart and bailed." Mrs. Bates smiled. She liked Barnett. "I don't know what happened to her, but I think he's still got the car. Wanna cup of coffee?"

"No thanks, ma'am. Did Duane have any guns around the house?" He continued to quiz her.

"Sure, several, but I don't know too much about guns. He and Huey both liked to hunt. And they had a couple handguns, too. I don't know what kind. I don't even know where they got 'em. Are you sure you don't want a cup of hot coffee? I just made some."

"Thanks, Mrs. Bates, but I've got to go." He gave her a friendly nod. "But I'll take a rain check on that coffee. I really appreciate the photos." He handed her his business card. "If you hear anything from them, you'll let me know, won't you?"

She grinned and he grasped her hand, holding it just a little longer than necessary, having had much past success with women like her with this parting gesture.

"I would like you to do something for me. I'd appreciate if you could make me a little list of some of the jobs Huey and Duane have done in the past year. Just think on it a bit and jot them down." He smiled and she readily agreed.

"Oh, by the way, does your husband or his brother happen to have a friend or know anyone named Ray Slankard?" He pretended it to be an afterthought.

"Ray?" She tipped her head and fluttered her eyes. "No. Nobody named Ray I know of."

He invented a drawl. "Well, just askin'. Thanks anyway, ma'am." He drove off, confident he had given her plenty of reasons to call.

The break in the case filled Ken Thompson with fresh resolution. He called Frank immediately and they met at the town cafe the next morning. Frank, with the strain evident on his face, was waiting at a small booth in the corner when the chief arrived. Ken sat down and called an order for pie and coffee to the waitress.

"How's the family, Frank?" He opened the conversation and offered his old friend a release.

"Joanna's a mess, so Weston and Jenna have moved back to the farm for a while." Frank turned his coffee cup over to be filled. "Hell, Ken, she doesn't know what she's gonna do. The whole operation revolved around Jeff and the stud."

"Yeah, I know. How's Chris handling this?" Ken had a special affection for the girl. She was bright and not easily derailed. The chief could see why Jeff had adored her.

"The first week, well, I didn't think she was gonna make it. Did you know Gabe Judd came up here and found her at the cemetery the night of the funeral? Let her ride Jake the next morning. I can't figure the poor old kid doing that."

"It's not surprising. Sheriff Edwards tells me Gabe lost his mother when he was sixteen or so. Suicide," said Ken, "so I checked up on it. She jumped into the river. They found her body about a week or so later and not too long after that, the little rented place where they lived caught on fire and everything burned."

Frank rocked back in the chair, putting the pieces together.

"You know, I sort of knew Cynthia Judd. I mean, I was acquainted with her work. She was a decent trainer. In fact, she trained Jenna's bay mare. I recall she had a boy, but I never knew what happened to him."

"Edwards' brother gave him a place to live and a job," Ken filled in the gap. "Of course, you know that's where he lives now and keeps the horse there."

"Well, we sent the mane hair off for a DNA test, so we should hear about that soon. I figure we'll get the colt back," said Frank. "You know, we sure do feel sorry for the boy. There's just no good end to a thing like this."

"Fate can be a ruthless thing," Ken said as he reached inside his coat for an envelope. He shoved the photos of the Bates brothers toward Frank, spreading them out on the table.

"Ever see either one of these guys?"

The waitress topped off the coffee.

"Nope. Can't say I ever saw either one. Who are they?" Frank folded his arms on the table and leaned forward, studying the photos. Ken reported Barnett's findings in detail.

"Of course, we're not sure about the one on the left. That's Duane," Ken explained, "but the car is registered to Huey, so we figure he was involved. The propane truck driver described the suspect as heavy with long scraggly hair. Looks like a match to me."

"Why in the name of God would these two Ozark yahoos want to kill the stallion?"

"Could be they were hired to do it. We'll turn up more information on them soon." Ken waved his fork emphatically. The seemingly cold trail had suddenly turned red hot and it gave him a great sense of satisfaction to report the progress to the family. "And then we'll put more of the pieces together. While we're talking, Frank, I'd like to ask something. Other than Ray, did Jeff have any bad deal goin' with anybody, owe anybody money, anything like that?"

"Barnett already asked me that. He asked Joanna lots of questions, too." Frank rubbed his forehead. "But I can't say Jeff had any problems with anybody. Nothing that would make somebody do what they did. Hell, there just ain't no reason for it."

The chief finished his pie and carefully tucked the photos inside his jacket. "I'll be in touch." He stood to leave.

"What's the next step here, Ken? What's gonna happen?"

"We'll be trying to establish some connection to Ray Slankard. Right now, he's the only one we know of with a motive." Ken clapped Frank on the shoulder and turned to leave. "And of course, we are doing everything we can to find him. It's just a matter of time. He'll turn up somewhere."

Ken left the cafe and drove slowly down Waterson Street. Ray's brother, Vernie, had lived in New Winston for years and while he had been questioned relentlessly since the murder, he claimed to know nothing about his brother's whereabouts. The chief picked up the cell phone and rang his wife.

"I'll be home in a bit. I'm going by Vernie Slankard's again. I got a feeling Ray knew these Bates brothers. Just a hunch, you know?"

He turned in the short driveway and approached the shabby house. It once had a screened-in porch but the screens had been torn away. Vernie met him on the steps with an anxious frown.

"My brother called me this morning. He said he knew the cops was after him and he wouldn't tell me where he was calling from." Clearly agitated, Vernie scratched his unshaven jaw. "If he don't want to be found, you ain't gonna find him, I'll tell you that right now. And I've told you, he didn't know anybody named Bates."

"How did he know the cops was after him? Is he psychic?"

"I don't know how he knew, he didn't say. That's all he said, and hung up." Vernie didn't like talking to the law and he didn't like his neighbors seeing a lawman at his house. "Hell, he probably saw it on the news and figured he was a prime suspect."

"He is, Vernie. What kind of jobs did your brother do last year, aside from working for Jeff Day and the Shaws?" Ken was looking for a thread.

"I don't know. Just jobs. After he got fired from the Day place, he worked on a roofin' crew somewhere. And he worked for a guy doin' some construction, for cash, I think."

Ken Thompson scribbled it all down in his notebook.

CHAPTER TWENTY-SEVEN

The Genesis Ranch near Pilot Point was a horseman's dream, but Rod Rollins' days in Texas were coming to an end. His employer had indulged in a love of quarter horses for years and invested no small amount of money in developing some fine colts. But his illness had weakened him and if he were to survive it, he must give up the ranch and absolve himself of the taxing job of running a thousand-acre operation. The management of the ranch would be passed on to his nephew, who would continue to raise cattle, but had no interest in a horse program.

Rod had mixed feelings about leaving the ranch, but going home to Missouri seemed somehow reassuring to him. He was gratified for the opportunity to know John Wyatt and campaign the Genesis horses, but an endless calendar of horse shows had exhausted him. He welcomed a break from it. Also, he knew the dissolution of the Genesis was the right move for Wyatt. A long winter of chemotherapy and radiation had left the ranch owner pallid and weak.

When Larry Wayne called with the Jeff Day-Invincible shocker, Rod hung up the phone and sat down in a stupor. He'd told Larry he would join him to fly back to Missouri for the funeral. But Rod wasn't thinking about paying respects to Jeff. He barely knew him. His concern was for Joanna Day and her impish, pretty daughter. Sitting there in the big chair in the small office at the ranch, Rod knew somehow, the probable conclusion of Genesis and the tragic end of Jeff Day's life were connected. The call from Larry had provided another piece to the puzzle that was his future. The Missouri River Valley was calling him home. He leaned back in the leather chair, stretched out both legs and thought about it.

***

After the funeral, Rod and Larry boarded the plane to return to Texas. Larry was silent during most of the flight, and Rod knew he was dealing with the appalling murder of his friend and the senseless death of the stallion. They parted in Fort Worth and Rod drove back to the ranch. He couldn't erase the image of Joanna and her family at the graveside. His brief glimpse of Chris at the funeral had amazed him. The theft of her horse and death of her father had robbed the girl of her trademark vitality and left her gaunt and wasted. But he was most preoccupied with Joanna. She was an exceptionally compelling woman and he had always admired her. Her face, ashen and beautiful in grief, was a vision he couldn't forget.

Two weeks after arriving home, he picked up the phone and called her. It was late and she was surprised, but seemed glad to hear his voice.

"Hey. It's Rod. I was serious about what I said about helping out. Things here at the ranch should be taken care of by the end of the month and if you need me ... "

"I thought about it after you left and the truth is, I'd like to discuss it with you more." She didn't hesitate. "I haven't mentioned it to Chris or Wes, but I know we can't handle this alone. I'm not making very good decisions right now."

"Do you think you want to keep up the breeding operation?" he asked, sensing her need to talk.

"I'm not sure what I want," she said, grateful for his concern. "I'm going to have to make some hard choices, though. Frank and Lil are getting older. My son and his wife are going to have a baby and they have their own lives. Our financial situation sucks and my paychecks aren't all that much. With Vince dead, there'll be no income there. I just don't know what to do."

"What about Chris, how is she doing?"

"Well, you know we found Jake, but that hasn't been resolved entirely." She sounded perplexed. "There seems to be some problem with Vince's DNA record. It didn't match Jake's at all. So, we sent some hair samples from a couple of other colts and those didn't match either. We don't know what's going on."

"The DNA record didn't match?" He was incredulous. "On any of 'em? Not possible!"

"We tried to contact the lab that did the test and it seems they're no longer in business. We found out they apparently changed management a couple of years ago. After that, the lab developed an unacceptable error rate with test results and none of the livestock or horse associations would accept any more records from them." The pitch of her voice rose as she released her frustration. "And they had a ton of lawsuits against them, so they went bankrupt."

"I can't believe it!"

"I found an old letter in Jeff's desk from the quarter horse association informing him they would no longer accept results from this lab and recommending we request a kit, pull hair and resubmit it directly to them. Just to be sure."

"It's hard to imagine Jeff flaking this off!"

"I don't have an answer to that. He probably just thought, 'piss on it.' I know we never had Vince retested."

"Damn! Well, there's sure no way to get another test done on him now," he said, fully realizing the dilemma.

She found it curiously easy to confide in him.

"It's a screwed up mess. Chris isn't about to give up, but truthfully, I don't know if we can get Jake back. I don't know what she's going to do, I just know I can't deal with it anymore. I've got too many other things on my mind."

"Do you think you might take the stud's insurance payoff and buy another breeding stallion?"

"Well, the problem is, all of our mares were selected to cross back on Invincible. The whole direction of where we were going has hit a brick wall." She sighed and then was silent for a moment. "Jeff's goals weren't really my goals. I need to think about what I want to do with all these horses."

"Maybe you need to take stock of what you've got and get the operation to a size you can manage," he suggested.

"Yeah. I think you're right. I've got two-year-olds that Jeff's been riding and yearlings in the pasture and babies that need to be weaned, and … God, all those brood mares. Most of ours are bred, but I had to send a lot of customer mares home."

"I can finish the two-year-olds and if you want to keep showing, I can do that, too," he found himself saying. "Don't worry about paying me. If you'll give me a place to stay and let me train some outside horses out of your barn, we can work through this. Mr. Wyatt gave me my choice of our show string, so I'll be bringing one with me."

"Rod, I don't know what to say, I … " she drew a long breath.

"If you can hang in there, I can finish up my business here at the ranch and be in Missouri by the middle of May."

To Joanna's relief, Rod Rollins was already taking control.

***

Several days later, Joanna called a family meeting.

"I'm laying it on the line," she said flatly. "I'm going to have to make some changes around here and I need to know everyone will support me."

Chris was mildly amazed at the authority in her mother's voice. "What kind of changes?" she said. "Are we going to have to sell the place?" This was now her worst fear.

"I'm not sure, but we're going to have to get some horses ready to sell. Whether or not we can keep this operation going depends on how much money we can make."

Joanna was anticipating this question from Chris and was ready with her best answer.

"As you know, Rod is leaving the Genesis Ranch. What I want to tell you is that he's coming here to help us out." She glanced around at her family's surprised faces. "I've already talked to him and he'll be here in a few weeks. We can give him the spare room and he can train out of our barn."

Chris was silent, thoughtful. Maybe Rod could come up with a way to get Jake back. Frank and Lil both nodded approvingly. Wes, however, rose and began to pace the room.

"I don't even know this guy! I do know he's a western pleasure trainer and probably doesn't know squat about a breeding operation."

"What breeding operation?" Joanna looked at him in disbelief. "Our stud is dead! And I've made up my mind. We're going to sell the brood mares in the fall and maybe that will give us enough money to go on. If we're lucky, we can keep a few horses to show."

Frank spoke up. "Wes. Listen to your mother. She's right. Those mares need to be bred back in the spring, and we can't afford to send them all to an outside stud. Most of them are in foal now and they ought to sell, even this time of year."

"I have some money in the bank," Jenna spoke up softly. "I have the money that Vic left me. And after I have the baby, I'll get a job teaching school and … "

Joanna rose and embraced her daughter-in-law. "You and Wes have to think of yourselves and your family. I appreciate the offer, Jenna, but I've made up my mind. You can't be bound to someone else's dream."

Jo's last statement struck Chris like a thunderbolt. She stood up and walked to the front porch where she sat alone on the swing. *Someone else's dream. Jeff Day's dream.* She understood with a heavy sense of disappointment her family had accepted the end of it. In her heart, she knew that dream was very much alive and that it had become her own. But she realized she was all alone there.

CHAPTER TWENTY-EIGHT

"Explain to me again about this DNA thing," Charlie questioned his brother as Edith passed the roast beef around the table. "Does this mean they can't prove it's their horse?"

"Here's what happened, as I understand it. Joanna Day got a new kit from the quarter horse association, and they took Jake's hair and sent it off. The association got the DNA test back and tried to match it to the stud's genotype, but it didn't match," Van Edwards reported.

"So it's all a mistake? Gabe's horse is not the Days' young stud?" Edith was hopeful.

"Oh, I think he's the Days' horse, all right," Van said as he reached for the salt. "But Ken Thompson told me they sent hair samples from two other Invincible colts and those didn't match either. So it's pretty apparent there's something wrong somewhere. I did some further checking on this deal and I found out this quarter horse association uses hair analysis now. When Jeff Day's stud was tested several years ago for a DNA record, they used blood."

Charlie's brother smoothed butter on his hot roll and continued. "So the Days' vet sent the blood off to an independent lab. Apparently, this lab used to be approved by the quarter horse association but failed to meet their standards and promptly got the boot. This lab either mislabeled the vial of blood or entered the information on the horse into the lab's computer wrong. Whatever. At any rate, the DNA record submitted by the lab was not that of the Days' stallion."

"There had never been any reason to check it, so nobody caught it," Gabe said, adding the details.

"So, are you telling me that with the stud and the black's mother both dead, Chris Day has no way to correct this situation?" Edith clasped her hands with relief.

"Seems to be the case. There's no legitimate parentage verification, which is what Christine Day needs to legally get her horse back."

Edith was beaming. "Thank the Lord!"

"Did the Day girl lose her mind when the DNA thing didn't go through?" Van said. While the news was good for Gabe, Edwards was genuinely concerned for Chris.

"Yeah, you might describe it like that," Gabe answered. "I felt sorry for her. But you don't know Chris. She still comes down and rides him every Saturday. With my luck, I'll have to share my horse with her for the rest of my life."

"Do you think she would have done the same for you?" Edith asked.

Gabe thought about it. "Funny thing," he said. "I have a feeling she would have. She's not like most uptown girls."

"How many uptown girls have you known, Gabe?" The sheriff laughed out loud and tossed him a hot roll. "Well, the black is a fine horse. Too bad you'll never be able to paper him. I guess he's worth a lot of money."

"No matter to me," Gabe replied.

"You know, you oughta go ahead and cut him, no need him bein' a stallion, then." Van said, looking across the table at Gabe.

"I might do that if I have to," Gabe said, "but he doesn't act like a stud. I think when he was turned out with those old mares before I bought him, they taught him some manners."

Charlie chuckled at this. "They no doubt worked him over pretty good. Hell, he was only a yearling. He probably went through some hell with them old biddies." He paused, fork in mid-air, and turned to his brother. "Remember that old coot down the road from us when we was growing up? His young stud ran out in the pasture with a half-dozen old hides. Never made a peep unless he was on a date. He knew his place in the pecking order!"

***

For weeks, the Day farmhouse had endured the despair of a family in mourning and patiently played the role of a gloomy abode. On the day of Rod's scheduled arrival, Chris awoke with a craving to exorcise this melancholy pall. She had spent all morning opening windows and placing fresh flowers in several of the rooms. Downstairs in the kitchen, Jenna busied herself trying to figure out what goes in chicken salad besides the chicken.

The upper level of the farmhouse was a pleasant blend of painted wainscoting and traditional print wallpaper. A long room at the top of the landing provided access to four bedrooms, the upstairs bath and a spare room. Chris finished making the bed in the spare room, surveyed the surroundings and was pleased. The room was rich with the character of angled ceilings and large sun-washed windows. She was sure Rod would find it comfortable.

At noon, his one-ton Dodge Ram and shiny aluminum trailer pulled into the drive and parked beside the barn. *How would she greet him? A handshake, a touch on his arm?* He didn't give her the opportunity to mull over it and pulled her close for a long hug.

"I'm parked in your space," he said, smiling. He pointed to the red sign on the barn that read "Christine's parking."

She winced, then smiled back. "It's all right. Dad got that for me at a horse show. I'll let you off the hook this one time."

"Where's your mom?" he said, a little too soon to suit Chris. "I talked to her on the phone last night and she said she might have to work today."

"Yeah, she couldn't get off. School will be out in a week or two then she'll be home all summer," Chris explained as he walked to the back of the trailer.

"How's Jake?" he ventured.

She kicked aimlessly at the trailer tire, then spoke. "I don't care what anybody says, he's mine and will always be mine. Gabe knows it. I know it. I'll get him back someday. Somehow."

He put a sympathetic arm around her.

"Remember that poor little pisser I rode last year at Columbia?" He changed the subject with a bright smile. "I think we got his leg problems worked out and when Mr. Wyatt gave me my choice of horses, I picked him." He unloaded the sorrel gelding and walked him in circles.

"It's been a long ride and he doesn't haul real good. But it looks like he's going to be okay." Rod handed the lead rope to Chris as he closed up the back of the trailer. "He may never amount to much, but I like him."

Rod was impressed with the barn and pleased Chris had prepared a stall for his gelding.

"What do you call him?" she said as Rod put the horse up and they watched him take a long drink of fresh water.

"Mister Cool, for short," he replied. "After a bit, we can turn him out to exercise. You can ride him any time you want. He's nice to ride."

They were interrupted by a loud clanging sound. Chris smiled at Rod's questioning expression.

"That's Jenna, calling us for lunch. We've got one of those iron triangle things hanging on the porch, and Mom and Jenna bang on it to call us up from the barn." She laughed. "You'll like Jenna. She and Wes have been staying with us, but my brother's got a lot of work in Kansas City so they're going back to the apartment tomorrow."

Rod adapted quickly to the routine at the Days' and within a week demonstrated the reason behind his success. He began riding a pair of two-year-olds started under saddle by Jeff. One was a chestnut gelding and the other a black filly.

Chris noted immediately that Rod's technique was different than her father's. Rod showed immeasurable patience and his lessons were quiet and productive. Rod never displayed temper and was seldom perturbed at coltish mistakes. He disciplined a young horse only when it was required.

"My primary goal is to get him to relax," he told Chris as he saddled the chestnut gelding. "And make him understand this is no big deal. A pleasure horse has to relax. We don't need to hurry along and give him so much to think about that he gets tense."

Unlike Jeff, who was forced to live an unorganized balancing act mixing his job with his barn duties, Rod was a man committed to precise routine. He came downstairs at the same time every morning, adhered to the same schedule every day and went to bed each night at the same exact time. Joanna was amused, and arranged meals around his schedule. Somehow, the stability of his personality was heartening. His presence provided a much-needed relief for her. She surprised everyone and began to take a vigorous interest in the horses again.

Within a month, the two-year-olds looked very sharp and a couple from Springfield bought them both, agreeing to leave them with Rod for training through August. Joanna deposited the checks ecstatically. The chestnut gelding brought a good price, and black filly had brought twice what Jo anticipated.

Late one evening, Chris sat in her room, curled up on the window seat of her alcove, writing a note to Jenna. Through the open window, she noticed shafts of light illuminating the outdoor arena and pulling the curtain back, she saw Joanna riding alone. She strained to see the horse and in amazement, realized Jo was riding Cherry. In the shadows, she saw a lone figure leaning on the rail watching. It was Rod.

***

Chris sifted through the bedding with a picking rake, and tossed the filth in the manure cart. Keeping the stalls clean required daily picking. Once a week, she stripped each stall down to its base, removing all of the used bedding and replacing it with fresh, clean shavings. It was a dirty, miserable job during the hot summer, and as perpetual and time-consuming as laundry.

In warm months, she cleaned stalls as soon as she had fed the horses, making the most of the cooler morning air. After the evening feeding, she picked them again, as she could not bear seeing a horse standing in a fly-infested stall, manure stains on his side from lying in its own waste. Stall cleaning was a wretched but necessary chore, and Chris went about it in a mindless, methodical fashion.

She wheeled the last tub of manure and dirty shavings out of the barn, wrestled the large container out of its wheeled frame and dumped it into the bed of the manure spreader. The wagon was full to the brim and would have to be emptied before she could tackle any more stalls. She climbed aboard the old tractor, coaxed the engine and it fired up. Easing it into gear, she wheeled the gray and blue tractor toward the lane leading to an open field, where she usually released the manure, spreading it over the grassy ground. Gripping the large steering wheel, tractor crunching through the gravel, she turned instead toward the orchard. Jolting over the bumpy turf, she approached the level corner where the wooden cross served as a memorial to Vince.

Jeff's everyday spurs hung on the cross by their old leather straps like sacred amulets. Tugging the gearshift into neutral, she pulled on the brake, slipped out of the seat and knelt. She lifted the spurs from the cross, held them to her breast. The sharp jab of pain she wanted and needed to feel was instead, a dull ache. This surprised and disappointed her.

"I'm standin' on the corner in Winslow, Arizona ... " she began to sing softly, tormenting herself until the tears came.

***

The following morning, she drove to Prairie Rock. It had been a week since she had seen Jake and she felt an inexplicable need to be with Gabe. He was tending the store when she arrived. A young woman in short shorts, sleeveless knit pullover and sandals leaned against the counter, talking to him. Inspecting the orange streaks of the girl's bottled tan, Chris noticed she had a tattoo around her ankle that looked like a barbed wire ankle bracelet. Gabe glanced at Chris as she walked in, but continued the private conversation with the girl. Charlie emerged from the back room and greeted Chris.

"Who's she?" Chris said. She was surprised to hear a trace of jealousy in her own voice. The sight of Gabe apparently enjoying the flirtatious conversation annoyed her.

"Just a girl who comes by here to see Gabe. She usually picks up some feed for her dad every week."

Charlie was unconsciously comparing Chris, in jeans and ball cap, to the attractive young lady whispering to Gabe. The storekeeper smiled, knowing without a doubt, which one Gabe would prefer. The girl picked up her little purse and made a cute goodbye gesture with just a wiggle of her finger, murmured something about Saturday night, then backed seductively out the door.

After the girl had gone, Gabe finally spoke to Chris.

"I guess you'd be wanting to ride."

"Go ahead, we're not busy, take a break," Charlie said. He walked to the cash register and waved them out the back door.

"Are you going out with that girl?" Chris blurted out before she could think.

"Maybe. What's it to you?" Gabe's face broke into a mocking smile.

"Nothing. I just wondered if she was your girlfriend." Chris was not good at being tricky, and she was confused by the reaction that had jabbed her when the girl left.

"Don't jerk me around," he said, walking toward the concrete building where Jake was stalled. "I know you don't care who I go out with."

Chris was silent as they led Jake out and saddled him.

"What's her name?" She couldn't help herself. She had to know more.

"Who? Tamara?" Gabe laughed out loud. "Divorced. Got a kid. Butterfly tattoo on her shoulder."

This startled Chris and the sudden pouty look on her flushed face provoked a reaction from Gabe.

"I know what you're thinking," he said, "but she's a nice girl. Don't look down on her just because she doesn't come from a hot shot family like yours."

"What!" She placed her hands on her hips and walked a small circle. "We are not hot shots and I don't know why you keep harping on that. Anyway, I didn't come down here to supervise your Saturday nights. I came as a friend."

"Don't even start! The only reason you come to see me is standing right here with this saddle on."

"That's not entirely true. I really came today to talk to you," she spoke truthfully. "I sort of needed to talk."

"What now? More problems? I swear, Chris, you are a pain." His pretended indifference was his only defense against the spell this girl was working on him. She stood with a demanding expression on her pretty face, in faded jeans with shredded knees, George Strait concert tee shirt three sizes too big and a pair of $300 boots. He was never quite sure if he wanted to kiss her or insult her.

"You know I told you about the trainer who was coming from Texas?" She continued to talk as he buckled splint boots on the front legs of the horse. "Well, he's here."

"And I suppose he wants to take the black colt and show him," Gabe said, not giving her a chance to talk. "Will you ever give up? You can come down and see him all you want, but you ain't gettin' him away from me."

"That's not what I was going to say!" She was getting vexed at him. "I'm really glad Rod came, but it's sort of like he's taking Dad's place. My dad's only been dead two months and Mom's just getting on with her life like it didn't happen."

"What do you want her to do, grieve forever? Don't sentence her to that, it's not fair." He worked Jake on the longe line for a few minutes while Chris watched.

"I saw them last night in the outdoor arena," she said when he returned. "She was riding! She had Cherry out and was riding! Her butt hasn't been in the saddle for over a year."

"So? Sounds to me like that was a good thing." He looked at her and his face softened. "Hey. Your mom is looking for her old self. Trying to get back to that person who was in control before all this happened. Let her be."

Chris thought about this as Gabe swung into the saddle and headed toward the back lot. Jake was testy and unusually playful, and Gabe worked him for at least thirty minutes before he relinquished the reins to Chris.

"He's being a little studly today," he muttered. "Watch him."

She walked and trotted him for a long while before nudging him into a lope. After the first time she had ridden him, the morning after Jeff's funeral, she had learned to pay attention to his every move. He was good-natured, but was still coltish. She had learned from Gabe what she'd done wrong that had unseated her that day. The colt was uncommonly ticklish in the flank area and even the slightest pressure there could put her in the dirt again. She was careful to keep her heels down and rode with her stirrups well away from his sides.

As she loped circles, he quieted a bit and dropped his head slightly, smoothing out and moving lightly over the ground. She opened the circle and made it larger.

Gabe smiled broadly as Jake cruised effortlessly past him. *She really was a pretty good hand.*

After she finished riding, they unsaddled Jake together. As they worked silently, brushing him and picking his feet, Gabe was keenly aware he had become part of an inextricable trio out of which there was no escape. He had possession of the colt. She had the papers. Legally, it had become a standoff, but spiritually, Gabe knew the black colt belonged to both of them.

"What if I come down later next Saturday, say, sometime in the evening?" she said, recalling Tamara's last words to Gabe and trying her best to be shrewd.

"Sorry. I'm going to be busy," he forced himself to say, looking away so she could not see the amusement in his eyes.

CHAPTER TWENTY-NINE

"All Cherry needs is a tune up and I think she'll be ready to go," Rod proclaimed as he stepped from the saddle. "Why don't we take her and my gelding and we'll go over to Illinois at the end of the month. It's a pretty good show and I know I can have her ready."

"I haven't been in the show ring in a while, you know, but I'd like to go." Joanna tried to suppress the mixed rush of doubt and excitement she felt. There was nothing she'd like better than getting back into competition with Cherry. She had a lot to prove to herself. *But what would people think?* She wanted to explain her uncertainties to Rod, but could not bring herself to say anything that would make him think it was wrong for them to be seen together. She decided to wait and by the end of the month, perhaps she could think of a good excuse to stay home.

At the end of the week, Rod took a call from a couple in southern Iowa who wanted to bring a pair of young pleasure horses for him to finish.

"They are started, but far from show ready. We heard you were back in Missouri and thought this might be a good opportunity for us. Can you take two more?" Whitt MacDonald liked Rod's work, but Texas had been too far to take his horses.

Rod hesitated as if checking a hectic calendar and replied, "Can you bring them down Saturday? I'll have two stalls ready. I'll need the regular stuff, health papers, etcetera."

"Fine! We'll be down about noon on Saturday," Whitt said. He was pleased. His two red roan geldings were very fashionably bred and he hoped one, if not both, would be good enough for Rod to consider campaigning.

Word spread fast that Rod had returned to the Midwest and soon he was riding six outside horses, Cherry and two more of Joanna's two-year-olds.

Wes and Jenna, spending the weekend at the farm, joined Chris and Uncle Frank at the outdoor arena to watch Rod work. It was hard for Wes to envision a stranger commandeering the barn, and he often suffered guilt pains when he thought about the future of the horse operation. But his farrier business around Kansas City had become full time, and he was committed to his role as the breadwinner for his soon-to-expand family. His marriage to Jenna and his unconditional obligation to the baby she carried were the only things in his life he had never questioned. He had mixed feelings about Rod's presence, but his newfound sense of business prevailed and Wes reluctantly told himself he must accept it. However, he wanted to see good measure from the new trainer, and was not disappointed.

"The guy's a machine," he admitted to Uncle Frank, as they observed from the rail. "You figure he's riding nine a day and each one gets an hour or so of his time, he's got a full day."

Jenna noticed a sudden stony expression in Chris' eyes as she realized Rod has passed the "Wes Test," and made a mental note to pry more out of her later when they were alone.

"He rides every day. He does his own shoeing, too. Each horse has his own damned chart!" said Frank, whose approval of Rod was not based solely on the relief it afforded his widowed niece. "After supper, he and Joanna go through the barn and mark up each chart. More feed, less feed, more hay, supplements."

After supper, Jenna found Chris in her room, kneeling on the window seat and peering through the lace curtain. She was watching Joanna walk toward the barn.

"She spends all her time at the barn now," Chris said, sensing Jenna's presence, but keeping her eyes on the barn.

"Isn't that what you want? I remember when you used to beg her to come to the barn at night," Jenna said gently.

"I know, but she doesn't go there for me!" Chris continued to watch until Joanna was out of sight. Then she turned and faced Jenna. "She's always with Rod. What's with her? Doesn't she miss Dad? Plus, she is almost ten years older than he is! I don't get it!" Chris flopped on the bed and stared at the ceiling.

Jenna had suspected a problem and already had a half-formed diagnosis of its nature. Rod's positive, even temper and sense of humor gave Joanna something Jeff had neglected. Around Jeff, Jo had been righteously dutiful. Jenna had always sensed Jo's words and very actions had been guarded to avoid his criticism. Rod had an unabashed admiration for Jo that seemed to give her confidence she had lacked for years.

"I love your mom so much, Chris. She is very special," Jenna said. She sat down on the edge of the bed. "Don't you want her to be happy? Can't you see how good she looks?"

"Yeah. But what's with that new do?" Chris moaned.

Jenna smiled approvingly. Joanna's long blonde hair was now permed and scrunched in a trendy new style that suited her. The sorrow was fading from Joanna's face and Jenna saw in its place, a new confidence. During her marriage to Jeff, she fought to keep herself trim and flat-bellied. Now, she had quit counting calories and ate chocolate when she craved it. She let laundry stack up when she didn't feel like doing housework. She was reshaping her life and rediscovering herself.

"I really don't think there's anything improper happening between Rod and Joanna. They barely know each other." Jenna was disappointed Chris failed to appreciate her mother's long suppressed self-indulgence.

"That's not entirely true. Last summer, we spent four days with him at a show in Columbia. I think he had some feelings for her then, before Dad was even dead." Chris turned her face into the pillow. "This is no new deal. He came to the funeral, you know. And that day he offered to come here and help us out. Did you know that? And then, bam! He just moves right in."

Jenna was genuinely exasperated with Chris' self-centered whining. "Stop that! What the hell is the matter with you?" She turned and was out the door.

When she found Wes, he had joined Rod on the porch. He had been waiting for an opportunity to talk to him and was anxious to discuss the murder investigation with the trainer.

"Mom says the investigation is taking a lot of time, and they can't find Ray anywhere," he began, "and that's all she'd say. Is there something I should know that she's not telling me?"

Rod sighed. "Not really. It's tough for her and she doesn't like to talk about it. She's trying to put it behind her. She's quite a woman."

"She's really into the horses again, I guess," said Wes, dropping the subject of the investigation. "That's good. When Dad was alive, she did everything for him. And of course, she was the queen of the horse show mothers. I like to see her doing it for herself now."

"She's a top-notch rider," said Rod with obvious admiration. "I'm putting together a schedule of shows for the summer. If I can talk Joanna into going with me, we'll be hitting the circuit hot and heavy in July and August."

Wes noticed that Jenna had raised one eyebrow a bit.

"What about Chris?" he asked. "Are you going to leave her home?"

"Sure, why not? She's twenty years old. She can handle things here, and she's got Frank and Lil."

***

"I think you need to talk to your sister," Jenna said to him later as they turned off the light in his old bedroom and climbed into the big bed. "She's very confused right now."

"I think she's always been a little looney," Wes yawned. "But I hear ya. She's not a little girl anymore and she don't want to give it up yet."

In the dark, his young wife smiled and spoke softly. "You mean there's a woman in her that's trying to get out, but the little girl won't let her?"

"Somethin' like that." He reached toward Jenna and drew her close. "I'll talk to her in the morning."

The next morning, Wes trailed his sister as she dumped feed to each horse. Jenna followed behind, tossing each a flake of hay.

"Do you see Jake often?" Wes asked.

"As much as I can," Chris said, suddenly bright. "I usually go over to Gabe's on Saturdays."

"Yeah, and Mom says sometimes you don't come back 'til late," said Wes in his usual frank manner. "You got something going with that guy?"

"No," Chris said curtly, cheeks on fire. "We're just friends. I don't think I'm his type."

"Hah!" Wes hooted at that. "Not his type? Good, I'm glad to hear it. I was worried there for a minute. My advice is to stay friends with him. He ain't got a pot to piss in. You can do better."

The old "Wes Test!" Her face darkened and she turned on him with a fury that sent Jenna ambling on down the alleyway to a safer spot.

"Damn you, Wes! You are just like Dad!" Chris screamed. "You just need to get to know Gabe!"

Wes put his hands on her shoulders and held her off, but she slugged him in the hard flat of his belly and sprinted toward the house.

He pretended to be hurt and doubled over, looking toward Jenna, who stood with mouth agape.

"Was that the little girl or the woman?" he groaned.

"The woman, I think," said Jenna, eyes wide.

"Good. I was sure she had some sort of little girl crush on Rod, but I guess her real feelings were for Gabe," muttered Wes with a wide grin.

"And there's nothing like a good squabble to help a woman make up her mind."

"You're missing the point," said his wife. "Yes, I think she has a new friendship with Gabe, and yes, she may have had a crush on Rod at first, but I think her real confusion is failing to understand Rod's relationship with your mother." Jenna caught his hand and waited for the reaction. "Rod and Joanna … "

"Bull crap! Mom couldn't have anything going with Rod. You're out of your mind," Wes pulled away from her. "Just because your mom buried Vic and moved Miguel right into the house doesn't mean my mom could do it."

"This has nothing to do with Claudia," Jenna said, remaining calm. "There is a chemistry between Rod and Joanna, and everybody knows it. Chris knows it, too. Maybe they are just good friends now, but if it grows into something more than that, I hope Chris can handle it. I hope you can, too."

Wes was silent, and she knew he was weighing his thoughts. Finally, he spoke.

"Whatever makes my mom happy, I'll support her, no matter what. As for daddy's little princess, if Mom's friendship with Rod goes any further, I guarantee the shit will be on."

CHAPTER THIRTY

Driving home from Prairie Rock, Chris watched the full moon inching its way along the horizon. It hung low, illuminating the worn asphalt of the old state highway and bathing the surrounding hillsides in tawny translucence. Her rides on Jake had been improving each week, but today, she took a step closer to the perfection she would need to take him into the show ring. She was brimming with the exhilaration of this ride.

She knew in three weeks, many quarter horse people would be attending a big all-breeds open show near St. Louis. It was a day of fun, barbecue contests and good prize money, luring many good riders. Anybody could enter. Although health papers were required, registration papers were not necessary. Chris calculated this would be the perfect place to challenge Brandon Penny, rumored to already be counting the jackpot pleasure winnings. She wasn't sure how she would persuade Gabe to cooperate, but the plan was firmly planted in her mind.

On Tuesday morning, she called him at the store. He was surprised, but pleased to hear her voice.

"Saturday's ride was so right! I've been thinking about something and I want to talk to you about it," she began. "What do you think about taking Jake to a big open show, just to test his wind? I really think he's good enough to win some money."

"Nah! Remember what happened the last time I showed him? It was at Victor City. Worst day of my life." He was quick to dismiss this idea. "Besides, I don't have any good gear and Charlie loaned the stock trailer to Edith's brother."

"So what?" she said. "I have a truck and trailer, and I've got the gear."

"I don't have any decent clothes." He still wasn't convinced.

"I'll ride him in the class. C'mon! Let's do it!"

He hesitated for a second, inclined to blow it off, but the thought of spending the whole day with Chris Day made him smile. It might be interesting. He agreed to think about it.

That afternoon, she loaded her show saddle in the front seat of her truck, tack box in the back and returned to Prairie Rock. She went directly to Jake's stall in back of the store and began to survey the job at hand. She found an electrical outlet, plugged in her clippers and went to work. He had been clipped numerous times as a baby and stood obediently as she trimmed his fetlocks, bridle path, face and ears. She brushed his tail and after spraying it with conditioner, she braided and stuffed it in a long sock, securing it below the tailbone. Next, she retrieved her thinning scissors and began to shape his long mane. When she finished, it was very short and neat, as style dictated. She was so intent on her work, she failed to hear Gabe approach.

"I just noticed your truck – damn! He sure cleans up good!" He stared at Jake.

"What do you think?" she said, heading for her truck. "Don't you think he's good enough to take on some competition?"

She hoisted the heavy saddle and show pad out of her truck and lugged it back to the stall.

"Wait until you see how this looks on him."

It didn't take much to convince him. By the time she left, her plan was in place. They were going to the show.

***

"Sunny and hot today, high near 98 … " crackled the voice on the truck radio. The sun burst through irregular ruptures in the shade trees, making patterns on the road as Chris pulled out on the morning of the show. Joanna watched her leave and thought how proud Jeff would have been at the way Chris had polished the truck and trailer to a gleaming finish.

Gabe sat on the back steps of the store waiting. Instead of the faded jeans and sleeveless tee shirt he normally wore, he was handsomely dressed in creased jeans, starched blue shirt and new straw Stetson. Jake, freshly bathed, was tied in the shade, legs wrapped.

"You clean up pretty good yourself," she called out as she climbed from the truck.

"Edith ironed my jeans and shirt for me," he shyly fielded the compliment, silently admiring her fitted black jeans and black and white striped sleeveless shirt. He noticed she wore makeup.

The show grounds were crowded and several people waved a greeting to Chris as they pulled in the parking lot. She scanned the lot for the Pennys' big trailer and parked on the opposite side near a row of trees, away from the other trailers.

"Maybe this will give us some shade," she said, as she maneuvered the big trailer in place. "We don't want Jake to have to stand tied in the sun all day."

She had anticipated plenty of familiar faces, but she had not planned on the response of friends and acquaintances when they saw her unload Jake.

"Does everyone here know this horse's history?" Gabe mumbled. Chris shrugged.

"Only everybody I've ever known." She retrieved a bottle of fly spray from the trailer's tack room and misted the horse's legs.

"Christine! It's so good to see you back. It was a shock to see you pull in with the trailer!" It was two women who were good friends of Joanna's. "We've missed you so much. Where's Jo?"

Chris forced a smile. "We had customers coming from Kansas, and she and Rod had to stay home."

Both women stared at the black horse tied in the shade.

"Oh, my God! Is that Jake?" One of the women exclaimed, admiring the colt. "He's all grown up!"

"We heard you found him but there was some kind of mess and you couldn't legally get him back."

"This is Gabriel Judd," Chris interrupted. "He has Jake now. But I've been riding him a lot and see him every Saturday."

"Sounds a little like joint custody!" said Jo's friend, with an optimistic smile. She and the other woman headed back to the trailer. "It's good to see you back! And it's nice to meet you, Gabriel."

Chris growled as they disappeared from sight, and Gabe laid a hand on her shoulder.

"Here's some advice you probably don't want. Lose the attitude. These people are trying to be nice."

"You're right, of course," she admitted. "Let's go longe Jake a little. He hasn't been around any other horses for a while, and he might be a little goofy."

Gabe offered to work the colt and suggested she study the show bill. "Find out when the two-year-old class is," he said.

"I'm not going to ride him in that class. This is an open show and we can ride him in whatever we want." Her words were full of intent. "And I want to take him into the jackpot western pleasure class. Okay with that?"

He hesitated, a bit confused, before muttering, "Whatever." He had learned mediocrity was not a part of Christine Day's personality. He fished the longe line out of the trailer and led Jake toward a large, open area where other riders were working their horses. Chris grabbed her purse and walked briskly toward the entry shack. As she stood in line to enter, something made her turn and watch Gabe and the stud.

She scrutinized Gabe's easy, long-strided walk, his suntanned face and strong jaw, eyes slightly squinting in the sun. Jake moved along beside him, neck arched and nostrils flared. The stallion's hair coat glistened in the hot sun and his large round eyes surveyed the scene. He was elegant, like royalty, but at the same time carried himself with the presence of an athlete. When they reached the warm up area, Gabe stood motionless for a moment, allowing the horse to think about it. In a coltish move, Jake took a half step toward Gabe and lowered his head. Gabe reached out and placed a quieting hand on the colt's withers. Chris was abruptly struck by a swell of affection that left her deeply perplexed. She couldn't discern if those feelings were for Jake or for Gabe. She memorized the sight of the two of them standing there.

She finally turned and picked up an entry blank, vexing emotions swirling inside her head like a dusty wind changing directions. She had come to this show seeking revenge on Brandon Penny. It was her intention to humiliate him in the jackpot western pleasure, challenging his rock-solid mare with an inexperienced two-year-old. This challenge, a moment she had long awaited, suddenly seemed trivial. Brandon meant nothing to her. Gabe was somehow now another matter.

She paid her entry fee and entered the jackpot class, writing in the name of the horse as simply "Jake." An hour later, she and Gabe were saddling the colt. She dragged out a large, expensive saddle pad with leather corners tooled in a basket weave pattern.

"I'll get him ready. You better dress." Gabe picked up the pad and wondered how much it had cost.

Stepping inside the trailer, Chris scanned the clothes rack for the perfect shirt. Never in her life had she wanted to look so right. She picked a white blouse, slightly padded at the shoulders, and trimmed in black ultra suede. She braided her ponytail and looped it into a neat knot. She adjusted her straw hat and touched up her makeup. Satisfied, she leaned forward and took a close look in the mirror mounted on the back of the trailer door. She marveled at the realization she was beginning to bear an unmistakable resemblance to Joanna. She quickly grabbed a pair of large silver earrings and held them to her ears. *God. I am becoming my mother*, she mumbled to herself as she put them on. Finally, with black chaps zipped and folded up at the bottom, she opened the trailer door and stepped down, posing with hands on her hips.

Gabe was slipping the headstall over Jake's ears. As he turned, she saw the centers of his hazel eyes betray amusement. It was not the reaction she hoped for and he sensed it. *Okay, so he's not impressed.* She managed a grin, dropped the seductive posturing and assumed her normal relaxed stance. A wide smile spread across his face.

"You're supposed to be speechless," she said, slapping the ends of the reins on her thigh.

"I'm just used to you in crummy old jeans and tee shirt to your knees." He was still smiling. "Hmm. I really don't know what I like best."

She pursed her pink lips and thought about this. He was a hard nut to crack.

"Pin my number on and don't stick me." She handed him the number and two safety pins. She turned her back to him, holding the reins as he fumbled with the pins.

When he boosted her into the saddle, he noticed she was wearing an old worn pair of spurs, heavy and partially rusted.

"They were Dad's," she said softly. He raised his eyes to her, questioning the use of this equipment.

"Don't worry, I won't jab him, but I gotta wear them!" She looked at him with a pleading face. "For luck."

"This ain't the time to try anything new on him," he said simply. She frowned.

"Take them off," he ordered.

"No. I gotta wear them." She began to move off, but Gabe grabbed the reins and held Jake in place. She was surprised at his stern face, but more surprised at her inclination to surrender to his wishes. She hesitated, then leaned down and unbuckled each one and handed them over. His face softened and he rested his hand lightly on her knee. Momentarily, she laid her own hand over his. He paused and then slowly withdrew it.

"Don't depend on luck to see you through this. It's all up to you and Jake," he whispered. "Go show 'em what you've got."

Their eyes met for a moment, then he stepped back and patted the horse on the rump as she moved off.

She was not in wonder that the jackpot class had so many riders. There was $500 added money, purse to go to the first five places. As she moved into the holding area, other riders had gathered and she spotted Brandon, straightening his tie and tucking his shirt in. He looked up and saw her, and as the recognition registered on his face, he was dumbstruck. Ironically, she didn't even care. His mouth fell open as he realized the horse she was riding was Jake. She couldn't resist nodding to him affirmatively.

The man at the gate called for twenty-three head. They began to file into the large outdoor pen at the trot. Gabe stood at the rail.

"Remember, go easy with your hands," he called to her. "Don't think about anything but Jake."

She acknowledged his instructions, took a deep breath and urged the black colt into a soft jog trot.

From the moment she entered the show ring, she felt unbeatable. She sat confidently in the saddle, feeling Jake glide down the rail. In her mind, a memory penetrated her concentration. A shivering newborn foal lunging frantically over the dead body of his mother. She relived the exact moment Jeff caved in and Jake became hers. And she became his. She blinked back a tear. *Not now*, she reprimanded herself and sharpened her focus.

After the judge inspected each competitor, he asked them to show their horses at the walk, jog, and lope. Chris was aware his eyes were on Jake. There would be no opportunity for even the slightest mistake. This judge was watching her too close.

Under the hot sun, the ringmaster was perspiring. He mopped his forehead and took his signal from the judge to reverse the horses and work them to the right. Chris trotted Jake in front of him, and found a perfect rail position for the impending transition. Although the class was crowded, she had nailed a spot on the rail allowing her at least ten feet between Jake and the horse in front of her. As she heard the announcer call for the lope, she looked forward, a suspended feeling of power rushing through her body. She shifted her weight and gave Jake a slight cue. He responded trustingly. In consummate unison with his fluid motion, Chris rocked into the lope. The judge, a short, stocky man, hadn't missed a footstep.

Abruptly, he held his hand up and stopped the class, having decided to eliminate some of the horses. After conferring with his notes, he handed off a list of numbers to the ring man for the announcer. All but ten horses were excused. Those remaining at ease on the rail had made the cut. Chris patted Jake on the neck and waited with the other riders for instructions from the ring man. Jake was hot and a little tired, but he stood patiently. The announcer then called for the riders to show their horses at a trot. One by one, each competitor eased into the soft jog.

Within steps, however, the judge gave a signal and the announcer asked the riders to go to an extended trot. An interested reaction rippled through the bleachers. Asking for this optional gate was perfectly reasonable, but was infrequently required in an open western pleasure class. Unless the horse competed in English as well, many western pleasure riders spent little time working their horses at this sweeping long trot.

Several riders appeared concerned and hesitated to move off into this ground-covering gait. Gabe, on the bleachers, stood up. He had seen Chris try this with Jake at home, but the colt was usually confused and broke into a canter or just trotted faster and became choppy. This optional gait, one she had not practiced much, could blow her perfect go.

"Oh shit," Gabe mumbled to himself.

He watched Chris' face, flushed from the heat, and thought he saw a subtle smile. He held his breath as she gathered a bit of rein, pushed herself forward a bit and urged Jake to move out. The black colt responded uncertainly to the collection and pushed off with some hesitation. Gabe could see Chris talking him through it. She closed her legs around the huge barrel of his body and Gabe closed his eyes. He was positive when her heels touched those ticklish flanks, she would be airborne. But in three steps, the black colt's stride lengthened and he began to cover ground. Perfectly balanced, he sailed down the rail, settling confidently into the powerful gait.

They closed in on Brandon. He was urging his mare to speed up, but at the same time holding her back with the reins to prevent her from a canter. As a result of the mixed signals, the poor mare was hopping along like a three-legged pooch. Chris guided Jake around them. Her hands made only the lightest contact with her horse's mouth and whatever words she was speaking to him served as the only control over his awesome energy. They swept majestically down the rail.

Mercifully, the judge did not work them long. Within minutes, the ten finalists were lined up and the announcer was placing them in reverse order. Brandon placed fourth, despite his lousy effort at the extended trot. Finally, one breathless rider and her dripping wet horse stood alone as the loud speaker called out.

"First place and winner of today's jackpot western pleasure is number 87, Jake, exhibited by Christine Day."

For one second, she leaned forward over the neck of the horse, arms extended, stroking him. Then she sat up, smiling, and threw a meaningful kiss toward the sky. She rode out of the lineup and toward the gate to collect the trophy and as she passed each section of bleachers, friends stood up and began to slowly clap their hands.

Gabe met her at the gate. She swung her right leg over the saddle and dropped to the ground, still hugging the trophy.

"What do you think?"

"Not bad." He shrugged, smiling.

"Not bad? What a ride! That was for Dad. He would have loved it!" She unzipped her chaps and hung them over the saddle horn. Gabe took the reins and led Jake back toward the trailer.

"Take my number off, will you?" she asked, turning away from him and leaning against the trailer. She liked the touch of his hands on her blouse. When he had unpinned the number, she faced him, blushing. Anticipating his normally impassive expression, she was startled to find herself locked in his torrid stare. He was deeply convinced she used him to be with Jake, but he couldn't help himself. He reached for her.

"You are so unpredictable," she whispered. "How am I supposed to ever know what you're thinking?"

He responded with a gentle push backwards, into the trailer wall. Blood had rushed to his face and his eyes flashed with a yearning that was exploding within him. He easily lifted her, setting her on the ledge of the wheel well and pressed his body close. As their lips touched, she wrapped her legs around him, inflamed with the heat of her own passion.

He clamped his eyes shut, then released her and backed off, trying hard to shake the feelings that were consuming him. Bewildered, she reached out and touched his face.

"You better finish changing your clothes," he finally spoke.

Flustered, she sought the refuge of the dressing room. There, she sat down on the tack box. When she eventually emerged, clothes changed, Gabe was nowhere in sight. She walked around the trailer and looked toward the show pen. She spotted him standing on the rail, watching the competition, his arms folded.

As she walked toward him, a familiar voice rang out.

"I suppose I should congratulate you. How about a little hug?" Brandon stepped in her path, arms extended. She pushed him away but he reached out and cupped her face in his hands. She stood glaring into his handsome face.

"You came here to beat me, didn't you?" He dared her to admit it. "I should really be pissed at you, Chris. Fourth place! In a damned open show. You made me look pretty bad out there. I'm better than that."

She shoved him aside and walked toward Gabe, who had turned away from the rail and stood frozen, watching them.

"I want to talk to you. Will you call me?" Brandon whined pitifully as she stepped away.

Gabe was quiet as they returned to the trailer and began to wrap Jake's legs.

"Who was that?" he finally said when Jake was ready to go.

"His name is Brandon Penny," she replied. "He's nobody."

"Go get your winnings and let's get the horse loaded," Gabe ordered in a monotone.

He was silent on the way home and when Chris attempted to talk, he turned the radio on and leaned against the window.

It was after dark when they pulled into Prairie Rock. Gabe unloaded the horse and put him in his stall, patting his shoulder and throwing down a flake of hay. His eyes avoided her.

"I guess I'll just go on home," she mumbled, thoroughly confused. He said nothing, so she climbed in the truck and started the engine.

He walked to the truck window, driver's side, and stared down at her.

"That guy wasn't just nobody. Did you go to that show just to see him?"

"In the beginning, maybe," she said truthfully, "I wanted to beat him. But after I got there, it didn't matter."

"You've been using me, haven't you?" Gabe's eyes narrowed, fixed on her face. "This whole day ... going in the jackpot, dressed fit to kill ... it wasn't for me, or Jake. It was for that guy, wasn't it?"

"No! You don't understand!" She began to protest, but he turned his back and leaned against the truck, arms folded.

"Oh, yes, I do. I understand perfectly." His voice was harsh. "I think you better go on home. Whatever you wanted to do today, I think you pretty well got your way. Go home and call pretty boy. He's probably waitin'. And don't come here again."

"Gabe! You don't get it!" She cried out and tried to climb out of the truck, but he pushed her back inside, slammed the door and walked toward the back door of the feed store.

Pounding her fists on the steering wheel, she dropped her head and clamped her eyes closed. When she looked up, he was gone.

CHAPTER THIRTY-ONE

Miguel's voice was tense and Jenna knew when she answered the phone he was upset.

"Your mother left here after that funeral and said she was going to Mexico for a few weeks," he told her. "It's been quite a while and I haven't heard a word from her. I'm kinda worried … "

"She went alone?" Jenna interrupted him. "And left you home?"

"I'm working at the dinner theater full time now, as assistant manager," he replied. "She wasn't really mad that I couldn't just take off and go with her, but she was having one of her anxiety attacks and said she had to get away. But it's not like her not to contact me."

"What about the house?" asked Jenna, not really surprised at Claudia's disappearing act. She was used to her mother's impulsive actions and knew she could work herself into a nervous breakdown over the wrong color nail polish.

"I'm paying the bills and keeping the house up." He sounded exasperated.

"You're paying the bills?" Jenna was surprised at this. "Miguel, I'm really sorry. My stepfather left half of everything to me, including the house. If she isn't paying the bills, that should be my responsibility."

"I don't mind, since I *am* living here," he replied. "I just thought you ought to know she left. I know you don't want to see her, and truthfully, I'm beginning to understand why."

"I'll bet five bucks she'll be back soon and she'll come breezing in with a bunch of presents like nothing's happened," Jenna reassured him. "I know her. She doesn't think much about other people's feelings."

"I guess she didn't care about me as much as I thought she did," he said. "But, I suppose I'll just hang out and wait. I've paid the utilities and the lawn service people. She left me one of the cars. I assume it's paid for since nobody has come to repossess it." She sensed he was genuinely fed up. "The pool guys have been here twice, so I guess she owes them money. They are a pair of real morons. Wouldn't leave a bill. Anyway, I'll keep in touch, Jenna." He hung up the phone.

"What's the deal?" Wes stirred on the couch where he'd been napping.

"That was Miguel. Mom's dashed off someplace and hasn't called him. He's upset." Jenna plopped down beside him. "He's a good guy, you know. He should just dump her and get someone capable of caring for him."

"Yep. I can't figure why he's stayed with her this long. Aside from the fact she's rich and sexy." Wes yawned. "So what's he gonna do?"

"He's going to stay at the house and he said he'd keep up the bills and stuff. You know, if he leaves, we'll probably have to move in. Somebody's got to stay there. And it's half mine."

"Nuts! That's all we need," he sat up. "And then one day your mom'll turn up, like a bad penny."

"I didn't say we'd have to go tomorrow!" She tried to soothe him. "Mom will probably be back soon and patch it up with Miguel and everything will be fine."

"Where do you suppose she went?" Wes wondered aloud.

"Miguel said Mexico, but that doesn't mean anything. She could be anywhere," Jenna said, flipping on the television.

CHAPTER THIRTY-TWO

Wes wanted to meet with Ken Thompson before returning to Kansas City. He and Jenna met Ken for breakfast at the cafe.

"Here's where we're at, Wes," reported the chief. "We've got a file full of information on the Bates brothers. And Tom Barnett keeps in contact with the estranged wife of one of the brothers. She's given us photos, details, background, all she can. We're up to our asses in leads, but we simply can't find the bastards."

"What kind of information is Mrs. Bates giving you?" Wes wanted to know more.

"Oh, such things as what kind of jobs her husband had, where he hung out, places he could have met Slankard. It's pretty clear these Bates fellas had nothing to do with horses and were just hired guns. This is purely speculation, but," he leaned forward, "I think they stole Chris' horse, found out they had screwed up, and dumped him off. Somehow, the colt ended up with the old man who ran him through the sale. Gabriel Judd gave us the old guy's name off from the Mintonville sale papers, but we can't find him."

"So, whoever hired the Bates brothers maybe told them to go back later and try again." Wes filled in the blanks. "And this time, they really messed up. They got caught by Dad and they panicked."

"Well, of course, we're not sure, we really think this is what happened," said Ken. "I don't think they intended to kill your dad. But they obviously intended to kill the horse. Hell, maybe they were told to shoot the horse this time, just to make sure they got the job done."

Jenna sat and listened to the dialog. It all seemed so unreal.

"So what do we know about the Bates brothers?" she asked. "Is there anything you know to make you think they are hired killers? Ray couldn't afford to hire somebody to kill a fly."

"That's true. We've not been able to connect anything to Ray ... any place they've been or any freakin' thing they've done. I don't know, maybe we were wrong about him being involved. But we are square on target with these Bates boys. Our profile indicates they did a lot of rat jobs for cash. These guys are crum-bums from the word go. There's no reason to think they'd have a problem taking money for shooting a horse in the head."

The chief motioned to the waitress for coffee.

"What kind of rat jobs?" Wes continued casually, trying to put his own pieces together.

"Oh, I don't know. Mrs. Bates said they hauled trash, did a little roofing. Last week she called Barnett and said she had jotted down some more jobs her husband did. Nothing unusual. He worked down south for a while cutting wood, and Mrs. Bates said he and his brother worked together somewhere around Kansas City for a while cleaning swimming pools for cash."

Inside Jenna's head, the chief's words collided with her last conversation with Miguel. *The swimming pool guys kept coming back to collect their money from her mother.* Her face paled and the coffee cup slipped from her fingers, clattering into its saucer.

Hours later, she sat in Ken Thompson's office, head bowed, hands folded across her round belly. Wes paced the floor behind her.

"Jenna, you said your mother knew Jeff Day before he married Joanna?" The chief's words were soft but deliberate. Thompson sat across from her at a large desk and Detective Barnett perched on the corner of it.

"Mom and Joanna were sorority sisters and best friends. Mother dated Jeff first. They broke up and he started going with Joanna. Mom was really in love with him, or obsessed with him or something," Jenna said in a very small voice. "She told me once he was my father."

Wes exploded, pounding the back of the chair. Ken quieted him with a wave of his hand.

"But I went to Montreal and found my real father … the man Mom was married to when I was born. He told me Mom lied. While I was there, we had a blood test. Dad said she never got over Jeff and was sick in the head."

Wes slid his hand through his hair, incredulous.

"Is she 'sick in the head,' Jenna?" said Barnett, narrowing his eyes to slits. She bit her lip and looked troubled.

"She's a total psycho," Wes answered for her. "A poisonous bitch! She wasn't invited to our wedding but she crashed the reception! Then she showed up at Dad's funeral in this stupid widow get-up … skirt up to her ass and a long black veil!"

Detective Barnett shot a look at the chief and made notes. After a moment, he looked up and continued questioning Jenna.

"Is she jealous of Joanna, then? Did she resent Jeff's marriage to her?"

Jenna nodded, confused. "I don't know ... she talked like they were all best friends. After my stepfather, Vic, died, Mom sent me to New Winston for the summer. She told me it would be good for me, and that Jeff and Joanna would take care of me. After I went back home, she asked me about them. I guess I told her a lot."

"Yeah, and then she was nutted out that Jenna became like a part of the family, and she and I started going together," Wes growled.

"Jenna, did you communicate with your mother much during the time you were at the Day farm?" Ken prodded her.

"Yes, I wrote to her all the time and sent her pictures. I sent her a picture of Jeff and Invincible!" She suddenly recalled this and began to cry softly.

"By looking at that photo, could a person tell that the horse was black with a white half moon on his forehead?" Barnett leaned forward with an intense expression.

"Yes, of course, and I described him in the letter." Jenna could hardly speak. "And I told her he was Jeff's pride and joy and ... how much Vince meant to him."

"Where is your mother now, Jenna?" Thompson stood up. "If you know, you better tell us."

"She doesn't know," Wes answered, standing in back of the chair with his hands on Jenna's shoulders. "Claudia's boyfriend Miguel calls every now and then. He said she disappeared after the funeral. She told him she was going on vacation to Mexico, but we don't know that for sure."

"She's learned to speak Spanish pretty well," added Jenna weakly, "she likes to go there."

"Mexico! Damn!" muttered the detective.

"Miguel is the one who told Jenna the pool guys had been by for their money," Wes said as Jenna began to rock back and forth in the chair.

She coughed and spoke softly. "I think he said they came twice. I'm sure Miguel will describe them for you. Would that help?"

"He can do better than that. We've got photos of the brothers we can show him," said Ken.

"The last time they came, did Miguel pay them?" said Barnett.

"No. They didn't even give him a bill. They wanted to see Mom," she said in a feeble whisper.

"Jenna, what is the address at the house?" The detective looked at her, pen in hand. "If this boyfriend didn't pay up, you can bet they'll be back. And with his help, we'll be waiting."

CHAPTER THIRTY-THREE

Duane and Huey sat handcuffed in the back of the patrol car with frowns of disbelief on their vacuous faces. The brothers had phoned Miguel on July 10 and made arrangements to come by the house, supposedly to pick up a payment from Mrs. Gambiano. The visit resulted in a swift arrest. The Day family was notified shortly after noon. Within hours, both of the brothers implicated Claudia in a sequence of crimes beginning with the theft of Chris' horse.

"I'm telling you, the deal was a goddamn screw up," Duane said. He was anxious to clarify this as if it would lessen the charges. "We had a picture of this stud, black with a white mark on his head. We was supposed to poison the sonofabitch. So we sneaks in one night and we finds the horse that matched the picture and I says to Huey, 'why should we kill him?' We figures we could take him and sell him and the old gal wouldn't know shit about it."

"So you didn't take him that night?" asked the interrogating officer with a deadpan face, tapping the eraser end of a pencil on the table.

"Naw, we had to find some way to move him. So, we borrowed a truck and swiped a horse trailer from behind the sale barn in Odessa and goes back the next night."

"What happened to the trailer?" The officer continued to tap his pencil nervously.

"We took it back and I don't think anybody even knew it was ever gone," Duane said. He sniggered his lip and grinned at his cleverness.

Huey Bates was questioned separately and told the same story. "We figured we'd wait a few months before we tried to sell him, so we just headed south with the horse. We was drivin' down south of Clinton where we used to hunt, and we found this old bastard way out in the damned sticks who said he'd keep the horse for a month for $25."

"Why didn't you go back and get the horse, like you planned?"

"We tried like hell! But, we had been drinking a little the night we snatched him and couldn't find the damned place again."

After several hours of methodic questioning, the detectives pieced together the events leading to the murder of Jeff Day. The brothers' nefarious mission had taken them to the lane, night after tedious night, watching the house for a pattern on which to base their course of action. They had been foiled by Jake's uncanny likeness to their intended victim. On their first bungled try, they had been confronted by Wes' dog and Joanna's unexpected "who's there?" from inside the dark barn.

On the night of the murder, Huey had parked the car in the lane, downed a half of a pint of cheap whiskey, and watched the house while his brother snored beside him. After several hours, it appeared no one was home and they decided to make their move. They drove through the gate and up to the barn door and hurried in to find the horse. Duane carried the gun.

"One shot to the horse's head and he went down. We was just leaving the stall when this guy comes flying out of the dark hallway," Huey confessed. "Scared the crap outta me. He was a maniac. We was caught off guard. He jumped on Duane and knocked him back into the stall, and the gun went off and the guy fell."

***

"The looney toon in the widow's garb was behind the whole thing?" Rita was in shock. "And Ray the scuzzball had nothing to do with it? Don't say another word, I'll be right there!"

She slammed down the phone and grabbed her car keys. Ten minutes later, she swooped through Joanna's front door and threw herself breathlessly onto the living room couch.

"Why the hell would she do it?"

"She never intended for Jeff to die. I'm sure of that. She just wanted to take something away from him. Something he loved. She's always been so damned extreme."

"Why would she want to mess with him like that? I thought she was an old friend of yours!"

"She was. She was also one of Jeff's old lovers ... God, that was so long ago! All those years and she was still obsessed with him," Jo said, lighting a cigarette with shaking hands.

"Why did she send her daughter to you for the summer? As an unwitting spy?"

"I think she sent Jenna to Jeff, not me. Maybe she thought Jenna would win some place in his heart she could never have. I don't know."

"And she ended up losing her only daughter to your son ... Jeff's son."

"It was right before they got engaged, we noticed someone watching the house."

"It probably pushed her right over the edge."

"God! Claudia!" Joanna moaned, clamping her eyes shut. "All these years and I never knew."

The following week, the Bates brothers were indicted. Claudia's whereabouts, however, remained a mystery. Mexican authorities had been alerted, but Joanna knew Claudia was probably not in Mexico at all. She was too shrewd to have dropped this clue to Miguel. Sloppy was not her nature.

***

A half a world away, a petite woman in a loose-fitting dress and large hat sat alone at a small table. The cafe bartender busied himself wiping the bar and tending the few customers, occasionally glancing her way. Soon, a black-haired young man crossed the white tiled floor and dropped into the chair beside her, drink in hand.

"Do you like the ocean?" he said casually, with a thick Moroccan accent.

"The ocean? I love it. The waves are very soothing," she answered, pulling off her dark sunglasses and revealing puffy eyelids heavy with mascara. She leaned forward, inspecting him.

"Is your name Rick?"

"What?" He was puzzled.

"Light my cigarette, Rick." Her words were slurred and he noticed her lipstick was slightly smeared.

"Will you be staying here?" he questioned, checking out her diamond rings as he held the flame.

"Oh, no. It's just someplace I always wanted to visit," she mumbled, eyes fixed on the lethargic motion of the dropped ceiling fan above her. "I don't really like the North African heat." Her voice was toneless.

"Word has it you are a widow."

She froze for just an instant and then threw her head back as a shrill peal of laughter escaped her red lips. He groped for words, alarmed by the lunatic expression on her face. She quickly regained her composure and elegantly touched his hand as he nervously played with the swizzle stick.

"Why, yes," she said, taking a drag. "My husband Jeff, is dead."

CHAPTER THIRTY-FOUR

Joanna sat alone in her bedroom waiting for the sound of Rod's truck and trailer to pull in the drive. He had called her that morning from Illinois, where he was showing several horses. In shocked silence, he listened to the news about the Bates brothers and Claudia Gambiano's involvement.

"Poor Jenna," Jo had told him on the phone. "She and Wes went to Kansas City to see Miguel, the boyfriend. He's pretty rattled. We all are. Chris went with them. They'll be back Sunday night."

"I'll load up and head home. The last thing you need is to be alone this weekend," he told her, estimating he would be home about midnight.

Marveling at her calm demeanor, he thought of her all the way home. It was nearly one when he entered the dark house.

Flipping off the kitchen light she had left on for him, he slowly ascended the stairs, careful not to disturb her, but the soft glow of light on the floor before her bedroom door announced she was awake. He hesitated at the door of his room, then walked down the hall to her doorway.

"I'm glad you're here," she sighed. She was sitting in the dim light, cross-legged, in the middle of her bed. Her eyes were painfully troubled.

"I know how you must feel ... I don't know what to say," he began. "But soon, it will be over and I'm sure they'll eventually find Claudia."

"They'll never find her," she said with a knowing smile. "She's crazy, but incredibly clever." She waved her hand, dismissing the subject.

"That's not all, is it?" He sensed there was more.

"No. Not really." The tone of her voice seemed strangely repressed as if those simple words were carefully selected and it evoked a nervous ripple in his gut.

"What is it, then?" He moved closer and stood at her bedside.

"The school board. They are making budget cuts or some such thing. They told me this afternoon." Her voice was flat. "I won't be going back this fall. I've lost my job. After all these years. I'm just ... gone."

The termination had initially angered her, but the combination of loss and rejection left her with an emptiness that replaced the outrage of being discharged. It was the nothingness that was far more difficult to accept. For Joanna, this development in her life had slammed the door on one of her remaining comfort zones.

"Tell me about it," he said, not knowing what else to say.

Girlishly, she drew her knees up under her chin and related the details of the impersonal notification. The release from this beloved obligation left her feeling precarious and strangely aimless and her face was a blank.

"I guess I just can't believe it. You know, I wanted to be a teacher, but all that got away from me," she confessed. "I quit college to marry Jeff. The closest I could get was my job at the junior high. I know it doesn't sound like it was any kind of impressive career or anything, but I truly loved every day of it. Without that income, I'm not sure what I'll do. There are very few good-paying jobs in this town."

In the hushed seclusion of the room, her words played on his senses like warm fingers. He didn't speak, but sat down on the edge of the bed. He wanted to touch her, but resisted.

"I feel as though I'm on a sinking ship," she whispered. "I never thought that this far down the line, I could be so lost."

He had nurtured a maddening desire for her for months, but had respectfully denied it. The notion of her drifting, displaced, rendered him defenseless.

"You're not lost. You've got me," he said, suddenly revealing a passion that jolted her.

She looked at him in surprise. He studied her face and recognized confusion and hesitation in her eyes. He held her hand to his lips, then stood up. Still, she made no move.

He gazed at her gently, accepting her cautious uncertainty. Disappointed, he turned and walked down the hallway to his bedroom. Alone in his room, he undressed and slid into the big bed, every nerve ignited, senses amplified. He had waited all of his life for a woman like her. For Rod, Joanna had led him to a remarkable threshold of discovery, as his only experiences had been with whimsical young women … women who wore him like an ornament, like some championship status belt buckle.

The stillness of the house was overbearing and he was acutely aware this was the first time he had been alone in the house with her. The clock in the downstairs hall struck two singular, echoing tones. Minutes later, a slight rustle revealed her presence at his bedside. It was the sound of her blue jeans dropping softly to the floor. He turned back the covers.

Her body was not hard and lean, but pliant and charitable, molding to his limbs, accepting his passion. Sex with her was not raging, but needy. She was a tender and wise lover and he felt not depleted, but replenished and infused by the degree of her generosity. Afterwards, an overwhelming tranquility coursed through his body. He had discovered the mysterious, seamless continuity of mature womanhood and lay in the dark with his new secret. He would forever cherish the beauty of it.

***

"You are in love with him, aren't you?" Nothing escaped Rita. Her best friend's life was more intriguing than any daytime soap and she relished being smack dab in the middle of it.

"I really don't want to talk about it," Joanna looked away. She had met her friend for lunch and knew after ten minutes Rita had sized her up.

"You feel like you're cheating on Jeff and people will talk. And you're too old for him and your kids will freak out." Rita kept it up. "Don't cut yourself out of a good thing, honey. Life's too short. Do you really have feelings for him?"

"Yes," Jo said simply. There was no doubt of this. "But there's more. John Wyatt, the guy that owns the Genesis Ranch, called yesterday. He's in remission and has moved back to the ranch. His nephew had made a mess of things and John's taking over again. He wants Rod to come back to Texas."

"And you think he's going to go?"

Joanna nodded. "He needs to go to Texas. Training is his life. It's too big an opportunity to turn down. He wants me to go with him."

"God! He's that serious about you?"

Jo stirred a puddle of ketchup with a French fry.

"Well, there's a college campus near the ranch and he says he'll work while I go back and finish school. He wants me to get my degree so I can teach. Can you believe it?"

Rita raised her penciled eyebrows and tapped the table with long painted, squared-off nails.

"You know I would *die* if you left, but I have no problem with some frequent flier miles. What about your family?"

"I don't know. That's my biggest dilemma. I don't worry about Wes. But Chris is different. She's having a tough time accepting my relationship with Rod. She thinks it's wrong, of course, and last night, we had a helluva battle. She's not speaking to me."

"It's not wrong, honey. It's just lousy timing. And that's something nobody can control. I think you should go. If it doesn't work out, come back home."

"I don't know what to do! This is all happening just too fast for me. I can't think!" Jo shoved her plate away, searched in her purse for a tissue and blew her nose. "I want to go with him so bad, Rita! But there's no way I can leave Chris."

"Can't Wes and Jenna stay at the farm with her?" Rita was trying to be helpful.

"I can't just dump the whole mess on them! They have other responsibilities. Since Claudia skipped out, Miguel has found a new girlfriend and he wants to move out of the house. Wes' business is good in Kansas City and it's a nice house, I guess. So, they'll be moving in next week. I know they are going to be just fine. But, I can't leave Chris with so much responsibility. She doesn't even have a job. And do you have any idea how much it costs to feed and care for all those horses?"

"Surely there's some money in the bank from Jeff's insurance?" Rita was blunt, as usual.

"Not really. He had a loan against his insurance policy! I knew *that*'d come back to haunt us. Truthfully, I'm almost broke."

"Jee-sus!" Rita rolled her eyes. "Then you *know* what you have to do. Sell the damned horses! That'll give you enough money to keep the place up. She can't take care of that many anyway."

"I guess I've known for months it would come down to that. And I've sold some of them already. It's just that – well, you know how Chris feels about the horses."

"It's simple. Give her a choice. She can go with you to Texas or she can sell the horses so she can stay here. Let it be her decision."

"As far as she's concerned, those aren't even choices." Joanna shook her head, perplexed by the situation.

"Joanna! There are no other options here! She's not a kid any more. Quit treating her like one! There has to be at least $100,000 worth of horses standing around your place and you're going to have to sell some whether you go to Texas or you stay. As for the deal with you and Rod, she'll get it over it. I know she will."

"Maybe you're right, Rita. She's so much like Jeff. Nobody can tell her anything. She wants everything to be the same as it was. And everything has changed so fast. It'll never be that way again." Joanna drew a breath and looked up with resignation.

"It's like the old Missouri River, baby," Rita soothed her. "Remember that old story about it changing course in the middle of the night? It's the rules of the stream. Sometimes life does that. And nobody can put it back the way it was."

"I just hate it that she's going to have to learn it the hard way. And I can't stand to think of her here alone."

"Joanna! She won't really be alone. She has Wes and Jenna! And Frank and Lil will always be nearby. And of course, she has me!"

"You're right, of course."

Rita fiddled with a dangly earring. "That settles it. So when are you leaving?"

***

Chris sat in her room staring at the wall as Rod's footsteps up and down the staircase told her he was loading up his belongings. His big Dodge truck sat in front of the barn hooked up to his trailer and his gelding, legs wrapped, stood tied to the side. Joanna's suitcases and several boxes sat on the front porch. He had attempted to say goodbye to Chris at breakfast, but she refused to talk to him and retreated to her room.

"Chris, we need to talk." It was Joanna. She stood in the doorway, eyes pleading. Her daughter sat frozen, jaw set, eyes focused on nothing in particular.

"I am trying to get on with my life! Can't you get that through your head? There is no future in the past."

Chris remained silent.

"I know you think we can make it work here, but you don't have any idea how much money it takes just to take care of this place and the horses. It's all I can do to hang on to the farm! If you're going to stay, the horses have to go."

"I'll find a way to keep them."

"Honey, there is no way. We're nearly broke! I've got to go back to school to get my degree so I can get a good job. Meanwhile, Mr. Wyatt has offered me a job helping Rod. I can send you a little money every week, but it's not nearly enough to … "

"Go on and go and don't worry about it." Chris walked to the window seat and sat down, staring out the window.

"It's really so very hard for me to leave you here alone, do you know that?"

"It couldn't be that hard. You're doing it, aren't you?"

Joanna began to speak again, but her voice weakened and trailed off helplessly. She backed away from the door and slowly descended the stairs.

Some time later, the slamming of trailer doors and crunch of gravel below announced they were gone. Chris walked to the window and watched the truck and trailer turn onto the road. Soon, it was out of sight and a sense of utter isolation gripped her. As she walked downstairs and through the hallway, the house seemed large and empty. It frightened her and she moved quickly toward the screen door, seeking fresh air. She was startled to find Joanna, sitting quietly on the porch steps, surrounded by her suitcases and staring forlornly down the road.

CHAPTER THIRTY-FIVE

Working side by side, not as mother and daughter, but as two women, they endured the next month. While Joanna gave herself tirelessly to the demands of the daily barn chores and the task of winterizing the aging farmhouse, her heart was in Texas. Every day, Rod called. He and Jo spent hours on the phone, nurturing a relationship that was becoming only stronger.

"I've been looking for a job in town, but no one's hiring," she told Rod one evening. "We're pretty low on cash, so I'm going to sell some horses. I don't have a choice, really. I know how much it's going to hurt Chris, but we just can't feed them all winter."

"She's a grown woman, Joanna! You act like she's still twelve years old!"

"So much has happened to her. Jake's gone, Jeff's gone. Don't you understand? I can't hurt her anymore!"

"Couldn't you just sell the broodmares? She's not so attached to them."

"I've got four left, but they're our best mares and Frank keeps telling me to hold off. They're all in foal and I've got to think about our future income."

"Well, if you'd come down here and get your degree, you'd be sure to have a future income," Rod replied. "I'm serious, Jo, I can't stand being down here without you. I think about you every damned minute. You better consider selling some horses. Maybe the yearlings."

After she hung up the phone, she walked back down to the barn to check on Lester. He had refused his grain for two days and had only picked at his hay. Tonight, he was standing with his head down, thick snot dripping from crusty nostrils.

"Damn it, Lester!" she moaned as she headed for the office to summon the vet. McGraw was there within the hour.

"Well, he's got some kind of virus. Pretty common this time of year," Doc said as he patted the colt. "Your older horses might not get it, of course, but keep an eye on the colts. This stuff is contagious as hell. I can't give him anything for the virus. It'll have to run its course. But he's got a little respiratory infection we might be able to help." Mike injected penicillin into the colt's hip, and patted him as Lester flinched from the needle.

He scrawled out a bill for his services and handed it to her.

"Just pay it when you can," he murmured, and then having said it, felt a little ashamed.

By the end of the week, one more yearling was sick and two weanlings were running a fever. She and Chris found themselves camping out at the barn, which became the farm's infirmary.

"Virus! What the hell?" Rod's voice exploded on the phone. "Where did that come from? You haven't had any of 'em out anywhere. How'd they catch it?"

"Al bought a couple colts at a sale and kept them here a week. I think Lester must have caught it from one of them. He was the first to get it. He's been really sick."

"Great. After they get well, they're gonna look so bad, you won't be able to sell any of 'em for at least two months!"

"Yeah, they've already lost weight," Jo lamented.

Later, Joanna and Chris finished cleaning stalls and together, lifted the last heavy tub of dirty bedding into the manure spreader. Joanna clambered atop the tractor and as it started up, the right rear wheel labored before it made a lopsided attempt to roll forward in the mud. Jo leaned across the steering wheel and buried her face in her arms. Chris stood silently for a moment. Flat tire.

Joanna abruptly raised her tired eyes and looked at her daughter's face, then climbed off the tractor and walked to the house. The sight of her wearily climbing the porch steps in her mud boots provoked a twitching sensation deep inside Chris. On the day Rod left, Chris realized how much Joanna had sacrificed. When she saw Joanna sitting on the steps, watching Rod's truck and trailer pull from the gate, she had forgiven her mother instantly. But in the ways of her father, Chris had neglected to say so. She offered up a vicious kick at the idle tractor and wished she could somehow change it all.

Chris had tried several times to call Gabe at the feed store. Charlie had promised to try to persuade him to talk to her, but his appeals were unsuccessful. At the end of the month, she tried again.

"I've got to talk to him," she pleaded.

"Sorry, Chris," Charlie told her. "He and Gil went to Kansas City for a load of feed."

"Will you make him call me?"

"Edith and I both have tried to talk him into calling you, but he doesn't want to hear it ... How's it going at the farm?" Charlie went on, not wanting to end the conversation abruptly.

"Like hell," she answered him simply. "We've been nursing sick horses for a month, but they're getting better now."

"Winter's on the way. Got your hay all up in the barn?" He tried to make small talk.

"No. Frank got it cut and we hired a guy to bale it. Mom and I were going to put it up, but a little rain came up and it all got wet in the field. I think it's all ruined."

She stopped herself, fighting the urge to tell him everything.

"Listen, Charlie. I've got to talk to Gabe. He has got to let me see Jake," she finally whispered. "Just tell him, okay?" She paused painfully and then hung up the phone.

***

Chris sprawled listlessly in the big brown easy chair in Frank and Lil's living room. She loved this old house and it had often served as her safe zone. Dozens of family pictures crowded on every wall in the place, and Jeff had always said Lil owned more figurines than anyone on God's green earth. The house always smelled like navy beans and fried potatoes and the television was always on, no matter what time of day it was.

Uncle Frank sat in the other chair, white stockinged feet propped up on a vinyl hassock, watching some guy on TV attempting a stunt with a nitropowered dragster.

He finally leaned his head back and turned the TV down.

"So, you want to send your mom to Texas? Well, missy, here's the way I see it."

Through the kitchen door, Lil looked up from her ironing to hear what he had to say.

"Joanna has put this off as long as she could, but it's reality time. You need to sell Zan and Cherry. As soon as they get well, you need to sell off the rest of the weanlings and yearlings. Lester, too."

He looked at her, surprised at the wistful resignation on her face.

"Try to keep your four brood mares if you can," he continued. "You'll have to keep Tess and Sheila, of course. Use 'em for riding lessons and open up the barn and take in some boarders."

"Board other people's horses? *Oh, man!*" She threw herself backwards in the chair, head in her hands.

Frank ignored her. "If you make it reasonable enough, you'll get some customers, 'cause you got an indoor arena. You got a good farrier, the vet's close, and the place never floods."

Lil finished the shirt she was ironing, hung it up and joined them.

"Listen to Uncle Frank, honey. You gotta have an income. Jo's been looking in town for a month and there's no work around here. You got to do something to get some money comin' in."

Chris sat up, twisting a lock of hair.

"Well, then," she said slowly as Frank and Lil exchanged glances. "Do you think if we took in some boarding horses, I could afford to stay here on the farm? I want Mom to go, but I know she won't unless I convince her everything here is going to be all right."

"If you sell your horses, you could make it to spring, and then you can start boarding. Right now, you don't even have enough hay to feed your own. Taking care of other people's horses is a full-time job, but Lil and I will do what we can." He looked at her evenly. "It's a seven-day-a-week deal. And you won't have time for any horse shows."

She leaned back and sighed. "No matter. I'll do anything to stay here."

***

Joanna stirred the scrambled eggs as Chris buttered the toast. Down the road, the distinct sound of a Cummins' diesel engine made Jo quickly look up, spatula in mid-air. Through the kitchen window, Chris watched Rod's big Dodge truck roll to a stop in front of the house.

Over her shoulder, she heard Joanna draw an astonished breath. In seconds, Jo was through the door, down the porch steps and locked in his arms.

"Hey! Surprised to see me, babe?" Rod stroked Jo's hair.

"You didn't tell me you were coming! I just talked to you yesterday and … "

She was interrupted by the squeak of the screen door as Chris stepped onto the porch. Rod acknowledged her with a grin.

"Yeah, well, I drove all night to get here."

"What took you so long?" Chris said, hand on her hip.

Joanna stared at her daughter. She began to speak, but Rod Rollins had knelt down on one knee and was taking her hand in his own.

"I've got something to say to you and I wanted to say it in person."

Joanna knew what was coming and shot a helpless glance at Chris, who was slipping unobtrusively into the house with a devious smile.

"Do you know about this?" Joanna called after her. "What's that look on your face?"

Chris returned to the kitchen and began setting the breakfast table for three. She was glad she had called Rod.

Later that morning, Chris finished chores and returned to the house. Rod was seated at the table, drinking coffee. Joanna turned to her and took a deep breath. Chris was ready.

"I am not sure what you're up to, but I don't see how I can leave you alone here." Jo spoke first, folding her arms and facing Chris.

"I won't be alone," Chris shot back. "I've got Uncle Frank and Aunt Lil and we've got a big job cut out for us to get ready for spring." She spilled out her plan.

Rod interceded. "I told you, you've underestimated your daughter. And I guess I did, too. She and Frank have a pretty solid scheme."

"The sooner you get going to Texas, the sooner I can get started." Chris spoke firmly, hiding her doubts behind her smile. "We've got some horses to get ready to sell, and I'm going to start giving riding lessons. Wes and Jenna said I could use Tess and Sheila."

"Riding lessons? You can't give lessons and still show in amateur classes! Are you ready to go into open competition? Honey, you know you'll be going head-to-head with the best trainers and the toughest horses …"

"I probably won't be showing anymore, so it don't matter."

"Do you mean that?" Joanna drew her close and scrutinized Chris' face.

"I couldn't be more sure," she said, unwavering. "You really need to get your teaching degree. It's your dream! With Mr. Wyatt's deal, you can make money while you're going to school. And you can be with Rod. You know you should be with him. When you want to be with someone really bad and you can't … well, it …" She paused as the words caught in her throat and were strangled there. A full minute passed before Jo spoke.

"If you'll help me pack some things, we'll leave in the morning. Rod says he needs to get back to the ranch." Joanna's eyes were still intent on her daughter's face.

"Okay, then. You'll need to take our good show saddle and some nice saddle pads. And your best show clothes."

Chris planted an assuring kiss on Jo's cheek. "You and Rod will be showing some horses and you'll need really good stuff, so you better take my chaps. And don't forget your lucky earrings."

Jo continued to search Chris' face for a shadow of indecision, but there was none.

"Your *good* chaps?" Jo repeated, her voice trailing off.

"I won't need 'em anymore," Chris replied valiantly and ushered Joanna upstairs to pack. It was an Oscar-worthy performance.

CHAPTER THIRTY-SIX

She hated late fall. The chilly north wind made her shiver and she rose from the porch swing and stepped inside. The house was deadly still and its dismal mood matched her spirits. Her truck keys lay on the front table, and she was tempted to drive to Prairie Rock and find Gabe. But she knew he wouldn't see her and this clutched at her heart. *When did she start loving him? Was it when he pulled her away from her father's grave that night in the cold rain?* She didn't know. It didn't matter.

Wandering slowly, aimlessly, across the living room rug, she stood before the rock fireplace and studied the pictures on the wall and the ribbons and trophies adorning the mantle. The pride she had always known when looking at these remnants of past victories had been replaced by a dull, aching humility. Lingering remains of an abandoned dream.

"I'm so sorry, Dad," she spoke to a large framed photo of Jeff and Vince. "I tried. But I just couldn't make it happen. Everything went so wrong."

Her eyes moved to a photo Jenna took of Cherry playing in the outdoor arena. Yesterday, the Jordans had come from Topeka to look at the horses for sale and when they left, they took two yearlings and Cherry. While Chris' all-consuming passion for Jake seemed to leave little in her heart to bestow on another horse, she realized the intensity of her attachment to the little chestnut mare when Cherry's legs were wrapped. Chris winced as the mare stepped innocently into the Jordans' trailer. *She doesn't even know she's leaving home.*

The weanlings, too, were gone. Chris recalled those happy months that she, as her dad's foaling manager, had fretted over each newborn. Now each was a memory. She suddenly felt very old, as if the better part of her life was behind her and she was standing on the brink of the rest of her years with nothing but a handful of failed hopes. The sale of Zan, Lester and the last four, and best, of her father's brood mares would give her enough money to keep the place up until spring. *What would she do then?*

Could she really take in boarding horses if it meant giving up raising and showing her own? She wasn't sure she could close the door on Day Quarter Horses.

She sat down at Jeff's big desk, switched on the tiny desk lamp slid open the bottom drawer where Jeff kept documents on the Day horses. She picked up the file folder marked "Registration papers and pedigrees" with her right hand, mindlessly closing the drawer with the left. The drawer refused to shut all the way. She jiggled it and pushed it hard. Still it refused to close. Irritated, she pulled the drawer all the way out and reached to the back. Her fingers found the culprit and retrieved it. It was an envelope addressed to the quarter horse association in Amarillo. Unsealed. No stamp.

Its contents astonished her and left her giddy. It was the kit with Vince's pulled mane hairs. Jeff must have just forgotten to mail it. With it, she could prove ownership of Jake. She opened the folder of registration papers and stared at the document on top.

It was nearly four when she flipped off the light, walked to her father's big stuffed chair and wearily fell into it. The only sound was the ticking of the old hall clock. Sometime later, she was shaken from her trance by a tap at the door. She stepped apprehensively to the hallway and saw a tall figure in faded jeans and old denim jacket standing on the porch. Through the screen, his eyes met her gaze and Gabe walked inside without an invitation.

She reached out and touched his arm. He abruptly drew back. She realized, with a painful stab, his wounds had made him wary of her.

"Charlie's brother had lunch with Ken Thompson yesterday," he said tersely. "And he told me you were selling the horses."

She took his hand and pulled him into living room, ignoring his reluctance.

"I guess it's true. I never realized how much money it costs to run this place. The feed bills, the vet bills. God! Winter's coming and I've got to get more hay and … "

She walked to her father's desk, picked up a paper and handed it to him. "So, I've made some hard decisions. This is a transfer report. I signed Jake over to you."

He was astonished at her announcement.

"Why?" he whispered. "Why did you do this?"

"Because I love that damned black horse." She lifted her eyes and spoke clearly, "but the truth is, I love you more."

Her admission stunned him. While his mind lurched helplessly, his arms acted on their own and reached out for her. She moved willingly to him and he felt her body trembling as he enfolded her.

"I was telling you the truth when I said Brandon Penny meant nothing to me," she blurted out. "It's a long story, but I did want to beat him with Jake. He hurt me once. But after we got to the show, I realized I didn't care enough about him to even enjoy kicking his ass." Her eyes were pleading. "It was the most perfect moment in my life and revenge had nothing to do with it. But sharing it with you had everything to do with it."

His mind hurtled back through nights alone in his attic, recollecting her flushed face after she'd won the class on Jake. And the kiss. The kiss that had consumed him, possessed him every night and day since her lips touched his. He bent down closer and drew her face to his, as if in slow motion, until his breath fused with hers.

"I brought you something," he finally mumbled, releasing her. She backed off, looking slightly confused.

"What is it?" Her voice was barely audible.

"Once you saved him. Once I saved him. Now, it's his turn to play the savior."

She felt her whole body convulse as she grasped the meaning of his words.

"Jake?" She strained for control. "You brought him home?"

"For the same reason you signed him over to me." The words were wrenched from deep in his chest. "Charlie said you still had four good mares left. Jake's the bloodline! Out of your dad's best mare and by your dad's stallion. With him and those mares, we can make it happen. You, me, and him. Jake's the real keeper of the promise."

He took her hand and pulled her outside. She stood beside him and looked toward the barn, trying to focus through her tears. Gabe's truck and Charlie's stock trailer were parked by the gate.

Down by the barn wall, tied to the hitching post, was Jake. Beside him, the red sign proclaimed "Christine's parking: all others will be towed."

The End

ABOUT THE AUTHORS

Native Missourians Sandi Soendker and Nicci DeMint are two friends with a common passion for horses. They began work on their first novel, "Rules of the Stream," in May of 1997. They invented plots and developed characters while passing the time at three and four-day horse shows, during road trips hauling horses and on the phone during late night foal watches. Both were born, raised and lived their lives in the Missouri River Valley.

CPSIA information can be obtained at www.ICGtesting.com
Printed in the USA
LVOW041730140912

298871LV00006B/89/A